P9-DVT-453

CORPSE BLOSSOMS

Volume I

limited to 500 copies

Edited by Julia and R.J. Sevin

CREEPING HEMLOCK PRESS

2005 – Gretna, Louisiana

This is a work of fiction. All characters and events portrayed in this book are fictitious, and any resemblance to real people or events is purely coincidental.

CORPSE BLOSSOMS: VOLUME I
First Edition

Limited unsigned ISBN: 0-9769217-0-7
Limited signed ISBN: 0-9769217-1-5
Lettered ISBN: 0-9769217-2-3

Cover design and art by R.J. Sevin
Interior art by Julia Sevin

A Creeping Hemlock Press book
Creeping Hemlock Productions, LLC
P.O. Box 2243
Harvey, LA 70059
www.creepinghemlock.com
admin@creepinghemlock.com

for the Bear,
when you're old enough

Acknowledgements

The editors wish to express appreciation:

To George A. Romero, for introducing us (so to speak).

To Stephen King, for building the sandbox in which we're all playing.

To the kind and brutal members of the Horror Writers Association, for pointing us in the right direction.

To Thomas and Elizabeth Monteleone, who set the standard.

To the nearly six-hundred writers who submitted their fine work to this, our first endeavor.

To every one of our twenty-five contributors, who gave us their best: you make us look good.

To Tim Lebbon, Matt Schwartz and the Shocklines family, Robert Weinberg, Stan and Heather at GillPrint, Jeff and Maria at Thomson-Shore, and Dennis Freeze.

To our families, for everything.

To everybody who lent their aid to us and other victims of Hurricanes Katrina and Rita, specifically William Bolen and his beautiful family, Greg Lamberson, Jeff Strand, Sean Lineweaver, Angie and Robert Craig, Patricia North, Darren and Julie Speegle, Carl and Amy, and the Gorumba family.

And finally to Nana Dot and Boppa Len: the Greatest Generation.

Contents

Introduction:
The Road Less Travelled

Joseph Nassise

For as long as I can remember, horror anthologies have been a part of my reading experience. From Kirby McCauley's *Dark Forces* to David Hartwell's *Dark Descent*, from Karl Wagner's *Year's Best Horror* to Stephen Jones' *Mammoth Book of Best New Horror*, I've eagerly acquired and subsequently devoured them all. Like a junkie in need of his fix, once I discovered them I couldn't get enough. *Masques. Borderlands. Darkside. Hot Blood.* Much of my appreciation for and understanding of the history of the horror genre has come from within their pages.

Why do I love anthologies so much? Quite simply because there is something special about a well written short story. Time in our hectic "hither and yon" culture is at a premium. After the demands of work and family, there seems precious little left over for personal relaxation. If I manage to find a few moments here or there to catch up on my reading, my preference is to work my way through a decent piece of short fiction rather than trying to rush through several pages of a novel, knowing I'd be forced to stop in the middle of a chapter or in the midst of the action itself if I chose the latter.

As a novelist at heart, I'm also envious of those who can capture the full essence of a story in a limited amount of space. Where I can happily dash off a 100,000 word novel, writing a 7,500 word short story is a real chore for me. Every word must be vital, every sentence irreplaceable. No long story arcs, no lengthy descriptions, no poetic meanderings. Just carefully chosen words inexorably pushing the story toward its conclusion. If I had followed that old adage about starting with short fiction before tackling something as big as a novel, I never would have pursued a career in writing.

But just throwing a bunch of short stories together does not give you an anthology that's worth reading. If it did, they would be a dime a dozen. What you need is a good editor.

No, wait, even that's not enough.

What you need is a good editor with a *vision*.

You see, even before the stories start to come in there are a hundred different decisions to make. Will the anthology have a specific theme or will it be simply a collection of stories without any common ties? Will you invite certain authors to submit? If so, who will they be? How many slots, if any, will be left available to open submissions? How many authors do you want in total? How many words each does that allow them to work with? What will you pay for the stories? What rights are you asking for? The list goes on and on. An editor with a solid vision for the project can make the appropriate choices, can guide the project right from the very start. Once all of that has been figured out, then and only then can the real fun begin . . . the submission process.

If you happen to believe that reading 500 submitted stories over the course of a few months is an exciting task, let me disabuse you of the notion right away. It is probably one of the most laborious tasks ever invented by man, second only to reading the slush pile at a major NY publishing company. If you don't believe me, try it sometime.

An anthology project that pays a fair rate will see an

average of 300-500 story submissions. A good 25% of them will be simply awful. Unreadable. So far off topic that you start to think they put the wrong story in the envelope. I'm not kidding. For a major anthology I edited two years ago, I even had one individual submit an idea for a story, rather than the story itself. Of course, the submission came to me without a title, without any identifying information as to who the author might me, and even without punctuation. Simply a "see there is this lamp a huanted lamp and this lamp blah blah blah", misspellings and all. At least that one was legible. We won't discuss the one I received handwritten in ink that had apparently been exposed to the rain a time or two.

Once you are past the simply awful, you get to the "what were they thinking" submissions. These are the ones where the writers have apparently decided to ignore anything remotely resembling your writer's guidelines and are sending you whatever story they happen to have available in their story file. Fantasy stories for horror anthologies. Horror stories for your latest romance oriented project. You get the idea. The one good thing about both of these categories is that you get to move past them extremely quickly, thereby lowering the outrageously high "to-be-read" pile that is taking up the space all around your desk. This usually encompasses another 10% or so of your submissions.

The next 50% of the stories you receive will be decent stories. They have a defined beginning, middle, and ending. They have characters that readers can identify with in some fashion. They have a plot that makes some logical kind of sense and the story itself is laid out in a decent fashion. Trouble is, they just aren't quite *there*. Something's missing, some spark, some sign of life that makes that puppy sit up and talk and practically scream at you saying "Buy me! Buy me!" These are good stories, told by decent writers, but they just aren't right for your project. These are often the toughest of the bunch, for as a writer yourself you want to take them apart, figure out why they don't work, and fix them. Which is quite out of the question, considering the still mile-high pile of submissions waiting to be read. You really don't even have time to dash off more than a quick "sorry, not right for us" note to the author and move on to the next story in the stack.

Finally, you get to the remaining 15%. These are the good ones. The ones you've been waiting for. The ones that hit the target dead-on. Characters that come to life as you read. Storylines that seduce you into believing they are real. Writing so crisp and sharp that it just jumps off the page.

Only trouble is, you've got 25 stories and only ten slots.

So you spend days agonizing over your choices, trying to find just the right combination of authors and stories that will leave you with a book that will be remembered long after the reader turns that last page. Just when you think you've gotten it right, you second guess yourself and start all over again.

Until finally, it's finished.

You've got a solid selection of stories that complement each other. Stories with unique voices and unique styles that somehow flow together in harmony, making the sum total better than its individual parts, creating a unique package all its own.

Like the anthology you're reading now, created by a pair of editors with a vision.

Truth be told, though, that's only half the story. You see, sometimes even a good project can often get derailed before it gets off the ground. As was *almost* the case with this one.

But before I can tell you about the anthology that almost wasn't, we need to talk for a moment about the First Rule of Professional Writing:

Money flows to the writer.

That's an immutable law for those of us in the writing industry, as certain as death and taxes or gravity's effect on a falling body. Writing is hard work. It takes time, effort, and skill. And like any other trade, a writer expects to get paid for what he puts into his creations. If I sit down and write 10,000 words on a given theme, I should receive compensation for the effort and energy I've put in from anyone interested in publishing that material. I don't care if they publish it on the web, in book format, as an audio file, as a comic book—whatever. Simply put, fair compensation for fair use.

In the case of a novel, a writer is typically paid an advance against royalties. When it comes to short fiction, like the stories found in this volume, a per word rate is usually paid upon acceptance. In the HWA, we set a bare minimum of five cents per word as a barometer of professional publication.

All of which boils down to that simple phrase again: Money flows to the writer.

Remember that. We're going to come back to it shortly.

As the president of the Horror Writers Association, the world's largest body of professional horror and dark fantasy writers, I come in contact regularly with people from quite a few different walks of life and at different stages of their writing careers. The HWA attracts a variety of working writers, from highly respected authors like Clive Barker and Peter Straub to newcomers who have made their first sale but have yet to make a name for themselves. Many of our members interact on the private message board the organization maintains, sharing everything from market news to the trials and tribulations of the writing life in general.

Just about three years ago, a new member began posting there, a fellow by the name of R.J. Sevin. R.J. was a personable guy, full of enthusiasm and excitement about being in the midst of an industry he found enjoyable and fascinating. Knowing that the markets for professional horror fiction were rather limited, R.J. decided that he was going to create a new market, one that would showcase some of the very best horror fiction currently being written. With much enthusiasm but also a small bit of naivety, R.J. created a webzine called The Web of Horror and invited all of the pros he'd recently become friendly with at the HWA to send him their latest creations.

The pay he was offering?

Exposure.

As you can no doubt imagine, R.J.'s offer went over with all the aplomb of a truck load of dead fish dumped in the midst of a Georgia debutante ball.

I can hear some of you asking already, what's the matter with exposure? Why wouldn't an author want that? Isn't exposure a good thing? Doesn't more exposure help build an author's audience?

Of course, it does. But unlike sex, which, as the old saying goes, is still pretty good for some people even when it's bad, the wrong type of exposure can be absolutely worthless. In certain situations, it can even harm a writer's career, rather than help it.

In order for exposure of a writer's material to be beneficial, the work in question must be exposed to a) the right audience and b) wide enough numbers to have a material impact. Showcasing a horror story on a romance web site, for example, would probably not be beneficial, as the majority of those exposed to the material wouldn't care less about it, if they viewed it at all. On the other hand, doing the same thing on a horror site is at least targeting the material to the right audience. This is where the second criteria comes in. Showcasing a horror story on a site devoted to the horror genre certainly makes perfect sense, but if that site is visited by the same ten people over and over again, it is next to useless for the writer.

Like many writers, I value each and every one of my readers. I appreciate the fact that they choose my work over the tens of thousands of other possibilities that confront them when they set foot inside a bookstore. However, giving away a story that I slaved over for weeks in exchange for the one or two new readers that might visit an amateur website does not seem like a fair exchange of effort to me.

Nor did it to the majority of HWA members who responded to R.J.'s post.

R.J.'s idea was well intentioned, there is no doubt about that, but he made one of the cardinal mistakes that those new to the industry often make—he didn't understand the basic framework on which it operated.

Unsurprisingly, a number of veterans let R.J. know exactly what they thought of his idea and why. Like most criticism, this was probably hard for him to take and quite possibly could have soured his enthusiasm for both the genre and the organization.

Happily, this did not turn out to be the case. Like a true professional, R.J. took the time to digest what had been said, to look into the issue with a bit more care and diligence, and then he came back with an entirely new idea, this time in partnership with his wife, Julia.

Our erstwhile editors recognized that in order to get the best work, you have to be willing to recognize the value it contains. Then they took it to the next level. They formed a publishing company called Creeping Hemlock Press and announced a new anthology project called *Corpse Blossoms*. When the submission guidelines landed on my desk, I was both surprised and delighted to see that not only was this venue a paying one, but that it was paying more per word than the majority of anthology markets available at the time. And not only that, but the volume would be released in multiple states including a trade edition, a signed slipcased limited edition, and a deluxe lettered edition housed in a custom wood and leather traycase. The Sevins created not just a well paying market, but an end product that any writer would be pleased to have in his collected works.

Sometimes adversity breeds triumph.

There are a wide variety of stories in this book. From the quiet horror of Brian Freeman's *Running Rain* to the gruesome nightmares of Kealan Patrick Burke's *Empathy*, there are tales here for every taste. Some will scare you. Some will make you think. Some are designed simply to entertain. But all of them, taken together, form a book that's worth reading.

What better compliment could the writers and editors receive?

Joe Nassise
Phoenix, AZ
August 2005

Foreword

This is no lottery.

This anthology was not thrown together with some haphazard flair, some foregone conclusion that good writing will inevitably shine, environment be damned. Nor was it organized to feature our more prominent authors and tuck the newcomers away in the pantry.

No.

These stories were arranged painstakingly and purposefully to complement one another by subject and voice, to vary from intense to languid, to carry the same general narrative thread from randomness to focused fear to madness to the end of the world itself.

Taken apart, *Corpse Blossoms* is a handful of snapshots. Arranged together, it is intended to be an experience. **We ask that you read these exceptional stories in the order that they appear for full effect.**

No, this is no lottery . . . but it's your lucky day nonetheless.

i: The First Handful of Dirt

White Shrouds of Memory

Ward Cary Parker

Tan on white on blue skirt beneath the card-strewn table
where he was not supposed to see it.

He had just decided to go to bed when the woman landed in his tangerine tree.

There had been a thunderclap, and, soon afterwards, a rattling of large objects hitting the roof. He wheeled himself to the patio's sliding glass door, flicked on the outside light, and that's when he saw her fall.

It was like someone had catapulted a mannequin into his yard. The body—so limp, so carelessly strewn—dropped from the sky and crashed into the crown of his beloved tree. The top branches were crushed, but the rest of the tree absorbed the impact, flexing like a bedspring. Unripe tangerines shot across the small yard and rolled to a stop beneath his single palm tree like green pool balls.

A body falling from the sky into his yard. It made no sense. Even as it dawned on him that there had been an airline disaster overhead, Thomas couldn't accept the fact that there was a body in his tangerine tree.

In the faint, yellow glow of his patio light, the dark figure was unmoving. He was sure she was dead.

Debris was still falling, slapping the leaves like the heavy drops at the end of a summer thunderstorm. He caught the acrid reek of burning fuel.

Lights appeared in the windows of his neighbors to the right and rear. Stanton, who hadn't yet gone to bed—evidenced by his blaring TV set—appeared at the low wall that separated their property.

"Oh, Jesus, Thomas. You okay? Anything burning?"

"There's a body in my tree."

Stanton glanced at the tree and crossed himself. "Oh, Jesus. This is terrible. All the people—God have mercy on them."

Stanton playing the moral Christian was hypocritical

in Thomas's opinion, but he excused him under the circumstances.

Fragments of paper, fabric and insulation floated downwards and dusted everything like snow. A cocktail napkin landed in Thomas's lap. It bore the logo of BargainJet Airlines.

"They blew it up," Thomas said more to himself than to Stanton. "The bastards blew it up just like that Pan-Am flight over Lockerbie. Goddamn terrorists."

"Maybe. It could have been an accident. A fuel tank explosion or something."

It didn't matter, Thomas thought. All these innocent victims had died for nothing. It was all so random and meaningless.

Stanton cleared his throat, as if trying not to cry. "Do you want to come over to my house until they take that body away?"

"I fought in Korea. I've seen plenty of dead bodies. Just help me cover her with a blanket for decency's sake."

Thomas rolled the wheelchair into the living room and grabbed the coverlet from the sofa. His wife had sometimes used it, but he never did. It only got in the way now that she was gone and reminded him that she had been stolen from him, even before she had died. Gazing at her cancer-wasted body had been far harder than anything he'd seen in the war or in his tangerine tree.

Stanton carried an aluminum extension ladder around the house from the garage and leaned it against the tangerine tree. He climbed up, covering the woman with the blanket unevenly due to branches poking up between her limbs. After he climbed down, he left the ladder standing.

"I'm going to check on the neighbors," Stanton said. "You'll be okay here by yourself?"

Thomas nodded and Stanton disappeared down the side of the house into the darkness.

The smoke was heavier in the breeze now, thick with wood smoke from homes on fire. He heard two distant sirens, but not at all the commotion he'd expect after an air disaster. He supposed things didn't happen as instantly as CNN would have you believe.

But how long would he have to wait for someone to take away the body?

Though he had claimed dead bodies didn't bother him, this one did. It didn't belong here. This wasn't a war zone; it was a quiet seaside community filled mostly with retired folks. And the fact that this poor woman had plunged over five miles to the earth—the fact that fate or physics had her land on his tangerine tree—seemed almost a message meant for him.

That death was winning in his world.

He took a long look at the body, a white hand dangling below the edge of the blanket and a white bare foot poking upwards. Then, pushing himself along the well-worn wheel grooves in the carpet, he went through the living room to the antique Chinese chest that served as the liquor cabinet. It had once been the center of good times back in the early days of his retirement, when Gladys had been healthy and neighbors were always coming by for drinks or bridge or more drinks. It was all a big party back then, with the exuberance of kids let out for summer vacation who haven't yet realized that vacations always come to an end.

Even now, with so many of their number gone, he still refused to accept that it was over.

His hands trembled as he poured the tumbler full of Scotch. It was too much to take down in one gulp and he nearly gagged until the warmth calmed him.

He glanced out the patio door and saw the blanket-draped body suspended in the tree. The blanket was white, which reminded him of the bodies in Korea—not the ROK soldiers, which you'd often find rotting by the roadside. No, white was the traditional garb of the peasants, farmers, villagers. He'd seen far too many of them piled in burning villages after the North Koreans had pushed through on their unstoppable dash to Seoul.

And he remembered others, beneath a railroad bridge. Mothers and children. White blouses blossoming with scarlet.

The memory was always just beneath the surface, struggling to break free, and he didn't want that to happen.

He took a large swallow of Scotch. Why was it, as he sat here waiting for a dead body to be taken away (because no matter how much he tried to deny it, he couldn't relax with the damn thing out there), that memories of the dead were returning to him now all at once?

The whiskey burned.

The white-clad children trying to hide behind their dead mothers. Gladys's white, almost translucent skin beneath which the blood vessels stopped throbbing.

He jumped as a figure appeared at the sliding glass door. It was Stanton, whose previously blanched expression had turned an angry red. He slid open the door without invitation.

"Can you believe there are no emergency teams here yet?" Stanton said, slightly out of breath. "There's no one here but the one volunteer fire department truck and some sheriff's deputies. There's got to be twenty homes on fire throughout the development, and the clubhouse is gone—wiped out. Nothing but a crater. One of the jet engines landed on it. We haven't found any injured residents, yet—thank God it's summer and half the homes are empty—but someone's got to stop the fires before this whole place goes up."

Stanton's New York accent was coming on strong, which it usually did when he was angry or complaining. He was tall with a full head of white hair, hawk nose and deeply lined face that made him look like the outdoorsman he was not. Women were unreasonably attracted to him. He'd been president of the homeowners association for five years straight and, apparently, was the self-appointed guardian of the community.

"And the bodies . . . sweet Jesus they're everywhere, Thomas. They're on roofs, in swimming pools, on cars.

Linda Levine down the street has ten bodies in her yard. It's absolutely horrifying and something's got to be done before there's a health hazard."

Thomas shrugged. "What did 911 say?"

"I've called them four times and they say the cavalry's on its way; but some drawbridges over the Intracoastal aren't working, so they're making a detour. This is ridiculous. It's as if they don't believe me. The last one said there's been no report from the FAA or anyone else that a plane's gone down."

"Maybe we're being too impatient," Thomas said, his fatigue slowing his words. "I know I am—I've got a dead body in my tree. Maybe this is the normal response time—maybe the FAA waits until they're absolutely sure there's nothing wrong with their radar or the jet's radio."

Stanton seemed doubtful. "The waiting period is over. Our community is burning down. Call me if you need me," he said as he stomped out the front door.

Thomas quickly made for the bar and poured another drink. This time he drank more slowly; he wanted to get drunk but knew it would be hours before he could go to bed. He turned on the TV and surfed through the channels, finding nothing about the crash. In the old days, every channel would be interrupted for a big story like this. Now the majority of these cable stations were oblivious to the world outside their music videos or tight-assed girls on exercise machines. Even if a nuclear bomb dropped on New York, they wouldn't interrupt their programming.

He settled on CNN and a local network affiliate, switching back and forth between the two to avoid commercials. But he soon grew bored. And glanced outside.

The dead woman in the tangerine tree moved her hand.

He was sure of it—the hand raised itself and then dropped down again. Now more of it showed from beneath the blanket.

Could she be alive? It was impossible. No one ever

survived an air disaster like this, though he did remember reading that they had found a fleeting pulse in a flight attendant after the Lockerbie crash.

That opened the disturbing possibility that this woman in his tangerine tree had been alive after the explosion. Did she have to endure the horror of an endless fall to the earth like Icarus? Had she been napping or reading when suddenly the cabin broke open and black night poured in and there was nothing but falling?

As if to answer him, her hand moved again.

True, it was only a very slight movement—it could have merely been swaying tree branches stirring her arm.

It could have been anything other than animated life moving that hand.

But he had to know.

Stanton answered the phone after the first ring.

"Oh, it's you," he said. "I just heard Mrs. Moore on Seahorse Lane died of a heart attack. Probably the shock of having bodies land on her roof."

"I'm sorry to hear that," Thomas said. "Could you come over? You speak of shock—I think the body in my tree is driving me . . . making me see things. I swear I saw her move her hand and I need you to check her pulse just to make absolutely certain she's not still alive."

"You've got to be kidding. How could she be alive?"

"Stranger things have happened."

"I'm not so thrilled to be touching one of these bodies."

"Please," Thomas said. "We've got to be sure."

It took Stanton twenty minutes to make it over, time enough for Thomas to finish a Scotch and think again about Gladys's hands. So delicate, so soft, so white. He had loved to touch her hands any chance he got—during movies, when taking walks, beneath the tables of restaurants. When he touched her hand he felt pacified; he felt reassurance flowing through her pores to his. When he woke up from the war nightmares, she would soothe him, hold each of his shaking hands between her palms and rub them as if warming them.

And his hands always trembled, like they had from the violent recoil of the .30-caliber machine gun. Shaking and shaking, round after round, until the barrel glowed red.

A lieutenant had put his hand on Thomas's shoulder. "You can stop now, Corporal. They're all dead."

All piled in heaps of white spattered with crimson.

The front door plunged open. Stanton entered as if this were his own house. Thomas had often wondered if he thought it was.

Normally, his neighbor would do his rooster-walk into the center of whatever was going on, but this time he was pale and unsteady. He reached into the Chinese chest, knowing exactly where his hands were going, and pulled out the bottle of Scotch. It rattled against the tumbler as he poured.

"Are you okay?" Thomas asked. "Has all this been too much for you?"

Stanton swallowed his drink and coughed. He collapsed onto the couch, a tear rolling down one cheek.

"I saw Maria tonight."

"What are you talking about?"

"It wasn't her, but it was," Stanton's eyes were pleading. "I can't explain. There was a dead woman in Mrs. Moore's yard, lying there on her back like she was sleeping. Completely undamaged, you know, like nothing had happened to her. Like she hadn't fallen from the airliner. And I took a closer look . . . and she was Maria . . ." He let out a single, painful sob.

"Shhh. It was just your imagination."

"That's what I'd say now, but when I saw Maria I *knew* it was her. She opened her eyes and they had hurt in them. They were accusing me of . . . well, it was like ten years ago," he cleared his throat and gathered himself. "I looked away and when I looked back she was gone—I mean it was some woman I didn't know with her eyes open in death."

"You don't have to check on the body in my tree if you don't want to."

"I've had enough of dead bodies tonight, Thomas. Are you sure you weren't imagining things like I was?"

"I'm sure. I would check her myself if I could."

"No, no, I'll do it." Stanton gave the sigh of the only one around to do a man's job. "If it helps you rest easy."

He went outside, across the patio, through the tiny yard to the tangerine tree. Thomas wheeled after him. Stanton climbed the aluminum ladder to the very top step and leaned over the branches toward the body, grabbing a branch in one hand to steady himself. He paused, then reached for her wrist.

Thomas, looking up, saw their hands touch. His tanned skin against her pale.

He remembered.

Tan on white on blue skirt beneath the card-strewn table where he was not supposed to see it. Sinatra was singing "Mac the Knife," and the four of them were drunk. Everyone was giggling at some stupid joke, except for Maria, whose dark eyes held foreboding. Stanton turned to Gladys and said something Thomas couldn't hear, but he could see a look pass between them and that's when he leaned back in his chair and saw the hands touching atop her skirt.

That's when their affair began and every bit of joy in life ended for Thomas.

He had done nothing to stop it. He knew he was a moody, difficult man to live with. His nightmares and the diabetes amputations that left him in a wheelchair made him too dependent upon his wife. So he tried to convince himself the affair wasn't happening.

But the rage festered.

"No pulse," Stanton said above him. "Are you satisfied now?"

"No. I'm not."

Thomas grabbed the wheels and lurched forward,

hitting the ladder with his shoulder. It tipped left, Stanton teetered right, and then both came down, bouncing on branches. The ladder fell off towards the wall. Stanton landed at the base of the tree, his neck at a funny angle. Thomas expected him to moan or shout in anger, but he merely lay there.

Thomas wondered how he could have snapped like that, as he bent over the body and felt the pulse flicker and then die.

He felt strangely empty. The people he had cared for and the man he had hated were all dead now. What was left to tie him to the world?

Screams pierced the night from all directions and the smoke was thicker in the air. As his numbness wore off, he began to be afraid. He returned to the living room and turned on the TV. He went through every channel and there was no mention of an air disaster or of a subdivision filled with retirees that was burning. The world went on, oblivious to their private nightmares.

The TV was snuffed out as the power died. He moved through the darkness to the front of the house, looking out the window as a man with a missing arm walked through the yard across the street. He heard glass shatter and a woman beg "*no*."

A shotgun fired twice somewhere down the street. The night sky glowed orange from spreading fires. He felt as if the world, at least here, were ending.

He went to close the blinds over the patio door but it was too late. He saw her move again.

She stirred lazily beneath the blanket as if she had overslept on a Sunday morning, her limbs stretching further as she awoke and lost her stiffness.

Thomas wasn't surprised, really. He was too far past trying to reconcile logic with what had happened this night. Still, he was relieved the blanket stayed atop her head.

Over the clicks of the blinds closing he heard her climbing down: branches snapping, tangerines thudding upon the ground.

For a moment he hoped that she would merely wander off into the night like the others were doing. But he peeked between the blinds and saw her coming toward the house, the blanket still hanging from her head like she was a kid pretending to be a ghost.

He checked to make sure the sliding glass door was locked but he knew it didn't matter. He knew she would get inside.

A dark shadow against the blinds. Fingers scratching the glass.

"Gladys?" His voice was hoarse. "Gladys, is that you?"

Just as Stanton had seen Maria, he hoped to see Gladys—Gladys here to take him with her to the other place where all their friends waited. He told himself it could be true.

He again peered through the blinds and got his answer. The hand that sought a way through the glass wasn't white after all. Then the blanket fell, revealing her face and the bullet hole that marred her forehead above her black, angry eyes.

She was a young Korean woman. He should have known it would be.

He unlocked the door anyway.

An Average Insanity, A Common Agony

Tom Piccirilli

He moved in the direction of the titty bar
wondering what new screw-up
he was headed for this time.

They thought it was just the funniest thing ever, bringing the old guy *and* his dog into the place. Three college jocks drunker than hell but with a real edge about them, carrying a harsh atmosphere inside with them from the street. Vin tightened in his chair as a flush of heat went through his belly. It only took a glance to know everything about them: a trio of starting line seniors but the pros hadn't come knocking like they were supposed to. Now at twenty-two these kids were already witnessing the fall of their dreams, the slow flat resentment angling up through their lives.

It's why they were so loud. Laughing wildly, easing loose with a little madness, pushing the blind man on, grabbing him roughly and hugging him to their barrel chests as if he were their greatest love. His cane tapped mercilessly, slapping at puddles of spilled beer on the floor. Even the guide dog walked warily beside its master, watchful, sensing a vague evil.

Vin felt it too. His scalp prickled and the sweat began to writhe at his temples.

The waitress came over and asked, "Another Scotch?" She had her body angled at him but she too continued glancing over at the scene.

A new song kicked on with a dully throbbing beat and she unconsciously swayed to it. He liked the way she held herself. Solid, with a real personality, an honest grin. She had a deeper strata to her disposition. Usually waitresses in strip joints felt a competition with the dancers, and tried to really throw it out there under the customers' noses. Blathering and flirting, putting a hand on your arm, giving the plastic smile. Everybody going for the same lousy buck.

The need to sigh rose in his chest but he crushed it

back down. She had a strong chin, a delicate cheek, and short brown hair that framed her heart-shaped face. A sudden jab of melancholy got him low, the way it always did when he realized he couldn't think sweet thoughts about girls like this anymore. They just made him into a dirty old man now, and he didn't know how it had happened.

"No, just a beer this time," he said.

"Charlie's on break," she told him, with a worried tone. It perked him up in his seat. She frowned in a brooding, little-girl manner, and he thought anybody who made her pout like that should be buried under the cesspools of hell.

"Who's Charlie?"

"The bouncer. It looked like a calm night so he took off with his girlfriend for a little while." She caught her bottom lip between two teeth and worked it for a second. "They're making fun of him, aren't they? And he doesn't know it."

"He knows it," Vin told her. "Even his dog knows it."

"He sells magazines on the corner with another old guy."

"I know, I see him all the time."

"I hope there's no trouble."

She'd been handing Vin his drinks for two hours, but the sudden shift in mood somehow brought them together now, alerted them to one another's presence. She gave him a hard look, the kind that took in details besides your face.

"What are you doing here?" she asked.

"What do you mean?"

"This is a dive," she said. "Mostly for drunks and bachelor parties and dumb kids who don't have the money to go see real erotic dancers."

"You don't show much loyalty to your boss."

"This is a stop-gap. I just got out of school. Fashion design. Visual merchandising. The real job in the city with *Truex & Balenciaga* doesn't start until the end of the month."

"Seventh Avenue," Vin said. "Quite a step up from this neighborhood." He shrugged and, almost with an air of surrender, nodded. "My father used to drink here with his buddies, back in the day. We lived around the corner. I still do, five houses down from where I grew up. This wasn't a strip joint back then, just a local pub. Not choice by any stretch, but some class, at least for the locals. A couple of the Brooklyn golden gloves champs, Johnny Tormino and Jojo Lebowski, used to hang around here."

"I don't know who they are."

"No reason why you should. Just a couple of guys who had some great stories."

"Are you a boxer?" she asked. "You look in shape, like you could do some damage if you wanted to."

"For my age?"

"You're not that old."

It was true, but it almost never felt that way. He'd turned some kind of corner not long ago and hadn't been the same since. He was thirty-nine and hadn't gone too far to fat yet, and he could still quote Browning and Keats when the mood called for it, but that didn't happen anymore. Perhaps it never really had.

Another eruption of scarcely contained malicious laughter, the kind of giggles the psychopaths on the ten o'clock news gave all the time. The blind man spoke quietly and they were still touching him, thumping his shoulder. Vin wanted to smash a bottle over somebody's face, but there still wasn't any visible reason for all the tension going through his guts. He wondered if he was starting to lose the nature of his character, the way his father had at about this age. Getting a little stupid, always sitting in the chair, silent and staring off. With almost no real identity at all at the end.

The jocks called her over and she went to take their orders. Vin locked up again. One kid put his hand on her hip, another pressed himself in close, showing off his teeth.

It always came down to this, the anger stirring inside

him, the jealousy about any woman he even looked at. He brought the glass up to his mouth but it was empty.

One of the flat-chested dancers walked across the stage and tried to make eyes. She swung around the pole and jiggled what little meat she had. You could count every rib if you wanted, and her nostrils were pink with flaring busted capillaries. Bony but with stretch-marks around her nipples. Another cokehead with a couple of kids being taken care of by her parents. She used pancake to cover over the bruises on her legs, but left the rug burns on her knees for everyone to see. Maybe it was supposed to be a turn-on. Vin was usually confused about shit like that.

The waitress moved by him on the run and said, "I'll get your beer in a sec."

"Okay."

The stripper didn't appreciate his lack of interest and really started doing her best slap-and-grind. It was so pathetic that he nearly laughed, until he realized what he must look like from the other side of the stage.

A graying middle-aged guy with his own scars and pockmarks, stubbled and squinting, the wrinkles around his eyes deep enough that they needed to be dusted. In a dive like this on a Friday night, with an overflowing ashtray and a couple of empty shot glasses in front of him, sitting around and waiting for money or happiness or fate to fall through the ceiling and into his fucking arms.

He handed her a five dollar bill and she gave him the imitation smile and wandered off down the stage.

She did the same shimmy in front of the jocks and the boys roared. There had been three just like them in college with Vin, twenty years ago. Del, Philly, and Bent. He was the bookworm anchor to their boisterous clique, and for a long while he'd admired them with a strange joy, sick with envy. Until one by one they'd all fallen away to pregnant girlfriends, factory jobs, and jail time.

Now here they were again, alternate versions of Del, Philly, and Bent, but so much like them in subtle mannerisms, down to their sharp movements and the near-hysteria in their laughter.

The German Shepherd swung its snout towards Vin and gazed at him with sorrowful eyes.

Still waiting for his beer, he looked down and saw that not only had the waitress already brought it to him, but he'd finished more than half the bottle.

Christ, just like Dad.

He took out a ten and left it for her, spun from his seat and moved towards the door. A growing anxiety kicked him along. As he passed the German Shepherd, he held his hand out and the dog licked his wrist, folding its ears back and cringing as the noise surged again.

The blind man was no longer smiling. He said a few quiet words Vin couldn't pick up, and then his lips appeared to weld together forming a bloodless line. His chest heaved as his breathing became rapid. The waitress came by with more drinks and the boys sucked them down, and another burned-out dancer commenced to stick it in front of them.

Vin got outside and the sudden cool air and silence was such a relief that he let out a gasp.

He stepped onto the sidewalk and crossed the street, looking at the cramped houses that lined the area. Once he could've named everyone who lived in each of them: the Danetellos, the Martinis, the Ganuccis, the Rorigans. He'd play stickball here with the rest of the kids, got into fights up the alley. The month he learned to drive he picked up his first lay, Jennie Bishop, right at the end of the road, and took her a mile down to the pier. It had been a reckless, mad night that ended with the challenge of manhood.

Maybe it had proven to be too great an ordeal. Vin walked back to his place but didn't want to go in yet. There wasn't anything for him inside. Not even a goldfish. Nothing that needed his attention or affection. No work that had to be taken care of. No real hobbies to consume the hours. No family left. Most of his friends had moved out of state, looking for cheaper family housing down south or out west.

The neighborhood had some kind of a pull on him tonight. You knew you were in trouble when you were this close to going through your high school yearbook and calling your old girlfriends. How sad was that.

He walked down the block past the house where he grew up and stared at the bedroom window that used to be his. A soft breeze drifted against his throat and he realized with a strangely immense yet common dread that he was as clichéd as every other man approaching middle age.

It doesn't take much to crowd you out of your own house.

When you were married it was the wife and her sister and mother and their busybody klatch. Later on it was the letters and endless phone calls and visits from her lawyer. The front door rattling in its frame from the fists of collection agencies, the pricks serving summonses. Then the drinking buddies, the clinging one-night stands who didn't realize the night was over.

He had all kinds of ghosts packed into his closets, and suddenly Vin backed up off the sidewalk, turned around, and had to fight to quell the desperate need to see that waitress again.

It was utterly stupid. The old man folly that had gotten hold of his father at the end was already at work on him. He wandered aimlessly through the neighborhood for about an hour, trying to work off the anxiety.

Instead, it had grown until he was on fire with it. His steps and body were driven forward. He moved in the direction of the titty bar wondering what new screw-up he was headed for this time.

By now he was almost jogging, and he heard the murmurs of a mob before he saw them. Then the flashing lights lending a peculiar glow to the street, flaring up against the nearby houses where people leaned over their windowsills.

Dozens had gathered in front of the bar. Two cruisers were parked head to head at the curb. They already had the crime scene tape strung around the door, the blue barricades blocking the sidewalk off.

The waitress, four dancers with flimsy robes on, and a musclebound guy who must've been Charlie the bouncer were all congregated by the police cars. They each took a turn talking with the cops. Vin slid through the throng, which was already beginning to fracture as folks broke away into the darkness.

Eventually he saw his chance and cut towards the waitress.

She let out a small moan when he touched her on the shoulder, then took his hand when she saw it was him.

"What happened?" he asked.

"Jesus, you just missed it." Her voice was heavy with emotion, and he saw she'd been crying. "It started two minutes after you walked out."

"Those three shithead jocks?"

"They started getting rougher with the blind man, shoving him, trying to get him drunk."

Vin thought back to the old guy who had looked as if his lips had been welded together, saying something quiet that Vin didn't catch. That frail chest heaving. "He'd had enough of their games."

"The dog growled and one of them spit beer at it. The blind man got mad and used his cane, waving it around, swinging at them. All three of those bastards started beating him up, got him on the floor and were kicking him, and the dog went crazy. It jumped and got one of the boys by the throat and killed him. Chomped on the wrist of the other. It almost took his hand off. The guy was spurting all over. He was bleeding out. It happened so fast it still doesn't seem real. I feel sort of high, you know?" Tears welled in her eyes but didn't fall. "Charlie came back and tried to tie a tourniquet on him but it didn't do much good. I called an ambulance. The third kid was screaming and kept kicking the blind man."

"Christ," Vin said, picturing it all, putting the names to the kids again, still identifying them with Del, Philly, and Bent. She started to tremble and then the shakes got worse. He took her by the shoulders, trying to lend her whatever he could.

"He got into a fight with Charlie and Charlie broke his jaw. The ambulance took both the boys away but I think that one, with the hand, is probably dead."

"Goddamn." He couldn't say anything more. The back of his neck was wet and icy with sweat. He was aware of feeling a certain amount of both horror and pride. Thinking about the dog and going, good for you, boy. Vin had no idea what that said about himself. Maybe he just hated everybody younger than him.

"The blind guy had a fractured skull, they said. He was having a seizure when they took him out."

Vin had known there was something foreboding about those guys, about the situation brewing, but he'd never imagined anything like this.

She actually came into his arms then, and he held her, trying not to show how startled he was. He tightened his grip as she wept. She struggled to get the words out. "They took the seeing eye dog away to the pound. He was so calm afterwards, just sitting there, his tail flicking a little. Three big dogcatchers came up on him with these poles with wire at the end and lassoed him around the throat. He was crying and whining, and the three of them practically strangled him and threw him into the back of their truck."

Pricks like that, they always had to move in threes. "The pound is only nine or ten blocks from here, down over from Ocean Boulevard."

She looked at him, the tears streaming on her cheeks, and he felt, for a second, very young again. "I know it's stupid but I want to help him," she said. "It wasn't the dog's fault. It shouldn't be killed. Do you think we should go there?"

"The cops are going to want to talk to you again."

"I already told them everything twice."

"They'll ask again with something like this."

Two kids dead, an old man possibly dying, but when it came down to it, he only cared about the girl's smile and the dog. Perhaps because he felt that, somehow, they were the only innocents here. Even the blind guy had been calling down his own trouble, drinking with the jocks and taking as much shit from them as he did. Hadn't he felt the charged possibility of violence from the start, the way Vin had?

"I'll go see what I can do," he told her.

She grinned at him, and the world seemed to be filled with a little extra potential once more. We all need a private mission to perform, a reason to take the next step. Easing his hand up, he touched the side of her face. She leaned in for a second and stirred against his him, and he almost kissed her forehead but didn't, and then the cops called her back over and she went.

Okay, Vin thought, let's go to the pound.

It was over on a cul-de-sac down by the beach, near the crumbling boardwalk and condemned pier. Vin started moving faster, until he was jogging again. When he was a kid his parents used to take him down here to go swimming. They'd build sandcastles and his father would make sounds like the seagulls, his voice echoing among the dunes. You couldn't do anything in these waters anymore. Too much sewage and factory waste.

Soon he was flat-out sprinting. It took five minutes and he wasn't even winded by the time he turned the corner into the cul-de-sac. Not too bad for an old man. He checked his watch and stopped short.

Jesus, it was almost 4:30 am.

But the lights were on in the pound, and a cruiser was parked in the street out front. No sign of the three dog catchers. Vin walked up to the front glass doors, tried them and found them unlocked. He stepped inside.

A cop stood there talking with a pregnant woman who'd obviously been roused from bed. Is that how they handled things like this? Nobody had to sign any papers, they just woke up whoever was in charge and they put the animal to sleep right then? Vin didn't even know how they did it. Gas? A lethal shot? Furnace?

Dogs whined in the back room. The cop moved to meet Vin, already looking pissed off. He was hardly older than the jocks in the bar last night. He said, "Who the hell are you?"

Putting him in his place right from the start. Keeping him in the box even though he hadn't so much as taken a step out of it. That's how they all did it to you. It wore down the skin of your soul until you were nothing but exposed nerve.

"It wasn't the German Shepherd's fault," Vin said.

The officer pulled a face. "I asked who you were."

"I was in that strip joint earlier tonight."

"Were you a witness to the attack?"

Which one? The kids on the old man, or the dog on the kids? "No, but I saw those boys getting out of hand. They were giving the blind guy trouble. The German Shepherd—"

"It killed one of them, did you know that? Another lost his hand. He's undergoing major surgery over at St. Mary's. He might die."

"Look, the seeing-eye dog was trying to protect its master. You didn't hurt it yet, did you?"

The cop gave him an expression of disdain, staring at Vin with his lips curling and his chin pulling back like there was a bad smell. Vin wasn't sure anybody had ever given him such a look of disgust before. Not even trying to understand, not listening at all. Talking about the kids, but not saying a word about the old blind man. How was he? Was he still alive?

The pregnant kennel worker remained silent but seething. She walked around Vin and went to the door, opened it so the cop could push Vin back outside.

It was as if they had rehearsed this many times before, like they'd been waiting for him, tonight and perhaps for all his life.

The officer laid a hand on Vin's shoulder, gripped him hard, and tried to turn him around. Getting up too close. Shoving.

"Quit pushing me, kid," Vin said.

"What did you just call me?"

One of them had been dying to get rough—maybe they were both spoiling for a match—and now the cop reached for his nightstick. Were they all just burning to beat the shit out of somebody? Was that the only choice anybody had left anymore? Or had it been that way from the beginning, but he hadn't noticed?

He'd never answered the waitress when she'd asked him if he was a boxer. He'd never stepped inside a professional ring, but as a teenager he'd spent a lot of hours with Johnny Tormino and Jojo Lebowski, training, thinking about putting his skills to the test. He'd thought about it and thought about it, and by the time he decided to give it a shot his chance had come and gone.

The cop held the nightstick out straight and pressed it against the center of Vin's chest, forcing him back. "Am I going to have trouble with you? I can smell whiskey on your breath."

"That was hours ago. I told you I was in the bar."

"Why don't you go sleep it off, buddy, before I have to run you in."

Run him in, like he was a second-story man. A purse-snatcher. There were mobsters living all over the neighborhood, but no, this one here was going to run Vin in.

"I haven't done anything. I just wanted to—to say that I was there—that I saw what was going on. It wasn't the dog's fault."

"Are you crazy, mister?"

Laying it out on the line like that, asking the big

question. Vin actually thought about it for a moment, wondering, is this insane what I'm doing here? Am I being that irrational? Is that what happens when you want a young fashion designer to like you?

Again with the nightstick in Vin's chest, harder this time. He let out a grunt and backed a step away. The woman held the door open even wider.

An abrupt rage swelled within him, igniting. The cop tried the move again, crowding him, driving the stick forward. Vin grabbed hold of it and smacked it aside.

That was all it took. The pregnant lady let out a little screech, and the dogs in back began to howl, and the cop's eyes got wide and he sneered like a maniac and started to go for his gun.

Vin said, "No."

He grabbed the officer's wrist, yanking him off balance, setting him up for a left hook. Vin let one loose and felt the kid's lips smear beneath his fist. It felt so beautiful and right that he gave a brief laugh. He cut it off, knowing this was the serious shit now, he'd just crossed over a line.

The cop hadn't gone down but had flown backward a few feet, doubled over holding his face with one hand, clearing the gun free from leather with the other. Vin stepped close and brought a vicious uppercut into the kid's chin. It lifted the officer two feet into the air and deposited him on his ass, out cold. The pistol spun across the floor.

There, he thought, that was all right.

He grabbed the woman by the forearm and said, "Take me to that German Shepherd."

"You're insane."

"Whatever, lady."

"You're going to go to jail."

"There's worse things," he told her, though he really wasn't certain. Was being in the can going to be worse than living on the outside with no purpose? Probably not.

She brought him into the kennel and led him to a cage. The German Shepherd sat there, ears back, looking terrified.

"Let him out."

"It'll attack."

"He's harmless. Do it."

She unlocked the cage and pulled away. Hesitantly, the dog stepped out and stood before Vin and licked his hand again. The woman said, "It's a killer. It still has blood on its fur."

"No different than any of us, lady."

"Why are you doing this?"

"Because it's time to draw a line."

The dog walked beside him and they moved back out into the main room. The cop was still unconscious. Again Vin felt that weird sense of pride, although he knew it would land him in prison. At least he'd thrown one good punch.

As they passed by the officer, the woman shrugged free and slowly drifted from Vin. So slowly that he didn't realize what was going on as she sort of squatted down. The hell was this? She held her belly with both hands and went to her knees.

Oh man, she's going into labor. Look at this, look what I did. Vin held his hands open to her, patting the air in a calming gesture, and asked, "Are you okay?"

It took another second for him to understand that she was going for the gun. He couldn't believe it. She was kneeling down reaching for the cop's pistol, had her hand on it now, looking back over her shoulder at Vin with furious eyes. The dog's tail flicked against his knee.

Had he really done anything tonight that was worth killing him for? Even if he was nuts, even if he deserved some jail time for knocking a cop on his ass, did he deserve to get shot for it?

He went, "Wait a second—"

She closed one eye like Annie Oakley and pulled the trigger. The noise started the animals screeching and barking again, except for the German Shepherd that sat silently beside Vin. She'd aimed too wide and taken a piece out of the door jamb behind him

Just like that. Without even saying anything. Telling him to freeze or she'd shoot. No, she'd just tried to put him down, another dog in the pound.

He ran at her as she sighted on him once more.

What a night, Jesus Christ. Vin slammed his arm down on hers and the gun went off again. She screamed and a searing pain drove through his gut.

Oh man, she actually did it. I'm shot.

But even that wasn't good enough for her. Damn, he thought, pregnant women are rough. She held the pistol up again, centering on his face. Not even his heart, she wanted to take out his eyes. Vin rapped her once in the chin and she sank on top of the cop.

He'd hurt a pregnant woman. Here he'd been inflated with some dumbass notion of gallantry, and instead of being a hero for a cute girl serving him Scotch, he'd punched out a pregnant woman.

What would Johnny Tormino and Jojo Lebowski say? What would Vin's father be thinking of him now, from the other side of the grave?

"Oh God, I'm sorry. I'm so sorry."

The German Shepherd followed him out the front doors. His guts were on fire but the pain didn't impede him at all. That was surprising. He looked down and saw he was covered in blood, but still it didn't feel all that bad. Shock. They always talk about shock at times like this. He didn't really know what it meant, but he realized when it wore off all that agony came flooding back in.

"Ah, shit."

He kept a stiff stride without any real notion of where he was headed. The dog kept up, panting and looking around, maybe searching for his master. In a couple of blocks Vin started to stagger a little, bouncing along parked cars as they picked up speed, as if heading towards something, maybe the purpose he'd been after.

The sound of breaking waves on the beach became

clearer and clearer, but they were leaving the neighborhood lights behind. It grew darker, and now it was as if the German Shepherd were leading him. He felt the boardwalk beneath his feet, the heavy resounding thump of his footsteps bringing him back to when he was a kid. When the pier was alive with families and laughter and his father making those silly seagull noises. When he had more ahead of him than behind.

Another noise strengthened beneath the pulsing sound of the ocean, and it took a second to make it out. Steadily it escalated. Sirens.

So I'm a fugitive now? Well yeah, of course he was. You slap around a cop and a pregnant lady and steal a killer dog, and sure, they're gonna want to come after you.

Vin felt it now, burgeoning within him. A boiling agony that was about to break free. He champed his lips against it and tried not to cry out. Held his hands tightly over his belly and felt the rip there. The crescendo of crashing waves broke over him with a roar and Vin turned and turned, unsure of his direction. That was nothing new. Sweat stung his eyes and the darkness had a weight that bore down. The German Shepherd barked an instant too late and Vin found himself falling.

He was underwater. It snapped him awake and brought him back into himself. He'd gone off the pier. Man, when you start down a fucking dangerous, ludicrous path, you really go all the way to the end of it.

Gasping, he rose and broke the surface and felt the German Shepherd swimming and scrambling along with him against the moorings of the pier. There was more light now. It was nearly dawn, and the horizon bloomed with a mounting orange. He saw a slime-covered, rotting ladder but the waves bounced him against the pilings and he kept getting beaten back. The dog in its terror started to bite him. It snapped at his throat and missed, then locked its jaws on his forearm. Another scream worked up Vin's throat but he felt it was important to keep it in, to keep everything inside. Letting it out now would prove he'd been wrong, that the dog was a killer and should be gassed, injected, burned. Once he started screaming he'd never stop.

"Hold on," he whispered, talking to the German Shepherd and himself, imaging his father just above on the boardwalk, leaning down and trying to help.

It hit Vin then that he didn't know the waitress's name.

Or the blind man's. Or the pregnant woman's. Or the dog's. Or even the three tough guy jocks who'd let the loss of their ambitions drive them to such foolishness at the wrong time.

Exactly like him.

Another bellowing siren somewhere nearby, but not near enough. Reaching for the ladder again he managed to grab hold of the bottom rung. He slipped off but dove and managed to clench it. He thought of the way Dad's arms had bulged with power. It gave Vin a moment of fire where he managed to heave himself up a bit, but the weight of the dog held him down. The tear in his belly opened wider. I am weak, he admitted, so goddamn weak, and it's brought me to this.

He didn't want to shirk the animal free. You don't kill your last friend. He couldn't feel his arm anymore, the dog's teeth deep in the muscle, severing veins. He turned back and saw that the German Shepherd still had its eyes open, blowing bubbles frantically from its nostrils. The dog was too panicked to swim to shore but wouldn't give up. Vin felt the same as they clung there together under the pier with the battering, crushing tide coming in, the eastern sky diffusing a wintry blue, the water growing a richer red around them, and yet despite all that had happened and might still happen before them, he would not let go.

Wednesday

Michael Canfield

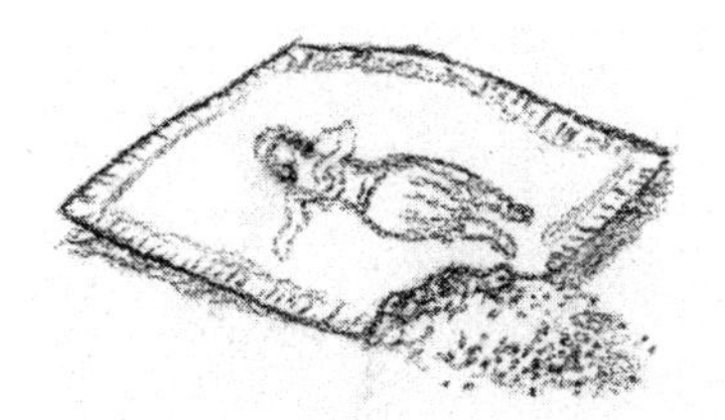

"'The likes of me'," he repeated.
"What a phrase! Very dramatic. But then you get paid to write the likes of that."

Name's Benjamin R. Willis and I used to write a bit. All that's over now. This last piece records where I was when it happened—specifically a small independent espresso shop in a major northwestern American City near the beginning of the twenty-first century. It was June, it was Wednesday, an hour or so after I had arisen—so that means around eleven. There was nothing significant about the day or time yet.

I ordered a soy latte. Let me explain that order. I started in with the soy a few months prior, and I don't remember why. It had nothing to do with the divorce. I do like the taste, and besides, I drink so many damn lattes regular milk was starting to give me problems. A lot of things have given me problems that I've done nothing about, so that alone doesn't account for the switch. Nor am I a granola-birkenstocks-ponytail type. I eat meat. Cows are cute, but I'd gladly dissect one with rusty boxcutter to get at a thick red cut of prime rib. When I drink, I drink what's on sale, not the filtered, micro-brewed stuff (unless you are buying—then what's your pleasure? Happy to join you).

Just like soy is all.

The woman at the counter was roughly between nineteen and thirty. I wish I could be more specific, as women are the most interesting part of this story. But I'm in my mid-fifties now, and I've steadily lost the talent to guess ages of people so much younger.

She didn't notice me. If the police had happened to come in later, seeking my description, I doubt she could have accurately recalled my drink order, let alone details of my person. I was invisible to her.

But she wasn't invisible to me. I remember freckles

on her nose. I remember the way her fingers danced with each hand motion, ten independent souls finding perfect harmony. Well, I'm supposed to be a writer, so I'm supposed to notice those things and relate them, but here my vivid recollect means more than that.

Had I know then what I etc., blah blah blah . . . I would have stood at the counter watching her fingers dance all day—or at least until those hypothetical police were called. She wore a silver crucifix. Jesus twisted on it, the Passion played out against the cleft of her collar bone.

What did she smell like? All I smelled was coffee.

By the end of her work day, probably coffee was just about all she *did* smell like. Picture her coming home to you after six hours, or whatever it is, pulling espresso. Coffee grounds under her nails, in her clothing. The smell of coffee in her hair. Think of that: the smell of coffee in a woman's hair.

Aw, fuck it.

I took my soy latte and headed to a table by the window. I was alone, but this makes the telling more difficult, so allow me to introduce a fictional companion for myself. This only makes sense dramatically, and you will thank me for it, if you decide to stick with this piece. The reading will go easier. He's a real-life person incidentally, he just happens to have been conveniently inserted into that afternoon for my purposes. Normally I would just do it, just slip my absent friend into the narrative without a word on the sly, but why bother to dissimulate any more? I'm past it.

Long as I'm embellishing, I'll shave a decade and some off myself and say that I am mid-thirties. Who the fuck wants to read about an old man in a coffee shop alone? I don't. And if I don't want to read it, then I can't very well expect you will.

While I'm at it, I'll give myself back my hair, erase my love handles, and add an inch or two where it counts. (I mean my height, you dogs.) I won't give myself washboard abs, or strengthen my weak chin, because there are limits to verisimilitude. Verisimilitude is the quality of appearing to be true. If I haven't lost you already, I'm about to, and those washboard abs might push it off the cliff. Everything else here is true, and by the end you will know, because once you hear my story (if you've any awareness of the world-at-large, that is) you will know that everything in this world-at-large changed for everyone that Wednesday.

I saw it change.

So as I was saying, I sat down and my hypothetical friend soon joined me. Barney's his name. Barney was crossing the street toward me mid-block.

Tires screeched. A driver had to crush her brake pedal to prevent flattening Barney. Barney awarded this lightning-speed reaction by extending his middle finger.

The driver returned the gesture and the smile lines around her mouth deepened, as she grimaced in disgust at Barney. I remember those lines around her mouth. Barney took his time stepping out of the way of her car. When he finally reached the sidewalk, she accelerated with a force equal to the one she'd used braking, and was gone.

Barney popped into the cafe, dropped his *New York Times*, National Edition, on my table and grinned. "Evening, Chief." I've already established that it was late morning, eleven o'clock, right then, not evening. That's just the kind of shit Barney says. Sometimes you get to know somebody and though you may not like him, nor particularly dislike him, your paths keep crossing, and before you know it you're friends. That's how it is with Barney and me.

Barney pulled off his sunglasses and dropped them next to the *Times*. I don't remember the headline that morning, though I do recall that whatever story it was seemed like a big deal then. It doesn't anymore.

Below the fold was a photo of the President and his senior foreign affairs staff.

Barney sat down and drummed his hands on the table a few times. He stared out the window. Looked at me, looked at my coffee, looked at the ceiling.

Without moving, he said, "Think I'll order."

"Good idea."

Now you'd think this would be the obvious course of action once entering a coffee shop and greeting your companion, but that's not the way Barney does things. Barney doesn't move from point A to point B. Ever.

He asked me what I was having and I told him.

"Still on the soy. Well you'll outlive us all. Got to be good for you because it tastes like shit, don't it?"

"No it doesn't. Try it."

"No. I've eaten enough shit today. Gonna get thrown out of my place. Landlady bitch."

"Found work yet?"

"Fuck no. I'll probably move. This fucking city. No jobs here. Good thing you don't have to worry."

There was an edge in that comment, but it was true . . . I didn't have to worry, so I let it go.

He looked at my coffee. "Maybe I'll try it," he said. I pushed the cup across. He lifted it, peering in like he was trying to divine a message from the foam oracle, before finally taking a sip.

"Well?"

"Not bad. Think I'll have a drip coffee."

"I'll buy yours."

"No, fuck no." He stood up and went to the counter.

Did I mention that the cafe was devoid of customers except for us? It was.

His footsteps echoed toward the back and I looked out the window, thinking I'd probably made Barney feel bad. I knew he was thin-skinned and should not have been surprised my offer insulted him. I shrugged; he'd get over it. Or he should get over it; whether he decided to or not was his business.

It had been sunny when I'd come in a few moments earlier; now a cloud cover swept in. Would be raining in a few minutes. It had been a nice spring, not much rain at all.

A beautiful woman passed the window. She was forty, I guess, had short auburn hair cut longer on one side. She wore a thin summer dress, her arms were slender and muscled, she had on dime-store grade pink flip-flops, and she carried groceries in one of those net sacks that recyclers like to use instead of plastic. What did she have in the sack? Looked like a bottle of olive oil, and one of wine. A baguette. With the dress and the groceries she looked like a vision from Paris, or Florence. Or anywhere but here, really.

Paris or Florence, thought I might go, once I finished my current project. Now that I was single again, why not?

Rain blasted down in a burst.

Drops hammered the pavement hard and fast, like nails hitting a drum skin.

The woman was passing right by me when it happened. She hadn't been expecting rain, certainly. Her shoulders hunched up in shock at the downpour.

Next, several things happened within an instant, but I remember them all. Clearly. Not entirely defenseless, she raised the netted sack above her head. She stepped closer to the glass, but the coffee shop didn't have any awning worth mentioning. Our eyes met and we had a moment . . . half a moment, maybe. She realized the absurdity of her situation—seeking shelter from a net sack and a pane of glass. She looked at me and laughed, I smiled back. She would come in and sit down; I would signal Barney to get lost. He'd be obtuse at first, but I could work around that.

Her eyelids fluttered against the pounding rain, then she bolted. She didn't go for the door of the coffee shop, but continued on her way, running through what was now a sheet of rain. She lost one of her flip-flops and I expected that would slow her down. It didn't, she kicked the other one off, and ran barefoot on the concrete. I wondered if she had far to go.

A sudden white light, coupled with the rain, impaired my vision. I lost sight of her.

At the time, that's what I thought.

What I really saw was too strange for my mind to wrap itself around. However, subsequent events prove that what I couldn't believe I saw that moment is actually the most logical, sensible thing in the world. It is the truth. No one else I've heard of, or read about, has ever reported seeing what I saw.

Her outline shimmered, dissolved, and she disappeared.

I repeat for clarity: her outline shimmered, dissolved, and she disappeared.

Here's something I learned, something to consider if you ever find yourself confronting a similar phenomenon and doubting it: people don't disappear all at once: first they shimmer. Then they start to dissolve. *Then* they disappear.

I stood up. I went to the door. I didn't run but I might have.

I told myself it was the rain, the lightning and the rain, I told myself I didn't see what I saw.

Barney came back without his coffee.

"It's not supposed to be raining," he said. "Where's the girl?"

"You saw her?"

"There's nobody up there," he said. I realized he meant the barista, not the woman I didn't yet believe had really disappeared for real in the rain.

"She was there a minute ago," I murmured.

"Is it self-serve now, or what?"

"Relax, she'll be right back."

"You don't know."

I don't know why he said that. I wish I'd asked him at the time, because he was right. I didn't—couldn't—know. "Sit down," I told him. "She'll be back." I sat down myself.

He sat and returned to drumming the table. "I'm supposed to sit here in public doing nothing? Without refreshment?"

"You're not doing nothing, you're watching me drink

my coffee."

"Lovely. Where were you about to go just now?"

"Woman lost her shoe."

The rain stopped. The men in the street stopped running, they came out from shops they had taken refuge in and continued on their way like worker drones. And every one of them had someplace to be that day, I realized. Everyone except me and Barney. I scanned the street. "I don't even see it any more." The pink flip-flop wasn't on the sidewalk now.

"So she picked it up."

"She didn't."

"Someone sharper than you picked it up and gave it back to her. You missed your big chance. Now you'll die alone."

"No, I would've seen."

"Let's get back to the bigger issue. The case of the missing coffee server."

It hit me that there was not a single woman on the street. What are the odds at any given moment on a busy weekday boulevard? I got up again and went back to the counter. There was something heaped on the floor and I leaned over to see what it was.

An apron.

I went behind the counter and picked it up. I caught a silver crucifix and chain as it slipped from the apron's folds. Barney joined me.

"Exhibit A," he said when he saw me with the apron. "She ain't here. Quit or something. Don't you tip good?"

"Would she have left this?" I showed the crucifix. "And we would've seen her walk out."

"They have a back entrance. I'm getting my own coffee." He joined me behind the counter. "Hey . . . if I man the place till whoever comes in to take over, do I get to keep what I earn? Is that ethical? For sure the tips at least."

I got it finally. "She disappeared. They all did."

Barney found a cup and put it under the drip dispenser. "She probably got a better offer, somewhere else. What's a little job like this to a kid? Plenty of better up and down the street. Well, not better, but no worse."

"I'm telling you they are all gone. I watched that woman in the street fade away, right out of existence. And her shoes? Where did they go?"

Barney took his coffee and poured about a pint of half-and-half into it.

I went out into the street.

It smelled of rain, and the street was bustling again. The sun had failed to return. I studied the faces of the men walking by. I looked into the windows of cars as they passed, and then into the windows of a bus. A few boys, a lot of men. No girls. No women.

Barney couldn't see the truth of what I was saying. "Go look in the street," I told him. "There are no women out there."

He smirked. "Well I'm not paying for this coffee. The cost must be ninety-percent labor anyway."

"Did you hear what I said?"

"There's no women out there. What do you want me to do?"

What did I want him to do? What *did* I want him to do?

"I'm telling you they disappeared."

"And nobody else has noticed this."

"Well, where are they?"

Again he smirked. I told him to stop doing that.

"Don't you think it's more likely that—just by chance—on this particular street, at this magic moment, there are no women around for whatever reason . . . rather than whatever you are thinking . . . that they all went away poof like in one of your stories?"

"I never wrote a story like this."

"Seems to me you did. I read one once."

"There's a science-fiction story set in the Amazon where the women—"

"That's not it."

"I haven't even told you."

"I hate science fiction, so I didn't read it, so that wasn't it. No, it was one of your stories. One of those brooding losers in a coffee shop things that you write. Where the dude's looking out the window thinking about his dead girlfriend and all the women remind him of her, and then suddenly he can't remember her face anymore."

"I've never written a story like that." I felt my cheeks redden. I hadn't but I could have. Barney's jab was clumsy but struck close enough.

He took his *Times*, looked it over and tossed it down again. I noticed something.

The picture below the fold. Previously it had contained the current President and his four top foreign-policy advisors. Now there were only three. His Secretary of State was no longer in the photo, and she was a woman. I didn't point this out to Barney, he would have claimed she had never been in the photo to begin with. Never mind. I did not need to convince him of anything. In time he'd see.

Sooner rather than later. Any moment someone was bound to miss their wife, or mother, their coworker or daughter. Cars formerly driven by women would be even now careening off the roads, or idling to stops in the middle of intersections. Planes would drop from the sky. It just happened that there was little traffic in that street right then. Out of my hands.

I realized I was still fingering the crucifix left by the barista. I put it away.

"What did you just do?" asked Barney sharply. "Did you just pocket that girl's pendant?"

"Not at all. Well, I guess I did."

"That's not cool. Not cool. What are you going to say when she gets back?"

Yes. They could come back, I thought.

"I'll give it to her."

His eyes narrowed, he looked at me through the thin

slits. "Are you trying to make a point or something? Okay, I'll put a buck down for the coffee before I leave if that's what you are hinting at. Just don't get up to your old tricks again."

"What does that mean? What old tricks."

He waved me off. "Don't get into it."

"I didn't bring it up, you did. You ought to explain yourself."

"Let's just say you've earned a reputation concerning the property of others."

"A reputation, you say. Explain to me this reputation. I'd be very interested to know what someone like you would know about reputation."

"If you want to have a pissing contest over it."

"I don't want to have a contest, pissing or otherwise with you. I merely expect you to tell me what you mean."

"Seen your wife of late?"

"Ex-wife, and what business is it of yours?"

"None, friend. I happened to run into her a few weeks back myself is all. Jesus can that woman talk. Gabriella; she has to hate it when people call her Gabby." He put his hands up. "Hard to resist though. When a shoe fits . . ."

"What would my ex-wife have to say to the likes of you?"

"'The likes of me'," he repeated. "What a phrase! Very dramatic. But then you get paid to write the likes of that."

"Just tell me what she said about me."

"She spoke very little about you, actually. Maybe her life doesn't center around you. Hm. There's a thought. Talked about her family, mostly. I didn't know she came from money."

"Is that all you think about?"

"Some of us have to think about it. Some of us don't have the means to sit around and prevaricate all day."

So that was it. "You jealous little shit."

"Yes. Absolutely. I am in fact a jealous little shit, but I've always stood on my own two legs, and I'm not a thief."

"I see what this is about. I'm not living off Gabriella's money. I'm doing quite well now on my own."

"As you say. *Now.* But there were some lean years. Years of struggling over the blank page, the faceless indifference of a philistine reading public, years when her family's vacation cottage provided much-needed weekend respite. When their fortune alleviated the soul-crushing need to keep the catalogue gig for grocery and printer ribbon money. When their New York contacts got your bullshit scribblings into the right hands . . ."

He trailed off, seemed distracted by the meaningless goings-on outside the window in the street.

"Finished?" I said.

"Did I tell you Gabby looks good? She's gone all new age with the crystals and the tarot and the wicca and all that stuff but it keeps her busy. It's kind of interesting actually, the wicca stuff. I'm sort of getting into it now too. She's dropped maybe fifteen pounds, but of course that extra weight had been smoothing out the wrinkles in her face. It's a tradeoff, I guess. Thank god I'm not a woman and have to worry about shit like that. But back to your artistic struggle."

"I never asked Gabriella to do a thing for me. She always offered."

"I know she did. The saddest thing is she was so proud of you at the time. She helped because she could, and a marriage is a partnership, right? But that's past now. You made the connections, you got the fat contract. You dumped the fat wife."

"What do you know about it? I've never seen any woman stick with you more than a fortnight. Wouldn't surprise me if you were gay."

Barney ran his tongue over his teeth. Affecting a grotesque lisp he said, "Even if I was I wouldn't suck your diseased dick, asshole."

I started to stand, and Barney pushed the table against me. The shock kicked me back into my seat, it disturbed—

but did not upset—our coffee cups.

"Oh what now? You're going to hit me?" laughed Barney.

"No," I said, seething. "I'm going to leave."

"Good. Stick with what works for you."

A figure came near the window outside and a shadow fell across Barney's face. I looked up and saw the barista staring at me. I don't know if Barney saw her or not, I wasn't paying attention to him at the moment. She was naked . . . then a moment later she wasn't . . . but I saw where the freckles on her collar bone disappeared into the ghostlike whiteness above her breasts. How could I see that if she were not naked at least an instant?

She walked inside slowly.

"I came back for something." She held her hand out toward me for it. "Know what it is?"

I stammered. I couldn't form words, so I shook my head.

"Crucifix. In your pocket. Give it."

I smiled. I'd forgotten I'd put it there. I found my voice. "He said you'd be back for it . . ."

"He?"

"My friend . . ." I gestured behind her, to Barney's chair, but it was empty. "That's odd. He was just sitting there."

She smirked, like she didn't believe me. There was something familiar about that smirk, that indifference to the truth. I didn't like it. "People leave," she said. "They just get tired of it and they go. My property please."

I gave her the crucifix. "I'm sorry," I said.

She closed her hand over it. "It doesn't matter, it's mine is all. I forgot it and came back. Now I'm leaving again."

"Where? Where did you go?"

She started to leave.

"Wait!" She turned around as if surprised to hear me still speaking. The gesture seemed almost regal, the Queen of England reacting having been addressed by a toad.

The expression didn't last, and she smiled—a little playfully, I thought. "Are *you* still here?" she said.

"Yes," I murmured. "Of course. Won't you have a coffee with me before you go?"

"No." she said. "I won't do that." Then she smiled again. A definite friendly smile. "But I will do this. Do you have a message I can give to someone? Anyone?"

I thought for a moment. The other woman, the woman I saw outside in the rain, she had also disappeared. I described her to the barista, and the barista's smile began to fade.

"Do you know her?" I asked.

"Possibly. If I do, what would you like me to tell her?"

"I would like you to tell her . . ." I faltered. What? Please come back? Did it mean anything when you looked at me, or were you just surprised by the rain? "Just tell her 'hello', I suppose."

"'Hello'? Is that all you've got?"

"Do you know her name?"

"Don't you have anything to say to Gabriella?"

"Gabriella, my ex-wife? You know my ex-wife?"

"Yes, I know your ex-wife." She paused, then mocked me. "'Hello', you say. And you call yourself a writer!"

She left, exiting the cafe and dissolving into the ether at the same movement.

I finished my soy latte, which had gone cold. That's another advantage of soy. Even cold in coffee it still tastes pretty good. I thought about what I would do the next time I saw Barney, if ever. I felt like punching him for the way he'd talked to me, but then I decided I just wouldn't speak to him. The one thing I haven't told you about Barney yet is he's always wanted to be somebody, but he could just never buckle down and do what it took. He'd play guitar for six months, and then the guitar would stay in the corner collecting cobwebs for the next decade. He dabbled in driftwood furniture for a while, and golf, and hypnotism. He once even tried to hypnotize himself into becoming a pro golfer. Now he was hanging out with my ex of all people and getting into, of all things, wicca with her.

In the street there were still no women.

Since that Wednesday I've spent a lot of time trying to find some women, or even one. But they're all gone. Even from photographs they have disappeared, and off billboards, televisions and film screens.

The thing I want to know—and this is why I'm writing even though there are no more girls to impress—is why has no one noticed this yet? Why is nothing else written about it, or broadcast in the media? Why does everyone, everywhere I go, look at me so strangely when I bring it up? Why is it just me?

Running Rain

Brian Freeman

The pipes behind the walls whine
like the pressure is so great they might burst.

Tonight is one of those perfect nights when he doesn't even need the streetlights.

The full moon illuminates the earth like the watchful eye of a peaceful deity and everything is bathed in the oddly beautiful blue light, enough light so that he can see for miles.

The trees along the sidewalk sway in the gentle breeze and a dog howls somewhere in the distance, setting off the other animals in the neighborhood like dominos toppling.

Tonight he runs.

Running frees him from the pain of everyday life, from the memories, from the nightmares.

Even with the chilled winter air nipping at his exposed skin, he runs.

He runs and he whispers the names: *Jeremy, Amanda, Susan, Michael, Andy, Beth, Lauren, and David.*

He crosses back and forth from one side of the neighborhood to the other, and he doesn't stop when he reaches the dead end where the woods begin.

He continues onto the path the kids clear every summer, the path that winds along the river, the path of frozen mud.

He runs and he keeps his head down, but when he reaches the river, he pauses to memorize the way the moonlight shimmers across the icy water.

The way the moonlight dances.

The first time he saw this river, he thought: *those waters are deeper and faster than they look.*

That thought has troubled him ever since.

When he returns to the small home he shares with his wife,

he is out of breath and his hands are shaking and his lungs are burning, but he's free.

He's been cleansed for another day.

He stands on the porch in the moonlight, bent over, his hands on his knees, and he breathes in the winter air.

He sucks in the coldness, and he feels so warm.

"How was your run?" his wife asks from the kitchen before he even closes and bolts the front door.

She's making hot chocolate. He can hear the water boiling on the stove.

This is their routine.

This is all they can talk about.

He stands on the hardwood floor in the living room, his heart still racing.

"Not bad. I took the path along the river," he says.

There's a sigh from the kitchen.

He knows what his wife is thinking, what she's going to say. So why'd he tell her where he went? Why didn't he lie? Why *can't* he lie about this anymore?

He has deceived his wife on purpose before, of course, but he can't stop himself from telling her this truth over and over again, and now she may as well just say what she's going to say. Then they can get on with the fighting. It's the only time they even talk to each other these days.

Each night they argue about him running near the river—but deep down, they're arguing about everything else.

Every secret. Every truth. Every lie. Every loss they share.

While he waits, he strips off his sweatshirt and unties his shoes.

Finally, with a trembling voice, his wife whispers, "Why don't you take a shower and have some hot chocolate?"

He doesn't respond. He heads for the bathroom.

Tonight she's holding in the words she needs to say, but he can hear the tears well enough.

The pipes behind the walls whine like the pressure is so great they might burst.

The shower fogs the mirror, and the heat feels good against his frozen flesh.

Goosebumps explode all over his body.

The act of running at night cranks his internal thermostat so high he never realizes how cold it is outside, but once the warm water hits his skin, he feels the night chill.

It's deep inside of him, and it's everywhere.

It's a coldness that will last for ages.

It's a coldness that digs into his heart and soul.

He imagines the block of ice inside his chest slowly melting, but his thoughts are interrupted by the bathroom door's hinges—they squeak as his wife opens the door.

He says nothing.

He stands under the pulsating hot water, surrounded by the rising mist.

He stands like a man lost in the fog.

A moment later the door closes again.

He turns off the water and grabs a towel.

The bathroom is thick with steam.

He steps out of the shower, and he's drying his hair when he looks at the foggy mirror.

I love you, his wife has written in the condensation with the tip of her finger.

He wonders if something happened today in her session with the therapist he refuses to see.

Maybe there was a breakthrough.

Maybe things are going to get better.

Maybe they'll be able move on with their lives.

When he reaches the bedroom, his wife is already in bed, under the covers, facing away from him.

He is very quiet. He does not turn on the light.

He slips under the covers and lays in silence.

He listens to his wife's deep, troubled breaths, and eventually he falls asleep—but only because he ran and repeated the names.

If he hadn't, he'd be up all night.

Not that his sleep is going to be easy, either way.

There are still the nightmares.

There are still the names.

There are still the memories.

Sometime after midnight he opens his eyes from a sleep so shallow it is worthless.

His wife is not next to him, that much he realizes right away.

He crawls out from under the covers, muttering to himself as his feet touch the wooden floor.

Wood floors dominate the home.

His wife loves them, but he thinks the wood is too cold. Tonight it feels like ice has grabbed his legs.

He puts on his slippers and a robe.

He moves through the darkness like a thief in the night. Each step is soft, as quiet as can be.

He stops short of the kitchen.

His wife is there, sitting on a tall stool. She holds a photograph; she clutches it to her chest.

She has lit a candle.

She sobs.

His cup of hot chocolate is still on the counter. He had forgotten all about it.

He watches his wife cry, and he considers his options.

A long moment passes.

Then he goes back to bed.

She doesn't need to hear his excuses, his reasoning for what he has done, and he couldn't find the words even if she did.

In the morning, the daylight sneaks past the curtains and burns his eyelids. He rolls over.

His wife is gone.

The school where she teaches is a forty-minute drive away, and she leaves an hour before he even knows a new day has finally arrived.

She'll be back.

She always comes back, even though most days she never wants to return to the house, to the neighborhood, to the town.

He knows this because he knows her so well.

She wants to sell the house, but he won't hear of it.

Why does he insist they stay in a place so alive with painful memories?

Maybe because he sees that look in the eyes of nearly every neighbor.

They understand the pain.

They understand the grief.

They understand the anger.

Even if they don't truly understand.

Everyone in this neighborhood has lost someone: a son or daughter or close friend.

They've all memorized the names of the dead.

Jeremy, Amanda, Susan, Michael, Andy, Beth, Lauren, and David.

The names of the dead still haunt them.

That's why he stays here.

Because anywhere else, he and his wife would be alone.

Here they can be haunted with everyone else.

He lies in bed, the hot sun burning a path across the bedroom, and he thinks about their son.

Jeremy was the first to go missing the previous summer.

He was not even out of high school.

The night Jeremy vanished without a trace, his father was in a bar—his father who would spend the rest of his life running along the river to absolve his sins.

But some sins just can't be washed away with a little rain and perspiration.

The night Jeremy disappeared, it was nearly two o'clock in the morning when he got home, and his wife had been waiting up for him. She was upset.

At first he was merely annoyed when his wife told him that Jeremy hadn't come home yet and she didn't know what to do.

He had just returned from drinking at Buddy's Tavern with his work friends on a weeknight—which might have been a problem in itself—and now his son was nowhere to be seen.

For some reason, he thought of the river.

Something about that river had bothered him from day one.

Those woods.

He had always warned Jeremy to be careful down there, but his wife said he was being overprotective.

The woods and the water, there was danger there.

Some part of his mind had been telling him that for years, ever since Jeremy was just a toddler.

Those waters are deeper and faster than they look.

Jeremy was eighteen the year he died, and in the months prior to his death there had been a lot of tension in the house.

When he wasn't with his girlfriend, Jeremy became depressed and locked himself in his room. He hadn't gotten into any of the colleges he had reluctantly applied to, and he refused to see a therapist to discuss his wild mood swings.

Anger to suicidal depression to crazed outbursts all became the norm. Yet there were plenty of good times, too. There was a strange balance to it all.

But when his parents pressed him about his plans for after high school, Jeremy simply said college wasn't his next step in life.

He said he wanted to be a rock star.

Or a movie star.

Someone famous.

Jeremy said if he had to, he'd run away to Hollywood and make a name for himself all on his own.

But Jeremy was never going to Hollywood, that much would soon become clear.

He asked his wife if Jeremy had said anything odd that afternoon, and she became even more upset, as if she hadn't really considered their son's words seriously until right then.

She replied: *Jeremy was really angry, and he said we were going to regret not supporting him more.* She paused. *Oh, Jesus! I thought he was just angry because we wouldn't send him to that rock star summer camp! You don't think . . .*

He interrupted his wife and asked her to call Jeremy's friends, even though it was so late. Some of them had to be up.

He sat in the kitchen, and he felt like he was waiting for a jury to return their verdict.

It came swiftly.

Jeremy's friends had last seen him by the river that evening, but they didn't know where he had gone from there.

They did know that Jeremy's girlfriend had dumped him that very afternoon. She was headed to Yale in the fall and he obviously wasn't going with her. She said it was time for a clean break for both of them.

And now Jeremy was missing.

Running to the river that night was the first time he had run in years.

First time since college, in fact.

He ran and his legs burned and soon he had to stop.

The heat of a million suns beat down on him even though it was night. The humid summer air soaked into his lungs and he had to walk the rest of the way.

When he reached the path at the end of the sidewalk, the path cloaked in darkness, he hesitated.

The night was piercing.

The darkness terrified him.

But he thought of his son and he pushed on, and when he reached the place where the path curved to follow the river, his heart slammed against the inside of his chest.

He noticed the way the moonlight lit the water.

The way the light danced.

He searched for his son, but found no one.

There was a rope hanging from a low-lying tree branch, dragging in the water. The swift current tugged on it with invisible hands.

He would think of that rope when the nightmares came.

When he returned home, his wife was hysterical.

He asked her to call the police, but he told her not to tell anyone what Jeremy had said before he left to meet his friends or what Jeremy's friends had said when she called them.

He didn't want anyone thinking their boy might have killed himself.

No one.

There had to be more.

He was right.

The police officers asked some questions and they said not to worry.

Teens stay out too late all the time.

Most runaways get tired and lonely and hungry and come back within days.

Jeremy was probably fine.

Don't worry folks, the one officer said. *We'll find your boy.*

The police never did.

Three days later, the first body turned up, but it wasn't Jeremy.

Those waters are deeper and faster than they look.

He just wanted to find his boy alive.

Hope and faith were all he and his wife had left.

They hoped for the best and they prayed that Jeremy had run off to pursue his dreams and would return someday—but once the killings began, hope and faith were fleeting.

There were seven other victims in all, and each was found tied to a low-lying tree branch hanging over the river.

They were floating in the fast-moving water.

A rope was wrapped around their necks. It had been used to choke them to death.

The killer must not have secured Jeremy's body well enough to keep the current from pulling the knots loose, and the water dragged him downstream.

That was everyone's best guess.

His body was never found.

Those waters are deeper and faster than they look.

Eight teenagers died over the course of the summer.

Jeremy, Amanda, Susan, Michael, Andy, Beth, Lauren, and David.

Then six months passed, and no more names were added to the list.

Everyone asked in hushed whispers who the Riverside Strangler could have been, but all they had to hold onto was that nickname given to the killer by the media.

The Riverside Strangler—another name no one in the town would ever forget.

The names of the dead compel him to run.

After the funeral for the fourth victim, he began to run each and every night.

By this point, he realized his son was probably dead. The body might never be found.

He started slowly, going just a few blocks, but soon he was called to the path and the river, and he answered that call.

It was his secret route. It was his secret place.

When his wife discovered where he was going, they fought.

He had known that would happen, but one night he just blurted it out when she asked how his run had gone. He told her the whole truth.

He didn't know why he was saying what he was saying, and he couldn't stop the words from spilling out of his mouth.

Now he couldn't stop telling her, over and over again.

He tried to assure her that he would be fine.

After all, by the time she found out where he was running, there hadn't been a murder in months.

No one knew for certain what had happened to the Riverside Strangler, but he had either died or moved on.

He certainly wasn't in the community. Everyone refused to believe that was even a possibility.

Someone so depraved couldn't have come from town.

The townspeople thanked the good Lord that the crazed killer had only taken the eight teens, and everyone prayed for the souls of his victims.

They knew the Riverside Strangler would get what he deserved in the next life.

The Riverside Strangler was just a name.

Every night, he runs and he whispers the names.

Jeremy, Amanda, Susan, Michael, Andy, Beth, Lauren, and David.

That's the only way he can fall asleep.

If he doesn't run, if he doesn't face his fears in the woods, if he doesn't remember every victim and not just his son, he can't sleep.

The nightmares will keep him awake until daybreak.

His thrashing and crying will wake his wife and that's not fair to her.

She's finally able to sleep without the pills.

All of this he remembers again and again while lying in bed, wasting the day away while his wife is teaching.

He drifts in and out of consciousness, and the nightmares are blinding.

In the early evening he hears the front door open and close and lock again.

His wife comes into the bedroom. She looks stunning in her work clothes. He misses that beauty. That radiance.

She says she'd like to talk.

We need to talk are her exact words, and that phrase has never meant anything good.

Not once in his entire life.

She says she wants their marriage to work.

She says she needs his help if that's going to happen.

He nods in all of the correct places, but he's still thinking, *if you had called the police right away, our son might still be alive and all of those other kids might be, too. Maybe the police could have gotten there in time to stop the killing before it even began.*

Once again he refuses to see the therapist—he refuses without words, he refuses with a strong shake of his head—but that doesn't seem to bother his wife the way it normally does.

She says she understands his reluctance, but at the very least he has to start talking to her.

They have to talk about something other than his nights spent running along the river.

She says she needs the marriage to work.

She says their marriage is all she has left.

He agrees, but doesn't reply.

Later he leaves for his nightly run, and his wife is crying before he even closes the front door.

Jeremy is dead.

He knows he has to accept that fact, has to move on with his life, but for now, all he can do is run and remember.

Jeremy, Amanda, Susan, Michael, Andy, Beth, Lauren, and David.

Tonight dark storm clouds are unleashing their rain in waves. In a few hours, the rain will change to snow and there will be no school tomorrow.

Maybe tomorrow is destined to be the day he and his wife talk—the day they discuss where their lives are headed, and whether they fit into each other's plans for the future.

But for now he runs.

He runs like the rain, free falling, free of the memories and the pain.

He runs and he ignores the thoughts trying to push to the front of his mind.

He runs along the path and he watches the rain strike the river like a thousand bullets.

He runs and he thinks: *those waters are deeper and faster than they look.*

He wonders if maybe there should be no tomorrow.

If he dies he'll never have to think about the secret he holds deep inside—the memories buried deep in the soil of his heart and soul; the memories he's fighting hard to keep buried.

He repeats the names of the dead, and he tries to forget what his son said the day he disappeared, what his son had wanted to do with his life.

He tries his best not to understand those words.

He tries to forget that his son had wanted to be famous.

He tries to ignore all the ways, both good and bad,

that you can become a household name in the modern world. Sometimes a nickname given by the media is enough . . .

He just repeats the names of the dead over and over, and the rain and the river whisper them back.

The river calls to him.

He never wants to remember what he discovered the very first time he ran along the path, just a few months after his son vanished . . . the truth he discovered.

If he responds to the river's call, he'll never again have to remember why the killing really ended . . .

And why he has the nightmares . . .

And why he has to repeat the names of the dead . . .

And what *really* happened to his son . . .

Those waters are deeper and faster than they look.

Whatever Happened to Shangri-La?

Larry Tritten

Blur your eyes just slightly
and an autopsy room might look indistinguishable
from the kitchen of an upscale restaurant.

for Susan

One TV show I don't watch is *Cops*. I know other cops who do, but as the Jewish comedian says, "Go figure." The applicable phrase here is busman's holiday. But I've got another theory. Masochism. I've seen more blood and tears in my twenty-five years on the job to fill a sea of sorrow, and the way I see it, it doesn't take a Freud or Jung to figure out that one of our society's primary urges is masochism. Maybe it's even up there with the sex drive and the need for food and shelter. The human craving for the balm of Angst ranges from the minimalist thrill of worrying a scab to the ultimate emotional *tour de force* for many, namely suicide.

I'm being pessimistic, you think? Sure, and hummingbirds audition at the Met. You live in a society that gives bright, colored medals to people for burning others alive and tearing them to shreds with hot metal fragments but views prostitutes and porn stars, who dispense pleasure that comes with a semblance of love, as morally *déclassé*. You live in a society in which all the downers (most specifically alcohol and a whole range of tranquilizing pills from the old Model-T of barbiturates, Valium, to the flashy new Mercedes of same, Prozac) are there for your consumption, but every manner of upper from marijuana to LSD has always been considered an enemy of the state. As if nobody had figured out that alcohol wasn't doing a bit more than *cannabis* to keep homicide cops like me and the doctors at Bellevue in business. But maybe you shouldn't even listen to me, for all you know I might even be smoking some of the aforesaid devil weed as I write this, just as you may be four fingers deep into a bottle of Jack Daniels or sailing around in an ersatz sky thrown over your consciousness by Stelazine as you read it. Never lose your sense of skepticism, gang, it's the most objective of all philosophical attitudes. Add to that Gide's cautionary, "Do not be too quick to understand me." And as long as we're roping dialectical steers, let me ante up something I think should be as ubiquitous in consciousness as the Universal Product Code is on products, Voltaire's (I believe) wryly expressed: "Once a philosopher, twice a pervert." Which is to say, *have the experience* before you presume to attitudinize about its nature or quality, and if you don't like it, *then* denounce the hell out of it. But if you haven't tried it (and this covers everything from cocaine to some of the more *outré* sexual practices), then no quasi-authoritative opinions, please!

Masochism? When I was a kid the monsters in horror movies were werewolves, vampires, and the like, and in the final scene the stake was driven or the silver bullet was fired, evil was conquered, and we felt good about it. But today's horror movies are about serial killers and other such types of human monsters who for the most part do their work with blades, and at the end of the movie Jason or Freddy is still there, invulnerable, ready for the next go-around; evil prospers, and the subliminal perk for the movie watcher is to experience a sustained vicarious sense of terror and lousy feeling. By the same token, it is almost mandatory for all future society movies to portray repressive, downbeat societies. Whatever happened to the concept of Utopia, or even the idea that things can get better? And just how did we get to the point where the bestseller lists are dominated by books instructing us how to accomplish the feat of feeling good? Feeling good didn't used to be such a heroic chore. The ultimate feel-good upper is arguably pornography, and I'm amazed that it was ever legalized in this country, but if you compare European with American pornography you can quickly see that the latter is practically a placebo, that it is to real sexual sophistication what a Big Mac is to the specialties at Le Cirque or The Four Seasons. There are a whole range of things that Puritanical old Krafft-Ebing labeled deviations and which are merely imaginative and playful sexual practices that are all kosher in European porn but are still as taboo in American porn as long pig at a Vegan picnic.

The point I'm making here is that in spite of all the societal conditioning we get not to feel good and the fact that I see so much rage and despair and so little love on my job, I'm still not a misanthrope. And, believe me, my job has given me all the credentials I'd need to make me a prize-winning antisocial misanthrope. While you get to watch the cinematic serial killers do their vicious deeds vicariously or get a so-called realistic dose of the hard cold world of crime via *CSI*, I get a front row seat at the *real show*. The censors aren't going to let you see the really bad stuff. Like what a beautiful fashion model looks like after spending six days floating in the East River. Or what a similar *soignée* beauty looks like as a rape-homicide victim, with torture and disembowelment thrown into the bargain, and maybe after rigor and livor mortis, putrefaction, and insect infestation have embellished the sight.

The fact that it's the beautiful women who wind up in these ways, dumped in the woods, left tied to a bed, or simply discarded on some floor like human litter, is what most makes me feel like shit. I adore women, always have. I have a beautiful wife and daughter. And I confess there's another beautiful woman in my life, outside their sphere. Too many really ugly crime scenes have put something of a psychic undertow in my joy of female beauty, but for the most part I manage to swim beyond its pull.

The phrase "serial killer" didn't used to be part of the language. But that was before this form of homicide became downright fashionable. Nothing motivates me to do my job well so much as a serial killer. We had a new one, who the press would soon be calling The Avenger.

I was there from the beginning. We got a call from the manager of the Celestial Hotel on the Upper West Side saying that a young couple had been murdered in one of the rooms. The killer had left the door of the room open and another guest on the same floor had discovered the bodies. It was Valentine's Day. All over the city men were giving women heart-shaped boxes of candy and bouquets of flowers, but this particular couple of young lovers were dead in bed, side by side, and when Jack and I got there *The Naked and the Dead,* oddly enough, was playing on the TV, which had been left on. I chalked it up to one of those ironic coincidences life is full of. Incidentally, they made a lousy movie out of Mailer's novel, but perhaps not as bad as what they did with the first film version of James Jones' *The Thin Red Line,* a movie about Guadalcanal that was filmed in Spain. Go figure.

The Celestial Hotel was the kind of place Willy Loman might have checked into toward the end of his career. It would be polite to call it inconspicuous. The better days it had seen were back during the time when Weegee had an office at Police Headquarters on Spring Street and was selling prints of murder victims for five dollars a pop to the *New York Post* and the *World-Telegram.* It was surviving, incongruously, between a New Age book store and a Japanese macrobiotic restaurant. There were no stars or moon to see in the real sky that night, but the fake neon one on the Celestial's sign was doing its best to compensate with three blue stars and one red one shining clearly and luminously in the twilight haze, although the crescent moon flanking them was burned out. Almost like an omen.

Room 603 held our dead lovers. There are times when entering a crime scene room requires you to brace your faculties for a sight of what a psychopath's imagination can deliver when he's doing his psychopathic best to have his kind of nice day, but we knew from the manager that this wasn't one of those scenes.

He was a good-looking Mediterranean type and could

easily have been cast in a daytime soap as a young lawyer who wasn't sure if he preferred surfing or skiing. She was so golden she could have been King Midas' daughter: her hair was the color of honey when sunlight shines through the jar in the morning—a short cut that capitalized on soft, natural waves and was shaped to create a flowing effect along the sides; her tan had the smooth radiance of a cup of first class tea; and she even wore a stack of simple golden bracelets on one wrist. She was as beautiful as anything life gives us, but she was now on the other side of the Styx and decomposition had already started to deal its ugly hand. There wasn't any evidence of how they had died, no wounds we saw, no weapons or pill bottles, no sign of a struggle. The medical examiner was on his way. Jack got engrossed in something Raymond Massey was saying in that awful movie, but I went for a walk on the block and located the car that had brought our dead lovers there. It was a brand new Mercedes S320, red as glossy lipstick. I looked in the back seat. Shopping bags from Bonwit Teller. I noticed the personalized license plate, IN LOVE, a plate probably made by some felon serving life for doing something that was conspicuously unloving, I thought. The medical examiner pulled his blue Ford Taurus up across the street, giving me a perfunctory honk of its horn. It was Warren Bain. We had worked together plenty. Dr. Bain reminded me a lot of Marcus Welby, the dedicated and caring doctor Robert Young used to play on TV. Except that he tended to undermine that image with a vocabulary that would have been more appropriate for a construction worker.

"Hi, Warren," I said. "I hope they didn't interrupt something enjoyable to get you out here."

He laughed dismissively. "Well, Evan, I was just watching a tape of an old John Wayne movie. *The Wake of the Red Witch.* But I've already seen it. It cost me twelve cents to see at the Dream when I was a kid. The tape rented for four bucks."

"Twelve cents doesn't go as far as it used to."

"What have you got for me, Evan?"

"Two dead young people, but we don't know how or why."

"Jack inside?"

"Yeah. Watching another old movie."

"Well, I assume your photographer will be hustling his ass along any minute. Let's go inside."

We went up to the room and Dr. Bain took a look at the couple and shook his head, and an unpleasant look narrowed his eyes. It was a mark of the sympathy of somebody who cares about people.

"Fuck," he said, his succinct summary of the raw deal the lovers had gotten. Then, "I suppose their parents won't be pleased about their residence in the Cocky Locky Hotel." It was his customary phrase for describing all tacky places like the Celestial. He might have expressed surprise of his own that they were here, but we both knew the reason could be anything. Keeping a low profile and avoiding being seen for one reason or another in their own *milieu*. Or cheap thrills slumming. Keller, our postmortem *paparazzo*, showed up, took his pictures, Jack's movie ended, and Dr. Bain quickly ascertained the cause of death. There was a scarcely discernible puncture wound in each of their chests, just over the heart. "A very efficient stabbing," he said. "No suspects of any kind, huh?"

"Right," I said.

The lovers lay beside each other supine on top of a bed still neatly made in postures so placid that not a hint of struggle was even suggested, the tips of their fingers just barely interlaced as if they had been holding hands in a warm post-coital communion when the assailant struck, the grip of their hands unlocked by a moment's trauma of pain and realization during an instantaneous slaying.

Dr. Bain looked around the quiet room, at the peaceful corpses on the unruffled bed. "I'm inviting you to an autopsy, Evan," he said.

Blur your eyes just slightly and an autopsy room might look indistinguishable from the kitchen of an upscale restaurant. Lots of shiny metal surfaces, tables, faucets, and the like. Immaculate walls.

Outside the room were the storage containers, rows of gleaming metal doors each of which opened into a dark hutch holding a gurney upon which reclined the corpus of one whose recent misfortune was to depart from the cast of the terrestrial drama, whether or not to be recast in a major transmundane musical forever being the speculation of those who remain. Our young lovers were for the moment enshrined in frigid metallic darkness. I followed Dr. Bain into this corridor, wondering if he would select the man or the woman. Necessity dictated no priority choice, and so he asked me for a coin. I handed him a quarter, which he flipped, spinning, into the air with his thumb, then caught, clapping it down audibly on the back of his other hand and, showing no emotion, handed back to me.

"We'll have a look at Jill," he said. He unlocked the door and hauled out the gurney, then pushed it along while I followed him into the autopsy room. As I watched him appraise his array of cutlery in a businesslike way I stared at poor Jill Nevins, whose parents had told me she and her current cell neighbor had been deeply in love, discussing marriage and the planning of a family, eager to commit to spending the rest of their lives together. They got the latter part of the deal in the lousiest way, and as I looked at Jill's blank face, which no longer seemed beautiful as it had when I first saw her because now death's process had given her a faceless anonymity almost as complete as that of old-fashioned department store manikins, I felt true pity. She would not again wear the black nylon stockings or lace-embellished black panties or snow white side-wrap coat-dress with gold-trim pearl buttons that had all been placed on a chair beside the bed in the motel; neither would I be compelled, since she had been naked when killed, to watch with an uneasily shame-tinged sense of voyeurism as Dr. Bain undressed her. I watched him go about the initial business of recording her description, then carefully examining her externally, looking for *something,* one never knew what. I was thinking how lucky my daughter Shari, approximately Jill's age and also in love and planning marriage, was. Dr. Bain was humming absently as he performed the external examination, and the fact that the tune was familiar but I couldn't place it irritated me.

At length, he took up a scalpel, placed its gleaming blade on Jill's left shoulder, slicing it deeply into the flesh and sawing down around the curve of her left breast up around toward the other shoulder, creating a great flap of loose flesh, then cutting down from her midriff toward the mons, laying all of the skin back then to reveal a full view of the bouquet of her internal organs, as brightly colored as hothouse flowers. This was the thoraco-abdominal or "Y" incision. After cracking the ribcage, he mulled over her heart, investigating it with his gloved fingers.

"Whatever punctured her," he said finally, "seems to have had the dynamic impact of a bullet, creating massive hemorrhaging. But it *wasn't* a bullet, Evan. It was . . . I don't know—a dagger, a screw driver, a . . ." He paused, shaking his head. "A projectile of some kind . . . an *arrow* . . . ? The wound is neat, tidy, *precise,* an absolutely mysterious puncture administered with extreme impact."

"An arrow?" I raised my eyebrows. "Wouldn't an arrow blade tear and gash?"

"Sure, the kind hunters use for game. But all the trees in the forest aren't pines, Evan. The arrows the Saracen archers used in the Crusades, for example, were needle-nosed things, no arrowheads or blades on them."

"Really?" I said, intrigued.

Our case didn't rate the front page in the newspapers. But two days later, in association with six other similar murders, it did. He was impressively busy the second night he struck: he killed a newlywed couple from Missoula, Montana in bed in their honeymoon suite at the St. Regis Sheraton, a newlywed couple from Harlem Heights while riding The Carousel in Central Park, and two gay men walking together in the glass-covered courtyard at the Frick Museum. In every instance the modus operandi was identical. Efficient instantaneous penetration of the couple's hearts by some sort of high-power projectile, but no witnesses, no signs of a struggle, no evidence of any kind, no suspects, no leads, nada. One of the tabloids came up with an ominous sobriquet for the murderer, the Avenger, extrapolating the motive of vengeance from the fact that all of the victims had been romantically involved and the killer was presumably vengeful as a result of being lovelorn or unloved—in any case, they were the pathological flip side of someone having a successful affair of the heart. It made sense. Jealousy is a powerful and flamboyant emotion and invariably seethes with the potential for cruelty. As a motive for homicide it's one of the biggies, neck and neck with homicide connected with making money. Jealousy is a theme that runs throughout the Ten Commandments. Check it out.

These killings were first-class puzzlers. The couples were all different kinds of people from different lives, and no significant connections could be made between them. Their romantic involvement was all they apparently had in common, and it didn't take a theorist in literary symbolism working out of Columbia University to see that the choice of Valentine's Day for the original killings was poetic commentary.

Four double homicides in three days. It left us cops stunned and put the city on the edge of panic, so you can imagine how things got when the Avenger struck again two nights after the second round of slayings by taking out *five* couples. A middle-aged divorced couple, who friends said had been thinking about remarrying, zapped in her bedroom on the Upper West Side. Two Latino lesbians found dead abed and among a cornucopia of dildos and vibrators (all of phallic shape, male chauvinist pigs take note). A couple of sixteen-year-old kids from social register families who friends had recently dubbed Romeo and Juliet, their hearts impaled while making love in her parents' bed while the latter vacationed on Saint Bart's. A bag lady and a wino, well known as The Lovebirds by all and sundry in their Times Square neighborhood, found in one of the doorways they resided in, huddled together for warmth. A male transvestite and a female boudoir photographer, mutually dispatched in her SoHo studio while in full libidinal rut in the rosaceous light of the dark room: not a good place for sharpshooting.

Every cop in the city was working overtime, especially homicide cops. There had never been so many theories in circulation about a crime since the assassination of President Kennedy. And what a formidable mystery it was. No evidence, no suspects. Most of the theories came from psychics and amateur hypothesizers. Forensic pathology was up the creek without an oar.

Three days later another couple was found dead in the same manner as the others. Two students at Cooper Union who had been dating found dead in the Hall of Ocean Life in the Museum of Natural History. Every lead we checked out was bogus, fanciful, or bullshit, and the tenor of daily conversation was starting to resemble the kind of stuff you might hear at a UFO conference. One thing was indisputably certain: most of the country's serial killers were in fair danger of being altogether upstaged.

Three days passed with the Avenger off the scope. Then he killed the six members, four women and two men, of two *menages á trois,* one trio wiped out while lounging post-orgiastically on an elegant *lit à la polonaise* in an apartment overlooking Central Park, the other three chilled while nobody noticed over iced mochaccini at one of the cozy, candlelit tables in the back at Gran Caffé Degli Artisti in the Village.

Nobody could offer any ordinary explanation for what was going on, so naturally it was the extraordinary possibilities that started to get attention. Those curio shops in ethnic neighborhoods that sell amulets and candles to dispel bad luck and wicked spirits did thriving business. What utter sense of horror we felt about the crimes was compounded by the fact that we were clearly dealing with a master criminal, impeccably efficient, infernally motivated, and virtually invisible. A week and a half had passed, we had twenty-six enigmatic murders, and every cop in the city, not to mention plenty of outlander hot shots from places like the FBI Academy at Quantico, was groping his way around as if in an impeding fog. And, as throughout all such bloodletting binges, everyone was thinking, as automatically as if they were watching a ball game, *what is the score going to be?*; although in this case the thoughts were attended with the fear of everyone who was in love. Love was under siege in the metropolis, and lovers were as eager to put an end to this demonic threat as Americans had been to rush to war after Pearl Harbor.

I notice that I've been using words like demonic and infernal, but I was not at the time inclined toward any acceptance of the occult. In fact, homicide cops are instilled with a regard for evidence and hard facts as much as scientists, and the philosophers I admired tended to serve up a combination plate of empiricism and rationalism, metaphysical fare to my way of thinking pretty much constituting the children's plate.

Little did I know that I was fated, as I was soon to be informed.

A call came in that they had a person in Bellevue who had confessed to the murders. When crimes that compel society's full attention are being committed there are always a certain number of attention-starved *schlemiels* out there who are willing to cop a phony plea. Another such confessor over in the Bronx was also being checked out. The one in Bellevue would be my afternoon's work.

Normally Jack might have gone along, but they had him on some other spoor.

Good old Bellevue. It is America's traditional symbol of the Nut House, which is to say it is generally thought of as an exclusively psychiatric hospital. I think the reason for that is Hollywood's longtime use of its name in such association. But Bellevue has plenty of departments other than psychiatry—gynecology, pediatrics, surgery, etc. The psychiatry building went up in 1935, ten years before Hitchcock's *Spellbound* would personify psychiatrists as brilliant sleuths and give the practice a romantic/melodramatic ambience embellished by Salvador Dalí and Edith Head. But Bellevue has been around a lot longer than psychiatry. A hundred and twenty years before Freud was born it was a six-bed infirmary. More than two-hundred years later it would have the first cardiopulmonary laboratory in the world.

But, to keep this story appropriately melodramatic, although no less true, Bellevue Psychiatry was where I was headed. I drove through Queens from my house to Manhattan, then along East River Drive to the hospital. The sprawling complex of buildings, both old and new, was familiar to me. I'd done my share of business there. I parked and took an elevator up to Ward 6, where I was met in the corridor by the chief resident, a tired-looking man of thirty or so who still managed a sort of a smile. He told me that the suspect had been arrested at the Port Authority bus terminal, that he had been drunk and attracted a crowd with a babbling, raging confession. He showed me to an empty conference room and said I could talk to the patient there in private, then went away.

My first thought when I laid eyes on him as he was brought in was that he was one of those bantam tough guys who had grown up in a rough neighborhood and had been overcompensating in word and deed all his life because of his size. He had the slight physique of a jockey. He was wearing a robe, pajamas, and hospital slippers. I pegged him at about fifty years old. Did I ever miss the mark on that one!

There was something in the quick satisfied look he gave me, seemingly of recognition, that made something fearful stir lightly in the back of my mind. In fact, I was brought to mind of the scene in *The Exorcist* in which the demon, knowing the priest is coming to confront it, croaks out in a chilling voice full of premonitory challenge, "*Merrrrrin!*"

We sat at a little table, facing each other, alone in the room. As I met his eyes the aspect of toughness seemed to go all at once out of his features, like a bulb dimming down.

"Hello, Evan," he said. "This meeting, you will see, was fated."

It didn't seem likely that anyone had told him my name.

"Hello," I said. They didn't have a name for him and he didn't claim one.

"I've been killing them," he said, "but I am through with killing."

"Why to both statements?" I asked.

"I stopped believing in love," he said. "In my time I have seen more of it, and what comes of it, than you can ever know, Evan. Somehow, reviewing it all, I came to the point where my attitude could be summed up by that J. Geils Band song, 'Love Stinks.' That one would have surely left a bitter taste in Cole Porter's genteel mouth, eh? Anyway, I was drinking too much. And hard stuff, too, which doesn't usually facilitate clear thought. Even so notable a souse as Omar would in a weak moment agree, 'You know, my Friends, with what a brave Carouse/I made a Second Marriage in my House;/Divorc'd old barren Reason from my Bed,/And took the Daughter of the Vine to Spouse.' I started thinking about my career, my role of declaiming and midwifing love, and in my cups I began to taste sour grapes." He smiled at me, not with any humor, and quoted,

"'The Brain within its Groove
Runs evenly and true;
But let a Splinter swerve,
'Twere easier for you
To put the Water back
When Floods have slit the Hills,
And scooped a Turnpike for themselves,
And blotted out the Mills.'"

"Emily Dickinson?" I asked.

He nodded, and repeated emphatically, "'But let a Splinter swerve'. My brain was sidetracked by a splinter of doubt!" He was quiet for a moment, then said, "I love Emily's poetry. Her imagery is full of metaphoric arrows, which I suppose is one reason why. 'I've got an Arrow here/ Loving the Hand that sent it/I the Dart revere'! Or how about, 'The largest Woman's Heart/Could hold an Arrow too'? Emily tended to think of the body as a pin cushion. And even life itself as a symbolic impalement, to wit, 'A single Screw of Flesh/Is all that pins the Soul'."

He didn't need to be drawn out and he wasn't having any trouble expressing himself. I showed myself to be attentive to his story, as I irresistibly was.

"I descended into hell when I stopped believing in the supremacy of love," he said. "Father Zossima said, 'What is hell? I maintain it is the suffering of being unable to love.' It was a belief that had sustained me for over 2500 years. I was used to the tragic suicides or lonely fates of unrequited lovers, I even got used to syphilis after it appeared. But AIDS put a terrible acerbity in the sweetness of the grapes. I began to dwell on all the brutality that thwarted lovers inflict. I brooded on how rarely a couple stays together permanently. I read somewhere that love often begins like a symphony by Beethoven but ends like a short story by Poe. That suddenly seemed as sad to me as the fate of Romeo and Juliet. In truth, it was the serpent of monogamy invading my Arcadian orchard. I was seduced by the idea that love dies when a couple breaks up rather than the fact that it merely goes into suspended animation. It would only die, of course, if one or the other emerged an obdurate misogynist or misanthrope, unable to find *new* love, which is usually what finally happens. Monogamy of the absolute kind and even serial monogamy both make emotion linear. Still, I began to view love as an absurd little *comédie rosse* produced by the brain and directed by the heart."

He gave me a bright, brittle look. "You know, at my work I was the best marksman of all time! Forget Robin Hood. Forget Sergeant York. Forget Annie Oakley and William Tell. Forget even Billy Dixon's legendary one mile shot at Adobe Walls in 1874. I *never* missed. Before the bitterness, my prospectus might have been summed up and symbolized by Bernini's *St. Teresa in Ecstasy*, in which the marksman's victim is in orgasmic transport, albeit in that case divine rather than carnal. My goal was to make a wound that would finalize love's power and presence, and thus to make those skewered, blood-dripping hearts that boys and girls and men and women adorn themselves with constitute *art*, not just anatomical *graffiti*. Valentine's Day was, of course, my favorite holiday. Heart-shaped boxes filled with confections—the sweetness of love symbolized! And bouquets of flowers—the sex organs of plants! I *loved* love, and I served it well. But when the bitterness took me, sharpened I suppose by over 2500 years on the job with no vacation, I suddenly began to enjoy depictions of Saint Sebastian and to admire dioramas of Crécy and Agincourt. The executioner's song began to lure my mind." He lowered his voice to a whisper as he said, "And so I decided to shoot to kill. Possessed and embittered, I began to execute lovers . . ." Remarkably, there then appeared in the corners of his eyes distinct tears.

"I'm sorry," he said, simply. He fired a quick glance at me. "Do you know who I am?" he asked.

"Cupid?" I said, without noticeable sarcasm.

It was the perfect moment for him to fill the ensuing gulf of silence by producing a golden locket, heart-shaped, on a golden chain and proffer it for my momentary glance before dropping it into my palm. A shadow passed over my heart in that moment. It was Shari's locket, I was almost certain, and I held it in my stone-like hand for seconds before opening it to see the tiny photograph of her and Carl.

"Don't worry, your daughter's alive," he said. "It was, in truth, the sight of her serene and ecstatic face in the soaring joy of orgasm, and the loving embrace of her beautiful legs 'round her lover's back, that stayed my bolt . . . that brought me *back* to my senses. I took the locket from her throat as she slept to remind me of my return to sanity."

Our eyes met and he transfixed me with the shaft of a compelling gaze, then said, "I know how much you love your daughter, Evan. And I know that you love your wife, no less than you love your mistress. The *pas de deux* of love can be shared with more than one partner. Did anyone insist that Fred dance only with Ginger? Surely not if they had ever seen him dance with Eleanor Powell!" He smiled. "If you attend my autopsy, make sure my wings are neatly folded." He reached back over one shoulder and I saw there the slightly distended shape of the pajama top. "And if you would remember me, let it be as Boucher painted me in *Cupid a Captive*. We *did* know how to party in those days!"

"Your autopsy?" I said.

He smiled wistfully. "The truth is, love doesn't really need me. Actually, I was never more than a sort of psychosexual hypnotist. But true love has its own vital and sustaining power. And I am, I confess, after all this time, *very* tired. Frost expressed it perfectly in 'After Apple-Picking':

'My long two-pointed ladder's sticking through a tree
Toward heaven still,
And there's a barrel that I didn't fill
Beside it, and there may be two or three
Apples I didn't pick upon some bough.

But I am done with apple-picking now.
Essence of winter sleep is on the night,
The scent of apples: I am drowsing off.'"

My gun, suddenly and magically, was in his hand. "On my grave," he said, "strew the appropriate flowers—bleeding hearts, love-lies-bleedings, and also anything red as blood, or pink, as pink as the vulvar shoals . . ."

He pulled the trigger.

The Avenger never struck again.

I left the mystery at Bellevue, for them to ponder. I told them that during the course of an incoherent confession he seized my gun. But before anyone came into the room, I took a look at his back, at the graceful white wings that had borne him in flight for all those many centuries.

Later, that night, I told my wife that I loved her, and after we made love I called Dawn to arrange a *rendez-vous* for the weekend, adding that I loved her. It wasn't really necessary to make the statement in either case. But the words had a pleasant taste, reminding me of how delicious they had always been to say, and how the most consuming love of my life, Fran, had once reacted to the declaration by whispering, in her lethal voice of volcanic ash and gold dust, "Say it *again*, it sounds so pretty."

Windows

Erin MacKay

Her shoulders were pressed down
from too many years of wanting,
her feet turned slightly inward
and her spine curved with it.

Nancy secretly wanted things. She never spoke of it, but inside her head was an accounting of everything she thought she ought to have, but didn't. Now that she had rounded the corner of thirty and her life was starting to congeal into its permanent shape, the wanting was taking on a shade of desperation. Only the ring of ugly words like *greedy* and *ungrateful* kept Nancy from admitting to herself how bad it was getting.

Besides, the things she wanted seemed small enough. Plenty of other people had them, after all. For instance, she wanted a frivolously fashionable pair of shoes, not ones classically designed to stay in style year after year. She wanted a car that was better than the best she could do with a meager down payment and her husband's lousy credit rating. She wanted to go to a cocktail party and talk to well groomed people and drink trendy wine, without once having to fight the urge to retreat into the kitchen and hang out with the help. Or leave early because David was bored.

She wanted to own a house, a house to which she possessed the only key, and into whose walls she could pound nails without calculating the cost per hole upon termination of said Lease. She wanted a house that she could become a part of, a place that a guest would enter and say, "Oh, this house is definitely *Nancy*." She wanted to choose the color of the carpet, or choose to have no carpet at all; she wanted to replace light fixtures according to her whim, to rip out prim boxwoods and plant pungent herbs and wildflowers instead.

But these things were hard for Nancy to want without getting mired in the same tarpit of futile desires that had worn her mother down; hard to attain without tying on the suburban straitjacket Nancy had sacrificed so much to escape. So when the wanting filled her chest like a swelling shadow, she swallowed it down. She told herself that there were children starving in Africa and cities burning in Iraq and she reminded herself, over and over, how damned fortunate she was.

Later, Nancy estimated that she had walked past the house at least a hundred and fifty times before she finally saw it. That was the porch's fault. Built in the last years before the automobile had transformed downtown Atlanta, the porch's steps led directly onto the wide sidewalk, convenient and inviting.

And it happened that Nancy's morning walk from the train station to her office building had long been the site of an uncomfortable battle between her pity and her finances. She wished no ill on the homeless, genderless beings who shuffled, dirty and tangled, down Peachtree Street, but she hated when they spoke to her. They asked her for money, always, and she had quickly figured out that if she gave money to every beggar who asked her, she would have to take a second job to support the extravagant habit.

So, she did the only thing she could do: She avoided them. She walked quickly down the street, her head low and her eyes focused firmly on the sidewalk a few feet ahead of her. Whenever she heard a rough voice growl, "Hey, miss lady," she shook her head, made a dismissive gesture with one hand, and tried not to feel like a horrible person as she scurried away.

At no point on the walk were her eyes lower and her pace quicker than when she passed the convenient front steps of that house. Even when the cops ran off the drunken vagrants perched there like pigeons, their offensive detritus remained—yellowed newspapers, Styrofoam cups rimed with mysterious substances, the cloying smell of human sweat, vomit, urine, worse—all things that made Nancy want to hurry past without thinking too hard about the ugliness swarming just outside her vision. So she had never seen the house.

Today, thanks to an early dentist appointment, Nancy found herself on that particular stretch of Peachtree Street at the sunlit height of the business day. The early morning shadows had melted away, as had the scuffling wrecks that lurked in them, and in full daylight, the porch steps were abandoned. Before she could stop herself, her gaze had found them and followed where they led.

She stood perfectly still, awestruck by the house's bedraggled, incongruous beauty. The last vestige of nineteenth-century Peachtree Street, it was rather more compact, like a townhouse, than the rambling structures Nancy associated with the Victorian period. The brick was red and warm and solid, the large windows set like jewels within it.

Despite its aged grandeur, the house huddled forlornly in the shadows of a six-story apartment building and a tattered strip mall, so tightly squeezed between the modern monstrosities that it seemed to be holding its breath to keep from touching them. Nancy didn't blame it. The house needed more space. It needed to relax, to brush against shade trees and a jasmine trellis, not fake stucco and a rusting dumpster.

Nancy drowned in a rainfall of bittersweet imaginings of when the house had been new, the pride of its owners, the envy of Peachtree Street: A man in a natty suit led a fashionably coiffed woman up the front steps for the first time. Letting her mouth fall open in delight, the woman clapped her hands, kissed her husband and declared the house perfect. A child in a white pinafore ran up and down the narrow staircases to ferret out the nooks and niches and stare out the oddly shaped windows, squealing gleefully at each discovery.

The woman wandered into the kitchen and leaned into the bay window to look at the shaded ivy and drooping wisteria, and beyond that, at the gracious lace curtains of the window next door. Surely she had closed her eyes in pleasure at the thought of her new home and the years of peaceful comfort ahead of her. Surely she had smiled in a quiet swell of joy to think that it was all hers.

Now the woman's bay window overlooked a sagging chain link fence and crumbling asphalt. Her front doors opened upon grimy, weathered blasphemers who drank grain alcohol on her front steps until they sprawled in senseless heaps. They woke up and pissed into the layer of rotting leaves that were once her flower beds, and let their befouled cups roll out onto the sidewalk she had swept clean every day.

Before Nancy finally forced herself down the sidewalk toward the train station, she indulged in one last look at the house. "If I ever won the lottery," she murmured, "I'd buy that old house and fix it up."

Nancy heard the futility in her own words the second they came out of her mouth. How many times had she uttered sentences that started with "If I ever won the lottery"? The familiar shadow of wanting rose in her chest, powerful and seductive. Biting her lip, she swallowed until the shadow faded and the wanting settled down.

As the crosswalk blinked yellow, the breeze brushed against her cheek and sighed down the street after her.

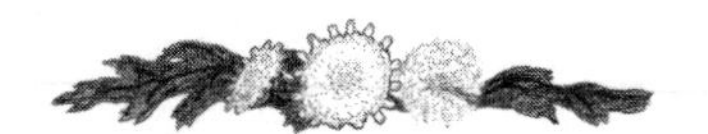

The next morning Nancy hurried toward her office, body bent against the chill November wind. Her hands were freezing through her worn gloves, and she thought longingly of her office's central heat and hot coffee. The cracks in the pavement flew beneath her shoes; the muffled mutter of some unfortunate soul wandering the perforated edge of sanity barely touched her awareness.

Then the gray morning light flickered as though, for a split second, the rising sun had been pushed back down below the horizon. Startled, Nancy looked up, and found herself in front of the house.

She knew she should look back down, hurry away before the ugly, unwelcome world asked anything of her. But instead, she stopped walking and lifted her eyes to the house—past the littered front steps, past the faded real estate sign clinging resignedly to the front door—to the oval window on the left.

Nancy stared into the window. At first, it showed her nothing, only the opaque reflection of the dim morning. But then, a glow like yellow lamplight slowly brightened the oval of glass, illuminating rose-and-ivory wallpaper and a slice of dark wooden stairs. Nancy could almost feel the warmth of a crackling fire, smell coffee brewing from somewhere within the house.

A black shadow leaped behind the window, shapeless and looming. Nancy gasped and took a reflexive step backward, but the shadow quickly resolved into the back of a little girl's dress: starched linen, lace and a broad blue sash tied in a bow. With a clatter of footsteps, the small figure darted up the stairs, corkscrew curls bouncing with every movement. Just before she rose past the level of the window, she stopped, leaned over the banister, turned her peaches-and-cream face to Nancy, and waved.

"Morning, miss lady." A cough like a rusty hinge drew Nancy's gaze down to the heap of clothes sitting on the front steps. It opened its broken mouth in a grin and held out a hand. "Spare change?"

Nancy looked back to the window, but the pretty, clean child was gone. As she watched, the shadow rose again, swallowed the lamplight and pressed against the oval windowpane. The glass frosted over with a chill darkness and a frustrated, aching hate.

The creature on the steps continued to stare at Nancy, waiting for her to respond. She stood serenely ignoring him, fascinated with her reflection in the cold, black window. She barely recognized herself. Hunched within her jacket, she looked small, afraid. Her shoulders were pressed down from too many years of wanting, her feet turned slightly inward and her spine curved with it. The wanting had made her eyes dull, her hair limp; it had sucked away at her youth like a disease.

The hate and anger seeped into Nancy. She hated the cold, littered street, the fouled morning air, the gritty train station, but especially, she hated the thing sitting on the house's front steps with its hand out to her.

Leveling her eyes, she met the dark stare beneath the greasy stocking cap. Her upper lip lifted in an expression her facial muscles barely knew, but instantly enjoyed. It made her reflection in the window stand a little straighter, and it made the shadow in her chest go away.

The body shifted nervously in its layers of clothing, and the dark eyes flicked downward. Nancy turned to face the wind and walked away.

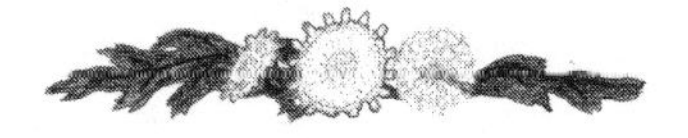

Tuesday morning, Nancy stopped at the newsstand in Peachtree Center to buy a grapefruit juice. Out of long habit, she bought a lottery ticket, too.

She forgot about the ticket in her backpack until the next morning, when the house stopped her again. Today an upper bedroom window lit up under its gable to show her a four-poster bed draped in a lacy canopy, and the delicate mirror of the woman's dressing table. The formless shadow rose and became the woman, using the mirror to tuck a strand of hair under a wide hat luxurious with ribbons and feathers. The woman turned, as though Nancy had called to her, and came to the window. She smiled down to Nancy in tentative greeting.

Nancy returned the smile, but it faded when the woman lifted her hand to show a small slip of paper she held in her fingers. Her bow-shaped mouth clearly mouthed the words: *You promised.* Then the woman dissolved, and the window surrendered to darkness. Nancy hurried onward.

At her desk, Nancy warmed her chilled hands on her coffee mug while her computer booted up. With fingers still a little stiff from the cold, she unfolded the lottery ticket and tucked it under a corner of her keyboard. When her computer finished booting, Nancy opened her internet browser and went to the Georgia lottery website.

She knew which link to click, but she let the cursor hover over it for a moment. This was really about to happen. Her life was about to change forever. All the petty debts would disappear, she would buy the house and kick the vermin on the front steps out for good. She would make the house beautiful and happy again. She had promised. Her finger trembled as she waited for the page to load up and confirm what she already knew, deep within her core: The house was hers.

Most days, Nancy shrugged when the numbers came up with not a single match, informing her that her life was the same as it had been the day before. But today, as Nancy read the numbers, so stark and indifferent on the white background, tears pricked at her eyes, and disappointment burned the back of her throat. She crumpled the ticket and threw it into the recycling bin.

She picked up her coffee mug to try to carry on her charade of normalcy, then changed her mind and put it back down. Moving her mouse to the search function, she typed in the name of the realty company she had read on the house's front door. Just to see.

Scrolling through the listings, her eyes tracked instantly to a thumbnail image of the house, touted as a *historical property, perfect for office space!* She clicked on the link and skimmed past the history and the architecture and the roster of once-prominent owners, hurrying to the bottom line: $1,200,000.00. Nancy blew out a small breath of surprise as she processed all the zeroes. In her mind, she repeated the words: One-point-two-million dollars.

The next day, she walked on the other side of the street. But the wind found her there, and it pulled at her hair and teased her with visions of an herb garden under the bay window—rosemary, lavender, lovely aromatic things that would bake in the summer sun and banish the fetid smells of the city.

"I don't have the money," she whispered to it. "You can't belong to me." The wind let go of her hair and flitted away.

The day after that, Nancy started getting off at the next train station down the line, so she could walk to her office from the south instead of the north.

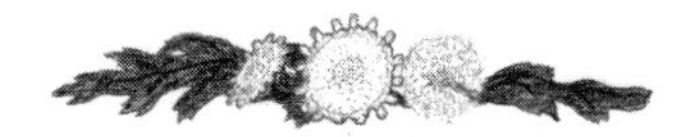

Nancy spent the day after Christmas at her father's funeral. Everyone agreed that perhaps it was better that the cancer had taken him so quickly; he was never a man who could have borne a long illness. But his death was still jolting. No one had seen it coming.

Nancy would never have imagined her father had stayed so well insured after her mother died. But after she dried her eyes, paid the funeral expenses and the estate debts, she was faced with the new reality that a bank account with her name on it had a balance with six figures. Barely six figures, but she didn't care, she could count all six of them.

She and her husband left the bank in bemused silence, neither of them quite able to grasp that the annoying car notes, the lingering student loans, the stubborn credit card debt were all about to go away. For David, the leash had been too abruptly loosened. Domesticated dog that he was, he had no idea what to do now.

Nancy knew what to do; she just wasn't sure how to talk David into it.

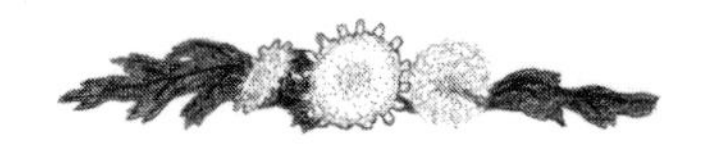

Nancy did not know what reaction she had been expecting from David. But the way he stood on the sidewalk, his gaze flickering from the house to his wife as though he were waiting for her to say she was kidding, was definitely not it.

"A million two?" he finally asked. "We've got a heck of a lot more money than we've ever had before, but we don't have even close to that."

"We have enough for a down payment, and we could get financing for the rest," she said quickly. If money were the only issue, surely she could make him see. The house would make him see. She kept waiting for a window to light up for him, for the little girl or the elegant woman to wave down to them, for the house to show him what it had shown her.

But the windows remained dark, chilled, silent.

"But that would just land us right back where we started, financially," he said. "Then there's all the work it would take to fix it up . . ." The sentence bogged down in skepticism and he shook his head. "I don't think so, Nance. I mean, it's a neat idea, someday when we're retired and have nothing to do but remodel an old house."

He came up with a dozen more reasons for her to put the house out of her mind, but she didn't hear any of them. While he talked, she stared at the shadow pressed against one black, gabled window and the wanting tightened painfully in Nancy's chest. She tried to swallow it down, and choked.

The black windows shifted their cool gaze from Nancy to fix on David.

Suddenly Nancy's ears were sick of his voice. "Yeah, you're right," she said, straining to speak around the wanting that had pushed into her throat. "Let's go home."

She walked slowly to the crosswalk, defeat pressing heavily on her shoulders. The breeze, catching up with her, began to whimper and fret. *You can't belong to me,* it whined in her ear, careful not to let David hear. *Can't-can't. Belong to me.*

Nancy opened her mouth to tell the wind to leave her alone, but some of the wanting slipped out between her lips and floated into the air like ink in a glass of water. The wind gathered it up and darted away with it, giggling all the way.

Nancy listened to it go, and pulled out her keys. "I'll drive," she offered.

"Okay. Thanks." David hated driving downtown.

Somewhere on the road home, the shadow became an empty delivery truck and the truck became a sail in a gust of wind, but the dotted line between the lanes remained just a dotted line. The crash tied up traffic on I-85 for hours.

By the time Nancy could walk on her own again, her limbs stiff and slow, the winter was dying and the driver's company had already made a settlement offer.

It was enough. But then, Nancy had known it would be.

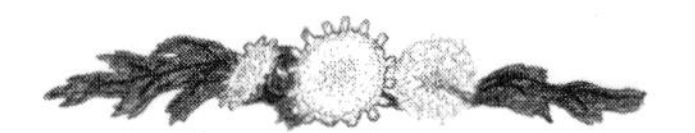

Nancy walked down Peachtree Street at sunset, the spring breeze laughing against her skin and dancing in the folds of her skirt. She laughed with it, her legs tired but her body empty and light. Her breath came easy in her chest. When she stood before the front steps, every window in the house lit up for her, golden with welcome. The little girl appeared in an upper window, clapping her hands and waving. *Do it,* the girl whispered, giggling and pointing. *Do it now.*

Smiling, Nancy waved back, then lifted her hand and dangled the key from her fingers like a hypnotist's charm.

"This is my house now," she announced to the sluggish garbage sprawled on the steps. "You have to leave."

Thick, croaking laughter met her ears. Slimy voices mocked her, dared her to make them go, described the drunken physical delights that awaited her if she stayed.

Nancy looked up. The little girl was gone, and the

windows were darkening. The house's revulsion and anger filled her emptied body, filled her up in the place where the wanting used to be. "Leave now," she repeated, her voice as cold and precise as a paring knife.

Then she turned around and walked back the way she had come. On Peachtree Street, the shadows lengthened and the breeze grew still.

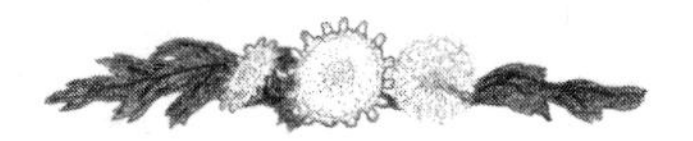

She came back early the next morning, when the sunrise was only a pink line in the east. The last piece of trash was crawling down the steps, gibbering and praying and crying. His face glistened, raked with bleeding scratches. When he saw Nancy, he pushed himself to his feet and stumbled away.

Nancy did not see him. She climbed the steps and used her foot to roll the two dead ones off the porch. They flopped down the steps and landed on the sidewalk, limbs splayed, their bodies leaking congealing blood.

But Nancy had already forgotten they had ever existed. The windows of the house sparkled with morning sunshine. She ran her fingers down the rotting doorframe, traced the porous mortar between the smooth, cool bricks. Her shaking hand fit the key into the lock, and she pulled open the creaking door. Looking into the lamplit foyer, Nancy opened her mouth in delight and clapped her hands together.

A man in a natty suit stepped out from the shadows of the parlor, and she turned to him with a smile.

"Oh, darling," she breathed. "It's perfect."

He grinned and extended a hand, beckoning to her. With a sigh of happiness, Nancy followed him into her new home.

Hexerei

Darren Speegle

. . . fields of tobacco, fragrant as blood
in the beautiful, flowering night.

As I sit here partaking of this strangely calming, strangely exhilarating thing I hold in one hand and contemplating the pen poised in the other, I realize I am no closer to finding a starting point than I was two and a half hours ago when I first opened my empty notebook to the waning afternoon. I've started my tale no less than three times now, from three different angles, three different points in time, and still Reiss's talk of sorcery and *Hexerei*, spoken only the day before yesterday, overlaps with Wagner's even more ominous words, uttered more than two decades ago to an eleven-year-old boy.

There is that sound again, fading in, a rhythmical central gear in a system of memories. As it increases I pull from the object in my left hand, pour from the instrument in my right . . . and it occurs to me that, instead of trying to work the prism's facets into some kind of linear sense, I should leave them just as they are. For essentially each is a beginning in its own right . . .

i

I wasn't sure what I had expected as I stood there, having just emerged from the trees, looking down on the forbidding structure that was Old Man Wagner's drying house. The vision was precisely as I remembered it, the planks of the tall barn stained dark against the painted afternoon sky and the lush fields of tobacco rippling in the early September breeze. A door at one end of the deep building stood partially open, revealing the nose of a rusty green tractor parked within. I imagined the rows of drying tobacco leaves hanging from beams above it. I imagined that and more, much more.

Scanning the valley and finding no disturbance beyond the ebb and flow whisper of the tobacco blossoms, I moved to the spot affording the best view of this place out of my boyhood and nightmares (if the one could be distinguished from the other). A pile of electric wire lay beside a deteriorated gate post, a former boundary of the pasture extending between me and the tobacco fields. Stepping across it, I dropped my bag, retrieved the beach towel I had packed and spread it on the grass. Next I dug out my notebook and pen, then the slab of *Käse* and the bottle of richly dark Neckar Valley *Wein* my new landlord had given me as a move-in gift. Lastly, the cigarette. A lone, filterless, machine-rolled cigarette that, when held up to the light, was touted to have none of the white specks of impurity an American cigarette had.

I wouldn't have known. I had never brought myself to smoke after playing as a boy among the aroma of Wagner's fields, an aroma I could smell now, more bitter than the cheese I unwrapped, more sweet than the wine I uncorked. The cigarette felt duly odd between my fingers. Odd as the face, the smile of Herr Müller as he'd produced it out of a metal container.

The lighter in my hand felt appropriate, the flame like prayer, incantation, its kiss in the blunt end of the packed tube a sort of saturating magic that could not be undone. Taboo like the orange-purple sunset melting in streams towards nightfall. Mojo like the fields inviting the old friendly trespasser back into their midst. Voodoo like the wrenching singing of swings and beams; the tickling of little girls' feet with pinkish blossoms; their last breaths, in a tall deep *Tabak* house with a green rusted tractor parked under a bestirred yield.

A cigarette under a flame. Smoke into my lungs, almost smoothly, as if I had been indulging all my life, of my own devices.

Then a murder of crows off to my left lifted as if spooked—in the process, spooking me. I watched the cigarette begin to shake in my hand. I had no idea why I had lit the thing to begin with. It was too early, too fucking early for symbolism. Three days it had been since I'd arrived back in Germany after the years, three days to find my way across the fields and forest to this place again. Three days to face my terrors. The cigarette could wait as I pinched it out unceremoniously, setting it aside in favor of the vine-purple wine, steadying agent, organizer of thoughts.

As I let the wine play its less-than-obscure part, the sun gradually fled from Wagner's property. Alcohol, nicotine, the being there brought the taboo into focus under the horizon—the voodoo, the juju, the mojo as the dark castle of hanging tobacco became a silhouette against the swelling dusk. The September sky became speckled with stars. I watched the structure with calm, restrained wonder. With every swallow I further suppressed the basic fear. But the expectancy, the watchfulness remained as the evening, in strange new effects, took hold.

The warmth of the wine seemed at odds with the startling sharpness of the crows that came and went at their fancy and with the fresh bent of the wind, seeming to warn of the coming hour. The warmth of the wine could not combat the threat and suggestion of the cold September night—its wrenching sounds, its laughter—and yet I found myself longing for that dark house where I had once been caught trespassing. I found myself . . . picking up the cigarette again, looking at it . . .

The light like incantation. And not a soul down there in the valley to disprove it, though I did begin to detect, fading in and out, a regular and cyclical sound. Like a wheel . . .

ii

Somehow I always knew I'd return to take over for my father when he retired from the *Heidelberg American*, the newspaper he'd started in '71, year of my birth. I'm not sure whether duty or nostalgia played a part in it or whether I was simply haunted. As my childhood had continued to linger through college and then a teaching job that barely paid for life, much less living, it could easily have been the latter.

My parents and their golf cart were already part of the Floridian landscape when I landed on European soil again to stay. Herr Reiss, who'd leased and then optioned to us the house I had spent the first twelve years of my life in, was gracious enough to put me in touch with an elderly neighbor of his who had an available apartment in the same lovely farming region southeast of Heidelberg.

The three of us met on the evening I drove my rental down from the Frankfurt airport, a round of schnapps sitting on the rickety table of the room I'd be spending the night in whether I thought the place worthy of my money or not. Other than the table, two rusty scissors-legged chairs, a small refrigerator, a few dishes, and a horrid orange-patterned sofa—my bed—the first-floor apartment was empty. The upper level of the functional two-story house constituted a separate apartment, as is common in Germany, but it remained empty most of the year, reserved for Herr Müller's relatives when they came to visit from Würzburg.

It surprised both men when I accepted the price without viewing the place by daylight. That it stood on the northern skirts of the village, accessed by its own small road—albeit a rough one—was enough for me. The stooped and venerable Müller actually clapped his withered hands at the news, while Herr Reiss, frowning at this sort of rash decision-making, offered to show me around in the morning.

"No need," I told him. "I remember the area like yesterday."

Reiss was there nonetheless when I rose from the deep and dreamless sleep that follows a transatlantic flight and opened the door to the new day. Framed by a clear September sky, he held a coffee in each fist, last night's frown replaced by the cheerful face from my youth—a face that seemed to have aged none at all since the last time I saw it.

"*Was hat denn das Leben so für dich getan*?"

I wiped the traces of oblivion from my eyes, accepting the mug presumably brought from his own cupboard. "Can't complain too much. I'm here, as they say."

"So you are, Reed." He put his hand on my shoulder, doubtless glad to have around some remnant of my father, with whom he had developed a friendship through the years.

As I started to invite him in he gestured with his coffee hand to his right. "Have you been around to the patio?"

"No, actually. You're the first thing I've seen this morning, Herr Reiss."

"*Albert*, Reed. Albert."

I felt a strange thrill at this luxury. The twelve-year-old boy had known him only by the respectful title due elders and landlords. "Then no, Albert," I said. "I've not visited the patio."

We walked along a footpath of octagonal stones, textured and substantial under my naked feet, to a tiled semicircular patio with a view that managed to take my memories and transform them into verdant lace. As we looked down over the rolling fields of tobacco capped with pink-white blossoms, I sensed both his pride and his unease.

"Old Man Wagner?" I said. "Is he still around?"

"Yes," he exhaled, seeming relieved to have it out in the open. "I hope you will forgive that this house borders his property. It was the only available apartment in Zuzenhausen in your price range."

"No problem," I said, choosing to withhold, perhaps even from myself, that this very distinction had been a selling point. Meanwhile the rational part of me was somewhat disarmed by not only his frankness about the matter, but also his considering it deserving of the sober look on his face. A far cry from my father's opinions on Wagner.

His next statement found a cold place retained from my boyhood. "The village has grown rapidly in recent years. North is the natural direction for expansion, but no one will live near him."

"Because of the murders?"

"Because of *him*. Has your father said nothing to you about this? Wagner has become a blight on the land. In terms of impact on the community, he is worse than the rumors describe."

I looked to my left where the edge of the village was just visible beyond the fields. "Wagner's still a sore subject with my father and me, Albert. From all the way back to . . . the girls, the hangings. He feels I wasn't truthful with him at the time and that I've never admitted to it."

He peered at me over the rim of his mug. "Benjamin never said anything like that to me."

"No, I'm sure he wouldn't. After all, who would want their friends to know about their deluded boy?"

"Deluded? Is my English serving me?"

"You know exactly what I mean, Albert. Don't pretend to miss the point in defense of my father. That's the kind of thing . . . never mind."

He gestured inside the house. "May I get the chairs?"

"By all means." Along with the table, they'd probably been patio furniture to begin with.

We sat looking out on the waves of leafy abundance, the rich odor of untainted tobacco riding in on a sporadic morning breeze. Albert seemed to savor the scene even as his words cast a shadow over it:

"The villagers speak of strange sightings on his property at night. They avoid any dealings with him. He has his regular buyers for the harvested *Tabak;* otherwise he is a social . . . what is the word for an outcast of this type?"

"Pariah?"

"That is the exact word."

"But what are the villagers' reasons? When I was a boy there were two sides: those who accepted the findings of the police and those who accepted the findings of the police with the stipulation that Wagner was nevertheless involved in some way." I swallowed. "Never mind what came after—his wife found practically torn to pieces in the fields while he was away at market."

Albert studied me a moment, having detected the lump in my throat. "Yes," he said, "the stigma on the Wagner name." He sipped his coffee, letting his gaze drift out across the fields, adopting a look that could best be described as one of remembrance as he proceeded to elaborate on the subject.

I had probably been too young to understand, he told me, but the attitude towards the Wagner family had gone back to medieval times, when they'd farmed rye, the food of the poor—quite the opposite of tobacco, which only the rich could afford when the 'medicine' of the New World natives became fashionable. During the fifteen- and sixteen-hundreds the Wagners were rumored to have been actively involved in *Hexerei*—witchcraft, sorcery, black magic. One story, at least partly based in reality, told of two of Gerhard —Old Man—Wagner's ancestors, a mother and daughter, being put to death as witches. In retaliation the husband/ father, along with his son, the village baker, intentionally ground ergot-infested rye with regular grain and poisoned the entire village.

Ergot, Albert explained, was the fungus from which the drug LSD was derived. It had been known at the time, even used by alchemists for various potions, but it hadn't yet been identified as the cause of outbreaks such as St. Anthony's Fire—attributed to the mass consumption of ergot-poisoned bread—whose symptoms ranged from hallucinations and madness to gangrene so severe in the body's extremities that people were described as having blackened stumps for arms.

Legend had it that the Wagners had known what they had, that they'd experimented with it, made serums with it, used it to practice sorcery. "While many of the locals," he said, "will claim they don't believe such nonsense, you won't find them taking a shortcut across his property. Not then, not now." He regarded me from under the shadow of his brow lest I mistake his meaning. "But tell me, Reed, what did you share with your father that he would not believe?"

There it was, on the table between us, rigid and naked as the coffee mugs. In the silence I heard what I thought was the duet of hooves and wood on pavement. His nod invited but did not encourage.

"I told him about seeing Old Man Wagner with the girls at the *Waldspielplatz* prior to their deaths, about watching him tickle their feet with flowers—tobacco blossoms—as they swung on the swing set. I knew Wagner hadn't killed them, that the M.O. of the accused and later convicted drifter was hanging young girls. But the removal of the eyes postmortem was another matter. I told my father what Wagner said to me when he caught me trespassing in his drying house after the girls were found. I was an eleven-year-old, you understand, and terribly curious . . ."

iii

If my mom had owned her own church bell she would have been ringing it by now. I could feel her worry, palpable as the odor of the fields, as I finally watched the lights go out in Old Man Wagner's barn, the tall skewed doors of the structure screech shut, locking in the bunches of dried leaves that looked (through the windows of the tilted slats) like so many cocoons for God knew what.

I had stolen over hill and dell to be here, chased by my mother's words:

"You're not to go past the stream, son. I know they caught the man, but the thought of how vulnerable a kid is out there . . ."

"I'll be alright, Mom."

". . . it simply kills me."

It simply kills me.

Driving words, though she hadn't realized it.

Simply.

As if it were so.

Kills me.

As though her own daughters had been found hanging there, with black and empty eye sockets. But only I had any such connections, having often played with the children, a kind of older brother to them.

As I walked down the lazy slope toward the barn, I willed myself to shed all the extraneous matter and focus on the object, which was to look within the building upon the site of the crime. Whatever deeper compulsions might have been at work, they too became extraneous, dissolving in the night like Herr Wagner as he wobbled away on his bicycle. I was a slave to my fear, and my fear was a slave to me. The drying shed was the terrible medium where the two realities clashed.

The house of planks and beams rose above me in dark mystery, reaching for the moon but settling for its syrup dripping over the suspended leaves of the product. A house of magic and terror, a young man's dream to be explored, its contents known. I squeezed my skinny body through the rectangular hole where one of the planks was missing, finding myself engulfed in a silver-tinged blackness. I heard my mother's voice, but it was a long, long way from Wagner's barn.

The stench of oil managed to seep through the sweetly pungent fragrance of tobacco, with the further elements of hay and chemical fertilizer and my own sweat. The mid-September air was cool, but my flesh didn't know chill from heat. Children I had played tag with had died here, carcasses among cocoons. I gingerly felt my way around the wall, the hulk of the tractor and the pods above my head the only shapes visible in the dusk. My hand found a wooden shaft; I let my fingers crawl up it until they found metal prongs. I removed the pitchfork from the wall, a warrior now against the place.

A noise from the other side of the tractor, a creaking like the wind forcing two tree trunks together, made me clutch my weapon more tightly. I made my way along the wall so that I always retained my bearings, touching the beams and planks with my right hand while the other held my pronged lance extended by my waist. My searching fingers found a ladder, the possibility of actually climbing up above the beams where the girls had been hanged, and I was compelled to take it. I was halfway to the first of the drying levels when the door to the barn scraped open. I let the pitchfork fall and scampered behind the cocoons, one foot planting on a wall brace, the other resting on a main horizontal beam. Tobacco bunches from the next level hung in my face, a reeking camouflage.

A flashlight searched the spaces as the visitor walked through the barn. I could tell my hiding spot was at least somewhat secure by the densities the beam had to penetrate. If I remained utterly still, perhaps I would not be discovered. Then the light froze beneath me. For several seconds there was no motion within the building except that of my heart against my feeble shield of a shirt. Then, the beam shot upward, swimming among the tobacco, wanting me. I watched it pass across the crotch of my jeans, burn in the tobacco leaves I straddled, then die as the main bulb of the barn came on, the light filtering through the bundles indiscriminately.

A hesitation ensued, a period of foreboding, and then the game took its inevitable turn as rusty tines stabbed up through the murmur-glow below. I heard the word but did not utter it. Instead I remained stretched across the spider's corner I had chosen, feeling the silky webs over my mouth like gauze. The tines appeared once more then slipped out of sight. I hung there like a bat as Old Man Wagner's thrusts now took the form of speech.

My two years attending a German school and learning the native tongue paid off now as they never had before.

"Hallo, Reed. Ich weis das du in meiner Scheune bist. Ich weis wo du dich versteckst."

—I know you're in my barn. I know where you're hiding.

"Dort habe ich mich auch versteckt und habe zugeguckt wie er die Mädchen von ihren Hälsen an den Balken wo du gerade draufstehst aufhing."

—I hid there myself and watched him hang the girls by their necks from the beam you are standing on.

"Willst du wie sie werden? Wilst du deine Augen weggeben und für immer mein Geschöpf sein, um mich zu dienen, wie sie mich dienen?"

—Do you want to become like them? Do you want to give up your eyes and be my creature, to serve me as they now serve me?

My legs were shaking so wildly I could barely stand up, much less maintain my position on the beams. If there had been any question as to my exact location, it was gone now as the clusters of leaves around me shivered with my own fear. Even as I squeezed my eyes shut, knowing the next thrust of the pitchfork would not miss, I wanted to act, to obey the instinct that seemed to find connections through my paralyzed body.

He spoke again, the German adding a certain coarseness to his otherwise unaggressive timbre. *The eyes, they are your liaisons in every transaction, physical and otherwise. They are your last link to the world. They are strange vessels . . . strange orbs to hold in the hand.*

It was too much to bear. I let go my perch and launched forward into the cocoons, praying that if the tines were waiting on me as I dropped, they find my exposed stomach, my chest, my neck, anything but my eyes . . .

The last thing I expected was to land on a vacant floor, with a terrifying though unimpeded path through the brightly illuminated barn to the open doors at the opposite end. I scanned the surrounding area for him, but nothing disturbed the fields except the tocsin of my mother's voice from the other side of the hill and forest.

iv

And maybe Old Man Wagner has been waiting on me all these years as I keep hearing that revolving wooden noise, inevitably bringing to mind the fate of Frau Wagner, who liked to go out for a horse-drawn buggy ride at around dusk, to enjoy the land, the sweet scent of the fields, the materializing stars. Like tonight. I wonder, as I take another puff, if she, herself, smoked of the product. If she looked over her demesne exhaling silver clouds and never imagining to die a brutal death among the crops.

The noise increases by the second, echoing in the valley, the wrenching sound of wood on pavement, rope on wood, hooves in oblivion. I don't want to be here. I have only been back in Germany three days and I don't want to be here . . . as I place the last bit of cheese in my mouth. Chase it with a swallow of wine. Draw from the cigarette yet again . . .

I see the buggy appear below, from the direction of the village. Frau Wagner might as well be driving it, the twilight hour remaining hers in death. But the lamp hanging above the carriage exposes that theory, showing Old Man Wagner in the driver's seat, a whip in hand, like a tendril of ribbon in the light of an invisible moon. At the barn he stops, waits. I watch, drawing from the cigarette again, alert—peering and alert in the undeveloped night. I smell something more bitter than tobacco, or even my half-drunkenness. I smell Herr Wagner. I smell necromancy.

The doors of the drying house open and out come three small figures, shadows at first as they approach the buggy, then golden-haired angels as they enter the glow of the lamp. I cannot move. My petrifaction is such that I can't bring my hand down to grip the bottle of wine. Even from this distance I can see the infinitely black holes that are their eyes, dense spaces that the lamplight fails to penetrate. The wind touches at their hair, lifting gold flames around their oval faces as they stand looking at their master, hands by their sides.

I watch the whip sing in the air and manage a gasp as the first lash meets flesh with an eloquent *schpack*! The next lick comes immediately behind the first, the ripping sound of its all too successful landing filling the whole valley. The girls react to the vicious spurs by dancing, but not in the way the recipients of such abuse might normally do. The leather in Wagner's hand acts like an instrument, an instrument of sorcery, long licking wand that lifts them in a rotating funnel from the ground—hair sailing on the night, sleeves of dresses clinging to flesh as the girls raise their arms over their heads in a ballet beyond reason. The whip/wand keeps spitting, snapping, cracking as the three, in their elegant, slowly spinning dance, rise beyond their reach, and then begin to move . . .

In my direction.

I hear the word but, again, can't speak it. The muscles of my mouth make the attempt. I feel the *No* form, but by now they are halfway up the slope, black figures contrasted against the early night, but still dancing, still posing in the slow-motion whirlwind of Herr Wagner's *Zauberei*. *Hexerei*. Before I can address the sudden alienness of my own body, the hole that reaches up out of my insides to eat me alive, they are descending. Black sockets finding me with every turn, mouths now opening perhaps in memory, perhaps in appetite. All I know is nothing. No thing can be known in this world as the funnel slows, and they touch down on my towel, the three of them staring at me out of blackest oblivion.

"Ines. Selma. Karin," I am somehow able to produce.

"It's me. *Reed.*"

But I have gone to hell; words are meaningless. There is only the searing agony in every nerve ending as these creatures surround me with their fathomless sockets. Suddenly—or so it seems to me—one of them, the oldest, Selma, reaches toward me. My blood chills as I can think only of what they did to Old Man Wagner's wife, indeed why he must have made them his slaves to begin with. But she merely extracts the nearly burnt cigarette from my paralyzed hand, long snake of ash falling on the towel. She puts it to her mouth and sucks. The inhaled smoke collects in her empty eyes. For a second I see pictures form, house, swing set, tractor, then the memories become a word on her lips.

"Reed?"

"It's me, Selma. Reed."

Her head snaps sideways, toward the barn below, where the lamplit buggy still sits, its owner anticipating the satisfaction the night's deeds should bring him. Perceiving my stare, he pops the wand in my direction, playfully, a little kiss of goodbye . . .

I look at Selma. She regards me a moment, if such a thing is possible, then turns to the other girls. "Reed," I hear in the strange wind.

And as one they rise up off the towel, briefly levitating there, looking down on me . . . then they are spinning over the slope, three black dancers on the night. I look in the direction they are moving and find Herr Wagner's whip now upon the flank of his horse as he flees across his fields of tobacco, fragrant as blood in the beautiful, flowering night.

Mysteries of the Colon

Steve Rasnic Tem

Everywhere was weeping and then he realized it was his own.

When you're a boy it's one of the few things you think you really understand. The first thing you figure out how to joke about. And in a house with three brothers and two sisters, the bathroom was the only place Brian had for getting away from all that family togetherness.

Then, of course, he thought he might live forever. He'd be the first. He'd start a trend. He was sure of his body—it worked awfully well as far as he could tell. He knew little of how it actually worked, despite Health class and those fancy transparent overlays in the encyclopedia set his parents bought with his future success in mind. "Perhaps you'll be a doctor," his mother had said, as if simple exposure to images of the interior would set him on that respected and lucrative path.

He'd never liked those human anatomy transparencies. They'd made him feel a little ill. He wasn't sure he believed them anyway—how did *they* know what he looked like inside? He didn't want to believe people were just sacks of guts. Bags of blood and containers of brain. Something that couldn't help but spoil if you didn't stick it into the refrigerator, and *soon*.

Now that he was in his mid-fifties, everything about the body was an embarrassment to him. Bathroom humor made him angry. He hated the way people his age talked about aging and its accompanying ailments, talked about going to the bathroom as if *it* were an ailment, although to his ever-growing shame going to the bathroom was something he thought about a great deal. How *conscious* a thing it had become, like eating or handwriting.

Like a little kid, he felt compelled to check out his stool. Looking for blood, or evidence of something worse. (He imagined there must be such possible evidence, but he had no idea what it might be.) He'd read somewhere that men his age needed to be aware of such things. *If caught early the chances of survival are good.* But it all seemed quite mysterious, and vaguely disturbing. There was a kind of blood that was invisible and required testing in order to detect it. *Occult blood,* they called it. Shadowy, invisible blood from some deeper place in the body, a sure sign that things had gone all wrong.

Practically every time he saw a male neighbor or old friend the conversation inevitably devolved into comparing their respective healths or lack thereof. How they were feeling these days, how they were getting along. What hurt and what had recently stopped hurting. What they'd read about that might someday *start* hurting.

That, and how the government was always doing things to make that hurt much, much worse.

"We'll never be able to retire, you know." Peter's face turned somewhat orange when he talked about money. "I figured it all out. Most of us will be dropping dead in our cubicles. The government's already funding a task force to study ways of keeping office morale up when that starts happening on a regular basis."

"I work in an out-of-the-way corner," Brian said. "They'll smell me before they find me."

They stood looking at the ground, suddenly sobered. Brian wondered if he could stand staring into a computer screen that many more years.

Of course it paid too well for him to ever quit, and at this point he wasn't sure he could do anything else anyway. Peter worked for software companies as well, and more than once they'd found themselves at the same company for a time, until the next round of layoffs. They'd never been close for all that, Peter being a little bit too socially awkward even for Brian's rather loose standards.

"You work there too long, and that place'll turn *you* into software!" That was Peter's favorite joke, told as he patted his belly. The joke had fallen a bit short of clever the first time Brian had heard it and it had gotten no closer through constant repetition. Peter, however, had appeared to squeeze the flesh over his stomach a bit harder each time the joke was told.

In fact Peter was more misshapen than fat, with flesh that hung as on one who had recently lost a great deal of weight. The problem was, Peter had never *been* fat as far as Brian knew. Over the years his skin had just stretched. Even the flesh beneath his eyebrows appeared to wobble and travel across his skull when he laughed. Of course Brian was no matinee idol himself. Just another sack of guts lying on the highway.

Brian left Peter there on the sidewalk with his features in migration. He hoped he hadn't been so abrupt as to hurt his old neighbor's feelings. He had been telling Brian some sort of whining complaint thinly disguised as a story, but Brian hadn't really been listening—he'd heard that tone before and immediately stepped out. Brian couldn't be sure if Peter had even finished his tale—his straining tone of voice betrayed no rise and fall of dramatic tension, no crisis resolved or finale approaching. But standing so close to the man like that, a vague smell of undigested meat issuing from some place improbably far down Peter's gullet, had left Brian feeling vaguely altered and desperate. He had to get inside.

Once on the other side of his own front door, Brian peeked between the front curtains. Peter stood out on the sidewalk, stepping first toward his own house, then turning away, looking at Brian's house, then looking down the street, stepping in that direction, then reversing himself. Talking to himself. As odd a bird as Peter had always seemed, Brian had never known him to do that before.

Brian had stomach acid problems that night, and he was alarmed to discover he'd forgotten to replenish his stock of a variety of antacids. How he could forget such a thing, with the severe esophageal reflux problems he'd had since reaching adulthood, was unexplainable. Certainly it wasn't the first time it had happened. More than once his doctor had expressed some degree of concern upon the revelation, but Brian tried to laugh about his forgetfulness. He honestly didn't know, and he disliked suggestions about a possible tendency toward self-destruction. He wasn't sure if he even believed in self-destruction. Certainly the world and innate biology did enough on their own to try to destroy you.

Maybe if the episode wasn't too bad he could ride it through, although his emotional capacity for tolerating the sensation of feelers of acid lapping at the back of his throat had diminished drastically over the years. He'd never quite been able to get his mind around it, this idea that your own stomach acid was dissolving you, eating away at you, a spoonful of skin cells at a time. He'd always suspected the true malady must be something else, and the doctors just hadn't figured it out.

He tried to sleep propped up as he had so many nights before, his arms wedged into the pillows so he might have a chance of remaining erect even after he dozed off. But he woke just after midnight lying on his back with acid burning through his nasal passages, and found himself crying over a sense of rudimentary betrayal. He ran to the bathroom and attempted to spit out what he could, trying not to throw up the acid in the process, which would have been far worse than what he was going through.

He rummaged through the medicine cabinets knowing nothing helpful would be there, but trying it anyway. He wondered briefly what some antiseptic cream meant for exterior skin burns might do, applied to a toothbrush and then scrubbed as far down his throat as he could reach. He stopped himself, frightened by his impulse. His nose and throat continued to burn miserably. He wandered down to the kitchen and took some orange juice out of the refrigerator. It had never made much logical sense but he'd discovered through trial and error that O.J. sometimes helped the discomfort, acid fighting acid. At least it disguised some of the bitter taste that had welded itself to the inside of his mouth.

He sat at the table fighting back tears. He imagined the acid leaking out of his eyes, etching through his cheeks. He could feel it continue to boil, expanding its presence and concentration in his stomach. As much as he hated the idea, he knew he was going to have to go out and find something to help himself.

The local grocery closed at midnight, and the all-night drug store was many blocks away. But he couldn't bring himself to drive; he was experiencing some intense light sensitivity, as if the acid were cooking his corneas, producing halos and eruptions. Nothing for it but to walk. He considered what he might wear, then pulled jeans up over his pajamas, making great cancerous bulges under the denim. A green canvas coat over his T-shirt was cavernous even at his size. Now suitably anonymous, he padded out of the house in worn-out sandals that left his feet cold.

It took a while to make the trip, and halfway there Brian felt better enough that he briefly considered canceling the errand and risking sleep again. But he knew how badly the odds had it in for him and focused on the yellow fluorescent gloss shining off the storefront a few blocks ahead.

He passed a wide alley behind the Italian restaurant on his left. Stared down the pavement to the figure sprawled there, his or her anatomy spilled out and glistening in the moonlight. An animal picking at what remained of the head.

He wanted to walk on, but stopped, unsure. "Hello?" he said foolishly. The only reply a rodent rustle in the grisly debris. He reluctantly stepped farther into the alley. Whoever was there was certainly past all helping—what did he hope to accomplish?

The head flopped over: a rotted shell of milk carton, a mass of eggshells the brain. The rest was pasta and vegetables and moving scavengers. Brian felt the acid laughing up out of his chest, turned and hurried toward the drugstore.

He got a refill on his medications, loaded up with a dozen bottles of his favorite liquid antacids. He studiously avoided the candy aisle, but picked up a couple of candy bars from a rack by the checkout, plopped them down in front of the cashier at the last minute, turned away slightly ashamed as she added them to the bag. He hugged the bag tightly against his chest as he left.

Outside he started thinking about the candy, decided it was just reward for the discomfort he'd had to endure this evening. He worked out the amount of time he'd have to stay up drinking the antacid before he could safely go to bed after eating just one bar, then wondered if he could manage an all-nighter at his age. Then thought the hell with it. He stopped in the alley again, gliding into the shadows like an overweight ninja. He ate both candy bars, washing them down with a pint of antacid after a toast to the victim of disembowelment who was not there.

When Brian got back to his house he saw the lights flashing gaily down the street, better suited to a party than the usual serious business they signaled. As he got closer he saw several of his neighbors out in the street, and tucked the top of the bag in a bit tighter to safely hide its contents. Then noticed they'd gathered together outside Peter's house. Peter came out a short time later, carried on a stretcher by two burly men with gigantic, misshapen arms and all-business faces. All Brian could see of Peter was his forehead above the edge of the sheet, almost the same color. But underneath that sheet everything shook.

At lunch several days later Brian ate a salad so spare the

small slices of tomato secreted pleasingly about its terrain seemed an extravagance. Elaine, the woman from two cubicles over who never ate "anything that once had a brain," sipped stingily at an odd-colored liquid between bites of something soft and spoiled-looking. He rememb-ered a conversation they'd had a few months back about her interest in yoga, the use of scarves to clean the passage from nostril to throat, and then she'd launched into a diatribe about the need to "cleanse" the colon, about how Americans, especially, didn't pay enough attention to their colons, their colons were still pretty much a mystery to them, and as a result the consequences could be quite dire.

Brian had had no idea what to say. The temptation was there to tell her he thought about his own colon almost constantly thank you very much, but of course he did not. He'd sat there, nodding pleasantly and sprinkling her with *oh reallys*. Not surprisingly, the break room had cleared out when she first began her lecture. Before he got away she'd pulled some brochures out of her purse and stuffed them into his hand.

Work that afternoon was slow—between projects Brian had virtually nothing to do. He always wondered when they were going to find him out, not that he was the only one in that particular situation. And if he were fired, well, it wouldn't make that much difference, would it?

He much preferred stretches of overwork to these lulls when everything seemed to drop away, and he was alone with this incessant cycle of humorless thought and lack of meaning and feeling desperate for no good reason. Feeling sorry for himself and ashamed of that evidence of his smallness. The narrow channel of emptiness that ran up through the middle of his body gradually expanded, wrecking bone and muscle and pushing organs aside in its progress though his pitiful remains. He gasped for air and felt the acid bubble menacingly.

"Did you read my literature?" Elaine had stuck her head around the partition.

Brian stared at her. "Literature?" Had she recommended a novel or something? Like everyone else in the office he tended to tune her out so frequently—she might have said almost anything.

"There, on your desk." She frowned.

Brian glanced at the brochures. "Oh, of course. I *will*, but I haven't had a chance yet. Things have been so busy, you know?"

She stared at him doubtfully. "Not in my department."

"Oh, really? You're lucky." Brian could feel himself grow red in the face, the increased temperature bringing back a taste of peanut buttery acid.

At that moment William walked by. "Brian, I'm taking a late lunch. If you haven't eaten yet . . . care for some Mexican food?"

"Great idea," Brian said, stood up and grabbed his coat. "Talk to you later, Elaine." He practically ran from his cubicle, from the definite look of disgust that had crept up her face.

Out with William he devoured a giant foil-wrapped burrito log. It lay heavy as a dead baby at the bottom of his gut. Back at work he dropped into his office chair, turned to check his e-mail, but could not bring himself to stretch that far. He leaned back, pinned.

The brochures were spread out in an appallingly neat fan on the edge of his desk. Like the chef's prize plate at a Japanese restaurant. He thought about sweeping them off the desk into his wastebasket but knew he'd never manage it. He leaned forward and peered at the cover of one: a crude drawing of a man with a long beard and turban, twisted into an impossible position, a roll of white cloth like a snake coiled at his side. Others had garish diagrams of the interior, some with rather neat, well painted illustrations worthy of a medical text. He pulled them forward with a tentative finger and read them one after the other.

The next brochure was face down, and appeared to show a variety of beautiful, decoratively spiced dishes. He thought perhaps he'd mixed a take-out menu into the selection, turned it over and saw the title *Diseases of the Colon* emblazoned on the cover in bright yellow letters. He thumbed through the pages a bit more carefully, not touching the pictures. The images were a bit disgusting, but not as much as he might have expected. There was something visually interesting, almost appealing, about them. Like rare, exotic plants in a colorful catalog.

Why You Should Have a Colonoscopy was much more businesslike, laying out pros and cons with bullet points, and so reasonable in its tone you might wonder why everyone didn't just rush out to get one. The cartoony illustrations were a little frightening in their direct simplicity: the corrugated tube of flesh with the shiny black, snake-like hose filling its core, the monitor showing the camera's progress through a passage that appeared to live and breathe (which, of course, it did), the cartoon head of a male brandishing a goofy smile because he'd just undergone this highly intimate exploration. The isolated image of the colon itself, its ends separated from their anchors, practically smiling at you with its flexible opening, perhaps having just delivered up some amusing reminiscence or fart joke. This is John's colon, indeed.

More bothersome still, however, was the list of "interesting facts about Colonoscopy." How polyps could be detected and removed at the same time. How a liquid bowel stimulant taken the day before ensured the colon's cleanliness. (Elaine no doubt had her own private stash.) How a digital rectal exam generally starts the procedure. How perforation of the bowel was only a remote possibility. How you may bleed from your "back passage" for a few days after. How you should inform your doctor if it's more than half a cup (*half a cup!*).

Brian took a break for fried cheese sticks served at a snack bar four doors down. To several fellow employees sitting at a nearby table he gave a halfhearted wave before sitting down alone to hunch over his reward for almost finishing the day. He bought a tall jamocha shake at a neighborhood drive-through on his way home.

Halfway up his walk Brian noticed a young man on the front lawn of Peter's house driving in a sign. When the man turned Brian recognized him as Peter's son although he couldn't remember his name. In a rare moment of sociability and public display of concern, Brian walked over smiling, still sucking up his shake. "Hi. I'm Brian—I know we've met. How *is* your dad?"

And then he saw the "For Sale" sign. Feeling stupid, he took another quick slurp of his shake, stumbled, and dropped it on the ground. Peter's son looked at it and made a move to pick it up.

"No, no, I'll get it," Brian said, and knew that his anxiety must have been evident as he raced for the cup ahead of the still-reaching fingers of Peter's son. Clutching the top edge of the cup, he glanced again at the sign. "So your Dad's selling the place?" He couldn't believe he'd said it, but he forced an awkward smile anyway.

"Dad died. Didn't you hear? The neighbors have all been dropping by."

Brian stared at him, struggling for a reply. The straw made its way into his mouth as if on its own accord. Embarrassed, Brian spat it out, spraying his hand with a mist of tan droplets. "I'm so sorry!" he said loudly, staring at his hand. "I've . . . I've been away!" The last syllable became almost a wail.

"Hey, it's okay." The son looked embarrassed. "You didn't know. You worked with my dad, right? I seem to remember . . ."

Brian interrupted. "He was practically my best friend! We were just talking the other day . . . what happened to him?"

The son held his hand out, fingers splayed. "A heart attack, officially. But multiple organs were failing, apparently. Cancer, some other things."

"Did he *know*? Had he been sick for a while?"

"I doubt he knew for sure. But people sense when something's wrong, don't they? It may be a mystery to them, but they at least feel if there's a question to be asked, don't you think?"

Brian kept his face perfectly still.

"But Dad hated doctors and hospitals. I don't think he'd seen a doctor in years. He never took care of himself. He never ate right."

Brian moved the shake around to the back of his thigh. He glanced to his side, saw Mrs. Miller out in her front yard, staring at them with her arms folded. She was always watching. Like Death and Santa Claus. He looked back at Peter's son, whose frown seemed more like disgust than anything else. Brian raised his arm as if attempting to wipe his cheek with his sleeve, surreptitiously smelling himself. He knew sometimes he waited too long between showers, or didn't notice how dirty his clothes had become. Or perhaps he smelled in ways only other people recognized. Your smell must become your smell, he thought. You didn't even recognize it as something that stood out from all the other background smells of the world: flowers and children's sweat, the wind through the trees, cooking meat and industrial castoff, or the low-lying decay that churned the ground and replenished matter.

Things that went wrong had a smell, he thought. And sometimes you didn't recognize it until it was too late.

"I'm sorry, I have to *go*," Brian said suddenly. "I have company coming," he lied. "Old friends—they'll probably stay with me a few days, catching up," he embellished unnecessarily. *Sometimes you find yourself trying to make an impression, and you don't even understand what impression you're trying to make.* "I have to go now. But you take care. You take care."

Brian turned quickly, afraid Peter's son would see something in his face, the same thing Brian saw in the mirror now and then just before bed or just waking up: that fear in the eye, despairing turn to the lip, that pattern of crease and wrinkle that said *I'm not doing well, I'm not doing well at all.*

He made sure he got into the house before Mrs. Miller could see him cry.

That night he cleaned house, clearing out of his life papers, books, forgotten mementoes of disappointing excursions, anything collecting or capable of trapping dust and disease, stuffed into heavy-duty trash bags and hauled out to the alley. In some rooms were cardboard boxes full of a variety of objects he did not recognize, in fact he was sure they couldn't have ever belonged to him. Sports trophies and love letters and collections of stamps, small ceramic statues of idealized livestock, volumes of poetry and photograph albums picturing families he'd never seen before. Where had it all come from?

With the boxes gone, the floors were layered in dust. Searching through the supplies in the kitchen closet, he realized he didn't own a broom. He grabbed the ancient mop in the corner and saw that its graying mane was actually dirtier than any of the floors. But he supposed that was the nature of mops and somehow they cleaned anyway. He filled the kitchen sink with water and stuck in the mop to soak. The fact that the water went instantly gray satisfied him that at least something was being accomplished. After a decent interval he pulled the mop out and swabbed the floors as quickly as possible. He didn't have any floor cleaners but figured people had been washing with water alone for centuries before the invention of modern chemicals.

While he was doing this work he drank glass after glass of water. He'd always heard how hydration was one of the keys to good health, how it purified and replenished you, *cleansed* you as Elaine might say. And he had never drunk enough water, in fact had always found it surprisingly difficult to swallow, as if his body instinctively refused to let the water in. But it was never too late to start a good habit. He forced the water into himself until he was afraid he might throw up.

The dirt moved around nicely into swirls and wavelike patterns. At one point he felt quite satisfied when he was able to write his name with the wet mop's trail. But at the end of it all, he had floors with ridges and giant fingerprint-like patterns of dirt, and realized the keys to the mysteries of cleaning had not yet made themselves known to him. He pulled up a chair in the center of one of the cleared rooms and sat staring at the puzzle, having no idea what to do. He should call some professional but he'd be too embarrassed to let them into his house.

He closed the doors to each of the rooms and wherever there was a lock he locked it. But each time he thought he heard a chuckle from someplace near, and eventually even bothered to search when he felt he couldn't ignore it.

He found nothing. And his own house, the house he had paid for month after month, dutifully, almost religiously, stood back and did nothing to help him. Stood back and was awful.

He had accomplished at least something, hadn't he? There were tons of objects out in the trash pile by the alley. Objects he did not recognize, objects he had never seen before, so obviously they did not belong. When had he accomplished even that much at work? He found a place in his still-cluttered family room and sat down in front of the TV. His stomach churned as if punched. He got on the phone and ordered two large pizzas with everything—he would obviously need their palliative effects for the difficult hours to come.

The pizza guy arrived forty-five minutes later, the two giant flat boxes stretched across his arms like slabs of building material. "Two large, right?"

Brian stared at the boxes. Either they were much too large, or his hunger had distorted them. The man stared down at him with reddish eyes peering from beneath a mashed down cap. "Well . . . yes. Could you bring them in? I just cleaned." Brian said it with more emphasis than intended.

"Yep," the delivery man replied. He started through the door then halted when the corners of the boxes caught the jambs. He glanced at one side of the door, tilted the boxes quickly, stepped through, righted them again. He set them down on the shiniest part of the ancient dining room table, which appeared to dull the remaining finish, as if a light had been extinguished. "Fifty bucks," he said.

"Fifty dollars for pizza?"

Brian watched as the bloody slicks of the man's pupils swam through the squashed yellow bags to fix on him. "They're *large,* sir." He glanced down at the pizzas which now almost filled the table. "Damn large."

Brian watched a corner of one of the boxes expand and curl over the table's edge. He searched through his wallet and gave the man three twenties.

After the pizza man left Brian pulled up a chair to the table and flipped up the lid to the first box. It looked nothing like a pizza. The crust had crept out of round, was now an oblong still rising over the lip of the box, its variety of meat and vegetable and cheese ingredients moving fluidly across its surface like continents separating from a primordial mother mass.

Brian thought just to scrape the pizza off the table onto the floor, but he'd spent so much time cleaning, it would be a shame. Besides he was ravenous now, the blend of rich aromas making his throat weep. *Probably just too much yeast,* he thought, although he knew nothing of cooking. But he'd never heard of anyone dying from too much yeast. He looked for the slice lines but they'd been obliterated. He grabbed a spoon and pressed it into the pizza to hold it down while wrestling off a slice with his fingers. It was quite warm, but stopped short of burning him.

There seemed no point to a plate and fork; the sloppiness of the food dictated a casual dining strategy. He shoveled food into his mouth until he choked. He reached two fingers into his mouth and tweezed out an unidentifiable vegetable stalk of some few inches. That out of the way, he began eating again, the excess dropping onto his chin and down his collar, showered the floor with increasingly fine bits. Finally he stopped, vertigo-eyed. A small fart loosened his colon, which seemed to stretch out inside his body like an exclamation.

"Jesus Mary!" he cried, muffled, tears streaming down his face. He tried to push away from the table but an odd blend of sadness and curiosity made him turn back, wondering just how many more bites he might contain. He leaned forward into the pizza as if to kiss it, ended with his chin and lower lip rutting it down to crust. As his eyes squinted close there was a moment in which he thought he must be seeing beyond the moment: his internal body laid open and flat as a field, a smaller version of himself erecting a cabin in the midst of everything he'd ever eaten, the sun setting low over the potato and broccoli hills, and somewhere someone was beginning to sing.

Brian didn't remember finally getting himself up and off to bed. He thought he might have thrown up at one point. Certainly, he was wide awake now, feeling as full as he'd ever felt in his life, the skin of his belly feeling ready to tear. Pale, elongated shapes with no eyes and huge, distended mouths floated and twisted overhead. Some sort of parasitic worm, he thought, but so large. Parasitic snakes, perhaps. Occasionally one would pause mid-air and gaze down at him, or rather, point its mouth down at him. Like a colon with teeth around its rim. All digestion and waste, it emitted a foul smell. Brian raised his middle finger and waved it in the thing's direction.

The parasite puffed out its mouth fourfold and dived at Brian's abdomen. Before he could move it had sunk its two-inch teeth into his lower left side.

The pain wasn't much more than a bee sting at first, but the burning increased gradually over the next hour, spreading into an ache and finally descending into agony. Brian crawled out of bed then, maneuvered down the stairs and stumbled out to the garage. He didn't know if he could drive, but he had to try. With Peter dead he knew no one to ask for help.

He did not remember passing through the hospital door, but what he would always remember was the brilliance and dampness of the corridors, his inability to stand or walk properly on the slick wet floors, or to hold on securely to the weeping walls, and the heavy hand squeezing his mysteries so hard now, squeezing with a fierceness and desperation as if to squeeze the truth out of him as he struggled with his need to scream.

"It's a gall bladder attack," God said from behind red-rimmed glasses as big as, or bigger, than his cabbage-sized head. He reminded Brian a bit of Elton John.

"What gall bladder attack?" Brian asked, looking around for the object in question.

"It's what's wrong with you. You've been asking the last hour or so. Hasn't your doctor talked to you about gallstones?"

"I don't see him anymore—I just call him up when I need a refill for my acid reflux medication."

"Really?"

"They think they're God. They have all this knowledge about what's really going on inside you, and they let you know only a little bit of it. Sometimes they flat out *lie,* at least I think they do, but who could know for sure? I've heard that when they open you up, if they don't like what they see they just close you up again. Then the mystery kills you and they just nod their heads and say that's just the nature of things sometimes, and they get away with it because they're gods." Brian quickly studied God's face for that legendary fury of his. "Sorry, no offense."

"No offense taken. Do you want it out?"

"Out?"

"Your gall bladder. It's not doing you any good, and it's inevitable that you'll have another attack."

Brian stared at God in his crisp, white, stainless smock that would show blood easily. "Can I think about it . . . doctor?"

"Absolutely. I need to go get you some painkillers anyway."

Once Doctor God was gone Brian got off the table and crept quietly down the hall. The halls were bright and shiny, but not slippery. Several doors were open, and Brian peered through the first few.

A man in boxer shorts sat in a chair watching television on a monitor high overhead. Two tubes looped from low in his back up into his heart. The liquid inside was a greenish yellow color and bubbled aggressively. A third tube ran out of his heart and into a heavily bandaged portion of his forehead. This fluid was amber and sluggish and barely moved at all. The man whispered constantly with his mouth closed.

In another room a woman cried and ripped at her sheets with hands that were turned backwards. She appeared to be pregnant, but the evidence of her pregnancy moved up and down her abdomen like a gigantic, quivering tick.

The object in the third bed appeared to be nothing more than long delicate *legs* of indeterminate sex attached to a loose pouch of skin. The pouch breathed in and out vigorously, as if in extreme exertion. Rashes appeared and disappeared across the paper-thin flesh like rapidly moving clouds in a beautiful sunset.

Brian hurried from the room and down the hall looking for the nearest exit. Doctor God came around the corner at the far end, a large bottle of the green/yellow liquid in his hand. When he saw Brian he dropped it, the splash and shards making a bright reflective sunburst pattern on the white tile floor. Doctor God raised his arm and pointed, head thrown impossibly back, mouth pulled improbably open, a scream tumbling out and crashing against the walls, followed by long flowering vines that wriggled and scraped against the ceiling tiles, tearing off leaves and shoots that dripped yellow across the floor, and security men suddenly filled the space on all sides of Doctor God, and they, too, pointed and shrieked like a chorus of sirens.

Brian raced the length of the hall and down two flights of steps. Finally finding an outside door he slammed through it and down the wheelchair ramp, the sirens filling the building behind him until it could not contain them anymore and they burst through the glass and filled the surrounding air.

He was in intense pain, his lungs screaming for air and his mouth struggling futilely to bring him some. Brian had no idea where he'd parked his car and no time to look for it. He found the closest unlit alley and ran in and through to the other end, not allowing trash cans or protesting bums to impede his flight. He came out reeking of garbage and worse, brushed the crawlies and the wigglies off and was almost run down in the intersecting road by a speeding delivery truck.

Footsteps came running up behind him then fell with a scream and a screech of other tires but he did not look around. He dived into the dark vein of the next alley and struggled through the suck and grab of outreached appendages he could not see, slapped them aside and was then into the next street, then into the next alley almost immediately. Everywhere was weeping and then he realized it was his own.

Finally into a brighter street lined with ancient brick walls of sharply defined shadows and Brian glanced to the side to see the black outlines of sacs and tubes and great fingers of flesh bearing down at him, pressing forward with their need to push themselves back inside him from where they'd at last escaped.

At last to his house again where the light still burned, the front door stood open and the ruins of out-of-control pizza moved across the dining room floor. He dodged the eager mess and escaped into the bathroom just ahead of what followed, slammed the door and set lock and dead-bolt, sat down on the toilet lid giggling, peeing himself in his hysteria.

His head ached from lack of air, his chest heaving through pain, flashbulbs going off in his eyes.

All was silent now except the groan of his own belly, full of pressure, now edged with pain, but he held himself and rocked muttering shush-a-byes and threats to keep his own body quiet.

Then his fingers found the sunken place, and his hand the empty place where his old sack of guts used to be. And he stood impossibly before the mirror, and saw that from the center of chest to just over groin there was nothing at all.

On the other side of the door his insides let loose their stench of death and despair. At the bottom of the door his mysteries began their ooze over the threshold. Everything he'd once contained seemed adamant now, would try every possible passage to find their way back in.

ii: Wilting Petals

The Man in the Corner

Eric Shapiro

She refills his coffee.
You wonder if he admires her tits.

The simplicity of your choice is alarming: either you pay your check and exit the café or you slaughter the man in the corner. There is no middle ground. You're not going to engage in a conversation with him, tempting though that may be. You're not going to walk by him and drop a snide remark, tempting though *that* may be. Your head swells with hot gas. Life has been good lately. Not fine, as it is most years, but good. The children have healthy skin. The wife has positive moods. The yard is electric green. The comment-ators on C-SPAN are stimulating. The hours at the office pass briskly. The sponge organ in your head feels soft and fruitlike. Laughter surfaces easily. Orgasms are hard and tender.

But the man in the corner can change this.

You stopped by the café for some tea because the heater in your car is broken. The waitress is a welcome rarity: a redheaded teenager. You suspect she has no reserv-ations about giving blowjobs. This gives you hope.

A Bruce Springsteen CD deepens the soundwaves. The walls are painted lavender. The paintings thereon give you ships, skylines, cute kittens. This is a swell café.

You turn your head and this brings you to the man in the corner. He sips dark coffee. He sits alone. He is without a left eye. Or a right ear. Your jowls tighten and your brain goes thick. You momentarily forget you have a body sur-rounding your head. Thoughts splinter and surge. Your eyes are dry cabbages.

Perhaps the lawn needs fertilizer and perhaps C-SPAN could liven up. And perhaps the waitress stops by to fill your cup, and perhaps you even allow her to, but this is without relevance. You will leave the café remembering

the man in the corner.

You recall a conversation from years ago. You were with your friend Toby.

Toby rambled as you drove toward the Poconos. You were on your way to a camp reunion. Autumn had settled in and the crisp coldness flattened your cheeks. The mountains sat like old uncles fat from a feast. The leaves seemed like fire. You recently entered college. A weekend of pot and unhooked bra straps lay ahead.

You recall that weekend in bits and pieces: Studying Lana's ass beneath the bed sheets after she dozed off. Making Brian crack up on the balcony. Chatting with Christine about your favorite Loony Tunes characters.

But until you saw the man in the corner, you forgot what Toby had told you on the way up:

"I once heard about this gang bang . . ." he had begun.

The rest of Toby's words are mangled by memory. He explained something such as: shortly before you entered college, there was a gang bang in a motel near Daytona Beach. Sixteen guys slipped some girl a roophie and took turns. The girl came around and refused to press charges. The girl's brother tried to persuade her to do so.

She utterly refused.

Her brother pondered revenge.

A Catholic man, vengeance was against his upbringing. He did not slay the sixteen culprits. But he found them:

Three lived near Daytona Beach. Four lived on the west coast. Seven were scattered around the Bible Belt. One was from Chicago. One lived in the Philippines.

The victim's brother made phone calls and maxed out credit cards. He traveled quietly, as to avoid attention from his family and the law. He brought along only the bare necessities: wallet, toothbrush, disposable razors, shaving cream, three shirts, three pairs of pants, three pairs of socks, three pairs of underwear, one pair of shoes, six rolls of quarters, and one small hacksaw.

The first rapist defecated when his eye was sliced and vomited when his ear was subtracted. The second one was asleep for the ear but awake and sobbing for the eye.

The third had to be chased seven blocks. The fourth begged for his life. The rest varied in idiosyncrasies, but:

All of them lived. Minus the left eye. Minus the right ear.

The brother spread his story via chain letters and thug circuits. He made certain the culprits would be recognized on sight. Some of them were:

One of the guys from Daytona was gunned down by a neighbor. The one from Chicago was knifed to death by a girlfriend. Two from the west coast are missing. The Filipino was executed by local law enforcement . . .

. . . which leaves roughly eleven. One of whom sips coffee in the corner.

You stare at your smoking tea. Your brain plays a psychedelic picture show, complete with tight purple dickheads and echoing high-fives. And the girl's closed eyes. And the cans of Molson Ice in the bathtub. *Too Close for Comfort* on the muted TV set. **Do Not Disturb** sign on the door. Best friends. Come shots. Loud one-liners.

Drawn tacky shades.

Black adrenaline clouds your concentration. The man in the corner cracks his knuckles one at a time. He is unaware you exist. You try to wonder about him. Your brain is stuck.

You feel like hurting him:

Resorting to ancient measures. Splitting from the program. A civilized notion arises: *You couldn't get away with it.*

But you could and you know it. You could wait for him in your car and run him down in the parking lot. Or locate his car and stuff a rag in the exhaust pipe. Maybe find out where he lives and sprinkle Ajax in his two-percent.

The redhead waitress approaches the man in the corner. He makes eye contact with her. She refills his coffee. You wonder if he admires her tits. You wonder if he envisions her pussy.

Your tea is far away. You're standing. Your blood climbs through the arteries in your brain. You float to the man in the corner. He offers a warm smile.

"I know who you are," you assure him. Your heart pecks at your rib cage.

The man smiles. He is deformed but has charm. "Who am I?" he wants to know.

"Daytona Beach," you mutter, right about the same time the man gulps.

The man's sole eye darkens. He's not looking at you. "I thought that was you," he says. "What is it? Larry, right?"

You forget your own name for a moment. Then you nod.

He lowers his voice and says, "I guess her brother never found you. He only thought there was sixteen of us."

You remind him, "I never touched her."

He laughs. A full and genuine laugh. "Oh, that's right. You stood in the corner the whole time." The man laughs again.

Your blood feels wet inside your veins. A tear scratches the back of your eye.

The man in the corner sips his coffee. He's finished with you.

You leave without paying your check.

Disposal of the Body

Marion Pitman

There was a smell.

We drove Mother down into Sussex for the funeral. We asked Mark and Lisa if they'd like to spend the day with friends, but they said they'd rather come with us. We agreed that John would take them off somewhere while Mother and I were at the ceremony.

It was a warm day, a bit muggy, but it didn't look as if it would rain. We took some sweets and crisps and cans of drink for the kids, and they wore their ordinary clothes, and John wore a dark suit and tie, and just Mother and I wore black.

We got away in good time for once, and before we'd been driving five minutes there was a hell of a thump on the windscreen. I jumped, and Mother and the kids screamed, and we saw a pigeon had brained itself on the glass. John swore and pulled over, and got out to clear it off, but he left a little smear of blood, and it kept drawing my eye all the way down there.

Anyway, the journey went smoothly after that, except Mother kept fidgeting and asking was I all right; and we arrived at the house, and kissed Aunt Jane and said Oh My Dear, and smiled and nodded to all the cousins we hadn't seen for donkey's years, or in John and Mark and Lisa's case not at all, and then we all got sorted into cars, and Mother went in one of the undertaker's limos—they had two, must have cost the earth—on account of being the deceased's only surviving sister, and not surprising as she was twenty years younger and he lived to eighty-nine; and I was fitted in with one of the cousins, so John and the kids didn't need to come to the crem at all, which was quite a way, it took us about half an hour.

I hardly knew the cousin, and I don't like trying to make conversation in cars anyway, so I looked out of the window and thought about Uncle Bert. I hadn't seen him for years, but when I was a kid, until I was eight or nine, I used to stay with him and Aunt Jane for holidays. I couldn't remember much about it. I'd recognized the house, and knew it had a back garden with a compost heap and a coal bunker at the end, and Aunt Jane had always given me Weetabix for breakfast, which I never had at home, and hated, but was too polite to say so. I couldn't even be sure of that, though; childhood memories get so muddled.

I found I was quite upset, and a few tears were running down my jaw.

The service was very brief, they had the crematorium chaplain, who'd never met Uncle Bert of course, and who gave the usual spiel about what a good chap he was, great gardener, fine husband and brother, and I found myself thinking, rubbish, he was a mean old so and so, and vicious with it; which was odd, because I'd never thought that before.

There was a nasty smell in the chapel, varnish and flowers and cold, and when we stood up for a hymn or something I felt quite dizzy and sick, and had to hang on to the seat in front, and I remembered I hadn't had any lunch. The hymn was very dreary, seemed to be all blood and innards, and Uncle Bert had been an atheist anyway. Well, I thought, if he's wrong he knows now.

The long shiny box slid through the curtains without a penn'orth of sound, and went to be incinerated, and we all filed out and milled about and looked at the flowers, and other people's flowers, and said good-bye to those who weren't coming back to the house. Uncle Bert's flowers were a poor lot really, but the next batch must have been for a young boy, there were floral arrangements in the shape of footballs and roller skates and even a rabbit, which quite upset me.

Then we all got reshuffled, and Mother and I were put together in the back of a different cousin's car.

I said quietly, "I thought Jane looked awfully

cheerful."

"I expect she's still numb," said Mother. "I was completely zombie for weeks—you remember, Karen, you helped me do all the legal stuff, and sort out his clothes, and I was awfully calm and efficient, just going through the motions, and then one night I moved something on the dressing table, and there were his keys, and a little pile of change, and his season ticket, and it just hit me like a train, and I cried my eyes out for hours."

"I know," I said. "You were still crying when I came round in the morning. I can't imagine Jane crying."

"Sixty years is an awfully long time to be married to someone, even if you didn't like them."

When we got back to the house I saw our car wasn't there, and I assumed John had driven Lisa and Mark off somewhere, and overestimated how long we'd be gone; or maybe they wanted to escape the relatives.

We went in, and Aunt Jane said, "So kind of you to come, Karen—I'd quite have understood if you couldn't have faced it," and gave me a glass of sherry and moved on.

I chatted a bit here and there, and drank the sherry, and then got a cup of tea and a ham sandwich, and I was looking round, the way you do, to see if there was anyone I'd be sorry not to talk to, and I overheard behind me someone say, "But of course, you never saw him strangle a cat."

I slammed down my cup and plate and ran into the kitchen, and just made it to the sink before I threw up. I felt dreadfully embarrassed, and carefully washed away all the traces, and rinsed my mouth and splashed my face and washed my hands. Fortunately there was no-one in the kitchen, and no-one followed me in, but I couldn't face rejoining them all straight away, and I went out of the back door, through the scullery of onions and buckets and wellington boots, into the empty garden.

I drew some deep breaths and felt better, and then

strolled down past the rows of late vegetables to the end of the path. I went round the coal bunker, and there behind the compost heap was Uncle Bert's body. The chest and stomach were open, and shoals of fat yellow maggots were crawling in and out; his head had been battered till it was misshapen, and all over black blood; and the flies moving over it, and one lidless eye staring at the sky. There was a smell.

I looked at the body for a while, impassively, and then I walked back up the garden. There was blood on my fingers, but I rubbed it off.

I went round the side of the house, and saw our car in the road, and thought, Oh good, John and the children are back, and I walked between the dahlias to the front door, which was ajar for people coming and going, and I pushed it open and came into the little hall. The door of the back room was open, and I could hear voices, and I saw John standing there with a crumby plate and an empty teacup, and he said,

"All right now?"

And I said, "Much better;" and he said, "Are Tom and Jennifer still out there?"

And I said, "What?"

He said, "Are they still in the garden?"

I said, "Who?"

He said, "Tom and Jennifer. Are they still in the garden?"

I just looked at him blankly, and he laughed—I never heard him laugh like that—and said,

"The kids, Janie. They went out with you."

And I looked round for Mother.

The Smell of Fear

Bev Vincent

Skin that was fighting valiantly to hold back time and contain all that blood.

I didn't plan to kill on my first day out, though I hadn't given it much thought. If I had, I might have guessed I'd take days to get around to it. I'm not normally a hasty person.

The bus dropped me off at an intersection, enveloping me in a miasma of smoke that tickled my arm hairs as it chugged down the street. I searched the neighborhood for landmarks. Much had changed in eight years. All the houses now looked the same, except some were white, some were blue, some brown, some green. Some had attached garages; some were two stories: subtle differences that made it hard to pick out the right one. Even if I'd remembered the street address, it wouldn't have helped much. I was never good with numbers. When I try to read them they turn into snakes or eels, depending on whether they're underwater or not, and I've never gotten one of them to tell me what digit it represents.

When I finally identified the house, I stood on the front porch, wondering whether or not to ring the doorbell. The button glowed darkly, daring me to stick my finger into it. The front door was dusty rose. Running my hand over the rough paint, I felt its warm color seeping into my fingertips, where it merged with the blood running just beneath the surface. Skin works hard, keeping all that blood from spilling out of your body, but it doesn't always do a good job. That's when the trouble begins. Or ends, depending on your point of view.

I put my suitcase down and gripped the knob, which felt like the way a bridge looks in a dense fog. Vague, like the cars crossing it might suddenly plunge into the water because it's not there anymore. The knob turned and the door opened. Not all by itself—I had to turn it with my hand, and I felt bad for all those drivers who I upset when I twisted it.

Eight years since I was last in a house, but it seemed like yesterday. Actually, it seemed like last Tuesday, unless today was a Wednesday, in which case it really did seem like yesterday. I struggled to control my breathing and stepped inside.

After all this time my arrival didn't call for a special ceremony. I hadn't expected to find anyone waiting for me at the bus stop or a welcome banner strung over the front door, or balloons bouncing from the living room ceiling. A cake with a heartwarming message handwritten in icing was more than I could possibly have asked for. Jolly tunes played by a marching band would have been completely out of line. Annoying, even.

Just as well that I felt that way, because none of those things happened. I dragged my suitcase across the threshold and set it beside a coat rack and a tidy row of shoes, none of which were mine. How long do shoes last, anyway? After eight years, maybe my old ones had turned to dust and blown away.

The living room wallpaper was different than I remembered, or maybe it was new and we'd never had wallpaper before. Squinting, I tried to recall exactly what the room used to look like, but I couldn't find a hook to hang my hat on. The furniture wasn't familiar. Either it was new or had been refurbished. Or maybe it had just changed. Things change over time. I know that, because I had changed, and the people I told that to seemed to believe me. Good thing, because I can't lie unless somebody else lies to me first. It's not in my eyes.

If the couches and chairs were exactly like they had been before, everything must have been rearranged. Even some of the walls had been moved around a little, which is an impressive feat. Looking into that room was like meeting an old friend decades later, and trying to detect the younger person who once lived in that skin. Skin that was fighting valiantly to hold back time and contain all that blood.

A corrugated river of sound flowed up the corridor from the back of the house. A radio, perhaps, or someone talking. The ripples made it hard to tell. I waded down the hallway, being careful not to disturb whatever was going on.

She stood with her back to me, talking on the telephone. Scattered newspaper pages covered the kitchen table, and lunch dishes were stacked beside the sink. Rather than interrupt her conversation, I watched for a while, enjoying the way she moved as she spoke. She ran her fingers through her long brown hair and waved her right hand in the air as if the person on the other end could see it. Maybe the other person could. How much had technology changed in eight years? Maybe it wasn't really a telephone but some sort of transporter, like on *Star Trek*, and any minute now she'd get sucked into it and reappear somewhere else.

My fingers were overwhelmed by the urge to run through her hair just like hers were doing. I closed my eyes and pictured those long strands sifting between my fingers like grains of sand. Her voice was a high-pitched drone, like bees buzzing around a hive. I couldn't make out who she was talking to, or what they were talking about. The conversation smelled disloyal and hateful. Still, since she hadn't visited me while I was away, I doubted she was talking about me now. She hadn't answered my letters, either. None were returned to me, so she must have read them.

Her voice droned greener. Bees swarmed inside my head, filling my nose with their thick honey, and I couldn't take it any more and I whispered *Shut up! Shut up!* perhaps a little louder than necessary.

She dropped the receiver and shrieked. I think she left the ground for a moment while executing an awkward double-axel. She landed poorly, twisted her ankle, and grabbed the chair to keep from falling down. The ice looked hard and cold, which would explain the skates she wasn't wearing but should have been if she was going to try a maneuver like that. Her face turned loud crimson and her hair grew wild and disheveled like a sandstorm. Surprise and rough, gritty fear captured her eyes.

That was a mistake. It's always best to hide your fear. She couldn't—I could see it.

I could smell it.

The bees receded, jabbering on the far end of the telephone line or teleporter. I ignored them, hoping they wouldn't suddenly materialize in the room next to me because I hate honey, especially when it gets in your nose.

I stepped toward her and put a hand out, but she flinched as if I'd offered her a branding iron. My hand, I must admit, may have been curled like a claw, like the gnarled, iridescent fingers of a strangler, but I only meant to take her by the shoulder or the neck and help her.

Really.

But she flinched, and I felt a new shriek coming on. My eyes couldn't stand another one of those. My nose, ah, my nose told me of her fear.

Another step and I was on her. I clasped my hand across her mouth. All I wanted was quiet, but she wouldn't stop moaning. She kept struggling, trying to twist away from me. Her chest heaved. Her eyes bulged. Her face was slick with sweat, and it smelled louder than before, penetrating my ears. A vein in her temple pulsed and I tasted the blood throbbing through it. She didn't seem to have enough skin to contain it.

What else could I do but strangle her? Beneath my fingers, her moans felt like dread. I had to shut her up, had to stop the noise. My hands encircled her neck. My fingertips recognized each other when they met. Her groans burned my hands while my thumbs squeezed the terror out of her. The stench grew louder for a moment, then it was gone.

She slumped against me like someone greeting a lover

at the airport and passing out at the last minute. When I removed my hands, she collapsed to the floor. The chair didn't help her this time. Her head made a hollow, melonish thump when it struck the linoleum. I dropped to my hands and knees and peered into her face. Her eyes were open and silent. My handprints glowed loudly on her neck. I placed my palm over one, comparing the shapes. I was afraid my lifeline might have transferred to her skin, but it was still there when I looked at my hand.

The buzzing was back. The receiver—or was it a transporter?—dangled nearby, and someone was yelling through untold miles of lemony wire. "Rachel? Are you all right? Rachel? Rachel! Is someone there?" I tugged on the cord, like I was trying to start a lawnmower, and the droning stopped.

I turned to find the lazy bitch stretched out on the floor, asleep. Maybe she had gotten older while I was away, but that was no excuse. No excuse. Her arms were at her sides and her head tilted slightly. If I hadn't been so irate, she might have appeared peaceful, but anger colored my vision. I straddled her stomach and shook her by the shoulders, trying to wake her up. I shook harder, but she wouldn't cooperate.

She should have answered my letters. Should have visited me. I bet she was talking on the phone the whole time I was away. Now she was lying on the kitchen floor and I had strangled her. Killed her in less than five minutes after being away for over eight years. That's what I call getting things done. No messing around, no wasting time. See something that needs doing and, by God, just do it.

A phone rang inside my head. It wasn't the one on the wall. That one went "Brring, brring." The one in my head made a funny chirping sound like a smoke detector when the battery is going blue. "You can't leave her like that. They'll find her and you'll have to go back," a voice said. The voice, which has green eyes, never lies. Sometimes it burns, setting off tangerine fumes that get inside my eyes, but it never lies.

I thanked it, and sat at the kitchen table to read the newspaper while I contemplated matters. I hadn't seen the news in years, but nothing had changed. The paper was still full of words marching down the page like rows of black ants. They kept shifting places, making up new stories as they went. Only one of the stories was true, but there was no way to tell which one, or when.

The ink felt rough and sour, so I got up, carried her into the bathroom and chopped her into little tiny pieces.

That may sound easy, but it wasn't. In fact, it was harder than I remembered. I had to make several trips to the well-stocked cellar for tools, though it took me a while to find things. Nothing was where it should have been, considering I didn't remember there being a basement before. Must have been something she added when she wasn't on the phone.

I also didn't remember there being so much red in the bathroom. She must have redecorated *everything* while I was away. Between the phone and making all those changes, it's no wonder she was tired. Whatever she used to paint the bathrooms walls wasn't very good, though. It seeped into my clothing like a disease. The phone voice told me to take care of that in case we had company. Scarlet is an impolite color for entertaining.

I stuffed my clothes into a plastic garbage bag. While I was at it, I got more bags and filled them with the bits and pieces of her body. She was such a messy person. Tired after unpainting the bathroom and everything, I showered. Afterward, I started to take the garbage out. Can you believe that she left several huge trash bags in the bathroom of all places? Hard work always makes me hungry, and I wanted a nap, but the voice told me that could wait.

I was standing naked in the middle of the hall with a garbage bag clutched in each hand when the doorbell rang. I dragged everything to the basement and stashed it behind the furnace. A pair of old coveralls hung from a nail at the bottom of the stairs. They were a little small, so they weren't all that comfortable, and I didn't have anything for my feet, but it was better than answering the door naked or dressed in red. I must have gained weight while I was away, because I don't think I've ever owned any coveralls. "Roger" was stitched above the front pocket, which might have been my name in a movie once.

The doorbell rang again. Why didn't she get it? She was probably on the telephone. Always on the phone or asleep.

Or redecorating.

I climbed the stairs and waded down the now-silent hallway into the living room. Two men stood on the doorstep. She was cowering behind them, halfway to the street, clutching her purse while trying to look around them. One of them glanced back at her and she shrugged. Alarm emanated from her, but not from the men. Her aura was fuchsia, which I can barely spell let alone identify. Being unsure how to spell her terror made me uncomfortable.

The badges they showed me felt as real as the ones on television. "Police," they said, almost simultaneously, but not quite. The guys on *Law & Order* never step on each other's lines like that, but they probably get more practice.

"I was just about to take a nap. Or eat."

They looked at me in a funny way, which made me chuckle. Remembering how I was dressed, I flashed my best smile—sometimes it works like a badge—and said, "I've been working around the house ever since I got here and I'm beat. What can I do for you?"

"Are you related to Rachel Birch?" one of them asked.

"You've come to the right place if you're looking for me."

He stared for several seconds. At me, I think. It would've been impolite to turn to see if he was actually looking at someone behind me, the way he had glanced at the fuchsia woman on the path.

"We had a call from a friend of Mrs. Birch."

I didn't like the way he paused, as if he wasn't sure the words were the right ones. Like he stopped to look at the words before they came out of his mouth and was confused by what he saw. He wore dark sunglasses and I couldn't see his eyes, but I was sure they were blue. Liars always have blue eyes.

"Do all her friends call you?" I asked. "That must keep you busy."

"They were cut off a while ago. She thought she heard an altercation in the background before the line went dead."

"I guess those new teleporters still have some bees in them," I said.

The nervous-smelling woman fidgeted with her purse, trying to make it look like she wasn't listening, but she was.

"You still haven't told us who you are," the man with the blue eyes lied. "Could we talk to Rachel Birch, sir?"

"If you'd been here a little while ago, you could easily have spoken with her. Right now, I'm afraid not." You have to be careful what you say to these lying bastards. They'll take what you say and twist it around. All of a sudden you find yourself spending seven days and seven nights every week in a place where the food tastes like water and the water feels like hot piss and everyone treats you like you're crazy. When you're not. Crazy, that is.

"And why is that, sir?" Only liars who want something from you call you sir. Otherwise they call you dude or man. I like being called dude, but I wasn't about to tell him that.

"If she's not here, she must have gone out, right?" These cops were stupider than the ones on *C.S.I.*, who could lift fingerprints off air molecules if you gave them the right shit to work with.

"Out," the man who probably didn't have blue eyes said.

"Out," I repeated.

"Would you mind if we looked around?" the liar asked.

"I'm hungry or tired. Could you come back tomorrow?"

"We won't take long," he lied. "Just a quick look to satisfy the lady."

For a kick, I was tempted to ask if they had a warrant. Everyone has them on *NYPD Blue*, but they're just sheets of paper with black ants crawling across the surface, and I already had enough of those in the kitchen. When I stepped back to let them in, I knocked over my suitcase.

"Going somewhere?" the quiet one asked.

I picked the suitcase up and carried it with me. "No, why?"

Although they both wore dark glasses, I could hear the glance they exchanged. It went *woosh* from one pair of eyes to the other and back again. I could have reached out and caught it. I'm fast, unbelievably fast, but that would have been rude. Besides, what would I do with a handful of glance? If you rub it on the legs of your coveralls, it leaves a stain.

I stood back, suitcase in hand, waiting for them to go about their business. "The bathroom's over there," I said, pointing with my free hand. "There's probably something in the refrigerator if you're hungry."

I saw red polish on one fingernail. It tasted like glossy metal when I licked it off. I couldn't remember putting any on—it's not my style. I used to know a guy who painted his nails with polish the color of water, but it took forever to wear off.

The one with blue eyes pointed to a picture on the wall. "Is this Mrs. Birch?"

Police work must be boring if this was how they spent their days. Strolling around people's houses, looking at pictures on the wall. They'd do better getting jobs on TV, where they only work an hour a week. I told him the picture was of whoever he thought it was, even though I'd never seen it before. I don't have blue eyes, but if he could lie then I could, too. It's only fair.

I wondered if they were hungry, so I slipped into the

kitchen. A little later, I heard one of them—it might have been the liar, but it could very easily have been the other one—yell from the cellar, "Charlie, call for backup."

I heard someone coming toward the kitchen, so instead of making sandwiches I decided to kill the woman in the front yard. She was a silly goose, after all. I snuck out the back door and circled around the house, the pavement's heat crimson against my bare feet. She was still gawking and gaping like a stork, trying to see what was going on without getting closer to the house. Seeing her like that, I just had to break her stupid little head. It was so much fun watching her leap with surprise. She was more graceful than in the kitchen, but maybe that was because the ice was better out here. She didn't twist her ankle or fall down, and got decent elevation. Eight point five from the Russian judge, but they always mark our guys down.

Her fear hit me like a bucket of chum, the kind that guy in *Jaws* liked to wear. It dripped down my face, clinging to the skin under my coveralls. It was hot and sticky, and I had to get it off or I was going to smother. My skin was confused. It was supposed to hold stuff like that in, and now it had something to keep out and didn't know which one to handle first.

I leapt at the fuchsia woman and knocked her down, but her aura stayed upright. It looked around in confusion and then drifted away in a haze of unspellable color.

The path was solid concrete, but no matter how hard I tried I couldn't chip it with her skull. Really good work, whoever poured the cement. A lot better than the interior decorating. She didn't scream much after the first couple of times her head bounced off the path. A few gurgles and she was quiet. I think she spat blood at me, but with women like that you just never know what they'll say. Talk on the phone all day long, but when they get you face-to-face, all they can think to do is cough up a little blood. Her sticky, noxious fear melted off me and pooled on the ground.

A crowd gathered on the street, busybodies who

didn't know when to mind their own damned business. Ogling and pointing, they reminded me of people standing in front of a monkey cage, which is really funny because I've never been to the zoo and I don't think monkeys really have business or mind being stared at if they do. Didn't they have anything better to do, like baking cakes or burying their kids in the back yard? I ignored them and slammed her head against the ground some more. It was making a deliciously disgusting slobbery, gooshey sound by this point.

Charlie and the liar—or maybe it was Charlie the liar and the other guy—barreled out of the house waving these big black guns around like they were planning to do the shotput or something. I didn't understand what all the commotion was about, but I was getting tired again, so I stopped and wiped my hands on the splintered grass.

"Don't move," the quiet one said. He pointed his weapon right at me, and I thought for a minute that he was serious about shooting me. The absurdity made me laugh and laugh. Cops or not, these guys were pretty good comedians. Except for the liar.

I was still laughing when someone tackled me from behind. It was probably one of the nosy Parkers from the sidewalk. Bastards just can't mind their own business. Then I tasted round copper-brass-bronze-silver as something sharp slid through my coveralls and into my right arm. While I slept, the telephone voice told me many things that didn't make sense at the time, but were completely colorful when I woke up.

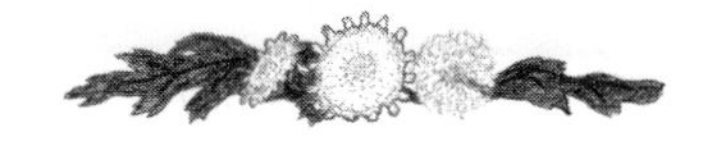

The doctor has blue eyes, so I don't trust him. I ask him when I'm going to get out again, but he's useless when it comes to giving answers. He's far better at asking pointless questions. He keeps asking me why I killed Rachel Birch, but I don't know who that is. I remember rolling around with her on the kitchen floor, though. She was so overjoyed to see me that she got off the telephone and then we were on the floor. I remember that.

I can't wait to go back. I was taking out the trash, but something interrupted me and now I'm here and the trash is behind the furnace in the basement and it's going to stink soon.

I hope I can find the right place next time, but that's up to the voice on the phone. It never lies.

Feed Them

Patricia Russo

There should be a smell, she thought,
especially with so many of them in one little room.

The last time Rita had met with her social worker, Ms. Mizukani started clicking her Mont Blanc ballpoint three minutes into the session. "Of course some days are tough," she said. "That's life. Some days will be tough, and some days not so tough." Click click click with the pen. Though she was pretty sure Ms. Mizukani was unaware she was doing it, Rita found it hard not to take it personally. "But if you start feeling a little overwhelmed sometimes, try thinking about what you have now, compared to, say, six months ago." Ms. Mizukani, who couldn't have been over twenty-five, couldn't have weighed more than 101, and always dressed as if she'd just slipped silently away from a Nieman Marcus display, smiled at her brightly. The only thing that could have motivated such a person to go into social work, Rita thought, was a raging case of the rich-kid guilts.

Okay, Rita thought, pacing in her tiny kitchenette, waiting for the phone to ring. Six months ago she hadn't had this apartment, which, crappy as it was, was still better than the halfway house. Kitchenette, living room, an alcove for her bed, a toilet with a shower. She'd actually enjoyed sitting in her living room, alone in the quiet, alone in a space that was hers, the first few months she'd lived there. Before the cold things had started to grow.

Six months ago she hadn't had a job, and though the one she had now was only stacking cans on the overnight shift at the 24-hour mega-mart, it was a paycheck. Six months ago she hadn't had the clothes she was wearing now, or the microwave glinting at her from the counter, or a phone. She hadn't had visitation rights with Daniel.

Rita stopped then, held herself still, and took a deep breath. Six months ago there hadn't been so many complications in her life. But no way, no way would she think of

Daniel as a complication. Daniel was the reason she'd finally gotten clean. She'd dropped out of his life only a few months after he was born. Maybe even before he had been born, if she were honest with herself. She'd stayed gone, even the few times she'd been physically present (one birthday, one picnic, one . . . some school thing, a play?) for the next eight years. Rita woke up at night drenched in ice-sweat, shaking over how much she'd lost, how much she'd never even know she'd lost, then crying tears so hot they steamed, tears of wonder that she'd managed to snag a second chance, and tears of terror that she'd blow this one, too. Nat, her ex, had fought her on visitation, and in defeat he remained suspicious and bitter. Barely civil to her on the phone. But she had won, and today Daniel was coming over for the afternoon again, her third unsupervised visit with her son since the judge had made her ruling and wished them all luck.

Daniel was not a complication.

Daniel was the reason she woke up in the morning and didn't drink, didn't go scrabbling through her beat-up backpack for the phone number of the MD with the fluid pen and liberal prescription pad, which she knew she still had somewhere.

Rita just wished the cold things hadn't appeared in her living room.

The phone rang. Her heart jumped into her throat, then started racing like crazy. Idiot, she told herself. Calm down. You were waiting for Nat to call before he brought Daniel over. It's Nat.

It was. Stiff, brusque. "I'll drop Dan off at two. Have him ready to go at six."

"Right," she said. Passive was best with Nat. Fighting with him was a total waste of energy.

Two o'clock. She glanced at the microwave's clock. Only forty minutes from now. Suddenly, that seemed like a suffocatingly short amount of time. She wasn't ready. Oh crap, she hadn't bought oranges. Daniel would want oranges.

The cold things had doubled in size since the last time Daniel had been to the apartment.

"Dan wants to say something," Nat said, and the next thing she knew her son was on the phone.

"Hi, Mom," he said.

"Hi," she said, her heart pounding.

There was a pause. Rita realized Daniel was waiting for his father to move away from the phone, go outside maybe, warm up the frigging car the way he always had to do for a full five minutes before driving anywhere. So uptight a blast from a fire hose wouldn't bend him over, that was Nat.

"Mom?" Daniel whispered.

"What is it, honey?" That was good. That was a normal Mom thing to say.

"Did you feed them?"

Rita was silent for a long moment. Then she said, "Yes."

Moms lie sometimes, too, don't they?

The cold things in the living room had sprouted overnight, six weeks ago, their emergence from the worn, well-scrubbed (by Rita, on her hands and knees) wooden floor-boards in the living room coinciding with Daniel's first unsupervised visit. He'd noticed them before she had, in fact, had frozen on the couch where he'd been squirming a bit, jiggling his foot and tugging on one of the upholstery's many unraveling threads while she tentatively asked him questions about school and soccer. "Mom," he said, and her heart leapt a mile, because he said it so naturally. "You got stuff growing here." He slid off the couch and crouched, then got on his hands and knees and put his face close to the floor. "Weird stuff."

Later, Rita wondered how she hadn't noticed the cold

things before Daniel pointed them out. They were all over the place, a clump of them under the TV stand, masses of them in every corner, enough of them pushing up under the coffee table right in front of the couch to look like a carpet. Maybe because she hadn't been able to take her eyes off Daniel. Even when she'd gone to the kitchen to get him a soda, she'd walked with her head turned, looking back over her shoulder, gazing at him.

Mushrooms? she thought then, slowly getting to her feet. The things were gray, or grayish. Most of them. Some of them were brownish. The ones in the corners were closer to white. They were all bulbous, and all more or less the size of fingernails. Convex, spongy, diseased fingernails. Daniel, halfway under the coffee table, stuck his face so close to the things his nose nearly touched one. "Mom," he said excitedly. "They're cold."

"Get out from under there," she said.

He ignored her. "What are they?"

"I don't know. Come on, Daniel, get up."

Daniel wriggled backward a little, then reached out a finger and poked one.

"Don't!" she cried.

"They're mushy. Cold and mushy."

Mushrooms, she was thinking, still thinking for a long minute there before everything changed. Mushy mushrooms. Some kind of fungus, some weird wood-rot she'd get on the phone to the super about. Only there was no odor. There should be a smell, she thought, especially with so many of them in one little room. Fungi stank. Didn't they?

Out of the corner of her eye, Rita glimpsed movement.

The things, the cold and mushy gray and brown things, were stirring.

Oh god, she thought, not mushrooms, not mushrooms, *alive—*

She snatched Daniel by the back of his T-shirt and yanked him out from under the coffee table so fast he yelped in fear. Scooping him up, she hugged him to her chest tightly. His feet dangled above the floor. Her arms were wrapped around his waist in a death grip.

Under the TV stand, the little cold things were crawling. Very slowly, but crawling. In the corners of the room, the little cold things were nudging each other in a languid but perceptible rhythm, the pauses between the touches lasting as long as it took to draw in a slow breath. Under the coffee table, the little cold things had begun to twitch.

Daniel threw back his head and burst into tears.

Then he started to shriek.

"Daniel, please. Daniel, stop!" Icy panic took hold of her. *I got clean for this. For nothing. The cops are gonna come. Social services. One afternoon, that's all they're going to let me have with him. They'll never let me see Daniel again.*

"Let me go!"

Rita was shaking, but she set her son down gently. "Okay, okay, Daniel, okay. Only don't touch them, okay? They're bugs, I'm going to get some spray—"

"They're not bugs," he said, with terrible scorn. He plopped down on the floor again, then reached up and tugged on Rita's hand, hard, until she knelt beside him. Her skin prickled all over. If they weren't bugs they were something worse, egg sacs about to split open, maybe, unleashing hordes of tiny ravenous stinging spiders—

"Look," Daniel said. He sounded fascinated, excited. Almost gleeful. His cheeks were still wet with tears, but he had forgotten all about them.

The little cold things throbbed. Rita, still registering them as creepy-crawlies of some sort, shivered. Grubs. Or pill bugs. Big-ass pill bugs. Daniel's face was glowing. But then boys liked bugs, didn't they? Bugs and worms and frogs and slimy creatures like that. "Don't get too attached to them," she was starting to say, her Mom voice coming back to her, "these aren't pets, they're pests," when she saw the legs.

And the eyes.

And the little, curled-up hands.

The bulbous bits were heads, or mostly heads. The appendages were tiny, unformed, maybe vestigial, the legs bent and drawn up, the hands lacking arms. Something like inchoate, miniature Humpty-Dumpties, she thought.

With open eyes.

"Oh, god, Daniel," she breathed.

"Aren't they cool?"

The eyes were pinpoints of black at the very top of the . . . well, not skull. The top of the curve of the dome was the head as well as the major body part, with two eyes, but so close together they gave the impression of being one cyclopean orb. The cold things had eyelids. She saw them blink.

The cold things had mouths, too, but Rita never saw them. She deduced their existence when Daniel snagged his glass of soda off the coffee table and deliberately spilled a few drops on the floor. The cold thing nearest the spill bunched itself up, then made a little rolling sort of hop directly into the liquid, which it then sucked up inside of a second.

Daniel spend the rest of the afternoon feeding the cold things soda, the entire two-liter bottle of cola she'd bought for him, plus the two cans of ginger ale that had been in the back of the fridge since she'd moved in. He stopped only when his father, idling at the curb, started blasting his horn.

The cold things had grown so much.

From the size of fingernails, to the size of pigeon eggs, to the size of new potatoes, to the size of old Brussels sprouts. Now a few were about the size of Rita's closed fist. She lifted her fist up, held it in front of her eyes. There was nothing she'd like more than to smash them all, flatten every single one of the cold things (their bodies would squish, she thought, like caterpillars), massacre them, sweep the remains into a garbage bag, scrub everything with bleach, and forget that the whole weirdness, this uncanny infestation, had ever happened.

Rita sat very quietly in the straight-backed chair, her legs up in semi-lotus, or as close as she could come to it. Every muscle in her body quivered.

The cold things were quite mobile now. Though their legs and little hands were still tightly drawn up to their Humpty-Dumpty heads, they had learned how to propel their bodies into fast rolls that could cover the length of the living room in under a minute, as well as how to inch themselves along in painful-looking creeps and crawls. They crawled for food. They crawled, a hands-breadth away from the group—they still huddled in groups, one in each corner of the room, one under the TV stand, and one, the biggest, under the coffee-table—to evacuate dabs of gloppy greenish waste. Right now they were crawling all over Daniel.

Nat had arrived at two p.m. on the dot. He didn't bother to park, just pulled up to the curb and let Daniel out. Nat didn't get out of the car, nor did he speak a word to her. Daniel had run up and hugged her; Rita was glad of that, thrilled that Daniel hugged her willingly now, and meanly pleased that Nat could not have avoided seeing it. But when they got upstairs, Daniel had broken from her side instantly, racing to the living room and flinging himself down on the floor, grinning widely even before the cold things began to twitch, then roll over, then creep toward him.

They were crawling all over him now, up and down his arms, into the sleeves of his T-shirt and out from the neckhole, struggling up his legs, attacking the rise of his hips like determined mountain climbers. Daniel was having the time of his life, giggling like a kid playing with a litter of puppies. Rita didn't ask him if the cold things tickled. She didn't want to know.

As the cold things had grown, the pinprick eyes at

the top of their heads had separated into two distinct orbs. More and more frequently now Rita caught the creatures looking at her, the same expression in all of their eyes.

So far they'd all stayed in the living room. They must be territorial, she thought, and tried to be grateful for small mercies, but part of her knew this small mercy could not last. They were getting bigger. Older. Growing up. Sooner or later they would venture out from their birthplace, start making forays into the kitchen, the bathroom, the alcove where she slept.

Rita clenched her other fist.

In the kitchen, under the sink, hidden in a brown paper bag concealed within a black plastic bag, Rita had accumulated a collection of poisons. The usual ant and roach stuff, but also herbicides and fungicides. She'd bought the canisters and bottles and boxes one by one over the last few weeks. Smash them, yes, she wanted to smash and stomp and squish them. But that way was uncertain, messy. What if one escaped? Poison was so much surer.

Daniel lay on his back, his arms stretched out, his hands full of orange segments. She'd peeled the oranges for him, before he arrived. Saving the peels, of course. The cold things seemed to like the peels even better than the fruit. Daniel had plonked a handful of the peels on his chest, another handful on his stomach. "Look, Mom, look!" he crowed.

"I'm looking," she said.

The cold things liked oranges more than they liked soda. They liked tuna fish and canned spaghetti, too, but oranges were far and away their favorite. Daniel had determined this on his last visit, after a couple of hours of earnest experimenting. Despite all the feedings, Rita had yet to catch even a glimpse of their mouths. The cold things ate face down, as it were.

"How's school?" she asked. "How's soccer?"

He answered easily, chatting about Mr. This who was making them do a project on volcanoes for Earth Science and Coach That who always bought the team pizza after their games. He talked about Mayiya, his stepmom, though Rita hadn't asked, and how the baby was a pain in the butt, crying all the time and no fun at all. Daniel said Dad said that would change when Timon got older, but Daniel confided that personally he thought that was a crock.

Timon. Possibly the stupidest name for a child Rita had ever heard. But then its mother was named Mayiya, so what could you expect?

"But I love him," Daniel said, serenely. "'Cause he's my brother."

"And you love Mayiya, too," Rita said. It was not a question.

"Sure."

"And Nat."

He looked at her then, tilting his head back, gazing at her upside down; even upside down, Daniel's expression said that was a really stupid question.

And me? Rita did not ask.

"Mom," Daniel said, "I gotta ask you something."

Both Rita's fists were still clenched. Her body was thrumming like a phone wire in a high wind. She tried to breathe deeply, she tried to center herself. She tried to unclench her hands. Her muscles were reluctant to cooperate.

"What is it, honey?"

Uncharacteristically, Daniel was suddenly tongue-tied. He wriggled his shoulders. He licked his lips. The cold things were still crawling and creeping all over him; the orange peels and orange segments were nearly all consumed, and the creatures began to move more quickly, eagerly hunting out the last scraps.

"Dad said not to tell you," he mumbled.

Alarm, instant as a thunderbolt. Panic like fire in her blood. Suddenly the cold things were the least of her fucking worries. Mutant mushy creatures sprouting and rolling and for all she knew mating all over her floor? Big deal. The danger, the enemy, pure and concentrated as a crystal of strychnine, was Nat.

Rita unlocked her legs from their semi-lotus. She put her feet on the floor. Fight or flight.

Fight. "Go ahead, honey, you can tell me." Rita made her voice warm; Daniel must not be able to sense the icy fear she felt. "You can always tell me anything you want, anything at all."

"Um," Daniel said, rolling his eyes back to gaze at her upside down again. "Um, we're going on vacation."

At first, at the very first, that didn't seem too bad. It was the beginning of June; school would be over in a couple of weeks. A vacation was normal. Nat, she remembered, had liked road trips. But as Daniel continued, growing more excited as he got into the details, it became clear that this was to be no week-long trip to the shore, no ten-day Florida or California jaunt. Mayiya was taking baby Timon to visit his grandparents, and for some reason Nat had wedged Daniel into the deal, too. All one big happy family. Staying with Granny and Granddad, for the entire summer, with Nat popping over for a weekend here and there.

Daniel wouldn't be back in the city until September.

He can't do that, Rita thought. Maybe she said it aloud, for Daniel slowly and carefully turned over on his side, nudging the cold things away gently, lifting off the ones who clung to him and setting them on the floor. He pushed himself up on to his knees. "Mom—"

Rita didn't remember standing, but she was on her feet, striding to the phone. "He can't do this. I have visitation rights. He's breaking a court order."

"He said you'd be mad," Daniel said, in a small voice.

She whirled, fury making her flush. Fury at Nat, of course. Not at Daniel. Daniel was only eight years old, and besides . . . okay, maybe she could understand why he wasn't exactly broken up about the idea of not seeing her for three months. Of course she could understand it. It was her own damn fault. But still—

"Oh, did he. What else did he say?" Because there

would be more. There would have to be.

"He said—" Abruptly, Daniel shut his mouth.

"Go on," she said evenly.

"He said you would get over it. If . . ." A trapped look appeared in Daniel's eyes.

"If," she prompted.

"If you knew what was good for you."

Son of a bitch.

Rita's hand was on the phone. She did not pick up the receiver. To go to court she'd need a lawyer. She could tell Ms. Mizukani, see if Miss Socialite Social Worker would help her get legal aid again, but nothing practical could be done before Nat actually sent Daniel off. And then what? Daniel would be out of state, but Nat would be working in the city most of the time. Could she have him arrested? Maybe. But no judge would give Rita custody of Daniel. Not now. Not yet. They'd go to court, have hearings and mediations and all that razzmatazz, and in the end Nat would get a slap on the wrist, but he'd wind up keeping custody. And he'd just mess with the visitation arrangement even more, in revenge. Rita worked it out, slowly, in her head, as she stood with her hand on the phone. Nat held all the cards, and even if she were technically in the right, that wouldn't help her much in the real world.

"Mom?"

So many . . . complications. If only things could be simple, for once in her life. Rita let her hand slip off the phone. She could call Nat and scream at him, but that wouldn't help, either. "Yes, Daniel."

"I need to ask you something."

That was how all this had started, she remembered.

"Look," Daniel said, and when she turned he was holding one of the cold things. One of the bigger ones, maybe the biggest; he needed both of his own small hands to hold it securely. The cold thing twitched slightly, but seemed content to lie in Daniel's cupped palms. "They're cool, aren't they?"

"I don't know about that," she said, as a glimpse of a silver lining to this black mess came to her. She could get rid of them now. Daniel would never know. In September, when he returned, when he visited her apartment again, she could tell him the cold things had . . . run away. Tonight, after Nat picked Daniel up, she would unleash the chemicals she'd stashed under the sink.

"You're gonna feed them, right?" Daniel asked, anxiously.

Rita froze. No, she thought, no. Oh, honey, don't make me lie to you again, don't make me lie to you any more.

"They're getting big. Look," he said.

"I see them." *I see them every minute of every day.*

"They're growing. I'm taking good care of them, right?" Pride in his voice, but worry creasing his forehead.

"You sure are, Daniel." Oh my god, she thought, he loves these horrible things.

He's eight. He'll forget.

A wave of coldness enveloped Rita, chilling her to the bone. If she touched Daniel now, she was sure she would freeze his skin, turn his marrow to ice. So she stayed back, even as he got to his feet, still holding the biggest of the creatures in his hands.

"This one's getting wings. See?"

And, horribly, it was, a thin membrane that might very well grow into something like the wing of a bat connecting the thing's still-bent leg to its head-body.

"That'll be really cool, when they fly, won't it?"

They won't stay in the living room then, Rita thought. She stared at her son. He was tense, she saw. The look on his face was half pleading, half fearful.

"Mom?"

He expects me to let him down, she thought. The coldness was so thick on her she wouldn't have been surprised to see her breaths puff out as clouds of frost.

"It's almost six," she said. "You'd better start getting ready to go. You know your father doesn't like to wait."

"Okay," he said, instantly. Too instantly. She hadn't asked Daniel a lot of questions about life at home, about Nat and Mayiya, about what happened in that house, what was normal there. That had been deliberate; those waters were still too risky. But she had noted that all Nat needed to do was clear his throat, and Daniel jumped. Two weeks ago, on his last visit, there had been bruises on Daniel's legs. Could have been nothing, of course. He played soccer.

Daniel set the cold thing in his hands gently on the floor, watched it as it crept to join its siblings again gathered under the coffee table. When he looked up, his eyes were full of tears. "You'll take care of them, right, Mom? You'll feed them and stuff?"

Oh god, he's crying. Rita started to shake. Let him not be crying, I can't stand it. Look away, she told herself, but she couldn't.

"Yes, Daniel," she said. "I'll take care of them. I'll feed them."

"You promise?"

The weight of history on one side of her, the weight of the future on the other, Rita said, "I promise."

They were out on the sidewalk at a minute to six. At six on the dot, Nat pulled up to the curb. Daniel hugged her before he got into the car. He waved goodbye at her to the end of the block, until Nat turned the corner.

Six o'clock. It was only six o'clock. There was the evening to get through, and then the long night. There was a summer to get through, before she saw her son again.

Rita checked her pocket. Yes, she had a five. Five dollars would buy a big mesh bag of oranges at the fruit stand on Miranda Place. Her feet seemed very far away from the rest of her; she felt like she was sinking into the sidewalk. Rita didn't think she could walk those three blocks. But slowly, one terrible, Atlas-heavy step at a time, she did.

The Weight of Silence

Scott Nicholson

The books were dead on the shelves, words for nobody.
The toys were dusty.

S*ilence isn't golden,* Katie thought. *If silence were any metal, it would be lead: gray, heavy, toxic after prolonged exposure.*

Silence weighed upon her in the house, even with the television in the living room blasting a Dakota-Madison-Dirk love triangle, even with the radio upstairs tuned to New York's big-block classic rock, even with the windows open to invite the hum and roar from the street outside. Even with all that noise, Katie heard only the silence. Especially in the one room.

The room she had painted sky blue and world green. The one where tiny clothes, blankets, and oversized books lined the shelves. Wooden blocks had stood stacked in the corner, bought because Katie herself had wooden blocks as a child. She'd placed a special order for them. Most of the toys were plastic these days. Cheaper, more disposable.

Safer.

For the third time that morning, she switched on the monitor system that Peter had installed. A little bit of static leaked from the speaker. She turned her head so that her ear would be closer. Too much silence.

Stop it, Katie. You know you shouldn't be doing this to yourself.

Of course she should know it. That's all she heard lately. The only voices that broke through the silence were those saying, "You shouldn't be doing this to yourself." Or else the flip side of that particular little greatest hit, a remake of an old standard, "Just put it behind you and move on."

Peter said those things. Katie's mom chimed in as well. So did the doctors, the first one with a droopy mustache who looked as if he were into self-medication, the next an anorexic analyst who was much too desperate to find a crack in Katie's armor.

But the loudest voice of all was her own. That unspoken voice that led the Shouldn't-Be chorus. The voice that could never scream away the silence. The voice that bled and cried and sang sad, tuneless songs.

She clicked the monitor off. She hadn't really expected to hear anything. She knew better. She was only testing herself, making sure that it was true, that she was utterly and forever destroyed.

I feel fairly *destroyed. Perhaps I'm as far as* quite. *But* utterly, *hmm, I think I have miles to go before I reach an adverb of such extremity and finality.*

No. *Utterly* wasn't an adverb. It was a noun, a state of existence, a land of bleak cliffs and dark waters. And she knew how to enter that land.

She headed for the stairs. One step up at a time. Slowly. Her legs knew the routine. How many trips over the past three weeks? A hundred? More?

She reached the hall, then the first door on the left. Peter had closed it tightly this morning on his way to work. Peter kept telling her to stop leaving the door open at night. But Katie had never left the door open, not since—

Leaving the door open would fall under the category of *utterly*. And Katie wasn't *utterly*. At least not yet. She touched the door handle.

It was cold. Ice cold, grave cold, as cold as a cheek when—

You shouldn't be doing this to yourself.

But she already was. She turned the knob, the sound of the latch like an avalanche in the hush of a snowstorm. The door swung inward. Peter had oiled the hinges, because he said nothing woke a sleeping baby faster than squeaky hinges.

The room was still too blue, still far too verdant. Maybe she should slap on another coat, something suitably dismal and drab. This wasn't a room of air and life. This was a room of silence.

Because silence crowded this room like death crowded

a coffin. Even though Led Zeppelin's "Stairway to Heaven" jittered forth from the bedroom radio across the hall, even though the soap opera's music director was sustaining a tense organ chord, even though Katie's heart was rivaling John Bonham's bass beat, this room was owned by silence. The absence of sound hit Katie like a tidal wave, slapped her about the face, crushed the wind from her lungs. It smothered her.

It accused her.

She could still see the impressions that the four crib legs had made in the carpet. Peter had taken apart the crib while she was still in the hospital, trundled it off to some charity. He'd wanted to remove as many reminders as possible, so she could more quickly forget. But the one thing he couldn't remove was the memory that was burned into her eyes.

And any time, like now, that she cared to try for *utterly*, all she had to do was pull the vision from somewhere behind her eyelids, rummage in that dark mental closet with its too-flimsy lock. All those nights of coming in this room, bending over, smiling in anticipation of that sinless face with its red cheeks, sniffing to see if the diaper were a one or a two, reaching to feel the small warmth.

And then the rest of it.

Amanda pale. Amanda's skin far too cool. Amanda not waking, ever.

Katie blinked away the memory and left the room, so blinded by tears that she nearly ran into the door jamb. She closed the door behind her, softly, because silence was golden and sleeping babies didn't cry. Her tears hadn't dried by the time Peter came home.

He took one look at her, then set his briefcase by the door as if it were fireman's gear and he might have to douse the flames of a stock run. "You were in there again, weren't you?"

She stared ahead, thanking God for television. The greatest invention ever for avoiding people's eyes. Now if only the couch would swallow her.

"I'm going to buy a damned deadbolt for that room," he said, going straight to the kitchen for the martini waiting in the freezer. Mixed in the morning to brace himself for the effort of balancing vermouth and gin all evening. He made his usual trek from the refrigerator to the computer, sat down, and was booted up before he spoke again.

"You shouldn't be doing this to yourself," he said.

Katie debated thumbing up the volume on the television remote. No. That would only make him yell louder. Let him lose himself in his online trading.

"How was your day?" she asked.

"Somewhere between suicide and murder," he said. "The tech stocks fell off this afternoon. Had clients reaming out my ear over the phone."

"They can't blame you for things that are out of your control," she said. She didn't understand how the whole system worked, people trading bits of paper and hope, all of it seeming remote from the real world and money.

"Yeah, but they pay me to know," Peter said, the martini already two-thirds vanished, his fingers going from keyboard to mouse and back again. "Any idiot can guess or play a hunch. But I'm supposed to outperform the market."

"I'm going to paint the nursery."

"Damn. SofTech dropped another three points."

Peter used to bring Amanda down in the mornings, have her at his feet while he caught up on the overnight trading in Japan. He would let Katie have an extra half-hour's sleep. But the moment Amanda started crying, Peter would hustle her up the stairs, drop her between Katie's breasts, and head back to the computer. "Can't concentrate with her making that racket" was one of his favorite sayings.

Katie suddenly pictured one of those "dial-and-say" toys, where you pulled the string and the little arrow spun around. If Peter had made the toy, it would stop on a square and give one of his half-dozen patented lines: "You shouldn't be doing this to yourself" or "Just put it behind you and move on" or "We can always try again later, when you're over it."

"I was reading an article today," she said. "It said SIDS could be caused by—"

"I told you to stop with those damned parenting magazines."

SIDS could be caused by several things. Linked to smoking, bottle-feeding, stomach-sleeping, overheating. Or nothing at all. There were reports of mothers whose babies had simply stopped breathing while being held.

Sometimes babies died for no apparent reason, through nobody's fault. The doctors had told her so a dozen times.

Then why couldn't she put it behind her?

Because Amanda had Katie's eyes. Even dead, even swaddled under six feet of dirt, even with eyelids butterfly-stitched in eternal slumber, those eyes stared through the earth and sky and walls to pierce Katie. They peeked in dreams and they blinked in those long black stretches of insomnia and they peered in from the windows of the house.

Those begging, silent eyes.

The eyes that, on dark nights when Peter was sound asleep, watched from the nursery.

No, Katie, that's no way to think. Babies don't come back, not when they're gone. Just think of her as sleeping.

Katie changed channels. Wheel of Fortune. Suitably vapid. Peter's fingers clicked over some keys, another fast-breaking deal.

She glanced at him, his face bright from the glow of the computer screen. He didn't look like a millionaire. Neither did she. But they were, or soon would be.

She almost hated Peter for that. Always insuring everything to the max. House, cars, people. They each had million-dollar life policies, and he'd insisted on taking one out for Amanda.

"It's not morbid," he'd said. "Think of them as life's little lottery tickets."

And even with the million due any day now, since the medical examiner had determined that the death was natural, Peter still had to toy with those stocks. As addicted as any slot-machine junkie. He'd scarcely had time for sorrow. He hadn't even cried since the funeral.

But then, Peter knew how to get over it, how to put it behind him.

"I'm going up," she said. "I'm tired."

"Good, honey. You should get some rest." Not looking away from the screen.

Katie went past him, not stooping for a kiss. He'd hardly even mentioned the million.

She went up the stairs, looked at the door to the nursery. She shuddered, went into the bedroom, and turned off the radio. A faint hissing filled the sonic void, like air leaking from a tire. The monitor.

She could have sworn she'd turned it off. Peter would be angry if he knew she'd been listening in on the nursery again. But Peter was downstairs. The silence from the empty room couldn't bother him.

Only her. She sat on the bed and listened for the cries that didn't come, for the tiny coos that melted a mother's heart, for the squeals that could mean either delight or hunger. Amanda. A month old. So innocent.

And Katie, so guilty. The doctors said it wasn't her fault, but what did they know? All they saw were blood tests, autopsy reports, charts, the evidence after the fact. They'd never held the living, breathing Amanda in their arms.

The medical examiner had admitted that crib death was a "diagnosis of exclusion." A label they stuck on the corpse of a baby when no other cause was found. She tried not to think of the M.E. in the autopsy room, running his scalpel down the line of Amanda's tiny chest.

Katie stood, her heart pounding. Had that been a cry?

She strained to hear, but the monitor only vomited its soft static. Its accusing silence.

She switched off the monitor, fingers trembling.

If she started hearing sounds now, little baby squeaks, the rustle of small blankets, then she might start screaming and never stop. She might go *utterly*, beyond the reach of those brightly colored pills the doctors had prescribed. She got under the blankets and buried her head beneath the pillows.

Peter came up after an hour or so. He undressed without speaking, slid in next to her, his body cold. He put an arm around her.

"Honey?" he whispered. "You awake?"

She nodded in the darkness.

"SofTech closed with a gain." His breath reeked of alcohol, though his speech wasn't slurred.

"Good for you, honey," she whispered.

"I know you've been putting off talking about it, but we really need to."

Could she? Could she finally describe the dead hollow in her heart, the horror of a blue-skinned baby, the monstrous memory of watching emergency responders trying to resuscitate Amanda?

"Do we have to?" she asked. She choked on tears that wouldn't seep from her eyes.

"Nothing will bring her back." He paused, the wait made larger by the silence. "But we still need to do something about the money."

Money. A million dollars against the life of her child.

He hurried on before she could get mad or break down. "We really should invest it, you know. Tech stocks are a little uneven right now, but I think they're going to skyrocket in the next six months. We might be able to afford to move out of the city."

She stiffened and turned away from him.

"Christ, Katie. You really should put it behind you."

"That article on SIDS," she said. "There's a link be-

between smog levels and sudden infant death."

"You're going to make yourself crazy if you keep reading that stuff," he said. "Sometimes, things just happen." He caressed her shoulder. "We can always try again later, you know."

She responded with silence, a ten-ton nothingness that could crush even the strongest flutters of hope. Peter eventually gave up, his hand sliding from her shoulder, and was soon snoring.

Katie awoke at three, in the dead stillness of night. A mother couldn't sleep through the crying of her baby. As she had so many nights after the birth, she dragged herself out of bed and went to the nursery. They had talked about putting the crib in their bedroom, but Peter said they'd be okay with the monitor on.

Katie's breasts had quit leaking over a week ago, but now they ached with longing. She closed her robe over them and went into the hall, quietly so that Peter could get his sleep. She opened the door and saw the eyes. The small eyes burned bright with hunger, need, love, loss. Questions.

Katie went to them in the dark and leaned over the crib. The small mouth opened, wanting air. The light flared on, stealing her own breath.

"What are you doing in here?" Peter said.

"I . . . couldn't sleep." She looked down at the empty carpet, at the small marks where the crib legs had rested.

Maybe if she cried.

"We should paint this room," Peter said.

She went to him, sagged against his chest as he hugged her. After she was through sobbing, he led her to the bedroom. He fell asleep again, but she couldn't. Behind her eyelids lived that small, gasping mouth and those two silent, begging eyes.

As she listened to the rhythm of Peter's breathing, she recalled the line from that movie, the cop thriller that they'd gone to see when she was seven months pregnant. The tough plainclothes detective, who looked like a budget

Gene Hackman, had said, "There's only two ways to get away with murder: kill yourself, or put a plastic bag over a baby's head."

What a horrible thing to say, she'd thought at the time. Only a jerk Hollywood writer would come up with something like that, so callous and thoughtless. Peter had later apologized for suggesting the movie.

"Is it really true?" she'd asked. "About the plastic bag?"

"Who knows?" he'd said. "I guess they do research when they write those things. Just forget about it."

Sure. She'd put that behind her, too. She wondered if Peter had been able to forget it.

He had taken out the insurance policy for Amanda a week after her birth. Peter had always wanted to be a millionaire. That's why he played the market. He wanted to hit one jackpot in his life.

She turned on the lamp and studied Peter's face.

Amanda had some of his features. The arch of the eyebrows, the fleshy earlobes, the small chin. But Amanda's eyes had been all Katie. When those silent eyes looked imploringly out from Katie's memory, it was like looking into a mirror.

Katie shuddered and blinked away the vision of that small stare. She pressed her face against the pillow, mimicking a suffocation. No. She wouldn't be able to smother herself.

She wrestled with the sheets. Peter was sweating, even though he wore only pajama bottoms. She pulled the blanket from him. He sleepily tugged back, oblivious.

She must have fallen asleep, dreamed. Amanda at the window, brushing softly against the screen. Katie rising from the bed, pressing her face against the cold glass. Amanda floating in the night, eyes wide, flesh blue, lips moving in senseless baby talk. The sounds muffled by the plastic bag over her head.

When Katie awoke, Peter was in the bathroom, getting

ready for work. He was humming. He was an ace at putting things behind him. You'd scarcely have known that he'd lost a daughter.

Why couldn't she show an equally brave face?

She made her morning trek into the nursery. No crib, no Amanda. The books were dead on the shelves, words for nobody. The toys were dusty.

"I'm going to stop by on my way home and pick up a couple of gallons of paint," Peter said from the doorway. He put his toothbrush back in his mouth.

"Was she ever real?" Katie asked.

"Shhh," Peter mumbled around the toothbrush. "It's okay, honey. It wasn't your fault."

Even Peter believed it. She looked at his hands. No. They would never have been able to slip a bag over a baby's head, hold it loosely until the squirming stopped.

She was surprised she still had tears left to cry. Maybe she would run out of them in a week or two, when she was beyond *utterly*. When she had put it behind her.

"Peach," she said. "I think peach walls would look good."

"It's only for a little while. Until we have enough money to move. The sooner we get you away from this house, the better."

The million wouldn't buy Amanda back. But at least it would help bury her, confine her to a distant place in Katie's memory. Maybe one day, Katie really would be able to forget. One morning, she would awaken without guilt.

She made coffee, some eggs for Peter. He rushed through breakfast, checking over the NASDAQ in the newspaper. She kissed him at the door.

"I promise to try harder," she said to him.

He put a hand to the back of her neck, rubbed her cheek with his thumb. "She had eyes just like yours," he said, then he looked away. "Sorry. I'm not supposed to talk about it."

"We'll be away from here soon."

"It wasn't your fault."

She couldn't answer. She had a lump in her throat. So she nodded, watched him walk to his car, then closed the door. After he'd driven away, headed for the Battery in Manhattan, she went up the stairs.

She reached under the bed and pulled out the keepsake box. She untied the pink ribbon and opened it. Amanda Lee Forrester, born 7-12-05. Seven pounds, nine ounces. Tiny footprints on the birth certificate.

Katie shuffled through the photographs, the birth announcement clipped from the newspaper, the hospital bracelet, the two white booties, the small silver spoon Peter's mom had given them. Soon Katie would be able to put these things behind her and move on. But not too soon.

She could cry at will. She could pretend to be *utterly* if she needed to, if Peter ever suspected. She could hide her guilt in that perfect hiding place, her disguise of perpetual self-blame.

Katie put all the items of Amanda's life into the plastic bag, then tied the box closed with the ribbon. She returned the box to its place under the bed. Peter would never understand, not a trade such as the one she'd made.

A million dollars to forever carry the weight of silence.

She clicked on the nursery monitor, sat on the bed, and listened.

Skeleton Woods

Ramsey Campbell

I'll be safe as long as I stay on the path.
Surely I'm not really feeling it stir
like a cocoon about to crack open.

They were never called that, but they seem to be now. When I manage to drag the warped sash high enough for me to lean over my old bedroom windowsill, I'm almost certain as I squint at the wooden arch daubed with moonlight that Skelton has acquired an extra letter. Under the moon the urban dell resembles a web that has caught the luminous worm of the stream. The woods look smaller than I remember, and even more secretive, no doubt because the trees have grown since I last took in the view. That's why the closest branches appear to be reaching for my attention until I back away and slam the window.

It's time to leave. I've seen all there is to see, which is virtually nothing. Every item of furniture has gone, even the lampshades and carpets. They were so faded they wouldn't have helped sell the house, but the stark rooms under the naked dusty bulbs feel stripped of all their memories. I switch off the lights on the upper floor and hurry past the rattling echoes of my footsteps in the darkened rooms as empty as my skull. Only the hall light remains to be extinguished, and I open the front door first so as not to feel trapped in the damp stale gloom. I jab the switch and am heading down the passage that has yielded its drab colours to the moonlight when I'm reminded of trying to escape before our mother could issue her instructions. "Watch out for Tim," she would tell me. "Don't let him get in any trouble, Philip."

At first I was proud to be trusted to take care of my younger brother—and I'm overwhelmed by such a flood of memories that I have to grip the scaly doorframe for support. I remember wheeling him in his pram through the woods, which our mother believed was safer than pushing him through the streets—old houses on our side of the railway, a cheap new estate beyond—that enclosed the reserve. I wasn't meant to take him in the tunnel that led the footpath and the stream underneath the railway, but of course I did, talking to him in a voice overgrown with a giant one that amused him. Once he graduated to a buggy I made him promise not to tell our mother if he ever wanted to go through the tunnel again, and now I realise I was teaching him to be surreptitious with me as well. I'm even more responsible for events I don't want to remember.

The worst of it is that we didn't need to deceive her. She walked me to school over one or the other bridge across the railway, but once I started taking Tim she encouraged us to use the tunnel; it would keep us clear of the children from the estate, at least until we reached the only local school. Relying on me let her work longer at the hospital, and soon she could afford to buy me a bicycle. In two years this passed to Tim, which seemed fair to me; it and its upsized replacement had been second-hand when I was given them for Christmas. But he didn't take long to see that it gave him the chance not to do as I told him.

Wasn't our mother to blame? People weren't supposed to cycle in the woods, but she thought the route was safer for us than the roads or even the pavements. "Just be careful of the old folk" was her only warning. Tim was too intent on leaving me behind to bother about them or anyone else on the footpath. I gave up shouting "Wait for me on the other side," because it simply provoked him to race faster through the tunnel and out of sight, leaving behind a mocking laugh that seemed to scuttle all over the glistening bricks in the dimness. If the stream was low he might cycle along it, stirring up ripples that sounded as though a dweller in the mud was sniggering.

Was the water already tainted by then? Tim was about that age when he began to call the place Skeleton Woods. That needn't mean anything, but I'm so enraged by the rest of my memories that I slam the door behind me and tramp out of the wild garden. I want to see how the woods have grown.

The entrance is directly across the road. Four-year-old Tim used to call them our garden. Whenever he said anything that delighted her, such as that, our mother would clap her hands and sigh. The memory slips away, because I can't see the letter that was added to the name carved on the arch. It must have been the shadow of a twig. "Skelton Woods," I repeat as I stare at the thin arch until it appears to be exuding moonlit clouds. I shake my head to dislodge the impression and step onto the path beneath the arch.

Trees close over the path as it slopes down to the stream. It's ribbed with steps and imprinted with shadows like traces of roots about to break through the earth. Where it levels out, the shadows merge into a mass of blackness, solid except for the glimmer of fallen leaves. As I pad down the steps, something clatters fast between the trees across the stream. Since nobody could be so thin, I imagine it was a squirrel. I try to drive off any other lurkers by adding weight to my tread as I reach the foot of the slope.

It isn't as dark as it looked from above. Leaves colourless as scraps of paper glow among the shadows on the path and hide a secret pattern in the dimness. The November trees have fastened their claws in the sky, so that I could fancy they're bringing the luminous clouds to a standstill. Apart from the whisper of the milky stream, the woods seem as fixed as a memory. I stride along the path, through the tangles of shadows. Perhaps I'll find Tim's and my den.

I found it one Saturday while I was cycling by myself. He was watching television programmes for children younger than he was. If I'd changed the channel his screams would have given our mother one of her headaches. Besides, she'd said "Let him have his favourite, Philip. You used to like that show." I didn't want to be reminded, and tried to be an explorer several times my age as I cycled onto one of the side paths that led deeper into the woods. A cluster of bushes at the intersection put me in mind of a jungle hut. There was just one way in, so low I had to crawl, but the interior could have accommodated at least a dozen tribesmen, while the green ceiling was high enough for someone taller than me to stand up. As a man walking beside the stream wondered why his dog was straining to reach the bushes, I realised I could watch and not be detected. Even better, the entrance to my hideout wasn't visible from either path.

I thought of hiding there from Tim, and then I realised I could make him do my bidding. I told him I had a secret that he would never learn unless he promised not to leave me behind again. I had to threaten to tell our mother that he'd been disobeying before he would promise. He knew she would accuse him of resembling our father or, worse still, the woman he'd gone off somewhere with that we mustn't name. Even so, he had to be coaxed to walk. I didn't want our bicycles to betray our presence.

As soon as he saw a woman on the path by the stream he began to call "You can't see us. We're here." How wise of me was it to persuade him just to make noises at people instead? Once he discovered that if he dragged a stick across the slender trunks of the bushes nobody could identify the bony rattling, he would play for hours. Now I wonder when he decided that it sounded like a skeleton.

He was already calling the dell Skeleton Woods. Our mother applauded and told him to carry on being himself. When he did in the schoolyard I saw his classmates laughing at him. "He thinks they're called Skeleton Woods."

"They are," Tim protested, clenching his fists and his small thin face smaller. "There are skeletons in them."

"There's never," one girl scoffed.

"Go when it's dark and you'll see."

"What'll we see? You making a face like that? Doesn't scare us."

"They live in the trees and they'll jump on you. When you hear the clicky noise that's them laughing, it's their teeth. And you'll see their shadows and think they're just bits of trees till they grab you and make you into bones like them. That's how it works, there was only one at first and it caught people and made them stay down there with it."

I couldn't judge whether his audience was impressed by all this or by how his eyes had glazed as if he was gazing inwards at the scenes he was describing. I was simply glad our mother wasn't there to deliver his biggest round of applause. Did he mean to frighten his classmates out of the woods? He had the opposite effect. Before long we heard children in the woods at night, giggling and whispering, sometimes crying out and running away. Perhaps they were fleeing the screams, not knowing they were Tim's response to not being allowed to go out after dark. "You're all I've got," our mother said, presumably including me.

He managed to content himself with daylight once he found it offered victims. I remember how his features widened with delight when he saw from our hideout two of his classmates who were venturing along the path, not nervously enough for him. He rattled the bushes and watched the girls shriek and stare about and dash away, and then he dodged out of hiding and ran after them, shouting "The skeletons want you. They'll be waiting for you."

A man out walking from the old people's home that overlooked the woods pointed his stick at him. "Don't stir things up, son. You don't know what you're doing."

Tim stared at him as the girls were surrounded by their own cries in the tunnel. "You'll be one soon," he said and ran off, leaving the old man to lean on his shaky stick.

I can't locate the den. I've forgotten which side path it was closest to, and all the clumps of bushes by the main one are the wrong shape, just crouching huddles full of gaps. I mightn't be able to recognise how it's grown, if it has even survived. I lower myself onto a bench that's too damp for me to rest my hands on and fumble a bottle of water out of my quilted coat. As I drain the bottle the pale rushes bordering the path finger the dim air with their fattened tips, though I can't hear the ripples that must be stirring the fleshless stalks. I could almost imagine that the stream is keeping some activity to itself.

How much was the water to blame? Hardly anyone seemed to give it a thought except Tim. Of course we may have been the only ones who saw the dog. There was gossip about a leak from a medical factory, but that was beyond the horizon, past an underground section of the stream. By then I was too worried about Tim to take much notice of the rumour. He was thirteen and using drugs.

At first I hoped that someone else had started hiding in our den. More than once I'd found the stubs of scrawny cigarettes under the bushes, on the carpet of fallen leaves that lent the interior a special secret glow. When I asked Tim about them he stared at me. Silence was his new response to much that he was asked, either to do or to answer. Our mother had been unable to keep him in at night for at least a year, and was reduced to sending me after him while she tried to relax with a bottle of wine. "Don't let anything happen to him," she would plead. "He's still your little brother."

He didn't seem like it to me. I thought he was determined to act older than I was, to do things I wouldn't dare. I knew it the night I trailed him to the den and saw greyness drifting out of the bushes. I tried to believe it was mist until I smelled it, which made my head swim. I dodged around the bushes and crawled underneath, bruising my elbows as twigs scraped my back. I lurched upright to see Tim suck most of the last inch of a thin cigarette to ash, then lick the remains and his fingers before dropping the blackened scrap. "What do you think you're doing?" I gasped.

When this was met with a wordless stare I stood up as straight as the branches overhead would allow and leaned over Tim, who was squatting cross-legged. "Where did you get that?" I tried demanding.

"Want some?"

"I don't, and you certainly shouldn't. Don't ever do it

again."

This time his silence didn't hold. "You're not my dad. I'll do what I like."

"Suppose I tell mother? What'll you do then?"

He glared at me so fiercely that even in the dimness I could see his eyes were red. "Go on, tell her. Like I care."

We both knew I wouldn't, and I wished I hadn't threatened to. "Why are you doing it at all? Don't you know what it can do to you?"

"Helps me is what." Before I was goaded to ask the obvious question, he answered it. "See things."

I attempted to laugh, though it made me feel like one of the scoffers in the schoolyard years earlier. "What things?"

"Like him."

Tim stared at the leafy canopy above me, which gave a loud creak. The next moment something clawed so viciously at my scalp it might have been eager to reach my brain. I ducked but managed not to cry out as I glimpsed a thin shape crouching on top of the branches. In an instant I couldn't distinguish it. I must have mistaken part of the tree above the bushes for a figure with a bird's nest for its raggedly perforated head after I'd stood up too far and scratched myself on a twig. "There's nothing. You're just making yourself see things," I said.

His mouth twisted smaller as if locking up a secret, but then he spoke. "That's all you know. It makes them come."

"No, it made me," I said, feeling clever. I felt less so once I followed him out of the den and was unable to locate the nest I'd thought was a head or even the branches I'd taken for limbs. Apparently the incident satisfied him in some way, because he headed home, which meant I had to worry that our mother would notice his condition. I was relieved when he made for his room without speaking and shut himself in with his headphones. I was even able to convince our mother that he had only been out for a walk.

After that I had to chase him most nights, always in the woods. He found it easier than ever to outdistance me on the latest of my old bicycles while I cycled warily along the twisted flickering paths. Sometimes he would linger in the tunnel to leave pungent smoke waiting for me in the dark. I never overtook him before he finished what he'd brought, until the night I almost collided with him as I put on speed out of the tunnel. He was so immobile that I grew even more afraid for him. "What's wrong?" I cried.

"Shut up. I'm looking."

When I peered past him I was reassured to see there was something to look at: a more or less Alsatian dog that was drinking from the edge of the stream. At first I thought Tim was fascinated by the way the glimmering ripples crowded back across the water to splash the dog's muzzle as though impatient to be swallowed. Then the animal raised its head and turned it slowly to survey the woods in an entirely uncanine fashion. I found I couldn't breathe until it finished and plunged its entire face into the stream for another drink. I wanted to intervene somehow, but I hadn't moved when the dog backed away and trotted along the path, swinging its head from side to side with great deliberation. "It's the water," Tim whispered.

"Well, don't you try," I said more loudly, feeling too much like our mother.

"Who's going to stop me?"

"It's poisoned, don't you realise? Do you want to kill yourself?"

"Maybe."

Though I didn't believe him, his saying it dismayed me. I was wondering if I would have to fight him to keep him from drinking the water, and how I would explain any injuries to our mother, when he cycled off at speed. I almost screamed at him to wait until I realised from the way he was peering about that he wanted to observe the dog's behaviour. I would have helped him find it if it kept him clear of the stream. I cycled after him as fast as I dared, but there was no sign of the animal, either on the main route or on the paths that wound under the trees, not to mention those that crossed the stream. Eventually Tim scowled at me as if I'd chased the dog away, and then he sped home.

Neither of us had anything to tell our mother. I hid from her questions in my room and gazed from my window at the furtive obscure movements of the woods. What was ranging about under the trees as if searching for prey? Was it the dog? If I captured it I could take it to someone for examination, and then they would warn everyone about the water. I could save Tim.

The next day was Saturday. While our mother took him shopping for new shoes to replace a pair he'd trodden holes in, I found a length of old clothesline in the back yard and hurried down to the woods. I walked every path, some of them more than once at least, but couldn't see or hear the dog. I was trudging back to the tunnel when I heard something less than footsteps descending a side path towards me. Once I saw that the cause of the thin relentless sound was the stick an old man was clutching, I had to cover a nervous laugh.

He grabbed the back of a bench overgrown with initials so as to poke his stick at me. "You'll never catch them with a rope."

Politeness required me to ask "What?"

He hobbled around the bench, pivoting on his gnarled fist, and lowered himself to sit. "Dray's the name. Yours?"

I felt as if I was being set a test. "Philip."

As he lifted his long face his neck stretched so thin that it looked barely capable of supporting his pale puffy head. "Weren't you the lad that was going on about skeletons?"

"That was my brother." In defence of Tim I added "He was just making up stories."

"You don't make things like that up."

I couldn't tell if this was a statement or a warning. "Why not?"

"They're underneath everything. They're under us now. Don't they teach you anything at school any more?"

I managed not to resent this, because I thought I could impress him. "You mean fossils and all that? I know about those."

"Well, give him a trophy. I'll bet you don't know nothing wants to be dead. It wants to be more alive, just in another way. Some things get together and help each other to be. And telling stories like that does."

By now I was lost. I wasn't even sure if he meant Tim's stories or this one. As I tried to make out what his face would have looked like with less of a profusion of flesh he said "So what were you chasing after?"

"Have you seen a dog? I think it's drugged."

"Good God, things just keep getting worse. Who did it? You or your brother?"

"We wouldn't ever," I protested loud enough to send some eavesdropper and its lanky shadow scuttling away behind the bushes. "It's the stream. Some kind of drug has got into it."

Did I imagine that I could call on him to deal with this because he was an adult? I didn't want to trouble my mother. His response wasn't encouraging, however. "That's all it needs."

I was too nervous for politeness now. "What are you talking about?"

"If it's like that on the surface it'll reach down. There are things that haven't even been alive yet. It'll dredge up worse."

I was more than sorry to have asked. I would have retreated except for the need to learn. "So did you see the dog?"

"I didn't, son. I've seen nothing you'd like to see." I was afraid he might expand on this until he said "I used to live round here, you know. It's all changed. I can't even find my home."

"You still live here, honestly. Keep looking and you'll

find it." I couldn't take him—I was already responsible for Tim. I hurried away, and when I returned through the tunnel Mr Dray had gone. I never found the dog either, just as I haven't found the den, and now I wonder if that's on the far side of the tunnel.

I mustn't be nervous of going through. There never was a reason. I push myself up off the bench and do my best to stride along the path, which has begun to resemble a trail of mist. Has it always followed the course of the stream so closely? Except for the substance I could imagine they're identical. The water glows as whitely as the sky that trickles between the entangled branches, so that I feel in danger of forgetting which is reflecting which. I'm almost glad when the darkness grows more solid between the trees ahead.

It's the railway embankment. For a few yards I can distinguish the glistening outlines of bricks arched over the stream and the path, and then there appears to be blackness for hundreds of feet, leading to the huddle of tree-trunks framed by the end of the tunnel. I don't need to see in order to walk through, even if the path is slippery with mud. The trouble is rather that as I pick my way I'm more able to discern it than I ought to be. It's as though the stream is carrying the moonlight through the tunnel, but if the water's luminous that might be worse. Can I really see ripples settling into stillness beside me in the middle of the tunnel before they come back to life some yards further on? How can any of this be possible? I'm halted by the notion that something is about to rear up out of the stagnant stretch of water, unless the water itself is preparing to leap at me. That's the kind of thing Tim would have imagined, and perhaps Mr Dray as well. The thought releases me, and I flounder and skid to the end of the tunnel.

The bare trees open out to the sky above the stream. Between the branches that overtop the banks of the valley, a very few windows are lit. I can tell by their smallness that they belong to the new houses, and now I remember another time I did. It was the night I found Tim with a girl in our den.

He'd stopped smoking, as far as I could establish, which only aggravated my unease. What might he be doing to himself now? He often didn't speak for hours, and avoided me whenever he could. Although I disliked resenting how his state didn't affect his schoolwork, mine was suffering from my anxiety for him. Perhaps our mother was aware of some of this, because eventually she asked "Is everything all right between you two?"

We were sitting in the kitchen with the fluorescent tube glaring down at the remains of that night's burgers from the Turkish fish and chip shop. Tim barely even shrugged, but I thought the twitch of his shoulders looked nervous. The best I could manage and try to believe in was "We're still us."

"I hope so." She let her gaze trail over me and then Tim as she drained another glass of wine from the box. "I see enough bad things at work. I don't want to come home to them."

When Tim sat up out of his crouch I was afraid his interest had been caught too well. Was he thinking there were better things to see and how to do so? Suppose he hinted or more than implied as much? My head was throbbing with the search for some remark that would forestall his when he shoved his chair backwards. "I'm going out," he muttered.

"Oh, where are you going now? What did I say?"

All at once I'd had enough—too much to be careful any longer. "That's right, Tim, where are you going? Why don't you say for once?"

He didn't bother looking at either of us. "I told you, out," he said and almost immediately was.

As the front door slammed I dashed into the front room, nearly tripping over his computer magazines strewn beside an armchair, and saw him making for the woods. Once his head dropped below the brink of the path I picked up a wineglass from the couch in front of the television and carried it to the kitchen. Perhaps I hoped the gesture would satisfy my mother in some way, but she was waiting with a question. "Do you think it's a girl?"

"I don't know," I said and tried to concentrate on clearing the table. I dealt with the washing-up as swiftly as I could, striving not to let her glimpse my concern for Tim. At least he wasn't cycling, and so I hoped he hadn't gone too far for me to find him. "I'll go out for a bit," I said.

"A bit of what, Philip?" Her smile couldn't keep up its slyness or even its shape. "Why don't you find yourself a girl too? I wouldn't mind."

I hurried out as much to escape her insistence as to discover the reason for Tim's eagerness. I'd followed the path beside the stream so frequently that by now it felt like a connection in my brain. I tried just to walk and ignore the surroundings. I tiptoed through the tunnel, and as I left the scrabbling of echoes behind I saw lit windows above the trees. They let me feel less apprehensive until I heard Tim's voice.

I don't know how far I'd walked—perhaps farther from the tunnel than I have now. I sit on a bench anyway and close my eyes so as not to watch the stream groping at the darkness with its reeds, because it feels as though they're reaching to snag my mind. At first it seemed that the bony tangles of branches were muttering. "I made them up," Tim was saying. "Skeletons are for kids."

I'd begun to wonder if he was talking to himself when a voice so high it reminded me of how mine still leapt an octave said "So why do you still call them Skeleton Woods?"

"That's what they are. The skeletons are everything that's here. Ordinary people just see them. When you know that's all they are you can start to see the rest. You're not just a skeleton, are you? Neither is this place."

I hoped the silence denoted boredom, but then the girl spoke. I heard admiration and apprehensive eagerness.

"What do you see?"

I couldn't stand any more. I shouted into the bushes "Never mind what. Why are you seeing things, Tim? What have you been doing to yourself now?"

I thought I'd shocked him into some kind of awareness until they both laughed. "Is that him?" the girl said.

"That's him all right. Big fat Phil. Phil the mummy's boy. Doesn't dare do anything she wouldn't like him to, or maybe that's what he wants her to think. Wonder what he does to himself when he's in his room with nobody to see."

"Nothing," I shouted and tried to part the branches, but they were as immovable as ribs, between which the darkness allowed me no view. "I can see you," I lied. "Stop that now."

I heard a kiss that suggested the darkness had developed soft wet flesh. Once his mouth was free Tim said "He's mad because he thinks this is his place."

"I found it," I declared and dealt the roots a kick that shook the bushes, rattling twig after twig.

"It was here first. You didn't make it anything."

"I thought I made it ours."

"Well, it isn't any more," Tim said and scrambled out so fast I thought he was going to attack my ankles like a dog. "So piss off and play somewhere else."

"I'm not playing, you are." Perhaps that was his worst betrayal, to dismiss my concern like that. "He's always made things up," I called into the bushes. "They're just like the stories he used to tell when he started school. He likes people thinking he's got more imagination than them, that's all. It's rubbish, everything he told you. There were never skeletons here and there aren't now."

By now Tim was on his feet. He brought his face so close to mine I saw his eyes glitter like coal. "You'll see," he said.

"Keep people like that out of there in future."

When I heard his companion crawling towards us I retreated alongside the stream; I didn't want a confrontation with anyone else. I lingered at a bend in the path long enough to watch the two of them vanish into the dark towards the new houses. I considered following them to learn what else they did, but I felt I'd done enough for one night. I was in bed before I wondered what exactly Tim had meant by "You'll see."

Did he plan to make me if I wasn't careful? I didn't want to think so. Perhaps he was trying to work on my nerves by passing me drinks at dinner—glasses of water from the tap. At first I told him I could fetch them myself, and then not to bother, and eventually just not to. Once I knocked over a glass he'd insisted on filling, and our mother burst into tears. He took that as an excuse to leave, and by the time I'd calmed her down and assured her that nothing was really wrong I couldn't find him when I went out to check on him.

We were at a new school now. Tim had taken to its size at once, and soon to the ways the girls were also bigger. At least it didn't involve passing through the woods. Instead I tailed him along the edge of the new estate. Sometimes he lost me, but after the night I caught him with the girl in the den I succeeded in observing him several times with one, presumably the same girl. In the schoolyard he had to share her with her giggling friends, but I saw them walk to school together more than once. The last time I overtook them and was able to watch them arguing. When they noticed me the disagreement grew fiercer, and they hurried off before I could hear what they were saying. It must have come to an unpleasant end, because when I asked Tim that night why he was walking home alone he gave me a look bordering on hatred. "Because I am," he said.

I wasn't sure this meant he'd finished with the girl. Whenever he went out at night I couldn't find him, even if I was cycling while he was on foot. Eventually I couldn't stand it, and waited for him outside the front door after dinner. "What are you up to now?" I murmured.

"Only one way to find out. Still want to see?"

"You aren't frightening me, Tim. There's nothing to be frightened of."

"Come on then, if you can keep up," he said so fiercely I felt his words condense like mist on my face.

When he dodged I thought he meant to run into the woods. Instead he hurried around the side of the house, and I was afraid he'd brought something too close to home. He was only collecting his bicycle. As I sprinted across the yard to mine our mother cried from somewhere inside the house "Can't you stay in with me for once?"

Tim glared at me as if I was to blame, and then he cycled fast around the building. I was about to follow when I realised that in the confusion, if indeed he was confused, he'd taken my latest bicycle and left its predecessor. For years that one had been too small for me, but I mustn't let him elude me. I squatted on it as best I could and wobbled alongside the house towards the woods.

I nearly lost my balance as the front wheel jerked downwards beneath the arch. Descending the steps felt like cycling over a giant's ribcage almost buried in the earth. Even when I reached the level path I couldn't help veering back and forth on it. Twigs clawed at my splayed knees while tree-trunks lurched at me as if they were bent on clubbing my skull. I might have abandoned the chase if I hadn't been able to hear Tim.

I heard my bicycle rattling along the path before it set up echoes in the tunnel. I could have imagined they'd barely ceased when I arrived at the downturned mouth. As soon as I rode in, the clacking of my pedals was multiplied by chattering in the blackness. No wonder I was so distracted that halfway through I strayed off the slippery path into the shallow water. I almost sprawled headlong on the path as I dragged the bicycle free of the stream. "Tim," I yelled furiously, but the only response was my own voice.

I righted the bicycle and pedalled awkwardly out of the tunnel. Even once I emerged from beneath the twitching of faint ripples on the bricks, I felt as though the stream was clinging to my feet and ankles. I did my best to shake off the chill as it seeped up through me while I tried to speed along the path. Then my flailing legs snatched both feet off the pedals, and as I struggled to regain control the machine toppled over.

At least I didn't fall on the hard path or in the water. I ended up with one leg under the bicycle on the damp grassy bank of the stream. As the clicking of the rear wheel wound down I saw that I was opposite the den. I was almost certain that I'd heard another noise—a stealthy creak among the bushes. I opened my mouth to shout at Tim, but instead I lifted the bicycle and used it to lever myself to my feet before laying it down again. I could be as sly as Tim if I had to be. I tiptoed swiftly onto the side path and dropped to all fours on the grass. Crawling into the den, I felt as if I'd won a game of hide and seek. "Tim," I said triumphantly, and looked up.

I couldn't see much, either despite or because of the pallor of the fallen leaves, but I knew at once that the figure craning down towards me wasn't Tim. For an instant I thought it was Mr Dray—thought I heard the scraping of his stick over the scattered twigs. His condition must have worsened, since he had more than one stick now; indeed, he sounded built out of them. He creaked and rattled closer, so that I glimpsed dimness through more than one gap in the looming mass of his head, and I scrabbled backwards out of the den.

I was floundering to my feet when I heard a commotion among the bushes. Whatever was in there sounded impatient to claw its way out, unless the figure Tim had cobbled together from bits of the woods in an attempt to impress me had collapsed against the branches. By the time I managed to conclude the latter, I'd staggered away from the den. "It didn't work," I called, and then I saw his bicycle lying beside the stream—my bicycle, that was.

Where was the one I'd ridden? How far had I blundered before I could stop? All that seemed to matter was that

Tim had to be nearby. I sensed that I was being watched. "Tim," I called and heard a surreptitious movement somewhere close. It wasn't among the huddles of bushes or in the gloomy labyrinth of trees; it was just the whisper of ripples around two small whitish rocks in the middle of the stream. In the moonlight they looked more than weathered. They looked—I searched for the word and grew dizzy with alarm as it came to me—scuffed. They were the toes of a pair of trainers, which led my gaze to the faint shape of a body in the stream.

"Tim," I cried and ran to the edge. The water was coated with moonlight, which virtually blotted out the figure lying on its back. I threw myself flat on the soaked grass and reached for its hands, but I couldn't find them in the unexpected depths. I was confused by an impression that the face was somehow wrong, though I couldn't distinguish its features, until I realised it must be upside down. I rolled up my sleeves and plunged my hands deeper but still found nothing to grasp. In desperation I lurched forward on the bank to immerse my arms all the way to the shoulders, and my head sank underwater.

A face rose to meet mine, but it wasn't Tim's face. It was too large, and luminous with moonlight or of itself. Its eroded piebald features reminded me of the moon too, except that they were blurred by an excess of flesh. I had a sudden suffocating notion that the figure I'd glimpsed in the den had swum or drifted to find me while putting on flesh. A drowned voice seemed to fill my ears. "Now you'll see," I thought it said. I was terrified that whatever the shape had for hands were about to seize mine and drag me into the impossible depths. I snatched my arms clear of the water and dug my fingers into the earth to haul myself away from the stream.

As I staggered to my feet and stumbled backwards onto the path I noticed that the objects poking up from the stream were only rocks whitened by lichen, and that's all I want to remember just now. Why did I come down here? I grip the bench, which feels spongy as a fungus, and stand up. When I hauled my face out of the water my surroundings appeared to have grown brighter—as bright as they've become. That's because my vision is feasting on the moonlight, and wasn't it then? All that matters is that there was nothing under the water or anywhere else, then or now. I simply want to leave because I've no reason to be here. I'm beginning to find the place oppressive, even the scent that looms out of the shadows. I plant one hand over my mouth and nose as I tramp along the twisting path.

The scent seeps between my fingers. It puts me in mind of an old woman's perfume in which she has doused her entire body to disguise the smell of burgeoning flesh. It's threatening to make me dizzy, which is why I'm confused by a movement in or on the stream. Either the insect was skimming the surface before I was aware of it or it has emerged from the water. It must be a kind of dragonfly, even if it's white as ice, with wings like traceries of crystal. It glides in my direction, and I lean towards it. So does a growth at the edge of the stream, a flower like puckered white lips on a stick. The plump wrinkled lips gape wide and close around the fly, and I seem to hear the faint fragile crunch of its wings as the swollen stem works throatily. Then I dash away along the path for fear of hearing the lips speak.

The scent keeps up with me. Perhaps it belongs to the flowers that pout at me alongside the stream, or perhaps the spiders in their cut-glass webs that span the bushes are exuding it. As I try not to watch, the spiders blossom, their luminous white bodies efflorescing with filaments and scaly petals while every leg twitches its web in such unison it might be a message. A chalky bird flaps out of a tree, and I hope I may be able to look at it instead, until I realise that although it's flying away above the stream, it's growing no smaller in my eyes, which has to mean that it's expanding with each beat of its wings. The trees are flexing their branches, drawing white flesh down from the bloated sky, slipping it on like fat gloves. I try to ignore the sight of the glowing tree-trunks as they writhe and gesture me towards them. I have to run in that direction, but only to pass them. I'll be safe as long as I stay on the path. Surely I'm not really feeling it stir like a cocoon about to crack open. At least nothing to either side of it can reach me if I keep to the middle—and then I hear something that can. There are footsteps ahead, around a bend in the path.

They're heavy and deliberate. They're coming for me. I know that before a voice calls my name. I stare about wildly, but there's nowhere to hide; even the shade under the trees is as bright as the clouds. Besides, I don't think I could bear treading on the restless white pelt that was the grass, never mind approaching the bushes that crouch forward to peer at me from beneath their pallid swollen convoluted fleshy scalps. I spin around again and almost fall against a tree, which is still trying to lure me with sinuous movements, although I can see it's old and cracked and scabby. Then the voice calls out again, too close. "Philip. Philip Dray," it insists, and the speaker strides into view.

For as long as he stands gazing at me I'm sure he's a total stranger. When he takes another step I realise that, despite the uniform, he's Tim. The recognition seems to bare everything at me—the litter caught in the broken trees, the avalanches of household rubbish on the slopes below the new estate, the objects like long whitish flattened glistening fingers under the bushes, a rusty bicycle in the stream. Perhaps the clump of splintered bushes beside us is the den, its branches charred, the ground beneath it glittering with syringes and glass. Is all this the skeleton? If that's the case, I don't want to know about it; I'd even rather listen to Tim. "Come on, old fellow," he says. "Let's get you home."

I'm not about to tell him I've forgotten where it is. I wait for him to take my arm and lead me along the path. I need some distraction from everything I won't look at, and so I say "How's mother?"

He doesn't answer until we're past the bend and I see the steps up to the road. "It all got too much for her, Phil," he says and seems to wonder if he should say any more. "She's gone. It was a long time ago."

I don't think his gaze is accusing me. It looks more like suppressed pity, but I don't want either. As he ushers me far enough to see his police car at the top of the steps I retort "You were the one who took drugs, you know. I don't care how you've changed."

He turns his eyes away from me. I don't know what they're withholding, and I'd rather not. I focus my attention on the path, and then I grin to myself so fiercely I can feel it hiding from him under my face. I'm looking at our shadows, and I see what he can't have noticed. At last I understand the real name of the place. He's holding me by the gap between the bones of my arm.

Need

Gary A. Braunbeck

To the attendants on the ward at the nursing home
where she will die quietly in her sleep,
Edna Warner will always be known
as the Where's-the-Beef? Lady.

"One can go for years sometimes without living at all, and then all life comes crowding into one single hour."

—Oscar Wilde, *Vera, or The Nihilists*

The letter, written on official department stationary, tumbles across the autumn sidewalk, skimming the surface of a puddle (soaking only the middle of the page, smearing certain portions of certain words) before the wind propels it against the base of a lamp post where it flutters, trapped, neither the wind nor the puddle nor the letter aware of their part if this brief mosaic nature is forming to amuse itself. A nearby rat, searching for nest material, sits up on its hind legs and regards the paper, then slowly moves toward it. The rat doesn't care about the needs of wind or paper, it is not aware of its own determined part in this mosaic, it only cares about its own need; for which this sheet of paper will do very nicely . . .

"I've got a special dessert for you guys tonight."

The two children look at each other and smile. It's been a long time since they've had a meal this good—hot beef tacos and now Mom says she's got a "special" dessert.

When the children don't say anything, their mother shakes her head and laughs. Now the children are very excited—Mom hasn't laughed in a long, long time.

"Well," she says to her son and daughter. "Aren't you even going to ask?"

"What're we having?" says the little girl.

Mom leans back in her chair and folds her arms across her chest, then looks at the ceiling. "Oh, Jeez, I don't know if I'm going to tell you or not, seeing as how you weren't interested enough to ask me in the first place."

The children give out with groans of disappointment and frustration—groans they both know Mom is expecting—and their mom laughs again.

"Okay," she says, leaning forward and gesturing for them to lean closer.

Mom whispers—like it's some kind of a big secret—"Chocolate mousse."

"Chocolate mousse!" they both shriek, delighted. This is their absolute, hands-down, no-question-about-it favorite dessert in the whole wide world.

"But only," adds Mom, "if you guys have another taco."

The children tell her how much they love her, grab up another tortilla, and spoon them full of the sliced beef for the tacos.

. . . now Charlie's going on and on about how no decent woman would whore herself out like that because that's what it amounted to and how that spineless scumbag was more concerned about his parents' money than he was about being a man and owning up to responsibilities so as far as he's concerned you don't talk about it with him, not ever, and Henrietta nods her head and smiles at him but not too widely, too wide a smile and he might think she's humoring him (which she is but mustn't let him know it) and get even angrier, and Charlie, you never have to do or say much to get him started on one of his rants, like today, all it took was Henrietta's letting slip with a mention of "the whore's" name (Charlie only calls her that, "the whore") and off he went, asking how could she still *talk* to that whore every week, and he was still going on, so Henrietta nods again and waits for him to storm over to the other side of the room (Charlie likes to cover a lot of ground while he's ranting), and when he does, when he heads toward the other side of the living room, Henrietta sits forward to look like she's really paying attention, like she's really interested, and as she does she slips one of her hands down into the space between the sofa cushions because just maybe Charlie or she lost some change down there, and it won't kill her, walking to the Bridge Club meetings instead of taking the bus for a week, she could use the exercise and at least the weather's been nice and as Charlie turns to make his way back her fingertips brush across the surface of something that might be a couple of quarters, so she continues smiling (but not too widely) and nodding her head because as long as Charlie makes eye contact he won't be paying any attention to her hand . . .

Inter-Office Memo
From: Paul Gallagher, Principal

Darlene:

I know you meant well, I really do, but several of the other teachers have expressed concern to me over your actions during 2nd Grade Class pictures last Tuesday. You did not have permission to take that girl off school grounds, let alone to the mall. We have a lot of children from poor and disadvantaged homes in this school, and anything that even remotely smacks of favoritism is frowned upon, not only by myself and the other teachers, but the School Board as well. Your actions—caring though they might have been—can be looked upon as "playing favorites". It is not our responsibility to make sure the poorer students have decent clothes to wear for their class pictures, and it is certainly not your responsibility to buy them (though I've seen the pictures, and the little girl looks like an angel).

In the future, please keep your more dramatic humanitarian impulses in check. You're new here, and I'm sure you'll learn how things are done in due time.

Albert Morse sits on the front porch of his house on Euclid Avenue. He's enjoying the warm weather and thinking that he needs to trim the hedges this weekend. Just because the house isn't in the best neighborhood is no excuse to let it all go to hell. The house is paid for, and Albert takes a lot of pride in that. He and Georgia have made themselves a nice home here, one that the kids and the grandchildren love visiting. At the end of the day, what more could a man ask for? Work your whole life away on the factory line, retire with a good pension and good insurance, own your own home, have the family over for dinner and holidays.

Why the city decided to build those goddamned government-subsidized apartments across the street was a mystery to him, and an even bigger pain in the ass some days. Not a day goes by when someone who lives on Welfare Row doesn't drag their business out into the street.

Like now, for instance; that young girl at the row of mailboxes, screaming "*Fuck!*" over and over again because of something she just read in a letter. Can't take your drama inside, no; you've got to play it out here in front of God and everybody like your problems are so much bigger and more important and painful than everybody else's.

Albert watches as the young woman continues screaming "*Fuck!*" over and over, louder and louder, until finally she breaks down into violent, wracking sobs. She wipes her arm across her eyes, shakes some hair from her face, reads the letter again, and then just tosses it away before starting in with the "*Fuck!*" and the sobbing again, right there in the middle of the damn sidewalk. She continues screaming and sobbing until a school bus stops at the corner; as soon as she sees this, she turns around, pulls some tissues from her pocket, wipes her face and nose, and turns around, puffy-eyed and smiling as a little boy and girl run from the bus to her side. She kneels down and hugs them, then holds their hands as they make their way back inside, behind closed doors, where any decent human being damned well ought to keep their troubles.

Georgia comes out and hands Albert a glass of fresh iced tea. "Just got off the phone with Cal. He and Rhonda are bringing the kids over for dinner Friday night. Cal says he wants to take us all out to see the new Disney movie."

"That sounds like fun," says Albert, taking the iced tea but staring at the letter the young woman had tossed away.

"What was all that racket a minute ago?" asks Georgia.

"Some gal over there," replies Albert, nodding toward Welfare Row. "I swear, honey, some of *trash* they allow to live there . . ."

"Don't get yourself worked up," says Georgia. "You don't need to go and get all upset about the way they act."

Albert shakes his head. "It just . . . it just makes this seem like such a rotten place to live, and it isn't, you know? Or it *shouldn't* be." He discovers that he can no longer see the letter; the wind must have blown it somewhere. "I swear, the *trash* . . ."

"I tried so *very hard*," says the drunk as he's escorted from the bar by Sheriff Ted Jackson, who's been through this routine enough to know that this particular drunk doesn't require handcuffs.

"I *tried*, I really did," says the drunk.

"I know you did," replies the sheriff, as he always does. He looks over his shoulder and sees Jack Walters, owner and proprietor of the Wagon Wheel Bar & Grille, standing in the doorway, shaking his head in pity. Jackson nods to him that everything is all right, just business as usual, and Walters gives the sheriff a mock salute before turning around and going back inside.

The drunk stumbles, almost falling, but catches himself on the trunk of Jackson's car. "It wasn't my fault. It wasn't." He reaches out and grabs Jackson's collar. "You know that, right, Sheriff? You know that it wasn't my fault."

Jackson removes the drunk's hand from his collar, and gently guides him into the back seat. "You need to sleep it off, Randall. We've got your usual bed ready, and in the morning, we'll get you fixed up with a nice, hot breakfast, okay?"

"Nobody calls me that," says the drunk. "I mean, she used to, once . . . like it was a pet name, you know? But nobody calls me 'Randall.' I always hated that name. I should have said something once I was goddamn old enough. Fuckin' sissy-assed name like that." He curls up into a fetal position on the back seat and begins sobbing. "I should've said something about that. I . . . I should've done a lot of things, you know? If I'd've stood up to my folks, then maybe . . ." He leans over the seat and vomits into the plastic bucket Jackson had put there earlier, in anticipation of the usual pattern. Once he finishes vomiting, he wipes his mouth, sits up, and hands the bucket to Jackson, who empties it in the gutter.

"I'm gonna quite wasting my time and get on with my life," says the drunk.

"I know you are," replies Jackson, as he always does, as he always has every few weeks for the last couple of years after Walters calls to say, "Same old song and dance, my friend."

Jackson closes the door, stuffs the bucket into a plastic trash bag, then, as always, tosses it into the trunk of the cruiser, thinking as he does that all the money in the world —and God knows that the drunk's got enough money, having inherited it from his parents—can't do a damn thing to make the nights less lonely.

From the back seat the drunk's sobbing grows louder

and more violent; the spasms wracking his body shake the entire cruiser, and Jackson cannot help but feel a morbid kind of awe. While there is the usual excess of self-pity in this puking, slobbering booze hound, there's also a depth of genuine anguish that Jackson cannot ignore—which is, he supposes, why people put up with this sort of behavior from the drunk.

There is some grief you never recover from.

to inf— you that, up— —iew, the Cedar Hill Dep—ent of Health and H—an

Having completed the required six weeks of training, this Wednesday is Daniel's first night working the Cedar Hill Crisis Center phone lines without backup. It is a little before eight p.m. when his phone rings for the first time. Taking a deep breath, he answers, and after identifying himself and telling the caller whom they have reached, listens as the voice on the other end says: "How can you go on living when all there is to look forward to is more yearning?"

The caller hangs up before Daniel can say anything.

He notes the time in his log, and in parentheses adds: *probable crank call.*

Still, the question finds him again, as it will continue to do over the course of the otherwise uneventful evening, as well as a few mornings later when he happens upon the article and photos on Page Two of *The Ally*; it comes back to him again and again as it will for the rest of his life, never leaving him, never losing him, no matter how much he tries to hide from it.

Detective Bill Emerson stares at the stack of mail on his desk, none of which is addressed to either him or anyone else at the Cedar Hill Police Department. There's the usual monthly detritus you expect to find in the mail—phone bill, gas bill, electric bill—only all of these envelopes are emblazoned with the words **Final Notice** stamped in bright red ink.

Emerson cracks his knuckles, then runs a hand through his thick gray hair, noting that he needs to get a trim. Between his bushy hair and equally bushy mustache, it's no wonder some of the other officers call him "Captain Kangaroo" when they think he can't hear them.

He riffles through the mail once again, tossing the bills to the left, the junk mail to the right, and everything else in the center. He's been doing this off and on for the last two days, his variation on walking a labyrinth for the purpose of meditating on a problem, and, as always, he comes back to the business-sized brown envelope that weighs more than all the rest and has way too much postage on it.

They should have used Priority, he thinks. *Four bucks and it's there in two to three days.*

He checks the postmark date against the report. Five days. Even with all the extra postage, it had taken this letter five days to reach its addressee. If they had used Priority, it would have only taken three to four, and that might have made all the difference in the world.

He drops the letter on top of the center stack, unconsciously wincing at the muffled *thump!* it makes when it lands, and stares at it.

He's still staring a few minutes later when his partner, Ben Littlejohn, comes in with dinner in the form of four cheeseburgers and two orders of fries from the Sparta. It smells great—the Sparta makes the best cheeseburgers in the free world, period—and Emerson looks up as Littlejohn sets the food on the corner of the desk.

"Still haven't opened it?" he asks Emerson.

"And your first clue was . . . ?"

Littlejohn wags a single finger back and forth. "Ah-ah, save the snappy banter for the rookies, not me." Littlejohn looks at his partner for a long moment, then says, his voice softer: "You want me to do it?"

"No. I was first on the scene, I found it. It should be me."

Littlejohn parks his ass on the edge of Emerson's desk and starts removing the cheeseburgers from the bag. "So . . . *when* are you and Eunice going to take that vacation she's bugging you about?"

"To London? Don't start, I'm warning you. She has talked about nothing *but* going there since she saw that damn *Notting Hill* movie. I rue the day Julia Roberts and Hugh Grant were born, because it set into motion the events that would lead to the making of that movie. My life has been endless misery since. Did you know they serve their beer room temperature there? Can you imagine that? No wonder we broke from the Crown."

"Uh-huh. Open the goddamn thing already, will you?"

Emerson picks up the brown envelope, noting again its weight, then looks at his partner. "You're a radiantly compassionate fellow, you know that?"

"I'm an intensely *hungry* fellow who's not going to be able to enjoy his dinner until whatever's in that envelope is out of our lives, and since that isn't going to be anytime soon—seeing as how you've put off opening it for almost two full work days—I'll settle for our knowing its contents."

"You should have seen it," whispers Emerson.

Littlejohn leans forward, rapping his knuckles on the desk to break Emerson's morbid reverie. "I *did* see it, Bill. I was only two minutes behind you."

"I know that, I'm not completely dim." He taps the envelope against his hand in a soft, steady tattoo that after only a few seconds annoys even him, but he doesn't stop. "Have you ever heard of something called 'The Observer Effect'?"

"That's a physics term, right?"

Emerson nods his head. "If I understand it correctly—Einsteinian whiz-kid that I am—it says that a person can change an event just by being there to watch it. They don't have to take any kind of physical action or what we think of as active participation, just *being there* changes it."

Littlejohn's expression grows concerned, albeit cautiously. "Okay . . .?"

"It was *different* after you came in. When it was just me, there was a . . . I don't know . . . almost a *peacefulness* there for a few seconds. But then you came in, and I saw your face and you saw mine and when we looked at it again, it was just . . . ugly and pathetic and sad." Emerson feels that last word fall from his mouth and land at his feet like a dead bird dropping from the sky.

"Bill," says Littlejohn, "I'm asking you now as your friend, not your partner, okay? I'm asking you to please, for everyone's sake, open it."

Not taking his stare from the cheeseburger bag, Emerson picks up the letter opener, slips it under the flap of the envelope (Scotch-taped, three times), slashes open the top, and removes the two sheets of paper inside.

The first sheet is blank, a twenty-pound standard weight of recycled typing paper that has been used to make sure someone couldn't hold the envelope up to the light and discern its contents.

You used a brown *envelope; no one could have seen through this, anyway.*

Unfolding the second sheet, he watches as the bills tumble down on the desk: two twenties, a ten, a five, and three ones. He reaches down with his other hand and arranges the bills side by side.

He looks at the letter, reads what it says—words written in a slow, unsteady hand (*probably arthritis*, he thinks; *a lot of older folks have trouble with that and can't write as neatly or steadily as they used to*)—but it's not the words that cause his throat to tighten, though they are bad enough, no; it's the two quarters, three dimes, one nickel, and four pennies that are taped across the bottom of the page (three pieces of Scotch tape, just like the envelope).

He blinks, pulls in a breath that is heavier and thicker than it ought to be, and hands the sheet to his partner.

"Fifty-eight dollars and eighty-nine cents," he says. "Who the hell sends someone fifty-eight dollars and eighty-nine cents? *Eighty-nine cents?* Why not just make it sixty dollars even?"

Before Littlejohn has a chance to finish reading the letter or respond to the question, Emerson speaks again:

"I'll *tell* you who sends someone fifty-eight dollars and eighty-nine cents, someone who only *has* fifty-eight dollars and eighty-nine cents. Someone who has to go through their purse or wallet, and then the pockets of their coat—hell, they probably even pulled the cushions off the sofa to see if any loose change had fallen down there, just to make sure they could send every *penny* they possibly could. *Anybody* could send you sixty bucks, but only . . . only someone who *cared* enough to scrape together all the money they possibly could would send you fifty-eight dollars and eighty-nine cents."

He realizes that he is almost on the verge of tears but doesn't care. "*Eighty-nine cents!* I'll bet that old woman had to walk to the store instead of taking the bus to make sure she could get that eighty-nine cents in there. Jesus H. Christ, Ben—*why* didn't she use Priority? That might have made all the difference in the world!" Emerson presses the heels of his hands against his eyes, takes a deep breath, then releases it slowly before wiping his eyes and lowering his hands, which aren't shaking nearly as much as he feared they would be.

"That was very moving," says Littlejohn. "Look at me—I am visibly touched."

"I'm turning into an old woman, aren't I?"

"No, you're just maybe possibly arguably a little too you-should-pardon-the-expression human for this job sometimes."

"And my cheeseburgers are probably cold."

Littlejohn shook his head. "Nope. I had them wrap everything in heavy-duty aluminum foil, just in case we didn't get to the food right away."

"I really *am* predictable, aren't I?"

"Let's call it 'dependable' and remain friends, shall we?"

"You're too good to me."

"I get a lot of complaints about that."

Emerson unwraps the first cheeseburger, starts to bite into it, then pauses and says, "Why didn't she use Priority?"

It is a question that will find him again and again throughout the rest of his life, never losing him, even when he tries hiding from it.

Edna Warner stands in line at the grocery store and thinks to herself, *The damn meat's gonna start thawing if she takes any longer.*

The young woman in front of her is riffling through a small stack of food stamps. The cashier exchanges a quick, exasperated glance with Edna, one that says, *I'm really sorry, ma'am, but there's nothing I can do.* Edna smiles in understanding, though it's a forced smile. Why does it seem she *always* picks the slowest line in the store? Just her luck, getting stuck behind a welfare case who doesn't have the sense to have her food stamps out and ready.

She takes a tissue from her purse and blows her nose, quietly, as a courteous lady is supposed to do. *Why* she felt compelled to stick her head in the pet store earlier would probably always remain a mystery to her, but that puppy in the window had been so *cute.* It never occurred to her that the pet store would also have cats. Edna was severely allergic to cats, couldn't even be near someone who *owned* the terrible things because people who owned cats always had at least a *little* shed fur on their clothes, and that's all it took to make her allergies go crazy.

Luckily, that was a few hours ago, and she's had a chance to take some non-drowsy allergy medicine, so now she's feeling much better, for which she is grateful. The last thing she wants is to be all stopped-up and red-nosed when Joe gets home from work. He always says it's hard for him to eat at the same table with her when she's like that, eyes all puffy and nose running like it was trying to win some kind of race.

Sometimes, her Joe can be awfully high-maintenance.

Edna busies herself with looking over the headlines on the tabloids in the rack by the checkout lane; this star has gained weight, another one has entered Betty Ford, someone else is having an affair. It's actually quite funny, when you think about it, how these newspapers try to make stars' lives seem even more dramatic than the characters they play in the movies; as if splattering all their troubles on the front page will make them seem like regular folks. *We have problems just like the rest of you,* these stars' faces seem to say.

Sighing, Edna checks her watch and sees that she's been standing here for almost five minutes. The young woman in front of her hears Edna's sighing, and smiles at her in apology. Edna is at first embarrassed to have been found out, then struck by how sad the young woman's smile is and—*Lord!*—how tired she looks. There are dark crescents under the young woman's eyes that stand out against her pale skin and make her smile seem even more cheerless. For a moment, Edna almost feels bad for having drawn attention to the awkwardness of the situation—*the poor thing looks like she hasn't slept in days*—then thinks again of the pot roast in her cart and how she hopes it doesn't thaw too much before she can get it home and into the freezer. If it thaws too much, she'll have to make it tonight, and Joe wouldn't like that; it's only Thursday, and Joe likes to have pot roast on the weekend. Feed him a too-heavy meal during the week, and he complains about how it keeps him awake and feeling tired all the next day.

Still feeling the young woman's eyes on her, Edna busies herself with the contents of her vinyl coupon holder, making sure that all the ones she'll need are in front, ready to go so that the cashier can scan them without delay. When she's sure the young welfare woman is no longer looking at her, Edna sneaks a peek at what she is buying. Edna's father always used to say, *You can tell a lot about a person by the contents of their shopping cart*, and over the course of her fifty-six years, Edna has found a lot of truth in that observation.

So she looks.

There is a coloring book with a torn cover and a bottle of over-the-counter sleep aids (both of which the young woman pays for with a handful of singles and change from her pocket), six cans of cat food (sliced beef in gravy), a quart of milk, a box of instant pudding mix (chocolate mousse, actually), a packet of taco seasoning (mild), and some frozen tortillas (corn).

The first thing that crosses Edna's mind is that she's not sneezing.

The second thing that crosses Edna's mind as she stares at the items is a commercial from the nineteen-eighties with that old gal—what was her name? *Clara Peller, that's right!*—where three old ladies are looking at a hamburger that's mostly all bun and Clara Peller starts squawking, "*Where's* the beef?"

Edna doesn't know why that, of all things, crosses her mind at that moment, but Clara Peller's famous question will find her again, during dinner, as it will find her again and again, for the rest of her life, never losing her, even when Alzheimer's Disease begins fragmenting her mind in another seventeen years: to the attendants on the ward at the nursing home where she will die quietly in her sleep, Edna Warner will always be known as the Where's-the-Beef? Lady.

Serv—s has, aft— —deration of y— indiv—l case (#AB765-L7) deter—d

In the basement of St. Francis Church on Granville Street, the Monday night Alcoholics Anonymous meeting is winding down, and Chet Beckman—twelve years sober, known to his friends as "No-Skid" because he's got the best record of any bus driver for the Central Ohio Transit Authority—is adding an extra spoonful of sugar to his coffee when one of the other fellows in the group says, "Where's that guy who was here last week? That fellow whose family . . . oh, what was his name?"

"Randy," says Chet, sitting back down and stirring the creamer until the coffee takes on that soft golden color that means it's just right. "And they weren't his family except in his head, and my guess is he's down at the Wagon Wheel getting stewed to the gills."

The fellow who'd asked the question seems genuinely disappointed. "How can you *know* that?"

Chet sips his coffee and smiles; it tastes perfect. "I can know this because Randy comes in here about—what?—every three or four weeks after he's gone on a real bad binge, and sits there and says 'I'm gonna stop wasting my time and get on with my life.'" Chet takes another sip of his coffee. "He's been doing that for damn near two years, and the pattern never changes, no matter how many sponsors we sic on him or how many quit or how many he fires. Hell, *I* was his sponsor for a while, when it looked like he might actually get past what happened."

"It sounded to me like it wasn't his fault, hear him tell it."

"That's what he keeps telling us when he bothers to

show up. 'It wasn't my fault. It wasn't my fault.' You ask me, he keeps repeating that because he's hoping that if he says it enough, he'll start to believe it." Chet shrugs. "Hell, maybe that wouldn't be such a bad thing, you know? Him starting to believe it."

The fellow who'd asked about Randy leaned forward. "Sounds to me like maybe you don't agree it wasn't his fault."

Chet sits back in his chair and regards the other fellow carefully. It doesn't do to get tempers flaring at these meetings; a bad argument's all the excuse someone needs to fall off the wagon, and this other fellow, the one who asked about Randy, he's only been sober five weeks and has got that desperate, anxious way about him that says he can go either way in a heartbeat. The first six weeks are always the hardest, and that sixth week is always the killer. Half the people AA loses they lose during the sixth week of sobriety, so Chet considers his words very carefully as he replies.

"Did you see that news story the other night about that avalanche they had in Colorado? The one that killed them two skiers?"

The other fellow nods his head.

"See, here's the thing about assigning blame to anyone or anything," says Chet, taking another sip of his perfect, golden-hued coffee. "I kept wondering—I wonder about shit like this sometimes when I can't sleep—I kept wondering, what if the snow itself could think like we can? I mean, imagine that every snowflake in that avalanche was able to think. Do you suppose any one of them would feel responsible for those skiers dying, or would they just tell themselves 'It wasn't my fault'?"

The other man thinks on this for a moment, then shrugs. "I don't guess I see your point."

"So what's responsible for that?" asks Chet. "Is there any one word that I just said that's responsible for your not understanding me, or was it *all* the words?"

The other man shakes his head. "You're fucking with me now, aren't you?"

Chet shrugs, deciding that he's had enough coffee for tonight.

that —— no longer qual— for benefits as outli— under Oh— Co— —— and

"Would you look at *this?*" shouts Steve over the roar of the garbage truck's compactor.

His partner, Marty, pulls the wax plug out of his left ear and shouts back, "What?"

Steve points to the contents of one of the trash cans they're emptying along Welfare Row. "This one bag came open. Take a look at this."

Marty peers over the edge of the trash can, looks at Steve, then back down at the contents.

The compactor finishes chewing up the last batch of trash, and howls loudly as it moves back into place for the next load.

"Looks to me like somebody's got insomnia."

Steve shakes his head. "That's more than insomnia, bud. There must be—what?—a dozen empty bottles in here. Fuck, that's enough to knock out Godzilla for a week."

"Is there anything else in there? Anything that might be salvageable? A busted radio or something we could maybe hock?"

Steve rummages through the rest of the contents. "Nah, ain't got shit."

"I guess that DVD player yesterday was a fluke, huh?"

"We were in a better section of town."

"Oh."

They toss the contents into the back of the truck, toss

the cans back to the curb, and run to grab the next ones.

all mon— and oth— — of ——— —all be immediately discontinued. If you h—e

The rat finishes shredding the paper for its nest, not caring that a large section of it has been caught by the wind again and is tumbling its determined way toward another role in a different mosaic that nature will soon form because of the need to amuse itself. The rat carries away the last of the shreds, knowing now that its nest is complete, is warm, is safe.

"So . . . how was dessert?"

"It was really *good,*" say the children.

"It was different than last time," says the little boy. "It was kinda . . ."

". . . kinda *crunchy,*" says the little girl.

"Yeah," says the little boy. "Like there was sand in there. It made it a lot thicker."

Their mother brushes some hair from their faces. "But it was good, wasn't it?"

"Oh, yeah!" they cry in unison. "It was yummy. And we at it *all!*"

"We sure did," says their mother.

"And you made so much of it!" says the little girl, laughing and yawning at the same time. "You never eat dessert when we have it. You're always saying . . . oh, what do you say?"

"That chocolate goes right to her hips," says the little boy, who's also laughing and yawning at the same time.

Their mother laughs, as well. "Well . . . tonight was special."

". . . sure was," says the little girl, fighting to keep her eyes open.

"That was the best dinner yet," says the little boy.

She kisses them both on the forehead, then the cheek, then hugs them and tucks them in for the night. She turns off the lights and sits on the floor between their beds, her right hand stroking her daughter's cheek, her left hand touching her son's shoulder.

She remains like that until they are both asleep.

She lowers her head and pulls in a deep, wet breath, then listens to their breathing.

She sees the coloring book lying on the floor at the foot of her daughter's bed. The two of them had been coloring in the pictures. They hadn't finished the last one.

It looked very nice. They played well together. They were each other's bestest friend.

They had loved the coloring book.

She listens to their breathing as she studies the colors, how well both of them stayed within the lines.

Later, she goes into the bathroom and runs hot water into the tub, lights a candle, unfolds the plastic bag, and measures out the duct tape.

"Goodnight," she whispers in the direction of her children's room. "Sleep tight. Don't let the bedbugs . . ."

She begins to undress, feeling groggy.

The Last Few Curls of Gut Rope

Steve Vernon

I am dying from caution. It is happening slowly.

I sit on a round restaurant stool, turning, turning.

Waiting.

I stare out the window at a dark nothing sky. Birds hang on the clouds like pairs of lonely scissors.

They tell me nothing.

What happened? Where did it begin?

I stare at the ring finger on my left hand. Something is missing. The pale white tattletale halo, once choked and hidden beneath a single band of gold. Missing. Like a silent telephone. Like a clapperless bell.

I've been up most of the night. Sleepless, chasing dreams. Another week of selling things I never believed in.

I sit and wait for breakfast. An egg. A beginning.

The restaurant is empty, save myself and the waitress walking towards me. Is she married? Is she lonely? Who am I trying to kid?

My heart is an empty shell. Broken.

I look about the restaurant. What might it clear on a good week? A little place like this ought to be a gold mine. Why isn't anyone here? How does it survive without customers? Do they draw a business crowd? Are the cook's burgers big with the construction crews? Truckers? Maybe the bums in the street scavenge empty beer bottles to trade in for a single slice of meatloaf.

If McDonald's requires the meaty devotion of a billion Big Macs bagged daily, how can a place called The Dirty Onion survive more than a half of an ill spent summer? Is it a hobby? The cook, an incognito millionaire with a fervor for the scent of burning grease? A front for a Mafia money-laundering scheme? Do those swinging yellow-white kitchen doors conceal a cache of terrorists?

It doesn't matter. It's a restaurant. A place to break, fast. A place to begin.

The décor is spartan. Dirty peeling tile. An out-of-date calendar, tacked to a grease-stained wall. Cigarette-smoke tattoos curl yellowly about faded pine moulding. Early American cheap.

It's eight in the morning. Somewhere people rise to sparrow song. Somewhere classes full of pregnant yogic women bend and stretch in perfect tantric pentameter, gonging their chis and filling their essence with a splendid tao of hot sugared morning tea.

That's somewhere else. Here, I sit and stare at a half-empty cup of watery coffee. It tastes like the bitter piss of Juan Valdez's oldest mule.

The waitress stands over me. I feel her shadow envelope me. The gravity of her cheap starchy ass. The apron of her aged boobs. She leans closer. Her back and shoulders stoop into a tired question mark. She clutches her hen-scratched order pad before her like a holy paper shield, a weary interrogative awaiting an answer.

"What do you want?"

Always the hard questions first. What do I want? Another life. A marriage that isn't in the dirtiest phase of a death-by-attrition divorce. A day job that doesn't involve selling my time and lack of interest. A shot at immortality.

"Eggs," I say. "Give me eggs, fried in sunny-sided optimism. Bacon, charred like St. Joan's pelvis bone. Toast as bland as a generic greeting card."

I give her my best smile. She ignores it.

"Eggs," she says with a nod of her blonde sprayed haystack-chaotic hair.

She's right. Why waste words?

She walks to the kitchen.

I sit. Waiting. The coffee gets colder.

Godot doesn't arrive.

I look at the ceiling. Try to remember the last time I was truly happy. It doesn't come to me. Memory never happens the way it happens in stories. It's confused, twisted, jumbled. Memory is a refrigerator that rarely gets cleaned. Once a decade you rearrange. Reprioritize. You check the expiration date on the milk. You sniff the eggs suspiciously. Throw out what cannot be preserved. You make compost offerings out of rotted fruits and forgotten jars of sauerkraut. There is strength in divesture. Sacrifice must be made.

I am dying from caution. It is happening slowly.

"Here you go."

She reaches over my shoulder, a reveille from reverie. She sets a plate before me. I feel the weight of one of her heavy breasts, soft against my shoulder blade.

It's a good feeling. Like being born again. Something moves deep inside me. A warmth I haven't felt for a long time.

"Enjoy," she says.

I see what's on my plate. Sitting there, like a coil of shit on a china cake platter, a large brown chicken pecks listlessly at a handful of indeterminate grain.

A chicken?

I look up at the waitress. Try another smile.

"Are you trying to pullet my leg?"

It's got to be some kind of joke. Maybe I've won something. One millionth customer to order chicken.

She looks at me. "I'm sorry?"

I hate that. People who say they're sorry, when they mean they didn't hear or understand. It's sloppy English. Wasted words.

"What's this?"

I point at the pecking bird. Instant Ice Age, just that fast. The waitress's face petrifies into a slow blank slate.

"Eggs," she answers in a flat monotone.

"Yes. I asked for eggs."

"Correct."

I point at the chicken. It snaps at my finger, like it was a large pink worm.

"That's a chicken. Where are my eggs?"

"They're coming."

"They're coming?"

She points at the chicken. I give her a grin to show her humor is appreciated.

I swear the chicken grins back at me.

"The chicken comes first," she says.

It's a joke. It's got to be some kind of joke.

"Who's on first?" I ask.

She stares at me. Maybe she isn't an Abbott and Costello fan.

"You asked for eggs," she says. "But the chicken comes first."

I'm hungry and pissed off. I hammer the table with the side of my fist to make a point. The chicken emits an indignant squawk. Apparently I've broken some point of poultry protocol.

"Where are my eggs?"

"There's a problem?"

A voice from behind me. It sounds big, and really close.

I turn around.

There's a large man in kitchen whites. A beak of a nose. A head, as bald as an ostrich egg. The cook. He scuffs his feet in front of me, like he's scraping off dirt.

"Is there a problem?" He repeats.

He bobs his head forward, tucks his fists beneath his armpits, a run-to-seed Mr. Clean attempting a sorry funky chicken. I ignore what I figure to be a pitiful attempt at physical wit, too busy trying to figure out what the hell is going on.

"Of course there's a problem." I point at the chicken. The bird pluckily snaps again. "Where are my eggs?"

"They're coming," the cook says.

I can't believe my ears. I rack my memory. Is this April the first? Maybe some national chicken holiday that I'm unaware of? The chicken clucks as if I'd tried to pluck it raw. Poofs its feathers up in an apparent attempt to emulate the waitress's amok bouffant. Stands and looks at its feet in surprise. There, upon the metal dinner platter, is an egg.

The cook and waitress point at what's supposed to be the answer to my problem.

"There's your egg," she says.

"I'm not eating that," I say.

"Why not?" the cook asks. "It's an egg."

"It came out of that chicken's ass."

"Well, where did you think eggs came from?"

"Not on my plate. Not at my table."

The chicken sits down.

"That's an egg. Fresh, too," The cook says. "I don't see what your problem is."

The chicken squawks. Puffs itself up and repeats the process.

This time when it stands, there are three eggs upon my plate. It's laid the last two at once.

"Two in one. That's rarer than double yolks. That's a good luck sign for sure."

I shake my head.

"I'm not eating those eggs."

"But they're your eggs. You asked for them. She laid them for you."

There's a sound. I listen. One of the eggs cracks.

"Is it hatching already?" The waitress asks.

A piss yellow chick pokes its wet sticky head from beneath its mother's feathered ass.

I can't believe my eyes.

"Oh my god."

"From whom all blessings flow," the waitress crows.

I hear the sound of more cracking, like static on an untuned radio.

"Praise him, egg and yolk." The cook calls out, with another furtive funky chicken step.

I stand up, nearly overturning my stool. Two more chicks peek out from the plate. The chicken squawks and lays a fourth egg.

I step right back.

The chicken hops from the plate to the floor.

"You can't go." The cook says.

"You can't leave your eggs behind," the waitress adds.

I move for the door, brandishing a butter knife: a salesman is trained in all forms of martial defense. "You can't stop me."

"You have to pay for your eggs." The cook repeats.

I shake my head and back away.

"I'm not paying for those eggs," I say. "They're raw."

"Correct," the waitress says.

"You have to pay," the cook says. "They're your eggs."

I reach behind my back to open the door. The chicken bustles past me, chicks in tow. I ignore the chicken rush. I've got more important things to worry about than chickens.

I turn to run. Feet, beat the street. The last thing I see of the restaurant is the cook standing in the doorway.

He calls after me. "Sooner or later you have to pay for your eggs."

It strikes me as strange, how calmly he says that.

No time for that now. I run. My car's back there, but so are the chickens. I'm not taking any chances.

It's hard to run down a busy city street. I feel like a salmon bucking the stream. People push past me like I'm not there. A mailman stares as I run past.

"You ought to pay for your eggs," he says, or maybe I just imagine it.

I run. My heart feels like it might break open, but I don't dare stop until I reach the bus stop. Home free, free for all, all the all the outs are free. I lean against the signpost, panting like a winded hound.

I'm free. I've escaped. What has been going on?

"Are these your chickens?"

I look up. A policeman stands there, his arms loaded with half a dozen fully grown chickens, and another armload and three pocketfuls of baby chicks.

"Are these your chickens?" The policeman repeats.

I try to explain, but the policeman isn't listening today. He pushes the chickens at me.

"I ought to take you in. You can't be running around with chickens. There are laws against the unlicensed exercising of barnyard fowl. Haven't you heard of the poultry flu?"

I shake my head, too tired to think.

"Chicken flew?" I ask. "I didn't know chickens could fly."

"You're darned tooting they can't. And that's why you're responsible for these eggs."

He hands me a hatful of eggs. I cradle them in the pockets of my suit jacket, my briefcase, and wherever else I can fit them. The bus hisses to a halt in front of me. I jump back, startled. The door levers open. I climb on board, holding my fare out with one egg-filled hand. The chickens clamber up the stairs behind me.

"Hey," the driver says. "You have to pay for your chickens."

I'm tired of arguing. I open my wallet and drop a twenty-dollar bill in the driver's hand.

"Keep the change," I say.

I stumble to my seat. The chickens heap in around me. They're soft and warm and somehow comforting. The bus moves forward. Someone sits down in front of me. I know who it is before he even turns around.

"Those your chickens?"

I look at the cook. Sitting there, so calmly. Like we'd just met. In a way, I suppose we had.

"I asked for them," I nod with a big friendly smile. I'm learning.

The cook reaches into his pocket. Pulls out a handful of grain. Of course. Everyone carries grain in their pockets. He probably wears beef jerky braided into his hatband and a dog chew stick tucked like a cigar in his vest pocket.

The cook keeps talking. "I like chickens. They're a holy animal in some parts of the world. A sign of wealth and security. If you own chickens you've got eggs and meat whenever you want them. Autonomy. Emerson would have approved."

"I don't want them."

"You asked for them, didn't you?"

He keeps feeding the chickens. One of them squats in the seat beside the cook and lays another handful of eggs. The eggs begin cracking. The cook keeps talking.

"Fecund little bastards, aren't they? The Persians believed that chickens were a form of immortality. New life every day. The sun trapped inside an egg. I needn't tell you about the giant who kept his heart inside an egg."

"Needn't you?"

I look at the eggs. There's so many. How many? I have to know. I begin poking them off, one-two-three.

"Don't do that." The cook warns.

"What?"

"Don't count your chickens before they're hatched." He smiles. It's almost a friendly smile. Almost friendly enough to make me want to smile back.

"Life is full of surprises," the cook adds.

Great. I'm traveling with a flock of chickens and Forrest Gump. I stare gloomily at the chickens.

"You're not just whistling 'Chicken Train'," I tell him.

The cook smiles, and winks, like I've cracked a very funny joke. He keeps on talking.

"They've been used for prognostication throughout the years. Priests would read the future in the windings of their entrails. A gypsy woman in Tirgu Mures used to lay a box of sand and pebbles and brightly colored rocks for a chicken to scratch in. She would read the future according to where the chicken scratched its tracks."

I listen glumly.

"They had a chicken at the World's Fair who could play tic-tac-toe and win, if you let it play first. It knew the secrets of life and death. Could guess your weight and age and peck out the numbers on an Underhill typewriter."

"Is that so?"

More chickens sprout and grow. It happens at a geometric rate. I wonder if this is some sort of alien invasion. Unidentified frying objects.

The cook keeps talking. "Shame what finally happened. Someone kidnapped the chicken. Held it for ransom. It died from a broken heart."

He shakes his great bald head sadly.

"He should have paid for that chicken."

The bus pulls to a stop.

"Is this your stop?" I ask.

"No," the cook says. "I've paid for further on."

Then he bows to me, like it's an honor for him to meet me.

I push my way to the front of the bus.

"There's more chickens here than you paid for," the driver notes.

"Put it on their bill," I numbly mumble.

I walk off the bus and down the sidewalk, a pied piper followed by a thousand feathered rats.

I'm no longer even trying to run away. These are my chickens. I asked for them.

I walk into the lobby. It's a tough trick to fit all of the chickens into the elevator, but I manage. We ride up four floors together, the chickens clucking softly to themselves, as if wondering about their destination. Their clucking is restful. Or maybe I'm just that tired.

I allow myself to be gently herded towards my apartment door. Apartment 505. I stare a long time at the zero. It's funny, how egglike nothing can be.

I open the door. I step aside to allow the chickens into my apartment.

"Make yourselves at home."

They clamber over the furniture. Perch atop my stereo and bookshelves. Clutter about the carpet and the laundry hamper.

I'm tired. I slump upon the couch. The chickens watch closely, their heads flicking like restless snakes. Who was it who defined a play as the moment when the chickens came home to roost? Tennessee Ernie Ford?

I can't remember. It's too hard to think of anything.

The chickens keep watching. Clucking softly, like a flock of conspiracy whisperers.

I watch them right back. At least they've stopped laying eggs.

That's funny. I cackle, startling one hen into a nervous short winged hop.

That was funny too. I decide to taunt them.

"A watched chicken never boils." I call out.

They keep watching.

"I'm not afraid of you."

They keep watching.

"You bunch of chickens."

I fall asleep with the chickens watching over me.

I dream of Colonel Sanders. The old Southerner, looking at me, all antebellum and sagacious in his dapper white suit coat, his carefully knotted string tie.

"There has to be a sacrifice," he whispers.

He pokes me with his gnarled black cane. There's a chicken claw on the head of it, clutching a great carved egg. The colonel pinches me, like a cannibal testing a would-be feast. Tenderizing me.

I awake beneath the weight of a chicken. It looks like the original chicken from the restaurant, but I can't be certain. All chickens look alike, even now. Is that some form of avian racism?

The chicken stares at me, its eyes like beads of red corn, hard and unblinking.

"Go for it," I say. "Let's play, chicken."

I keep staring. It stares right back.

Minutes pass.

Sweat beads and crawls across my brow.

"I'm not cracking," I warn the chicken.

The chicken keeps staring. Then it pecks a button from my shirt.

Ha. The damn bird is trying to break my concentration.

No way.

I keep staring.

The chicken pecks another button. A second bird lands upon my left arm. A third rests heavily upon my right.

I keep on staring, determined to get the best of this chicken. I can't let them beat me.

The chicken pecks another button. My shirt flops open like a loosened wound. Two more chickens mount my arms. I feel others on my legs. How many more, I can't be certain.

I try to move, but I've sat still for too long. My limbs are number than rubber chicken wings. It doesn't matter. I keep on staring.

The chicken pecks at my bellybutton.

"Damn!"

I snap. Try to rise up. The chicken pecks again.

More and more.

I struggle beneath the weight of all these chickens. Pecking. Pecking. There are chickens all over me. Jamming their beaks into me, like dirty orange pincer hooks, tearing, ripping, tearing, pecking.

I scream into a mouthful of beating dusty feathers.

The birds keep pecking.

I thrash and flap my arms. Try to stand up.

Pecking. Pecking.

I look down and see the bird with something long and wet and sausage-like in its beak.

Spaghetti?

The bird tugs. I feel a sharp pain. Inside me.

Damn.

It stands there staring at me, the first coil of intestine caught in its bright orange beak.

"There we have it."

I look up to see who is speaking, knowing who before

I even see him.

"There we have it for certain sure."

The cook. Standing over me. Like a god, or a living judgment.

He even does his little funky chicken strut. A victory jig.

Then he squats down beside me. Digs at me. I feel fat fingers root through my open wound. They feel cold, as if his hands are made of ice, yet I know the cold isn't the cook's fault.

He catches hold of my exposed gut and begins to unravel it. Like a long wet skein of yarn, twisting, long soft rubbery wet sausage spools, dumping it link by link into a small iron cauldron, whistling softly through his teeth.

"There we have it," he repeats.

"Have what?" My voice is a husk, empty and dry.

"The end of your tale."

He pulls the last few curls of gut rope from out of my gaping stomach. Then he pinches out a lump of something hard.

He shows it to me.

For a minute it looks like a moon. A tiny golden moon, but it's an egg. A solid golden egg.

"There it is. Rent for the next year."

He smiles. His teeth, all tiny and even like kernels of fine white corn.

All I can do is stare. I should be dead.

Shouldn't I?

How long does it take to die?

I have to say something.

"What's it all about?" I ask.

"Shh," the cook soothes. "Don't waste your words."

I open my mouth and cough out feathers.

Try to speak.

Nothing.

Not a sound.

The cook hooks the cauldron onto the end of an old-fashioned balance. Shifts weights and stones, like an ancient checkers player readying his match.

"Hmm," he says. "Heavier than a heart, but lighter than soul meat."

"What's it all about?" I ask.

He looks down at me. Smiles, like a tall tree of a saint.

"You have to answer the questions," he explains. "You have to pay for your eggs."

He reaches down with both of his hands. They are large and capable and merciful.

He cradles his palms about my temple, as if he were about to deliver a long wet kiss.

Then he smiles, as soft as a lonely wet sunrise.

"What came first?" he whispers.

"I'm sorry," I answer.

The cook squeezes his hands together.

The last sound I hear is the cracking of an egg.

iii: Bitter Fruit

Finding Father

Bentley Little

He stared at the obscene declaration, filled with a growing sense of unease.

He found it in a shack in the desert, a horrible thing of jellyfish and claws, scales and squid, bound into shape by strands of dark kelpy seaweed. It was sitting in the center of the rotted wood floor, and under his gaze it shifted, moved, tried to slink away beneath a sandy bench, all the while making a hideous squeaking squelching sound.

"Dad?" he said.

Jack pulled into the rest area outside of Barstow with as bad a case of the runs as he'd ever had (*Damn that Del Taco!*). He locked up the rig, ran to the bathroom, hurried into the stall, pulled down his pants, sat down on the toilet and with great relief let go. He closed his eyes as his bowels evacuated and for several minutes afterward tried to force out whatever else he could to guarantee that he wouldn't be caught short on the road, but his intestinal distress seemed to have disappeared with that one comprehensive purge, and when it became clear that the storm was over, he gratefully relaxed his straining muscles and sat there for a moment longer, recuperating.

He opened his eyes. In front of him, in black marker on the gray metal door, were the words *I took a shit here*. He wouldn't have thought much of it, would have assumed it was a piece of random graffiti, albeit one more pointless and witless than usual, but he recognized the hand, identified it from the letters his mother had saved.

It was his father's writing.

His father had been here.

It was an inescapable conclusion, though it left him baffled. Why would his father write such a thing? And why here, in the middle of the California desert, a continent away from his last known address? Jack stared at the rude, obvious declaration. It made no sense. But then again, he didn't really know his father, had never met him, and any personality traits he attributed to his dad were the result of wishful thinking. His mother had never mentioned the old man except to say that he was a worthless self-centered son of a bitch who had dumped her after she'd gotten pregnant. Jack would not even have seen the letters had he not found them buried deep in his mother's closet one day while looking for a shoebox in which to put his cassette tapes. She'd snatched them away from him when he asked what they were—angry, flustered and defensive—and until he'd rediscovered them while sorting through her belongings after the funeral, he'd always assumed she had destroyed the letters.

But he'd looked at them often since then—in some misguided effort to be closer to his parents, he supposed—and now he easily recognized his father's script.

I took a shit here.

Who had he been trying to impress with that message? Who was his target audience? What point was the old man trying to make?

And he *was* an old man by now. Assuming he was approximately the same age as his mother when they'd been dating, that would make him about sixty-five.

What kind of sixty-five-year-old man scrawled messages about his bathroom habits in restroom stalls?

Nothing about this sat well with him, and Jack quickly wiped and flushed and exited the stall. On impulse, he checked the two empty stalls to either side of him, but the graffiti there consisted of the typical insults and homophobic rants, and he saw no sign of his father's handwriting. Without trying to be too obvious, he scanned the concrete wall above the occupied row of urinals but saw nothing familiar there, either.

He left the restroom, went back to his truck and hit

the highway, heading for Salt Lake. The message in the bathroom bothered him, though, and even the gaudy lights of Vegas at twilight could not dislodge it from his mind.

I took a shit here, too.

It was his father's script again, this time in the restroom of a Fina gas station in Gallup, New Mexico, just across the Arizona border. He had almost convinced himself that it hadn't really happened, that he hadn't seen what he thought he'd seen, but the idea of a vague similarity in writing styles he'd been cultivating for the past two weeks disappeared the instant he saw the scrawled notation on the stall wall.

He stared at the obscene declaration, filled with a growing sense of unease. He realized that he'd been avoiding going to the bathroom as much as possible, drinking less, because he'd been both dreading and expecting to find this in every public restroom he visited. Now that he had found the message in his father's handwriting, he was disturbed by the fact that it was here, in this nowheresville truck stop town, and that out of all of the toilets he could have used, he'd chosen this one. It was coincidence, it had to be, but it didn't feel like it, and just the thought that this might be planned or preordained gave him the heebee-jeebees and made him quickly leave the gas station bathroom and go to McDonald's next door.

Back in his rig, back on the road, he tried to figure out what it all meant. Or if it meant anything. But he had no context for this, and he remained confused and frightened as he rejoined the convoy of trucks driving east on Interstate 40 toward Albuquerque.

He wasn't quite as freaked out by the message in Springerville the following week. He supposed that was because he was getting used to it. He even stopped at a convenience store, bought an overpriced disposable camera and returned to the gas station to snap a picture of the words, intending to compare them with his mother's old letters to determine once and for all if the handwriting was identical. Of course, he knew the answer already, but something about the logical steps he was taking and the rationality of this experiment brought reason to the chaos and made him feel a little more in control. He used up half of the twenty-seven shots, taking the photos from various angles, with the stall door open, partially open and closed, and saved the remaining pictures for his trip back to Bakersfield.

Just in case.

As it turned out, however, he did not need the camera. The restrooms at which he stopped were clean, and he made it home without encountering any words from his father. He had a lot of time to think on the way, but everything was confused and jumbled in his brain, and the only thought that remained clear and constant was that he wished his mother was still alive.

Back at the house, he dug through box after piled box in the garage until he found the one containing his mother's letters from his father. Why she had saved them all those years was a mystery. He had read them over and over again and found nothing even remotely compelling about the hastily scrawled notes. There were no fervent declarations of love and eternal devotion, no brilliantly memorable turns of phrase, only mundane greetings and brief prosaic descriptions of daily routines. They were far closer to the generic epistles of uninterested pen pals than love letters, and the only thing Jack could figure was that she'd kept them because they reminded her of him, because despite her obvious bitterness she still had tender feelings.

He picked up a letter at random and started to scan through it, when something about the missive caught his eye. He had never been much of a reader, but on the road, at night and in truck stops for lunch or dinner, he liked to do word puzzles. Jumbles and crosswords. His mind was trained to look for patterns in alphabetical arrangements, to see letters as elements in a composition. And he saw a pattern here. When read as a column, from top to bottom, the first letter of each line combined to form words. A sentence with paragraph indentations for spaces.

I took a shit here.

A chill passed through him, a deep icy dread that radiated from within and caused gooseflesh to rise on his skin. The note itself made perfect sense, expressed coherent thoughts and opinions in a believably natural way. But . . .

But the first letter of each line spelled out a secret message.

I took a shit here.

The first *and* the last. He realized with horror and fear that, impossibly, the last letter of each line, when read as a column, spelled out exactly the same thing.

He felt as though he'd stumbled onto some buried truth, a dizzying secret knowledge meant to be kept permanently under wraps, a wild electric unreality that pulsed just under the thin veneer of everyday life. He checked another letter. And another. As he'd feared, as he'd known, they were all exactly the same. Despite the discrepancies in time, despite the variety of subject matter and length, they each contained columns of hidden messages. The exact same message: *I took a shit here.*

But what did it mean? And who exactly were the words aimed at? *You,* a voice within him whispered, and Jack quickly refolded the letters and placed them back in the box.

He called his aunt Elizabeth and his uncle Garrett to ask them if they'd ever met his father. He and his mom had lived with them for the first eight years of his life, and though Jack still remained in casual contact with his aunt and uncle—birthday phone calls, Christmas cards—he had never asked them about his dad. That seemed strange now in retrospect, particularly since he had spent a goodly portion of his childhood in their home, that portion of his childhood when the absence of a father would have been felt most acutely. He was not sure now why it had never come up, why his missing parent had been a taboo subject, but he intended now to make up for lost time.

It was Elizabeth who answered the phone, and after the customary greetings, he just came right out and asked: "What was my father like?"

There was a long pause, as though his aunt was finally having to face a question she had known he would eventually ask, one that she had been dreading for many, many years.

Maybe it was all in his mind, however, because her answer seemed honest and real. "I never knew your father."

"What about Uncle Garrett?"

"Neither of us ever met the man." The words still sounded legitimate. Her voice, though, was old, strained, and he thought to himself: *She's lying.*

"Did my mom ever say anything about him? Did she ever talk to you when they were dating?

"That was a long time ago, Jack."

"I know. But he could still be alive. Probably is, in fact. What if I met up with him one day? I'd like to be able to recognize him if I ran into him."

She sighed tiredly. '"No, you wouldn't, Jack."

"What do you mean?"

"He wasn't good for anybody. Not your mother, not you, not . . . anybody. He wasn't . . . good."

"I thought you never met him."

"I didn't have to."

"My mom told you about him?"

"She didn't have to." But Elizabeth refused to say any more, and even when he told her that he'd been receiving written messages from his father, she would not talk about it, and for the first time, when the two of them hung up, they were mad at each other.

Barstow. Gallup. Springerville. Socorro. Ruidoso. Wilcox.

There'd been six sightings so far, and Jack had taped a road map of the western U.S. to the ceiling of his cab, marking off with little red stars the locations where he'd found his father's handwriting. A line could be drawn between them, two converging lines, really, and ignoring the chronology of their discovery, assuming that they proceeded from west to east (there'd been no *too* in the Barstow bathroom, indicating that it was the first), they led toward the barren expanse of east central New Mexico or, possibly, west Texas.

The last one had been signed, *Dad*. And he had the horrible feeling that the next one—wherever he found it—would be addressed to him: *Jack*.

He had long since given up the theory that this was coincidental, that his father simply had some bizarre compunction to record his bowel movements wherever they occurred and that he himself had stumbled on those restroom declarations accidentally. There was nothing accidental about this.

His father was calling to him.

And pointing the way.

Jack looked up at the map on the ceiling. Where next? He didn't know why, didn't know when, but somewhere along the line he had decided to be an active rather than passive participant. Rather than wait until he stumbled upon another message from his father, he was purposefully trying to figure out where that next message might be.

Lincoln or Roswell, he thought. Maybe Artesia.

Unfortunately, he wasn't scheduled to haul anywhere near New Mexico. His next three trips were in California: a load of solenoids from the dock in San Pedro to the Kragen

Auto warehouse in Sacramento; lawnmower parts from LA to San Fran; garden tools to various hardware stores from the manufacturer. Right now he was delivering fertilizer to Yuma, and for the next several weeks that was likely to be as close as he would come to his father's next restroom rendezvous. He tried to think of some way he could trade routes with other drivers hauling east, even considered taking his vacation now in order to explore New Mexico on his own time. But neither plan was feasible, and he resigned himself to the fact that it would probably be close to a month before he'd be in a position to seek out his dad's messages. And who knew how many there'd be by that time, who knew how cold the trail would grow?

He ate lunch at a Whataburger. Afterward, in the bathroom, above the urinal this time, he found it: *Jack, I took a shit here too. Dad.*

It made a mockery of his map, tore the hell out of his carefully calculated estimations. He stared at the words, at the handwriting he could now recognize in his sleep. There was no pattern, he realized. His father remained one step ahead of him, but he could show up anywhere at any time. The old man wasn't leading him anywhere. He was playing with him. And in his anger and frustration, Jack took a handful of paper towels from the dispenser, pumped pink hand soap on them—and used them to wipe the words off the tiled wall.

It had been two months since he'd last read his father's words, and Jack had begun to think that it was over, that his father's acknowledgement of authorship and kinship was as close as he was ever going to get to his dad. He regretted cleaning the message off the Whataburger bathroom wall, even considered the idea that it had been a test, that his father had been watching to see what he would do and that he had failed the test and been cut off forever. A whole host of crazy ideas went through his mind alone at night and during those long stretches of empty highway on the road, but none of them seemed to offer any real answers.

He was well past Tucson, traveling through southern Arizona on his way to El Paso, when he happened to glance over at an abandoned and only partially constructed building on the right side of the highway. In front of the rootless cinderblock structure was a For Sale sign reading: *Zoned Commercial. 200 Acres.* On the unpainted unfinished wall that faced the highway was graffiti, and although he sped past too quickly to make out all of the words, one jumped out at him.

Shit.

He was suddenly suffused with a feeling of apprehension, the certainty that he should not have driven this route. Out of the comer of his eye, he thought he saw spray-painted letters, and he looked quickly to his right to catch the word "*Dad*" on a boulder.

His heart was pounding, and he glanced out the windshield at the empty highway and barren landscape before him, suddenly sure that his father was close. Playtime was over. Whatever was going to happen was going to happen here. And now.

There was an overpass up ahead. He knew from previous highway signs that the next turnoff was the Armbruster exit. But as he approached, he saw that another rig had smashed into the sign, taking out the left half of the green rectangle, leaving only a crinkled mass of metal and the letters "uster."

Uster had been his father's last name.

A shiver passed through him. He was far beyond the point where he would consider something like this unconnected, and without thinking he immediately turned off the highway and onto the road. To his left, the lane crossed the highway on the overpass but only to provide access to the westbound lanes. On the other side of the bridge, past the onramp, the road ended at a guardrail.

To his right, the two-lane blacktop wound into the desert toward a series of low rocky mountains, and it was in this direction that he drove. The rig took up nearly the entire width of the narrow road; if he met someone else traveling in the opposite direction there was going to be trouble, but as far as he could tell, he was the only one on Armbruster.

Armbruster.

Why was it named that? After a landowning family or a rancher, as was so often the case in the west? Or after a local politician whose patronage led to the creation of the road? The fact that this exit had been named years, perhaps decades ago, and that the sign had been recently hit, leaving only the partial word "Uster," his father's name, made him wonder how involved this plan to lead him here was, exactly how the logistics of it were arranged.

The road went over a small rise, and all of a sudden the pavement disappeared. He was on a dirt road, and the wheels of the rig slid suddenly on the washboard surface. He downshifted, gripped the steering wheel tightly and weathered the transition. Jack knew he could be fired for taking the truck on such a trail, but he was far beyond the mundane considerations of job security.

Ahead, near the foot of the mountains, he could see buildings, what appeared to be a community of some sort. He couldn't afford to break down here in the middle of nowhere, so he was taking it slow, the truck gradually decreasing in speed until it barely registered on his speedometer.

The community ahead grew closer.

He thought at first it was a ghost town. The buildings on the main street were deserted, in disrepair, and seemed to have that weathered wood look so prized by the makers of Hollywood westerns, with even a few false fronts thrown in for good measure. He saw no cars, no people, no signs of life. Behind that, though, on a partially paved street behind the empty businesses, was movement: a young man walking into a garage, two boys riding bikes back and forth over a makeshift jump ramp, an old woman carrying a basket of laundry into a dilapidated house, a group of kids huddled on the cracked remnants of a sidewalk.

There was no way the rig could turn sharply enough to move over to that second street, no way it could fit on the narrow alley-sized roads anyway, so Jack parked it in front of an abandoned livery, locked the doors and got out. The temperature was hot, but that was to be expected. What was not expected was the stillness of the air. He could hear the voices of the children, but they were far more muffled than they should have been, as though coming from behind a thick invisible wall.

He would not have been surprised to run into some sort of force field, but there was no impediment to his progress as he passed between two empty buildings and walked across the sand and gravel to the inhabited section of the town. The ground appeared level, but an almost imperceptible downward slope made him quicken his step, and by the time he reached the bleached, cracked asphalt of the second street he was almost jogging. He stopped on the sidewalk, looked around. The kids huddled together. The boys on their bikes. Two women chatting over an unpainted picket fence separating their barren yards.

All of the residents looked like him.

He knew instantly what that meant, though he didn't want to admit it. In the faces of the children, the faces of the women, the face of a young man who strolled around the edge of a tool shed, he saw himself. He saw . . .

His father.

He was *their* father, too. They were his brothers, his sisters, and the fact that they were all here, gathered in this ghost town, living together way the hell out in the middle of nowhere, disturbed and frightened him. Still, he pressed on, walking forward, moving up to the group of children and offering a false-hearty "Hello."

The kids turned briefly to look at him, then returned

to what they were doing. He peered over the huddle of small shoulders and saw a brown-haired girl of about eight or ten who could have been his cloned daughter drawing on the cement with chalk. Her artistic skills were quite extraordinary, and he watched as she fleshed out a rather impressive-looking caricature of a serious, distinguished older man.

Her dad.

His dad.

He wanted to ask her about him, wanted to talk to all of them about their father but before he could say anything, the girl, clearly the leader of the group, held out her hand and another child handed her a small container of lighter fluid. Without speaking, she went over the chalk lines with the lighter fluid and then used a match to set it ablaze. There was a sudden whoosh! and for a brief, fiery second, her father's face was etched in flame. Then the other kids stomped out the burning face, smearing the picture until it looked like a jumbled mess, a blackened charcoal sketch of a corrupted amoeba. With wordless cries, the children bolted, scattered, ran.

"Wait!" Jack called. "Where . . . ?" But they were dashing between buildings, behind boulders. For a brief moment, the girl stopped on the sidewalk, turned and looked at him. She pointed up the street, silently, then ran away, disappearing into a shabby grocery store.

He looked down at the smeared burnt picture before him and something about it gave him the willies. It was not just the ritual that had been performed but the picture itself, the confused disarrangement that the drawing had become. He glanced up the street where the girl had pointed, saw a smattering of small dirty homes, a closed liquor store, an open laundromat, a neglected barn. Beyond that, the street ended at the base of a low dirt hill, and even from this far away he could see at the top of the small hill a wooden square on a post, about the size of a realtor's sign.

He broke into a jog, passing a man who could have

been his twin and an old lady who looked like the man's mother.

How old was his father?

Old, he thought.

He nearly tripped over an obnoxious barking dog that had run out to intercept him, and he stumbled, caught himself, looked down.

The dog's features resembled his own.

He ran faster, not wanting to think about it, sprinting up the dirt hill, his shoes kicking up dust behind him. At the top, he stopped to check out the sign and catch his breath. Written on the wood was a chalk arrow pointing down into the desert, away from town, and ahead, shimmering in the heat, nearly lost amidst the similarly colored dead brush, was what 1ooked like a rest area bathroom.

Beneath the sweat, his skin was cold, and he wanted to turn around, speed back to his truck and drive away. But he moved forward along the barely visible trail, too tired to run now, walking down the hill and onto the plain. As he drew closer, he saw that it was not a public restroom after all but a house, a shack, though a small one by any standards. *An outhouse,* a voice in the back of his mind said, but he ignored it.

The stillness was back, and while there weren't really any sounds to hear other than his own ragged breathing, it seemed as if both of his ears had been plugged with cotton. A predatory bird circled silently overhead.

Jack stopped in front of the rundown shack. The door, a weathered piece of plywood, was unlatched and swinging slightly though there was no breeze. Inside was darkness. This is it, he thought. He was frightened but determined, and he moved forward, pulling open the plywood door as wide as possible. Sunlight entered the windowless shack, illuminating a rotting wooden floor, a rusted freestanding sink and a sand-covered bench against the side wall. In the open center of the floor was . . .

He had no idea.

There was movement and it appeared to be alive, but attributing consciousness to the small horror on the floor violated all known laws of physics, biology and decency. It was an abhorrent amalgam of the slimiest, most alien sea creatures, compelled into some semblance of coherent form by dark stringy strands of kelp.

He stepped onto the decayed wood and the sickening thing moved away from him, making a hideous high-pitched noise as it crawled across the floor in a creeping, skulking fashion.

"Dad?" he said, but the repellent creature did not respond, moving further away from the door, seeking refuge beneath the bench.

Dad? This couldn't be his father. What the hell was he thinking?

He watched as it inched under the bench, squealing. In the center of what appeared to be a dome of jellyfish flesh, he thought he saw a gelatinous eye blink cruelly at him. Beneath a hard-shelled claw, a beaklike mouth opened and shut.

He turned and ran.

It was an instinctive reaction, he couldn't help it, but he stopped less than a yard away from the shack and after only a moment's hesitation turned back. That slimy scaly monster wasn't his father—it could not have impregnated his mother, could not have written those numbingly prosaic letters, could not have defecated in restrooms throughout the southwest and then scrawled messages announcing it in toilet stalls—but it was connected to his father somehow, and wherever this led he had to follow through, had to see it to the end.

He pushed open the plywood, walked back inside.

It was gone. Whatever it was, it was no longer under the sandy bench. It had disappeared, and to his surprise he felt a terrible sense of loss. He was suddenly filled with the certainty that he had blown his last chance—his one and only chance—to meet his father. He tried to recall the specifics of that slinking slimy horror, and he found himself comparing, trying to see if there were any physical similarities between himself and the creature, between that monster

his father

and the people who populated this town.

To his dismay, he identified a certain familiar cast to that cruel gelatinous eye, recognized a head shape in the jellyfish dome.

"Dad?" he called. His voice sounded too loud in his ear but it died in the air, swallowed by the stillness.

The plywood slammed behind him, and he jumped, his skin erupting in gooseflesh.

"Dad?" he said again, but there was no answer.

He could not stay here a second longer. The fear was back, the instinctive primal terror that had made him dash out of the shack in panic, only this time it was sharper, stronger and accompanied by the certainty of physical danger. He was hot and winded but he ran all the way back through the desert, all the way up the small hill, all the way back to town. He only slowed down when he reached the pavement. The kids were out again, he saw, huddled in groups of two and three along the sidewalk. Other people were out as well, lurking in doorways, peeking from yards, waiting for him.

He ignored them, kept walking. He passed by the smeared chalk drawing, glanced down . . . and stopped.

It looked like the thing in the shack.

Again he had the feeling of being in the grip of something deeper than he was able to fathom, caught in currents he did not, could not, comprehend. He stared at the sidewalk. The lines of the original drawing, the familiar large nose and wide eyes and severe cheeks that he recognized from his own mirror, had been smudged into an almost shapeless mass that resembled the slimy scaly horror he had last seen slinking toward the bench inside the shack.

Maybe that sickening creature *had* been his father at

some point.

This, too, was intentional. The chalk drawing on the sidewalk, the skittishness of the thing in the shed, the realization that it looked like the smeared burnt caricature: all of this was meant to lure him back to his father's home, to make him return for . . . what?

The thick air was even more silent than it had been before, and he realized that the town's residents were holding their breath awaiting his decision. The boys on the bikes had stopped jumping and were watching him. Two young women were staring silently at each other over a picket fence, their conversation paused.

No. He would not fall for it. He would not participate. Whatever was in store for him, whatever his father had planned, he would not cooperate. It took every ounce of will that he had, but he turned away from those lost souls

his brothers and sisters

and started back toward the abandoned front buildings, toward his truck. Behind him, he heard the sound of small running feet, then felt the tap of fingers on his elbow. He stopped walking and turned to see the girl who had made the sidewalk drawing. She offered him a piece of chalk, her mouth set in a grim line, her eyes dark, unreadable.

Fuck you! Shit on you! I did not *take a shit here!* A whole host of possibilities passed instantly through his mind, things he could write on the sidewalk, on walls, but he did not take the chalk, did not take the bait. Part of him wanted to, part of him needed to, but he thought of that kelp-bound monstrosity in the shed, and he understood that sometimes it was better not to know.

He walked away from the girl and returned to his truck. In the second before he climbed up to the cab and slammed shut the door, he looked back between the buildings and saw the girl still standing where he'd left her, tears running down her cheeks, sobs wracking her shoulders. He imagined he could hear from that small sandy shack the echo of his father's high-pitched scream.

For some unexplained reason, that made him feel good, and he smiled as he started the engine and put it into gear.

Empathy

Kealan Patrick Burke

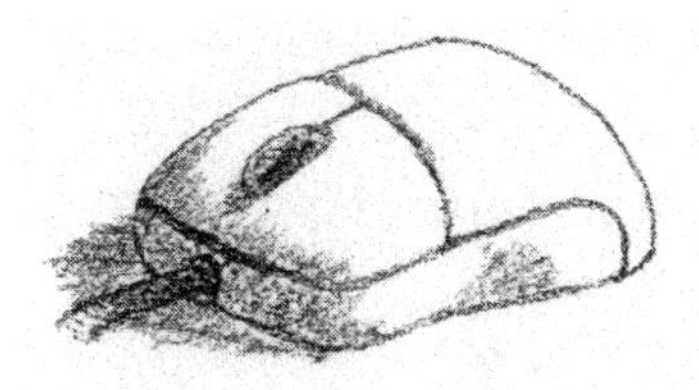

As he watched the sunlight crawl across the walls, he squeezed his eyes shut, praying nothing but dark awaited him there.

Will Chambers heard the muffled thump in the upstairs bedroom and sighed. He'd hoped his absence wouldn't wake Melanie but here she came now, trudging down the stairs, eyes narrowed at the light, auburn hair tousled, dressed in nothing but an old LAPD T-shirt and a pair of black silk panties embossed with roses. Ordinarily the sight of her—long pale slim legs, unhindered breasts pushing against the material of the shirt—would have been enough to arouse him and force the worries from the forefront of his mind.

But not now.

Dear God, not now.

He watched her shuffle to the table and yawn as she withdrew a chair and plopped down into it. "What's wrong?"

He shrugged, offered her a feeble smile. "Couldn't sleep."

"Me neither."

He suppressed a laugh at that. When he'd left her in bed, she'd been snoring softly. As always, his absence had roused her, like a silent alarm.

"You must be working too hard," he said, and took another drag on his cigarette. Smoke threaded its way upward, only to be shredded by the frantic whirl of the fan. He followed the nicotine with a slurp of coffee and sighed.

"Maybe, but what's *your* excuse?" Melanie asked again, crossing her legs and playing with a lock of her hair, her eyes filled with the memory of sleep. He knew she hadn't meant her words to sound as snide and accusatory as he took them. He'd lost his job at the *Delaware Gazette* almost a month ago now, replaced by some hotshot young kid who'd come straight from Penn State armed with "fresh and innovative ideas," as Will's editor had put it. So far, Melanie hadn't confronted him about his prolonged unemployment, or when he might start taking steps to rectify the matter. In truth, he was afraid to tell her his plan. Writing was all he was good at, and the thought of working as a salesman or security guard disturbed him—not because of the work involved, but because of how stifling it would be to his creativity. What he wanted to do was write a novel, but he had not yet summoned the requisite courage to announce to Melanie that she would have to support them while he tried his hand at it.

"I couldn't stop thinking, that's all. You know how it is sometimes. Stupid brain won't shut down long enough for me to get to sleep."

She nodded in sympathy. "Yeah, I know. Did you try reading for a while?"

"Yeah. I grabbed that horror novel you'd left on the nightstand. Talk about the absolutely worst possible book to choose on a sleepless night."

She grinned, exhaustion still clinging to her face like a well worn mask, and spoke as if addressing a child. "Aw, did it scare you, honey?"

I was already scared, he almost said, but returned her smile instead. "It was a little on the violent side."

"It's a horror novel. What do you expect?"

He stubbed out his cigarette, clucked his tongue when the air from the fan encouraged it to stay alight and mashed it until tobacco erupted from the filter.

"I think it's out," Melanie said. Her hand slid across the table to rest on his forearm. "What's the matter? Tell me." He offered her another shrug, but she squeezed his arm. "You've been walking around with a frown all week. Even when I say something funny enough to get a laugh out of you, it sounds like you're doing it to keep me satisfied. Something's bothering you and you know I'll plague you until you tell me what it is."

He slid another cigarette from the gaping box by his left hand. "It's that video."

"The one you watched on the Internet?"

He grimaced around the cigarette and nodded.

"I can't understand why this is staying with you," Melanie said, rubbing her fingertips along his wrist and across his palm. It tickled, but Will was afraid if he told her so she'd take her hand away, and right now he desperately needed her touch, needed to feel the blood, the *life*, ever so softly pulsating beneath her skin. "I mean, it was a terrible thing to see, but in fifteen years of reporting for the *Gazette*, I'm sure you've seen worse—"

"No I haven't," he said, with a bitter smile. "I've seen accident victims, murder victims, all the awful aftermaths. This wasn't an aftermath. I've never seen anything even remotely like that."

She sighed, leaned forward so her elbows were on the table. "It'll go away eventually," she said softly. "You just need to get it out of your system."

"Maybe, but what I saw on that screen isn't the worst of it."

Melanie said nothing, waited for him to continue.

He swallowed the fear that seemed to force the words out of him and cleared his throat. "Those people . . . that woman who died . . . the woman they killed . . ."

Melanie nodded, encouraging him to continue.

"When they . . . when I close my eyes, I see what they did to her, in more detail than they showed on that tape."

Stop now, he thought in one dazzling, desperate moment of panic. *Don't go any further with this. You'll scare her.*

Melanie's hand found his fingers, squeezed them tight.

Will lowered his gaze to the tip of the cigarette. "I see every minute detail, from the blade touching skin, to the blood pooling around her head as they begin to cut. It won't go away."

"Honey, don't—"

"I hear her screaming and . . ." He swallowed again, but this time it was bile he was forced to restrain, just like the first time he'd seen what his mind now replayed in vivid detail. "Tonight, in bed, it sounded so clear it could have been playing at a low volume on the radio." He gestured emptily. "The sound changes when they saw through her vocal chords."

Melanie's face had lost all color. Her free hand now covered her mouth. "Jesus, Will. Stop, please," she mumbled.

But he couldn't. Now that the door had been opened, he was powerless to stem the flow of words. "She whimpers." He gasped for breath as the panic that came with remembering seized him. The cigarette began to tremble in his fingers at the realization that talking about it—something he had hoped would help—only served to make them clearer, more vivid. "She sounds so childlike, as if . . . as if the pain is so incomprehensible it reduces her to an infant . . . oh God . . . that *sound* . . . and . . . and when it's over . . . when it ended, up here, *tonight*," he whispered, tapping an index finger against his temple, ". . . they take her head and raise it to face the camera . . . but . . ."

"Will . . ."

"But it's not her face."

"Please stop . . ."

When he looked up, there were tears in his eyes. "It's yours."

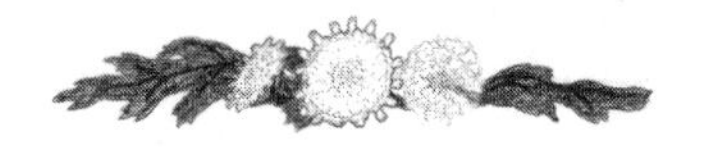

She stayed with him until dawn's sepia-toned fingers parted the blinds and painted bars of fire on the wall. They'd moved to the sofa, where he lay on his back staring at the ceiling, Melanie nestled against him, her hand on his chest. He stroked her cool skin while she slept, occasionally squeezing her closer to him, though they could be no closer, smiling now and then at the pleasurable moan she gave when he drew his fingers down her spine. He felt as if the only way to smother the horror that seethed within him was to pull her inside him, so perhaps she could fight the terror with him, so he wouldn't have to fight it alone. For now, she was a slender, sleeping figure, oblivious to the nightmare that danced across his eyes with every breath, every blink.

He was scared, and it was a preposterous fear. But knowing the foolishness of it didn't lessen its severity and now he felt as if the simple act of watching an execution, something not meant to be seen, had broken something inside him; that a rudimentary shield, essential to preserving a man's sanity, had ruptured under the weight of shock, and now the world had shriveled and dimmed, become a dank dark cell, a steel cage with razor-edged bars.

As he watched the sunlight crawl across the walls, he squeezed his eyes shut, praying nothing but dark awaited him there.

A knife grinding through muscle . . . a gurgled moan . . . Blood plumes, squirting upward and blinding him . . .

His eyes flew open, blinking in time with the stuttering thud of his heart.

"Oh fuck," he whispered shakily. "Oh *fuck*, God, why won't this *stop*?"

A sob so loud it frightened him burst from his mouth and Melanie jerked awake, startled, her eyes searching the room before she blinked once, twice and looked at him. "Will?"

Tell her it's all right.

But he couldn't. He could not tell her it was a dream, a nightmare, something that hurt and frightened him for a while only to flee with the realization that his imagination was to blame.

Instead he said nothing, but covered his face with his hands and wept.

"Will?"

But even in the darkness behind his hands, he saw

shredded skin.

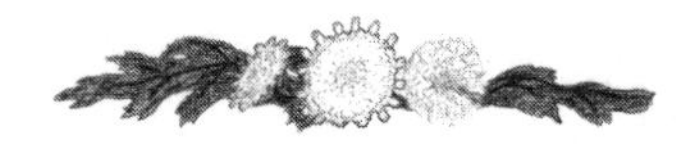

"I could stay home," Melanie said, standing behind him and massaging the concrete tension from his shoulders. Will shook his head, and stared at his hands, at the faint trembling there. He was coming apart.

"No, you go. It won't do you any good to sit around here looking at me feeling sorry for myself."

She was already dressed for work, and looking more beautiful than ever. In truth, he did want her to stay—the thought of being alone filled him with cold panic—but he knew it really wouldn't help. She couldn't chase away the shadows that capered behind his eyes no matter how much light her company brought with it.

She gave his shoulders a final squeeze and went to fetch her purse from the kitchen counter. "Okay, but you call me if you need me and I'll come home."

He nodded. "I'll be fine. Don't worry."

She turned and watched him for a moment. "You'll get over this, Will. I promise."

He wanted desperately to believe her, but the fact remained that she hadn't the slightest idea what he was going through, how much his world had changed in so short a time. If he could only let her see the nightmare that had corrupted his thoughts, if he could, just for a moment, share the images that relentlessly invaded his sleep, only then might her words mean something. As it stood, her attempts to make him feel better sounded trite and absurd in the face of his overwhelming fear.

Alone.

Melanie was a mere whisper of light in a room full of shadow.

"Call me," she said and kissed his cheek, her lips cool against his skin.

"I will." He did not look at her as she waved goodbye from the door, afraid if he did, he might see a thin red line forming around the base of her throat.

She left and silence took her place in the kitchen.

Exhausted, frightened and already beginning to feel the dark creeping back to the forefront of his mind, Will quickly turned on the television.

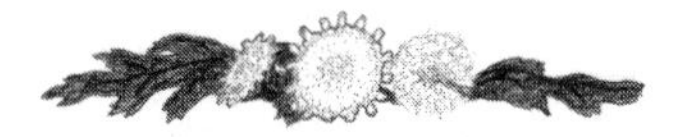

He would not watch the news.

He would not watch a movie.

He tried to watch cartoons but even the animated violence quickly brought to mind the echo of what he had seen.

He switched to *M*A*S*H*, only to change the channel when a fount of arterial spray blinded one of the surgeons.

He settled on a vapid sitcom—surely a safe choice—but soon even the wisecracking characters clustered around the bar began to lose their heads and bleed into their drinks. The audience laughed.

In the end, he stabbed the OFF button on the remote so hard his fingernail cracked. He lay on the sofa, finger throbbing, struggling to fill his mind with benign images: a sunny beach, the gentle hush of waves, a parade filled with grinning clowns and people in animal costumes; then a carnival, a place taken from a box marked 'harmless' in his memory: dour-looking barkers plying their trades, starry-eyed children clutching prizes, spinning lights, the scent of sawdust and cotton candy, and the deafening sound of screams

of screams

of screams

Until the scream was his and the room grew silver teeth.

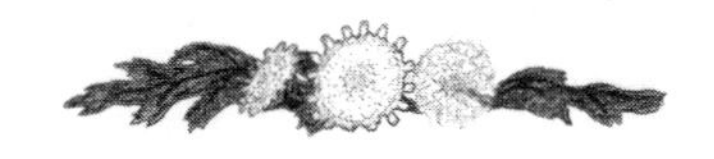

"Is this going to cost me?" Will said.

Don dropped his considerable weight into the armchair across from Will, and smiled. "Relax. You're one of the most together people I've ever met. I doubt this is going to have me running to write you up for the *Psychiatric Times*." He shrugged off his sport coat and scowled as he draped it over the arm of the chair. "I need a new suit."

"Heal thy friend and I'll buy you one."

"You couldn't afford the type of suits I wear," Don said. "Even I can't afford the type of suits I wear, but I have an image to maintain, you know?"

"What kind of image is that? Overweight, balding forty-something on the verge of a midlife crisis, too fond of Scotch and not fond enough of his second wife?"

"People like you negate the need for an autobiography."

They shared a smile, then Will sat back and sighed. "Thanks for coming over. I couldn't think of anyone else to call. I need your help."

"So you said on the phone. What's the problem? Nightmares?"

"It's a little more than that. Actually, it's a lot more than that."

Don relaxed into his chair and tented his fingers over a large paunch. "Tell me about it."

Will gave him a tired grin. "Now you sound like a doctor."

The big man shrugged. "I've been impersonating one for over twenty years now, my friend. Sooner or later it starts to come naturally. But, as I say to all my *paying* patients, don't think of me as a shrink, think of me as someone who owes a small fortune in alimony and has nowhere better to be right now."

"Comforting."

"Works every time."

There was a moment of companionable silence, then Will cleared his throat. "Someone sent me an e-mail a week or so ago. In it was a link to a web site called NobleSacrifice.com."

"Doesn't sound like porn," Don said.

"No. It was a website of banned movies and images."

Don frowned. "Movies and images of what?"

"People being killed. Accidents filmed by people who just happened to be there with a video camera, footage from wars, public dismemberments, disasters . . . I guess all of the things they don't . . . *can't* show you on the main evening news. There were films of soldiers being tortured and killed in various conflicts . . . a lot of war stuff."

"And you looked at all these?"

"No . . . God, no. There were descriptions beneath all the links, more or less telling you what to expect if you were brave or sick enough to watch."

Don grimaced. "Sounds like tons of family fun."

"Yeah, everything from celebrity autopsy photographs to videos of massacres."

"Isn't that stuff illegal though? I mean, how can something like that be available for public viewing?"

"It had a warning . . . can't really remember what it was . . . and a bunch of legalese saying they were protected by FirstAmendment—one word, with a link to whatever they were talking about."

"Jesus. What kind of sick fuck watches something like that?"

Will averted his gaze.

Don's bushy eyebrows rose. "Ah, I see."

"If you're thinking of asking me why, don't," Will told him. "I don't know. I'm not one of those freaks who gets off watching people being killed. I don't even know why I followed that fucking e-mail link in the first place. Morbid curiosity, I guess. But the point is, I did, and even as disgusted as I was by all the videotaped atrocities I saw were available, I still, with everything in me resisting, clicked on one. It said: "Nadejda Petrovna's Execution."

"Who's Nade . . . whatever-the-name-was?"

"A Russian reporter. That's all I know, except of course for the fact that Chechen rebels captured her, and videotaped themselves beheading her. "

"Christ."

"Yeah."

"And you watched this?"

"Not all. What I saw was enough though. I threw up right afterward and I haven't slept since."

"I'm not surprised. That would be enough to fuck up anyone's sleep."

Will nodded. "When I do sleep, there are nightmares, except I see the people I love being hurt, not that woman."

"That's to be expected," Don said.

"Why?"

"Well, because what you have to realize is that you witnessed a murder. How many average Joes can say that? Just because you watched it on a computer screen doesn't lessen the reality of it. You might as well have been looking through a window. And as any murder witness will tell you, it takes some time for the shock to wear off. Even after it does, they find themselves unable to shake off the horror, the stark reminder of just how tenuous this life of ours actually is, and the guilt."

"Guilt?"

"The guilt of watching that poor woman die, the guilt of giving in to that morbid voyeuristic impulse that exists in all of us, and, of course, guilt for not doing something to help her."

Will frowned. "But I couldn't!"

"Exactly. Had you actually been looking at her through a window, you could have tried to help, or called the police . . . something. But you weren't. Remember that this technology—the ability to watch such things from oceans of time and distance away—is relatively new. You wouldn't see it on the news. The movies make it fake enough for you, but when you're essentially *there,* when the atrocity takes place inches from your face, the mind, sitting in the front row, demands intervention. The impotency that follows as a result of inaction leaves a clear path for guilt, self-disgust and depression."

Will pondered this for a moment. Don had the complacent look of a man impressed by his own wisdom, but despite it, Will felt a swell of gratitude toward him.

There was, however, another problem.

"How does knowing all this help me to deal with it? How does it make me stop seeing death and violence every time I close my eyes?"

"It will pass eventually. That I can assure you. My advice is to find something positive in all of this." Will made to say something but Don halted him with a raised hand. "I know, I know. What could *possibly* be positive about it, right? Well, how about the fact that death, to you, is no longer something that happens to everyone else? Maybe from now on every time you hear about some tragedy you won't—like most people do—just shake your head and cluck your tongue before getting back to your crossword puzzle. Maybe now it will actually *mean* something to you."

"That can't be all," Will said, feeling the familiar barbs of panic writhing through him. "I mean . . . just feeling bad about death can't be the only reason this is happening."

"No, the reason this is happening is because you watched a woman getting her head sawn off."

Will felt his hope dwindle. "So in the meantime I just sit around and . . . what? Isn't there something you can prescribe for me?"

"Other than patience, no. At least nothing that would do you any good."

Will rubbed his hands over his face. "Shit."

"Look, Will. You made a mistake watching that damn video. But it's a mistake you'll get over with a bit of time. The cost of it is suffering through this little nightmare show for a while."

When Will dropped his hands from his face, his eyes were hollow, haunted. "And what if that *isn't* all?"

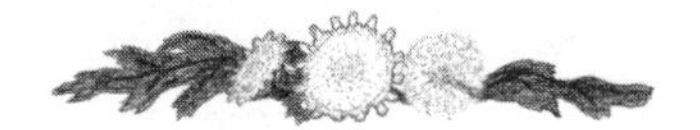

That night, Melanie dragged him from his turbulent nightmares with her lips, and her tongue. He moaned in pleasure as she tended to him, rocked his hips as she moved to straddle him, her hair hanging in her face, eyes twinkling in the gloom. The streetlight filled the window behind her with moonlight blue, making a silhouette of her.

"I love you," he whispered.

She didn't reply. He sat up, embracing her and crushing her heavy breasts against his chest; the nipples were hardened points against his own, her legs like a vice around him, locking him into the soft wetness of her. She breathed in short sharp gasps as he ran his fingers through her hair.

"You feel so good," he told her.

Her breathing caught. She stiffened. Another silhouette rose behind her.

Will froze, his erection wilting immediately.

Slowly, slowly, Melanie threw her head back as if in the throes of orgasm.

And her neck split with a horrendous zipping sound.

As her body fell away and rolled heavily off the bed, Will found himself staring into the still-watching eyes of his wife, his fingers, still tangled in her hair, now the only thing holding her head aloft.

"Help me, Will," she gurgled.

Will screamed.

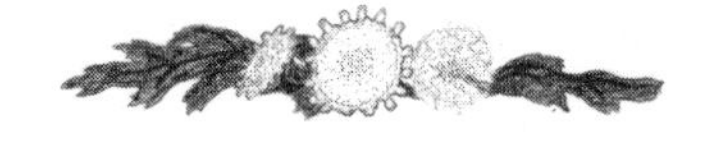

"Don?"

Static crackled over the phone. Will frowned.

"Hello, Don?"

"Hey buddy, you there?" Don said. "I'm on my cell phone, let me call you back when I get home, okay?"

"Okay. Thanks."

"Give me ten minutes."

Less than ten minutes later, with Will standing in the hallway, chewing his thumbnail down to the quick and frantically avoiding his reflection in the hallway mirror for fear of the ghoulish visage he might see staring back at him, the phone rang and he snatched it up. This time the line was clear.

"How's my favorite non-paying patient doing?" Don said.

Will cast a glance at Melanie, who sat on the sofa in the living room, nursing a cup of coffee and looking worried. He felt such a swell of love for her he thought it might reduce him to tears, and an equal pang of regret that she should have to bear witness to whatever was happening to him. Although she hadn't said anything about last night, he had caught her more than once massaging her scalp and wincing, which made him wonder how hard he had pulled her hair. Guilt forced him to look away, and he turned his attention back to the phone.

"Will?"

"I've been better," he told Don. "Last night was the worst night yet."

"More nightmares?"

Will sighed shakily. "No. They're more than nightmares. Hallucinations, maybe. I find myself watching . . ." He lowered his voice, aware that Melanie was within earshot, ". . . watching them killing Mel."

"Watching *who* killing Mel?"

"I don't know. Whoever I saw in that video killing Nadejda Petrovna, I guess."

A rumbling sigh. "Jesus, bud, this has really burrowed its way into you, hasn't it?"

"Yeah. Big time. I'm walking around in a daze from lack of sleep, afraid to close my eyes for fear I'll see the same thing over and over again—some shadowy figure cutting my wife's head off." He heard the faint rustle as Melanie rose and moved away into the kitchen. "I can't do this forever, Don. There has to be something you can do for me."

"I suppose I could prescribe some relaxants for you. Maybe some Valium."

"Will that help?"

"Well, from the sound of it, anything would be better than lack of sleep. If nothing else, it'll help calm you down, siphon off some of that anxiety. It could be that the apprehension and fear is prolonging these 'hallucinations'—you're expecting to see them, so your mind is obliging. I think maybe one calm, uninterrupted night's sleep will do you a world of good."

"It'll take care of the nightmares?"

"It should at least take the edge off them."

"Okay, great," Will said, relieved. "So do I come down there to pick it up, or what?"

"No need. There's a CVS around there somewhere, right?"

"Yeah, over on Sandusky Street."

"Good, I'll call them from here and have them set you up. They'll call when they have the goods for you."

"Thanks a million, Don. Really."

"Don't thank me yet, bud. There's no guarantee this will help, but it *should*."

"It'll work. I know it will." He ran a hand through his hair. "So what do I do in the meantime?"

"Hang up, light a big fire, grab a bottle of wine from the refrigerator, get Melanie drunk as hell, then take her to bed and teach her the ancient art of bang-fu."

Will lowered his voice. "A note from my doctor might help the request. After last night, I expect she'll be a little gun-shy."

"Gun-shy? Man, Freud would have had a field day with your sorry ass. And what happened last night?"

"Coitus interruptus, in the worst possible way."

"Ah, well . . . say no more, and that's a command, not a request. If I start getting envious of your *failed* attempts at getting laid, it'll only serve to remind me how empty and pitiful my own sex life is."

The burgeoning strains of cautious relief threatened to turn Will's laughter into a fit of weeping. Melanie returned to his side, put a hand across his shoulder, her eyes wide with concern.

"Thanks, Don," he said into the phone, his voice unsteady.

"For what? I'm well aware that you do this shit just to irritate me, to get me working harder than I care to. Then you stiff me and I'm the one left depressed. Textbook emotional osmosis, pal. Thanks a bunch."

"Would you knock off the wisecracks? I'm serious," Will told him. "I think I'd have gone completely insane without you."

"Bullshit. My ex-wife said the exact same thing and now she's getting porked by pool boys down in Maui, *on my tab* I might add. Now get off the damn phone and see to business."

"Okay, okay. I owe you one."

"Right. Give Melanie one for me and we'll call it quits."

"Tell him I said 'hello'," Melanie intoned.

He nodded. "Melanie says 'hi'."

A rumble in the distance and a sea of static erupted from the phone. "Don?"

There was silence, then the dial tone stuttered in his ear. With a slight shake of his head, Will hung up.

Melanie turned him around to face her, her hands seeking his face. "Are you all right?"

He summoned the best smile he could muster and wrapped his arms around her. "I think so."

She kissed him, a long passionate kiss he didn't want to end. But after a moment he broke away, staring at the small arched window at the end of the hall. Dark clouds had obscured the sun, leeching the light from the day. A moment later, rain began to fall, pattering against the glass and tapping on the roof.

"What is it?" Melanie asked.

Will looked at her, at the slender oval of her face, and forced a smile. "Do we have any wine?"

Some time later, with a full-blown storm battering the house and premature night pressing against the windows, the phone rang. Sluggishly, already regretting the half-bottle of Cabernet Sauvignon he'd consumed before taking Melanie to bed for mercifully uninterrupted and frenzied sex, Will strode naked to the phone. Through the staticky crackle on the line, a voice laden with practiced cheer informed him that his prescription was ready. He hung up, quickly dressed, and hurried out to his car, the wind wrenching and tearing at him, the rain needling his face.

As he drove the short distance to the store, the wipers working frantically to keep the windshield clear, he realized he already felt better. No hallucinations had spoiled his and Melanie's lovemaking, no shadowy specters had risen from their bedroom floor and afterward, when he'd dozed, there hadn't been any nightmares waiting to thrust him back out of sleep. The dirty feeling still clung to his skin, inside and out, however, a repulsive sensation he knew would take much longer than a day to dissolve.

He allowed himself a sigh and, one hand on the steering wheel, reached over and popped the glovebox. An almost-empty pack of Marlboro Lights tumbled out into his waiting hand. He checked the road ahead and fished out a cigarette, then straightened and thumbed the lighter on the dashboard.

Spindly-legged lightning, like negative images of dead branches, briefly turned the rain on the windshield to glimmering jewels. Will coughed, cigarette clenched between his teeth, and drummed his fingers on the steering wheel.

To his right, the CVS sailed out of the dark, and he flipped the indicator, letting the car coast to a stop as he reached the intersection.

The lighter clacked its readiness and he reached for it.

Then froze.

The hair rose on the nape of his neck. A chill scurried down his spine.

I didn't, he thought, fingers still poised before the lighter. *I didn't see anyone in the mirror.*

A gust of wind buffeted the car, rocking it on its axles.

Closing his eyes, but only for a moment for fear unseen hands would grab him from behind, he whispered further reassurances to himself. *The trick is to* believe *you didn't see it, not just to tell yourself,* he imagined Don telling him. *Force it out of your head, and you'll be okay, bud. Trust me.*

Will nodded slightly, as if Don were with him in the car to see the gesture, and he swallowed. Straightened in his seat.

A car honked behind him, making him jump.

"Just a second, you son of a bitch," he muttered.

The rearview mirror was inches from his face, awaiting him like the sheeted body of a loved one in the morgue. He did not want to look, for ignorance granted him the ability to deny what he thought he'd seen, to deny what might be there.

He cleared the knot of anxiety from his throat and wiped a trembling hand over his face, barely heard the rasp of stubble.

Melanie will complain, he thought. *She'll have beard rash.* He almost smiled, but another angry burst of sound from the car behind him jerked the thought from his mind. Headlights filled the window like glaring eyes, attempting to blind him, as the impatient driver let his car drift closer to Will's fender.

"All *right,* asshole," Will said, and straightened in his seat, eyes squarely on the rearview mirror.

For a moment, he saw nothing but the pebbled rain on the rear windshield as the light made fleeting ghosts that fled across the tan upholstery. But then, there was a woman sitting there, as if she had every right to be, as if she'd dashed in for shelter out of the rain and had just forgotten to thank him, or apologize for the intrusion.

"No," he moaned and yet could not turn away from the horror that exploded within him at the sight of her raising her bony white hands in front of a face that was slowly slipping to the side, as if she were merely nodding off to sleep. He blinked rapidly, demanding his eyelids scrub away the apparition, ghost, hallucination . . . whatever the hell it was.

But the woman remained, her eyes deep dark hollows in a moon-shaped face. And "*Help me, Will*," she whispered, before the angry red wound that circled her neck began to yawn open.

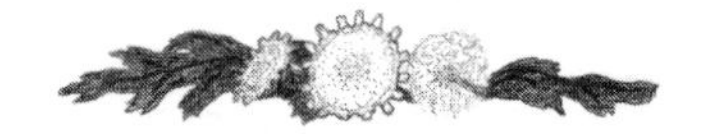

"Sir, are you okay?"

"Valium . . . um, Will Chambers . . . My psych . . . my *doctor* called earlier, called in a prescription for me, for . . . for Valium . . . Don Loach . . . *Doctor* Loach . . . My name is William Chambers."

"Is everything alright? Would you like a glass of water?"

"Please, just the fucking pills, *please* . . . I'm sorry. Please hurry."

"Are you going to be all right? Sir? *Sir*, are you—?"

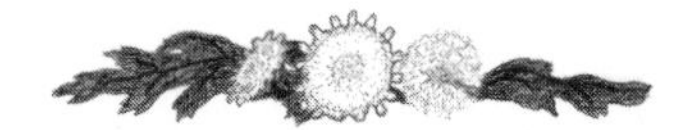

I'll get home, he thought in a panic. *I'll get home and they'll be in my house. Those men, those things, those* animals, *and they'll have my beautiful sweet precious Melanie kneeling on the floor before them. They'll have their hands in her hair and a saw to her throat, and I won't be able to stop them. I won't be able to do anything but regret for the rest of my life that I was fucking stupid dumb piece of shit idiot enough to leave her on her own. They*

tricked me . . . this is what they wanted . . . this is what they wanted to do all along . . . getting inside my head . . . invading me so I'd leave my wife ripe for them to come and cut her fucking head off . . .

He got home and barely thought to put the car in park before he was racing up the driveway and yelling his way into the house, not caring that he was dripping rainwater onto the carpet, not caring that he had left the front door open, not caring, when at any moment the lights might go out, the power might fail and he'd be left alone, in the dark, with the monsters who had most certainly slaughtered his wife.

The door clattered against the wall and shuddered its way back.

Then the house gloated with silence.

"Melanie!"

No answer. He put his hands to his face, nails primed to tear the skin away if it turned out that his nightmare had taken his wife away from him, if the poison that had marred his soul had reached out and murdered her, if—

"Honey, what's wrong?"

He almost collapsed with relief. Melanie, eyes narrowed at the light, hair tousled, was slowly coming down the stairs, tying the belt on her robe to hide her nakedness from the cold, or from *him,* who he imagined must look like a terrible phantom standing crazed in the hallway.

"Oh Jesus," he breathed, the relief draining him, the adrenaline slowly ebbing away. He leaned back against the front door. "I thought they'd got you," he whispered and with the admission came a huge whooping sob that set Melanie hurrying to cradle him in her arms. "*I thought they'd got you,*" he wept, trembling.

The tears made the dead woman behind his eyes appear to swim.

"Don will call to check on you tomorrow."

Will nodded, already feeling drowsy. The Valium would work. It would have to. The alternatives were looking grimmer by the second and the renewed onslaught of gruesome images was now sharing head-space with thoughts of institutionalization and white padded rooms with screams for cushions and dripping faucets for music.

The bed felt soft and eased the rigidity from his muscles. Beside him sat Melanie, one hand propping up her head, the other stroking his hair like a violinist playing a muted lullaby.

"I'm sorry," he told her, as the shades began to creep down over his mind's window. "I'm so sorry this is happening."

"Hush," she soothed. "It will be better after you've had a good night's sleep. Tomorrow we can have a nice breakfast and maybe go for a walk. How does that sound, hmm?"

He composed a smile, but it was not heartfelt. "Good," he said, feeling a warm tide rising in his chest, lapping at his throat. "Sounds good."

"Try to sleep now," she whispered, and her whisper had an echo. He wanted to point this out to her, but the tide had reached his tongue and seized it. He was not alarmed, for it felt sweet as honey and he let it fill him until he was lost in its thick, comforting folds.

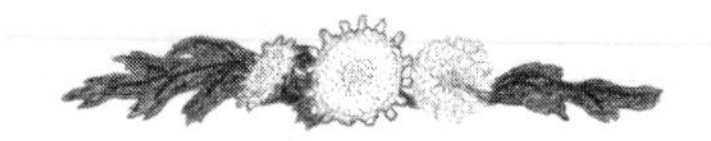

The phone rang.

Melanie dropped the paperback she'd been valiantly attempting to read in an effort to forget what was happening to Will and hurried into the hallway. With a shaky sigh, she snatched up the receiver. "Hello?"

"Mel. It's Don. Is Will still up?"

"Hi, Don. No, he's asleep. Should I wake him?"

"Absolutely not. Let him sleep. He needs it. Besides,

it's you I wanted to talk to anyway."

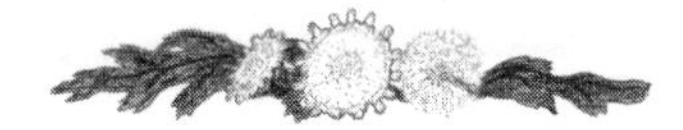

"Wake up, pig."

Frowning, Will's eyes snapped open and he coughed, wheezed and watched in amazement as what appeared to be dust rolled away across a stone floor. He shivered as a deep chill settled into his bones. Suffused white light pulsed across his vision, quickly followed by an acrid tang that was wholly unfamiliar.

"Where—?"

A sharp blow to his stomach propelled him backward and he yelped in pain as his back collided painfully with a solid wall.

Only then was he truly awake.

Jesus . . . he thought, the now-familiar terror clawing its way through him with icy nails. *Jesus, they're here. They came while I was sleeping. Melanie . . . oh God, where's Melanie?*

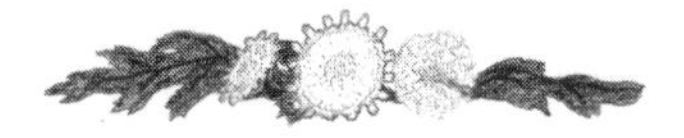

"You're familiar with Post-Traumatic Stress Disorder?" Don asked her.

"Yes, it's fairly common in soldiers, right?"

"That's right, but it's actually more common than that. Any victim of shock or trauma can suffer from it. Rape, molestation, accident victims . . ."

"Okay."

"The reason I mention it is because I'm starting to think that's what Will's suffering from."

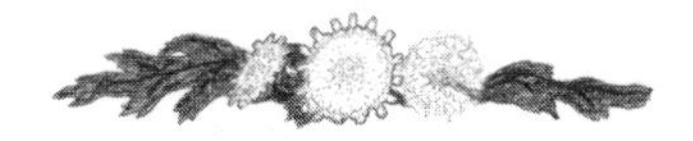

Before him stood a tall thin man, dressed from head to toe in black.

"Who are *you?*" The questions pushed against Will's

tongue like water through a crack in dam. "How did I get here?" For it hadn't taken him long to realize that he was no longer in his bed, or anywhere near it.

The man said nothing, but despite the headgear he wore, allowing only his eyes and the wide bridge of his nose to be seen, Will knew he was grinning.

"Get up," the man ordered then, in a clipped accent Will had only ever heard before in spy movies. *Russian*, he thought.

"Why am I here?" Will pleaded with him. "Tell me, please. What . . . what are you going to do to me?" He was trembling so bad he thought he might rattle himself to pieces. The cold gnawed at him—a merciless freezer cold.

"Stop asking question." It emerged as: 'Stup asging kesschun.' The man leveled the large assault rifle strapped across his chest in Will's direction. Distantly Will found the fact that he could discern not even the slightest tremble in the man's hands incredibly disturbing. It suggested a callousness only obtained by familiarity with violence. Whoever the man behind the mask was, this was a role he had played often.

Will moved, slowly, toward the man, and as he did so, he realized he was wearing clothes he'd never seen before, and certainly hadn't donned himself—a shapeless, ill fitting suit of the kind he'd only ever seen on the news. Prisoners in penitentiaries wore them. His heart thumped in his throat hard enough to make his head hurt, eyes brimming with tears.

"How did I get here? Please . . . tell me."

"Stand," said the man. "Stand *now!*"

Will quickly obeyed, the dusty floor ice-cold against the soles of his bare feet, making his toes curl. *I'm dreaming*, he thought. *Those pills did something to me and I'm dreaming*. But he knew, though he wished he didn't, that whatever was happening now was the proper end for whatever horror he'd been suffering, that this was where it had been leading him. And that it was no dream.

I'm going to die, he realized and felt his legs threaten to buckle beneath him.

The armed man nodded his satisfaction and thrust a hand in the center of Will's chest, knocking him back against the wall. Will, winded, looked around at the small room, at the fall of dust motes illuminated by harsh sunlight that slanted through the bars of the room's sole window.

The man muttered something unintelligible and a narrow door opened at the far side of the room.

Three men entered. All of them were dressed in the same garb as the gunman. One of them held a video camera by his side; another held a pistol.

Will felt his skin crawl.

The third man held a saw.

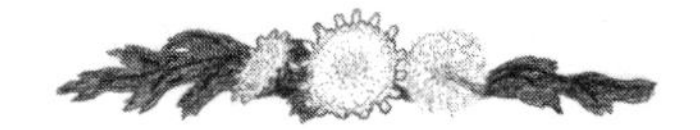

"The symptoms of PTSD are numerous," Don told her, "hallucinations, anxiety attacks, night terrors, memory loss, insomnia, erratic moods, lapses in concentration, depress-ion . . . sound like anyone we know?"

Melanie sagged. "So what do we do about it? Is there a way to treat it that doesn't involve a tight jacket and a cushioned room?"

"Of course. There are Neuro-Emotional Techniques, a relatively new form of 'power therapy' that have proved far more effective than 'talk therapy.' They target the mind through the body using systems borrowed from the Chi—"

Melanie rolled her eyes. "Don."

"Sorry. But that's your answer. There are numerous treatments available." He sighed heavily. "What I think happened to Will is that after seeing that video, he almost immediately began to visualize the murder, only with you and I'm guessing *himself* in that woman's place. You can imagine what persistent visualizations like that can do to the nerves. To 'cure' itself of the guilt and horror, and to save the imaginary victim, the brain can become convinced that *it's* really suffering the agonies the eyes have only witnessed. It can even start reproducing the sensations associated with such a death. In short, it can make the person suffer on someone else's behalf."

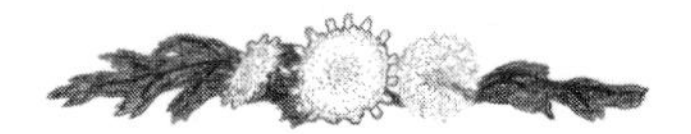

"Oh no," Will moaned, his body vibrating with fear as the tall man lunged forward and grabbed him by the collar of his jumpsuit. "*Now!*" he shouted into Will's face and flung him toward the other men, who had stopped in the center of the room. The one with the pistol pointed it at Will's head and said something in his own language.

The video man busied himself with setting up the camera, his ministrations oddly calm—he could have been fixing the machine for a kindly old lady, instead of preparing it to film an execution. And Will had no doubt that was exactly what was happening. What was *going* to happen, and that in a few days or weeks, his death would be appearing on a sleazy website he'd once had the misfortune to visit. A horrendous snuff site that justified its existence by claiming it had a responsibility to show the world what they were trying so hard not to see, that they had *no business* seeing, when in actual fact, it had a far more sinister purpose.

Will knew that now.

What he *didn't* know was how it had been done—how he had gone to sleep beside his loving wife and woken up in a strange place surrounded by masked men who spoke a foreign language.

He supposed it didn't matter now.

He was shoved to his knees, but on the way down, he caught a glimpse of the world beyond the window, and it was not his world at all, but a cold, stark landscape of faltering buildings and slush-laden roads.

Not my world at all, he thought with a flicker of calm.

Not my world. I'm not here. They can't hurt me they won't hurt me they can't.

A surer voice rose like a bloated corpse to the surface of his mind.

But they will.

He thought of Melanie, stroking his hair last night, and felt a debilitating wave of sorrow at the thought of never seeing her again, of her never knowing how or why her husband had died.

I love you, baby, he thought, willing the words to cross time and space and distance, to penetrate the veil of the real world so she would hear them. *So very much.*

They bound his wrists and ankles with thick heavy rope that smelled vaguely of motor oil.

"Please don't," he pleaded, trying in vain to shuffle away from them. "I didn't do anything to you. I don't even know who you are." Tears spilled down his cheeks. "Please. I have a *wife* . . ." Terror unlike anything he'd ever known swept through him.

Somewhere beyond the room, a church bell tolled.

Cold steel bit the skin on the back of his neck.

"Don't . . ." he sobbed, as he struggled.

The camera began to whirr.

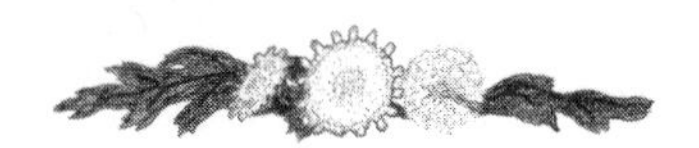

"Don. Why are you telling me this? Nothing like that is going to happen to Will."

"I know, I know. I'm not saying it will. I use it only to illustrate what the mind can do to someone when it manages to convince itself it's what the body deserves. Atonement for not being able to prevent someone else's suffering. It's a remarkable and tragic condition, but all the seeds are showing themselves in Will, and that's why we have to monitor him closely. You need to stay with him. He needs you now, Mel. You're the only link he has left to the outside world."

"Outside world?"

"Yeah, the *real* world, because for all intents and purposes it would appear he's losing his grasp on it at a frightening rate. Either that, or whatever dark alternative world he envisions in his head is tightening its hold on *him*."

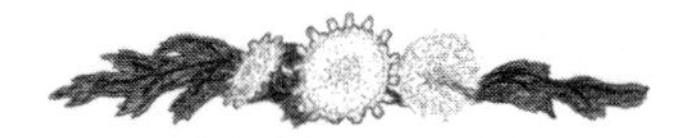

Melanie hung up, and hugged herself against the unmerciful cold that Don's phone call had left with her. My God, could it really be so bad? Could she wake up one day to find Will had utterly and completely lost his mind? What would she do? How could she save him?

No, she decided, brushing a single tear from her eye. She would never let that happen. Never. She was stronger than that and she knew Will was too. She'd help him climb his way back from the dark valley into which he'd stumbled.

As she made her way to the bedroom, she brushed the chill from her shoulders. It almost seemed as if the house itself had grown colder. She guessed it was her imagination but told herself to check the thermostat anyway when she returned from checking on Will. A fat lot of good she'd do her husband if she let the heating go berserk.

She cracked open the bedroom door, slicing a wedge of yellow light from the dark inside. "Honey?" she whispered.

Will didn't answer, but she fancied if she strained her ears she could hear him breathing deeply, though it was hard to tell with the rain drumming on the roof. Nevertheless, she allowed herself a slight sigh of relief. It was fiercely encouraging to see that he wasn't tossing, turning or screaming at ghosts. Perhaps the pills would do the trick after all. She prayed they would.

She opened the door a little wider and entered the room. Will was lying on his back, facing the ceiling, eyes closed. Slowly, she lowered herself down on her side of the bed, wincing at the faint squeak from the mattress springs.

I love you too, she thought, reaching over to stroke his hair, then realized how odd it was that she had responded to a prompt he hadn't given her. Her fingers found the soft curls and lightly brushed over them.

He turned his head toward her, eyes still closed, and she quickly withdrew her hand, annoyed at herself for disturbing him.

"Hush," she whispered.

And watched in stunned, numb horror as Will's face met the pillow and blood began to flow from his partly open mouth.

"Will?" She quickly stood, and shook him. "Oh Jesus! *Will?*"

His head rolled free of his body, tumbling down beneath the covers on her side of the bed. Melanie gasped, clutched both hands to her chest as if fearing her heart would burst through it at any moment, and felt the strength leave her.

"Will?" she croaked, staggering back, away from the bed and the ragged bleeding neck still poking up from the covers. She collided with a dresser and fell heavily to the floor, a trembling hand rising to her mouth. Briefly she tried to get up, a scream trapped like angry wasps in her throat, unable to break free. And then the world went black and she fell willingly into its soporific depths.

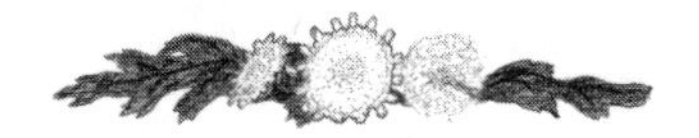

Melanie stared into her coffee, the steam rising like sinuous ghosts from a black pond, and remembered Don's words, spoken over the phone on the last night she'd awoken from yet another hideous and terrifying nightmare.

This has to be more than a coincidence, Don. What's happening to me?

Her fingers trembled as she traced a line around the rim of the cup.

Cold white sunlight pressed against the windows of the kitchen. From the television in the living room came the sound of a solemn voice relating the details of another atrocity. Melanie put her palms to her face and closed her eyes.

An impassive, bloodless, *familiar* face shrieked at her in the dark.

She jerked upright in the chair and looked at her hands, at the intensified trembling in them and stifled a sob. Will was dead. Almost five weeks had passed and still she expected him to come waltzing into the kitchen, unshaven and yawning with a dopey smile on his face. She missed him so much, missed the smell of him in the house, the *feel* of him in the house, a house she would soon lose if the police got their way. Their suspicion and doubt accompanied them like an unseen partner every time they called, or came to visit, which they did with increasing regularity. Though they had found no weapon, and could prove nothing yet, she knew they were committed to doing so. The implausibility of Will's death hadn't been lost on them, but she had been unable to satiate their demands for a reasonable story. The truth was an impossible nightmare they didn't believe.

But none of that mattered now. She'd lost Will, and nothing that lay ahead of her could hurt her more, even if she spent the rest of her life in prison. Even if they put her to death. At least it would kill the grief, and the soul-freezing fear that had possessed her over the last week or so.

Trauma, Mel. The reason it seems so familiar is because it is. It can manifest itself in different ways, but essentially it's the exact same thing Will went through.

She rubbed her fingers over her temples, chewed her lower lip.

So this is what he had to suffer. You know . . . I wished for his pain. When he was sick, I wished I could take it from him. Now I don't want it. What kind of a person does that make me?

Human, Don had assured her. These days she felt anything but.

Next to her coffee cup sat an unopened pack of cigarettes. She quickly tore the plastic off, discarded the foil that was all that stood between her and the panacea of nicotine, and quickly withdrew one. She lit it and inhaled deeply. She considered calling Don again, but resisted. Sooner or later she would have to conquer the fear on her own, and maybe it was better to start weaning herself off his aid now before she grew to depend on him so much he tired of her constant phone calls and referred her to someone else. Someone less caring. Someone who didn't *understand* what had happened her husband.

I've thought long and hard about it, Mel, Don had told her a few days after the funeral. *And it all keeps pointing to the same thing, though professional skepticism prevents me from buying it outright.* She hadn't wanted to hear it, but let him continue. Closure, she knew, was needed, or she would forever be haunted by the mystery of Will's death. Would never be able to stop blaming herself unless someone offered proof that it hadn't been her fault. An irrational need, perhaps, but very little about her life these days was rational.

You've heard of stigmata, right? When people, usually religious folks, start showing the wounds of Christ on their bodies? Bleeding feet and palms, and all that jazz?

She'd told him she had and he'd proceeded to inform her of various examples in which ordinary people had suffered extraordinary tortures, with no apparent cause.

There was a colleague of mine in Washington who documented a case in which an eight-year-old boy, after witnessing his mother's arm being torn off by a Rottweiler, almost immediately began to develop bruises and small wounds, consistent with bite marks, on his own arm, the same one his mother had lost, though he'd been nowhere near a dog. Three weeks later, the arm was hanging on by strings of flesh and little else, with no physiological explanation for why it had done so. In the end, psychiatrists were brought in to study the boy; they concluded that the boy's trauma at what had happened to his beloved mother was so great, it somehow lent him the ability to experience her pain, by subconsciously willing her wounds onto himself. I imagine if a boy can "borrow" his mother's wounds to punish himself, then a devout follower of Jesus Christ could conceivably do the same.

The phone rang, jarring the thoughts from Melanie's head. She ignored the persistent shrilling and finished her cigarette. As she'd hoped, it had calmed her, but not nearly enough. She rose and went to the bathroom, locking the door behind her out of habit. As she tugged down her panties and sat on the cold oval of the toilet, she pondered Don's theory, and, as she had when he'd first proposed it, decided it was impossible. But then, wasn't the manner of Will's death also impossible? No matter which way she looked at it, something unnatural had occurred in their bedroom that night, and yet she couldn't force herself to believe that her husband had willed his own death. Trauma could be overcome. Shock would always fade, and people didn't just decapitate themselves in the dark without a weapon, as the police persisted in reminding her.

Nothing more sinister than empathy.

She covered her face with her hands and moaned. Her body ached, the muscles in her back like taut wires beneath a trembling sheet. There had to be a rational answer to her nightmare but she was no longer sure she wanted to know it. Perhaps there was safety in mystery. Shaking her head, she opened her eyes.

There was a man standing before her, his shadow thick and cold.

Melanie's breath snagged in her throat and she looked up, tears threatening to blur her vision, fear like a snare around her throat, tightening, tightening.

Something hit the floor, and rolled and when at last she gathered the courage to look upon it, she found herself staring into her husband's glassy eyes. The body stood weaving against the wall.

She screamed and grabbed her hair, her nails digging, then dragging down her face, drawing blood, as all the horror, the loss, and the grief erupted, spewing from her open mouth as she slid from the toilet to her knees, even as instinct tried to tug her away from the head on the floor and the still, silent form of the dead man it belonged to.

And still she screamed.

"Help me, Mel . . ."

And screamed.

Until the scream became a tortured gurgle as a slim but deep wound began to draw its way across her throat.

The God of Discord

Steven E. Wedel

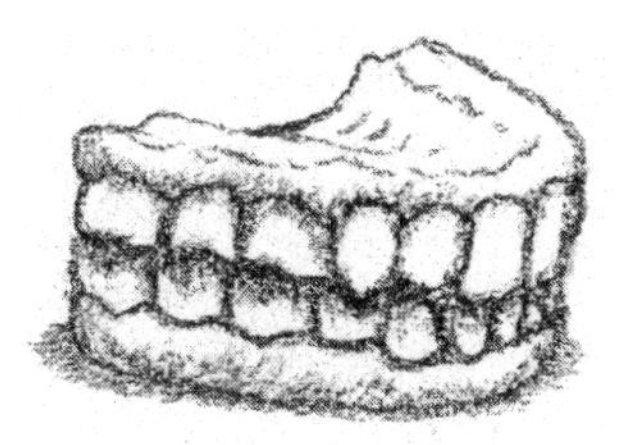

I never knew surgery was so hard.

My daughter was bad luck from the very beginning. She was conceived in the backseat of a 1976 Monte Carlo when I was seventeen years old. At the time, I was sure she had ruined my chances of ever amounting to something. Still, I didn't think she could bring about the end of the human race.

But that's possible now that . . . now that we've been noticed.

It wasn't Tina's fault. Not that it matters anymore. She's dead. We killed her a couple of days ago. She's stinking up the apartment now. Her heart is drying up and shriveling on a Corningware plate on her bedside table. The cockroaches have enjoyed the feast. I keep her body covered. I can't stand the thought of the roaches getting into her ruined body.

The smell of her burned lungs is still pretty strong in here. When the neighbors came knocking, I told them Lori, my wife, had burned our dinner.

Tina was a mistake and a pain in the ass most of the time, but I loved her. She never meant to do wrong. She was just stupid. She was like her mother that way.

My wife is hanging by her neck over our bed. I disemboweled her, letting her guts slide in a slippery, glistening pile onto our bed sheet.

Still, it isn't enough. *He* has seen it all. *He* has watched my sacrifices. *He* approves, but he will not be satisfied. He is coming. He is eternal, older than language. And he's tone-deaf.

I am sitting here, watching him watching me as he moves through the universe toward Earth, toward Man, toward me and the end of all that I have ever known. I will record my tale and then I will die—an appetizer for a god.

It's better than dying in an industrial accident or being run over in the street.

Tina is—was—in seventh grade. She was in the Longfellow Junior High School marching band. She plays—played—the clarinet. She wasn't good at it. She was terrible. I used to thank the god I once believed in that I got her clarinet for just $25 in a pawnshop and didn't pay hundreds for an instrument I knew she'd never master. She began playing last year, in the sixth grade, at Coolidge Elementary School. I don't know why she ever got into the band. She always hated sucking on that clarinet's wooden reed. I guess she didn't know about the reed when she chose the instrument.

I only have two Valium pills left. The damn doctor won't prescribe any more until the end of the month. The other pills, the red ones I use to supplement my Valium supply, are all gone. Rudy won't sell me any more because I owe him money. I wish I could take these last pills and go to sleep. But, even when I close my eyes, I see the god's eye in the dark, looking into my soul . . .

I'm not there yet. I'll come to that soon enough.

Tina was horrible on that clarinet. The first year, she practiced every night for at least an hour. It sounded as if she were slowly squeezing the life out of a kitten with a very high voice. I had to leave the house a lot because I just couldn't stand to hear the cacophony she made. I get migraines so easily, anyway, and hearing her torture that instrument always set me off.

She didn't practice much over the summer, but picked it up again once school started in the fall. I wouldn't have believed her ability could have deteriorated if I hadn't heard the sound for myself. I considered smashing the clarinet to bits and pieces when she left it home one day when there was no band class at school. I couldn't do it, though.

That's right, world. I couldn't do it. It would have broken my little girl's heart. Well, that heart is turning black and hard on a dinner plate now and we may all be doomed because I didn't have the balls to smash a clarinet.

On December 21st, the first day of winter, Tina was practicing for a concert the band put on during the last day of school before the big Christmas break. She was playing—trying to play—"Silent Night." She hit a series of wrong notes that made every hair on my body stand on end. A chill passed through me—a chill that seemed to turn my bone marrow to slush. I looked at my wife and saw that she also felt it. Her hair was standing up and I guess the sudden chill made her wet herself. Lori never had good bladder control after the pregnancy.

Oh, but the strangeness was just beginning.

The apartment building seemed to . . . stretch and groan, like a man waking up after a long nap. The hallway outside our apartment filled with people running toward the stairs and I heard the word "earthquake" several times over the agonized sounds of straining wood and cracking brick.

Tina ran out of her bedroom, the accursed clarinet still in her hand. Her hair—her stringy reddish-blonde hair—was white. Her skin was like a marble statue, as if all the pigments had been sucked right out of her flesh. The spattering of freckles on her nose stood out like drops of old motor oil. She tried to say something, but when she opened her mouth it was full of blood.

"Oh my dear God!" Lori shouted. She ran to Tina and got there before I could. She made Tina open her mouth, asking her all the time if the reed had cut her, had she bit her tongue, did something fall on her, had Daddy hit her again . . . what happened?

Tina's teeth fell out when she opened her mouth that time. There was more blood. A lot of blood. Or maybe it just looked that way because it was mixed with so much saliva. It seemed like a lot at the time. The stains are still on the carpet.

We ran out into the hall with Tina. We had to get her to a doctor. The building was still groaning and trembling.

The hallway was empty, but we found most of the people from our floor and the six floors above us crammed into the stairwell. It took us forty-five minutes to go down five flights of stairs, then another two hours to get through the panicked streets to the hospital, which is just eight miles from here. By that time, Tina's mouth had stopped bleeding and she'd fallen asleep in Lori's arms in the back seat of the car.

The doctor couldn't tell us anything. He was just a kid—still had pimples on his face and probably couldn't have grown more than peach fuzz on his chin if he tried for a week. He said he'd never heard of such a thing but guessed it was probably related to her diet. Tina was skinny, but she ate like a horse and didn't gripe if you gave her vegetables or candy bars; it was all the same to her.

The world changed that night. Do you remember it? Those assholes in Washington, D.C., have been trying to cover it up, but I saw the stars falling, felt the earthquakes and smelled the rising oceans and the stink of the famine dead. I know the world changed that night.

No one—not even me—knew that my daughter had attracted the attention of an entity that had never before taken notice of this spinning little ball in the universe. No one knew that we were now being watched. No one knew that he would come for us.

But he is. I first saw him the night after Tina made her musical mistake. I was sitting on the narrow ledge our landlord calls a patio. Tina was in her room, crying over her missing teeth and the fact she couldn't play in the band concert because the lack of teeth made it impossible for her to blow in that damnable instrument. I got tired of her wailing and, instead of whipping her for making all the noise, I put on my coat and went out to the patio.

I was sitting in a chair out there, not doing anything, really. I took a long drink of Bacardi. I'm a working man—or, at least I was before the damn layoffs—and I deserve to have a moderate drink if I want one. I took a drink, tipping my head back . . . and saw the red eye looking down at me.

I spewed rum over the ledge of the patio and almost dropped the bottle. I couldn't believe what I saw. I looked again, and there it was . . . a giant, round red eye with a slitted black pupil, like a cat's. It was just out there—in the deep darkness of space. But it was looking at us. Looking at me.

I made Lori come out on the patio and look at it. At first she said she couldn't see it. I finally had to take her head in my hands and point her face toward the eye. I was scared. Maybe I was a little too rough. I didn't mean to bruise her. But, it worked. Once I pointed her in the right direction, she saw that great big fucking eye looking back down at us.

I suggested we call NASA. Lori didn't like that idea. She said people who reported things flying in the sky disappeared if they told the government. She was right, of course. We decided not to do anything. We'd wait and see if the thing was there the next night.

You guessed it. It was there. But it was bigger. No . . . not bigger. It was *closer*. The eye was moving toward us. It was more than double the size it had been the night before. Its gaze was so intense I thought I could feel it reaching into me and feeling around, like a laser beam.

This time, I did call NASA. It took me a while to find the toll-free phone number, but I got through. I told them what I saw. A man—a lieutenant, I think—said they'd get some telescopes pointed in the direction I described and see what they could find.

That night, the god got into my mind, into my dreams. His name is Dhargolmet. He told me that. He told me he had heard of my race but he'd always believed we were beneath his concern . . . until one of us had played the sweet music that had caught his attention. He said he was coming and he would enslave us and make my race fill the universe with the music he had heard coming from my home.

That music! It was a series of wrong notes bleating through a horn held by an inexperienced child. It was an accident!

But what could I do?

I tuned into the news the next day. I watched CNN for hours, but there was no mention of NASA finding anything unusual. Maybe, I thought, just maybe it had all been an illusion.

Lori took Tina to Wal-Mart to buy some hair dye that day. Lori had convinced herself that Tina's hair turned white because of a peroxide accident . . . never mind the earthquakes and other shit I told her had happened.

They also went to the dentist. The dentist took a mold of Tina's mouth to make her a set of false teeth. Tina was happy about it. The dentist promised to have the teeth for her before the break from school was over.

A lot of good they'll do her now.

The eye was not, of course, any illusion. That night it was there again, closer than before. The first night, it had appeared as a thing about the size of my fist. This time it was as big as a tractor tire. It was out there, staring at us, at me, its slitted pupil unblinking, unflinching . . . emotionless.

I called NASA again. This time I talked to a woman who was not so sympathetic. She asked if I was under the influence of alcohol or drugs. I slammed the phone down on the bitch.

Lori would hardly even glance out the patio doors. She took a quick look and agreed with me that there was an eye in the sky. The bruises on her face had turned a dark purple and I felt bad about it.

That night, he came to me again in my dream. I begged for mercy. I begged him to spare all humankind. I begged . . .

He told me that as long as one among us existed who could create the music he had heard, he would come for us. He would fill the universe with that sound. The only alternative was a sacrifice made in his name.

Sacrifice . . .

We murdered my little girl on Christmas Eve. Lori

was reluctant. Sure, she said, she'd seen the red eye watching us, but she hadn't had any visitor in her dreams. No one had told her to kill Tina. She said I might be sick, that maybe I'd been taking too many pills with my rum. She started to get hysterical and I had to . . . make her be quiet. I regretted hurting her, especially since her face was still bruised, but what had to be done was bad enough without her screaming that I was crazy.

I ground up two of my Valiums and put them in a glass of Coke for Tina. She was asleep before the glass was half-empty. I carried her to her bed and lay her down as gently as I'd ever done when she was an infant.

Thirty minutes later, I had her heart in my hands. The sweet child never stirred when I came to her with our best butcher knife and a smaller paring knife I got for free after listening to a cutlery demonstration at the local grocery store.

I never knew surgery was so hard. I didn't how to get through the rib cage. I had to go in through her abdomen. I cut a slit in her soft little tummy and reached into the hot wet wound, working my way up until I found a hard lump that I knew had to be the heart. I pulled. I had to pull hard to bring it low enough to cut it free with the paring knife.

It was so small. So warm and slippery . . . that little engine that had kept my girl alive.

I put it on the plate very carefully, then held the plate over my head and said, "Dhargolmet, I offer you this sacrifice. Show mercy on my race." Then I put the plate on Tina's bedside table.

I was about to leave the room to wash my hands when I saw Tina's clarinet case on her dresser. The god had not given any specific instructions on the sacrifice. I realized it wasn't the heart that would please him. It was my little girl's lungs that had produced the air that created that accursed music.

I reached into her belly again, feeling around until I found her lungs. I cut them out. I knew they had to be destroyed, so I took them to the kitchen, put them in a cake pan, poured a bottle of rum into the pan and dropped a match on it.

The heat from that fire was incredible. It was so hot that I felt sure I had taken care of the problem. Mankind was safe! I washed my hands, told the neighbors to fuck off, and went to the patio for a drink.

The slitted red eye was as big as a school bus, like a bright round patch sewn onto the fabric of the night sky. I remember crying. I drank the rest of Tina's Coke and went to bed.

The god laughed at me that night. He said I had destroyed one source of his beautiful music, but my wife could easily produce another. His first task, he said, would be to impregnate her with his own seed so that she would bear a child better able to play the music he loved.

Of course, I couldn't allow that. Lori wouldn't take my Valium-and-Coke cocktail. I had to crack her over the head with a lamp. Groping around in Tina's body had been bad enough, and I had known what I wanted then. I couldn't bring myself to do that to Lori. And, I don't know enough about female biology to know exactly which parts make a baby.

So I put a hook in the ceiling over our bed, tied a rope to it and fastened a noose around her neck. Then I cut her open, like I'd seen a hog cut open in some movie, and everything just sort of slid out and plopped in a sticky, steaming mess on the bed.

I dug around in the stuff until I found some things I didn't recognize. I figured those had to be her reproductive organs, so I burned them in the same pan—now blackened and warped—where I'd burned Tina's lungs.

The neighbors came pounding again. I ignored them. It had been a harrowing few days, so I took a nap.

Dhargolmet came and laughed at me while I was asleep. He was not just a voice and an eye in the darkness of my dream this time. I could see him. He was huge. Bigger than huge. His slimy bulk was a solar system of ropy tentacles that looked like the entrails of my wife and daughter. The tentacles slithered, coiled and unfurled around a body that seemed to be a solid, living piece of nighttime, with that one monstrous burning red eye planted in the center of it, making the darkness all the more black.

I awoke in the early evening. My head ached terribly. I took a Valium, noticing how few of the little blue pills were left. It was still Christmas Day, so I plugged in the lights on our tree, but the little blinking bulbs reminded me of eyes in the dim room, and they made my head hurt more, so I turned them off. Well, I knocked the tree over, which pulled the electric plug out of the wall. The lights were off.

I dreaded the night, but soon it was upon me. As the light of the sun faded, the red eye of the god became increasingly visible. It was the size of football field and I was sure I could see it actually growing as it moved closer to Earth. Closer to me.

Praying did no good. I prayed to the god I grew up with, but that didn't help. I prayed to Dhargolmet himself for mercy, but he only laughed into the confusion of my mind. I looked up again and saw that his eye was even closer. The very stars were as insignificant as floating motes of dust that he ignored in his progress toward this planet.

I guess I passed out then. The next thing I remember, I woke up this afternoon, still on the patio, with the afternoon sun shining down on me. I was very cold because I'd gone outside in just my clothes and a jacket. When I began writing this, my hands were almost too stiff to hold the pencil. But, the warmth of the apartment and a fresh bottle of Bacardi have thawed me out.

Not that it matters now. I know what I have to do. I have destroyed the innocent child who played the accidental notes that attracted this monster. I have destroyed the womb from which she came. The only thing left to do is destroy the man who produced the seed that fertilized that womb and created the girl who played the notes.

Deep night has come. Dhargolmet is close. His great round orb fills my view of the sky. If I do not destroy myself, he will use me to create more misguided musicians like my sweet daughter. If I am dead, perhaps he will be without hope and will turn away from the Earth.

Perhaps.

He is watching me now. I feel that he knows what I am about to do. I can feel that he is nervous and angry. He is shouting into my mind that I should not, that he forbids it. That is all the proof I need that what I am doing is the right thing.

Someday there will be statues to honor me. I will take my place among the saints and martyrs for my willingness to make this final sacrifice to save my fellow man. As it turns out, the mistake made by a daughter who was herself a mistake will turn me into a hero.

I will go to the edge of the balcony now and throw myself into the night sky, toward the watching red eye.

On behalf of my entire family, I apologize for this brush with extinction.

Because Afterwards, They Pull the Shades

Clifford Brooks

From a distance, we look like a couple of drunk buds.
If that's what you need to see.

The pain is beginning again. Subtle at first, like a pinch in the gut from a lover. My balls tighten, pull up and nestle in the protection of my thighs. For the time being, they are out of harm's way. If only it were that simple, like a child, I would cover my eyes and hide in plain sight.

They watch her die. All of them. Nobody helps. Nobody lifts a finger to stop me from doing what I do. From violating her. Right there. Out in the open. In the park.

I use a small knife. One with a whale bone handle and a tempered steel blade. I punch her with it. Blow after blow after blow. And the sound, like the beating of a rug, is punctuated with puffs of expelled breath.

Still they watch. As if the futility of their actions is a foregone conclusion.

The thought thrums through the fat one's mind like angry wasps. *What the fuck is she doing in the park at night? ALONE!* He looks to his buddy, but before their eyes align, like like-poled magnets, they repel. The fat one looks back at me, at what I do. His face is pinched and lined, like he's just bitten into something sour. *She is so fucking stupid, man. Where did she have to be so badly that she'd walk through* this *neighborhood after dark?* He shakes his head as if he has all the answers. *Nowhere.*

Near the basketball court she falls to her knees, gripping her stomach, trying to keep her insides inside. She looks up at me through locks of hair plastered to her face with blood and sweat and tears and saliva. A face washed free of blame and guilt. It is the visage of the victim—one who can do no wrong, one who has done no wrong—that brings a smile so wide that it pushes my face into a triangle of need.

The middle-aged marketing manager *Just came out to the park to play a friendly game of basketball* and his boss stop their late night game in observance. *I've got a wife and kids* his Nike basketball shoes and pressed Adidas shorts confess, as he holds the basketball before him, like he's just birthed the most precious of excuses.

She hears a sound and somehow she makes it to her feet again. She doesn't know that it is the four-stroke idle of an engine—to her, it is the sound of salvation.

The biker and his chick pull up along the curb. He keys the cycle into silence. They are close enough to watch the tableaux, yet these are not box seats. They look at each other and shrug their shoulders in unenlightened unison. Their faces are as blank as if they'd just been asked the Final Jeopardy question, and to their chagrin, it had nothing to do with consumer grades of leather or roadside attractions.

The woman's hair is blond, like the victim's, and her well-traveled skin is scarred and crossed. The side of her nose is infected red; the result of a failed piercing. The biker is a large man, and though still straddling the bike, I can tell that he's got two to three inches on me. His hair is shoulder-length and as silver as the bike's handlebars.

They get off the bike, the woman first, followed by the biker. He is careful to steady it on its stand before they move, indecisively, a couple steps closer. The man shoves one of his large hands in the back pocket of his woman's tight jeans, and rests the other on the leather-fringed seat of his Excelsior.

I yank my mind from their reality and force my full attention into the victim. I jab her with it, between thrusts of the blade, and she wonders which intrusion is worse. Her eyes begin to roll, teeter-tottering up and down in her head as she tries to hang on.

The spark is still there, behind her eyes, taunting me with its resiliency. I've lost track of how many times my blade has pierced her flesh, but she hasn't. A part of her brain is doing the math, tallying each blow up and scratching it, indelibly, into her brain. The pain no longer radiates from specific loci, she can no longer say that her stomach hurts, or the cut in her cheek is killing her. It is the strength of her denial, nothing more, that keeps her from falling limp upon the pavement.

Using the bloodied blade, I lift her chin and look into her glassy glaze. "You are dead," I whisper, then push the tip of the blade into her throat. She tries to swallow it, gurgles up blood between her lips and around the blade, and her eyes roll in her head like they're on axels.

One of the onlookers, a grocery store clerk, pulls the cell phone from the holster at her hip and calls the police. She closes her eyes to the sight as I begin to eat my victim. It is too much for her packaged-goods mentality: *Lean Rump Roast $1.99 a Pound—Butcher's Special.* Her stomach rolls over the thought *Shit, they're not going to believe this tomorrow. No way.* Then she thinks she should puke. So she does. All over her Doc Martens.

The attending officer scrutinizes them with his questions. It never occurs to him to ask why it took them so long to call, or why, after it was all over, they bothered to call at all.

They turn as the ambulance pulls up; its sirens blaring like a Type-A dinner bell. But dinner has already been eaten, and the siren's wail seems superfluous. The sound fades like realization as the ambulance pulls through the ring of police cars to where the victim lies.

There are pictures to be taken, hair to be combed, samples to be collected.

But nobody knows the killer. Nobody can pull me from a lineup. Their combined composite incriminates half the men in the city.

Patches of hair cling to the old man's scalp like silver lichen. Though it is late September and the freezing rains have yet to start, his steps are slow and measured, like he's afraid of stepping in a patch of black ice. Truth is, he's already stepped in it, and at 12:23 at night, he wonders *How am I going to deal with this?*

"You see anything?" I ask, walking after him, slowing myself to match his pace. He jumps. He would have left his skin in a bloody pile on the concrete if it hadn't been tethered to his bones with arteries and muscle. And nerves.

"Huh," he mutters and drops his keys. They clatter on the pavement like discarded wedding bands. His aged body bends at the hips, like a plastic, jointed-doll as he reaches for them. Unbalanced, the slightest push will make him fall on his face. My hand twitches. Nails bite into my palm.

"The chick in the park, did you see what happened?"

As he straightens and pushes the keys into his front pocket, he looks up at me, as if he doesn't understand my words. As if I were speaking a language that was completely beyond his comprehension. He shakes his head; not a 'no' or a 'yes', but merely a shake, as he looks toward his old, dusty sedan. It's the only car left in the public area of the police department parking lot. *If I just keep walking, maybe he'll leave me alone.*

"No." I say to his unspoken plea. Startled, he looks back at the police station and quickens his pace. I see the pain in his joints as he pushes them beyond their years.

"You scared, old man?" I ask, trying not to laugh. He's trying to run now, but it comes out more like a waddle. I barely break a trot. "What scares you?"

He stops then, his chest rising and falling like he has just run a marathon. His car is barely ten feet away. Fear stretches the wrinkles from his face. He almost looks healthy for a moment.

"What do you want from me?" he asks. "I don't have anything . . ."

I smile at that. Funny how they never seem to know what they've got. Not until it's too late. Until they feel it slide wetly between their toes.

"Just wanna talk is all," I say, raising my hands before me. My hands are empty. Nails manicured. Palms facing out. And I give him my best grin. "You know—shoot the breeze? Talk shit about women? Whatever. I just don't want to be alone tonight. Ever been there?" He looks at me, deep in my eyes.

"You have, haven't you?" I say and smile. My tongue darts out of my mouth, licks my bottom lip, and disappears within.

"Wuh . . . wuh . . . why?" he says.

"Buh . . . buh . . . because," I answer, then laugh because sometimes I'm so damn clever I slay myself.

"You know me," I say.

"No", he says, and tries to look away. Too late though. My eyes have grabbed his and they won't let go.

"You know me," I repeat.

"No . . . no . . ."

"Tell me who you see." I lick my fingertips, brush my sideburns, then turn and give him my strong profile.

A tear bubbles in one of his eyes. He palms it away. A single word slips out. From deep in his chest. His lips barely move. "Death?"

I laugh at that. It's so damn theatrical. And the kicker is, I think he really believes it.

"You think death is a mean son of a bitch?" I ask, but don't wait for his answer. He's too close to the car now. So I move in quickly and grab him by the collar of his London Fog. The lapels are sixties-wide and the coat is old, spotted with dark patches of what looks like oil. His smell is medicated moth balls.

A car passes. The driver gives us a quick, curious glance. From a distance, we look like a couple of drunk buds. If that's what you need to see.

"Are . . . are you going to hurt me?" he asks. I notice the tang of sweat mixed in with his tenacious pharmaceutical odor. I pull him closer, until the air between our noses is charged. And I lick first his right eye, then his left.

He tries to back away and stumbles over his own feet. I'm practically carrying him by his lapels now, keeping him from tripping over his fear. His teeth begin to chatter.

"You like coffee?" I ask.

"Yuy . . . yuy," he chatters.

"Donuts?"

He nods.

"I know a place where you can get the best donuts. Man, these donuts are so fine . . . like the finest set of tits you ever saw. 'Cept twice as fattening."

He shakes his head. I think. The chattering is so violent it's hard to tell.

A Midwest wind pitches the double Ferris Wheel. A sixteen-year-old girl dies. Her boyfriend is paralyzed from the neck down. A dozen others swear that they will never go to another carnival as long as they live.

I like it here.

Small cornfield-bordered town. People milling around. Some hugging to keep warm; others seemingly ignorant of the temperature. Guys in rolled up T-shirts throw softballs at lead-bottomed bottles while every other light on the Tilt-A-Whirl blinks a seductive come hither. The smell of popcorn and beer and cotton candy and grease is so thick that every breath contains six calories.

I like it here.

"Not too much further," I whisper into the old man's ear as I guide him through a group of teenagers who are talking and laughing and posing over the blare of their boom box. My arm is draped over his shoulder, real chummy-like, as I lead him on. No one gives us more than a casual glance.

"Quiet now. No crying. No screaming. If you do, it will give you away. Reveal you. Do you understand?" He looks at me. His eyes watery with age and emotion. His bottom jaw quivering. And in response, he swallows dryly, his Adam's apple working overtime. It is enough.

I lead him to a dimly lit stand with a hand-painted sign that says "Elephant Ears". It is fronted by a case full of flat, glazed, plate-sized pastries and a tray under a heat lamp of powdered sugar-coated French waffles. The man behind the case, sitting in a lawn chair, looks at us through dark shades.

"Hey, Jory. What's up, my man?" I say.

The man stands slowly, grins a grin bereft of teeth, and says, "Not unless I sees you first."

I laugh like I'm gonna bust a gut.

"You slay me," I say, then shake the old guy. "Ain't he funny?"

The old man shakes his head like one of those rear-window dogs. Like his head's full of nothing but air.

"You got any titty cakes?" I ask.

Jory grunts, bends down to a shelf beneath the case, out of sight of the paying customers, and pulls a badly battered tin pan. "Got three left," he says, placing them on the counter. The pan clatters and rocks to and fro on its uneven bottom, until it finally settles. The cakes, mounds of glazed dough capped with raisin nipples, are Jory's specialty.

"I'll take 'em. Bag 'em up, would you?"

Jory puts the cakes in a small white bag. "Who's your friend?" he asks. "New guy?"

"Yeah, new guy," I say and give the old man a squeeze.

Jory grunts. "Don't talk much."

"No, that he don't. How much?" I ask, pulling a Minnie Mouse zippered coin purse from my back pocket.

"Shit, they're a dollar each. You know that."

"When they're fresh!"

"You don't want this shit?" he says, picking the bag up off the counter.

"No, be cool, man." I say as I fish in the little purse. Keys, a compact, a bottle of Charley perfume, some crumpled bills and a cracked tube of black lipstick. I pull out a badly wrinkled five and hand it over. It's smeared with foundation and smells of perfume.

"Damn!"

"Spends," I say to him.

Jory grunts, pulls two bills from his front pocket and hands them to me. His nails are caked with grease and sugar; they look sweet enough to suck. But it's getting late and the Klondike Brother's Carnival is going to close soon. Not before, I hope. So I usher the old man on, trying to get him to pick up the pace a bit. But it's little use. "You're gonna love these cakes," I say, holding the bag in front of his face. "Take a whiff. Nice, huh?"

I can see it now: Vanity's House of Mirrors. It's the most garish attraction at the carnival, and probably the oldest. Outside the small wooden building, a twenty-foot-tall fat woman, made of plastic and fiberglass, beckons visitors with a hearty laugh and a wave of her massive hand. Loudspeakers, located to either side of her head, pump out her static-filled laugh. A motor in her right arm raises and lowers, like she's blowing kisses, while a second motor in her upper torso moves her head back and forth, banging it repeatedly against the wooden peak of the Victorian house front.

Blow, bang, blow, bang

We enter through the shadow of her thighs. The room is dark and humid. It takes a moment for our eyes to adjust to the weak lighting. It is a maze of mirrors, floor to ceiling, and there's just enough light to make out the reflected images, but not enough to see where one mirror ends and another begins. The old man stops, losing his bearings, as we're surrounded by dozens of clones.

"Ever been to a house of mirrors?" I ask. He doesn't respond at first. "Look around. Dozens of us—everywhere we go, more." He says something then that I don't catch, but he doesn't repeat himself.

"You know, the funny thing is, every time I come in here, there are fewer of me," I say, looking around, making direct eye contact with myself. It's an odd feeling, one I can't shake, but I know that there is one less image of me here than there was the last time. "Damn, one day I'm going to come in here and not see nobody." I laugh until I wake the pain. It's sharp, and I want to double over and grab my stomach. I don't though.

I push the old man before me, hiding from my own image as we make our way through the glass maze. We make a number of sharp turns in a row, spiraling back upon ourselves, moving deeper within the deceptively narrow room.

"Here we go, right here." I move him aside. It's like moving a plank. And then I push a glass pane and it moves just as reluctantly, revealing a small corner room. The room, no bigger than a closet really, is outfitted with a chair, a candle, and a tin of small utensils. The back wall is the only wall in the entire house that is not mirrored. There is a curtained window in it, and the curtains, as usual, are open.

"Nobody hardly ever comes back here. This is where I do my work. See," I say, pointing above his head at a maze of mirrors angled from the ceiling. "The mirrors in here are like a freaking periscope gizmo—they cast my image into the hall of mirrors even though I'm back here in my place. The rubes don't ever see the real me. I put on a real spook show for them sometimes. Really freaks 'em out. Sometimes they cry and try to run from me. But they can't escape me." I look directly into the old guys eyes. I wonder if he's still with me—if my words are still triggering synapses.

"Look," I say, pointing at the mirrors, "we can see them and they can see us, but they can't get back here." I flip the bird at a couple of girls, they giggle and run off until it's just us again. "See," I say, but it's hard to tell if he does.

I help him into a sitting position. His limbs are heavy and stiff. Like he's got rigor mortis or something. I turn and walk to the coffee can where I keep the silver and fish through it until I find the steak knife. "This will do."

I pull the shades closed, all the way, so only a sliver of light slips beneath. It is still dark outside, but the light from the attractions give it the feeling of early morning. It is the long white pull cord that I want. That I need. Using the steak knife, I cut the cord from its pulley system.

He doesn't flinch as I wrap the cord around his wrists and then his ankles. A guy and his girl watch, pointing with a hundred fingers as I hog tie the old guy. The girl laughs, partly at me because my ass is sticking up in the air, and partly because she senses something isn't right here *I've been through this thing three times, and I've never seen scary stuff in here.* I turn and growl at her and she jumps. Now it's her boyfriend's turn to laugh. After a moment, she tugs on his sleeve and they make their way further into the maze.

The old man doesn't fight me as I tighten the cords, nor does he speak. "It will only matter for a while. Everything changes, you know?"

"Who . . . are you?" The old man says. It surprises me. I don't expect him to speak.

"Here," I say, and reach over and put a hand on his shoulder. I sit down beside him, almost on him, so I can place his tied hands on my belly. He tries to pull away, but I hold his hands in place. Then the shifting begins and his eyes grow large as the mass beneath my skin makes itself comfortable.

"You feel that?" I ask. My eyes squeeze shut for a

moment, then reopen. The time is now, I can feel it. I look over at the old man and see that his fear has metamorph-osed into something bigger. Something uncontrollable.

It begins to move again, rippling beneath my skin. The flesh of my stomach bunches, raising rills as thick as my forearm. Involuntarily, I arch my back as it twists around my insides.

And then it is still again.

"What . . . what is it?" He asks. I have forgotten he is there. I mop the sweat from my brow before speaking.

"It's me." I say, and I know that that's not enough. Not nearly enough. Not now.

"You felt it. It's what makes me me. Defines my world and provides its boundaries. Like these mirrored walls—it shows me things."

"A serpent?" he asks. His bottom lip quivers over the word. It comes out "sur-fent". It's as good a name as any.

"Somehow it's attached itself to my spinal cord. Made room for itself. I think it thinks me."

He looks at me, confused. "Your thoughts . . . it's taken over your thoughts? Makes you do bad . . ."

"No." I shake my head. "It thinks me."

He seems to accept it this time, even though he doesn't understand. Or maybe he realizes the connection is not one that can be easily put into words.

"It gets hungry sometimes," I admit. "So hungry. And so it begins to eat me from the inside—biting and tearing tiny chunks from my insides. Until there's nothing else to do. Nothing I can do but feed it. I get it what it needs."

"You fed it . . . tonight?" he asks.

"Not enough." I lick my lips again. They are dry and chapped and beginning to bleed. "But afterwards, after it's eaten what I've eaten, the pain subsides. It lets me rest. Let's me do what I have to do."

A little girl, lost and crying, reaches out to our images. I smile back at her, happy for her, because the tears are temporary. They'll end soon.

She runs toward where she believes I am and slams into a mirror, bounces off, and falls hard on her backside. Then she begins to wail.

A boy, only a few years her senior, rounds a corner and takes her hand. Rather than comfort, he laughs as he pulls her roughly to her feet and guides her, dozens of times, through the glass hallway.

The thing beneath my flesh begins to writhe again. Its pain is mine, and I double up, grabbing at my stomach. The pain spirals through me as the beast thrashes about in my belly. It feels like it's going to burst its way through. But I know better. It thinks me.

The old man looks on, dumbfounded, as I begin to retch. He tries to scoot away from me but his binds make it difficult for him to do more than tip over on his side.

My throat is full and my face red. Breathing is difficult. I claw at my bloated throat, trying to force it back down.

I spit up a lungful of blood as the baby's fist-sized head pushes its way between my teeth. My jaws pop at the exertion, like I've just yawned a bit too widely. Fortunately, I have a big mouth, and the baby, lubricated with my blood, is able to push its misshapen head through.

I grab it, right behind its head, and pull it the rest of the way out. It is a foot long, maybe eighteen inches.

"Keep that fucking thing away from me!" the old man yells. But there are tears clogging his throat and the command is weak and useless.

The thing inside me, having given birth, moves deeper in my belly. My breathing passage is clear again. I cough and spit blood and suck in breath like a drowning man. The baby wiggles in my grip. It does not like the cold world of the outside.

I grab the old guy's shoulder and pull him back into a seated position. I sit beside him, still breathing in gulps of cool air as I hold the baby up so that we can see it clearer. Its body is lumpy with vestigial growths; like some kind of missing link still trying to sort itself out.

"You're lucky," I say. "It's small . . . it won't need much for a few years still."

He understands then. Realization colors him like he's just been dumped in paint. He shakes his head from side to side. His eyes wide, his mouth twisted. He is more awake than he's been in years. His is a transcendent awareness. It is one of those moments.

He continues to shake his head. Strings of spittle fly from the corners of his small mouth.

His small mouth.

The baby begins to shiver. It's cold. It can not take the night air much longer. I coil it around my neck and it snuggles under my chin, absorbing as much warmth as it can. Its skin begins to dry, to flake.

My hands now free, I reach over to the old man and caress the back of his head. "You have a very small mouth," I say. And he begins to cry big fat hiccupping sobs.

It takes both hands to break the old man's jaw. One on the uppers, one on the lowers. And still, I have to put my back into it. The sound of bone breaking is loud and sharp, not unlike the pop of a midway light burning out. His body jerks, screams the screams his busted jaw no longer support, then folds in on itself.

There is no blood, for I am careful. His jaw hangs limply to the right. His eyes are sealed tightly shut, his temples tensed. His thoughts are a jumble of color and flashes as he slips in and out of consciousness.

The baby begins to quiver. My neck is no longer enough. It will need to eat soon, so I pull it from my neck. The whites of its eyes are muddy, the baby blue pupils full. It opens its mouth with a little cough and I can see four pointy little spikes. It will not have a full set for a year or so.

"Sylvia," I say, christening it with a name that comes to me from within the jumble of the old man's head.

"Sylvia," I whisper, so that only the old man and our reflected images hear. The old man doesn't seem to notice as I kneel before him. I reach for his broken jaw with one hand and force it open to its fullest. He jerks awake, the pain tensing every muscle in his body.

I force the baby's head between his teeth. The baby knows this is good. This is what it needs, and it wiggles free of my hand and pushes its way in.

The old man's eyes lock with mine, but I know he doesn't see me. The baby's tail lashes the old man's face as it pulls its body in. Blood and saliva spill from the old man's small mouth as the baby works its way in deeper. The old man's face purples as he tries to breath around the obstruct-ion.

It doesn't take long. The tail vanishes between his lips and the lump in the man's throat travels downward until there is nothing left to be seen of the baby. I wipe the blood and saliva from the side of the old man's face with an old rag I stole from the tattoo artist. I can see it in his eyes. It is happening already. The paradigm shift.

I reach for the white paper bag, remove one of the titty cakes, break off a piece and push it into the old man's mouth.

"This one's for you," I say as I work his broken jaw and make him chew.

The Chatterer in the Darkness

Lee Clark Zumpe

He looked into its eyes, and he knew
it was beyond saving.

Fat droplets of blood spattered across his face.

He worked frantically, trying to wrap the animal in a towel as it wriggled furiously on the pavement in a blur of matted fur and groans and snapping teeth. It whined sharply when he tried to pick it up. Its little body shuddered, and it kicked at him with its hind legs.

He looked into its eyes, and he knew it was beyond saving.

Delicately, he carried the stray mutt to the side of the road and set it down again gently. The dog's cries had tapered into faint groans. Its head rested on the ground as it lay panting, and its body twitched convulsively. He stayed with it, feeling utterly helpless, his hand stroking its neck tenderly. The dog never looked away, never let its gaze fall from his eyes.

Death did not hesitate.

At first he thought he would leave the carcass on the side of the road. The thought of scavenging ravens picking glistening entrails from the bloated dog made him shudder, and he soon found himself neatly wrapping the dead thing in the towel and lowering it gently into his trunk. He would dispose of it properly when he got home.

As Andrew climbed back into his sedan, he felt a tear spring from the corner of his eye and glide down his cheek.

He hated himself at that moment. Had he not been so immersed in his own selfish problems, he would have seen the poor thing in time. He could have swerved to avoid hitting it, even if it had meant damaging his own car. Even if it had put his life in jeopardy.

He kept thinking about a faceless boy who would undoubtedly be waiting for that dog. He would stand on his front porch well into the night, abandoning the television, waiting for the dog to come home. Even after his mother had sent him to bed, had reassured him that the creature would come home in the morning and that everything would be all right; even then that little boy would sit by the window until weariness finally forced his eyelids down and sleep overtook him.

And everything would not be all right.

Andrew brushed the sleeve of his flannel shirt against his cheek, dismissing the tears. The bitter cold of a late November night in the Appalachians infested the car. He fingered the A/C control, spinning it around until the pointer was buried in deep red territory.

He squinted as the road narrowed. With a flick of his wrist, he sent his high beams plunging forward into the darkness. Another forty miles lay between him and home, and the mists of the Blue Ridge had already started to flood the mountain highway.

Andrew made a fist and pounded the dashboard.

He could not banish the image of that moment from his mind. It played itself over and over again in a perpetual loop. The sun had sunk only minutes earlier, dusk was just beginning to paint the night. Had he not been so consumed by matters he should have left behind at the office, had he not been so involved in building strategies to cope with bureaucratic obstacles, he would have seen the ball rolling out into the street; and he would have seen the boy running after it.

No, the dog.

It was a dog he hit, not a boy.

The boy was at home, waiting for the dog.

Andrew's foot eased off the accelerator momentarily. He puzzled over the slip in his stream of consciousness. The blood staining his shirt, covering his arms, drying on his fingers; the blood came from the dog in the trunk, not from a boy who had blundered into the street chasing a ball. Not from a boy playing alone in his front yard after the sun had set, a boy whose parents should have called him in when it had gotten dark.

Now Andrew sped up. He shook his head anxiously, and muttered aloud, "no, no, it was a dog, it was a dog," and the trees rushed by on either side and the houses huddled along the ridges spat light through windows and dotted the darkness, and the distant crests of mountains pitched their bulk against the remorseless twilight.

The sedan raced down the winding Appalachian road as Andrew fled from the indistinct horror festering in miles and minutes gone by. It had not even happened, he told himself, none of it. No dog, no boy, no accident.

His rubbed his fingers against his thumb and felt the warm stickiness. He glanced down at his shirt and saw the dark splotches. He saw the ball on the floor on the passenger side. Had he picked that up, too?

He heard something chattering as he turned north on Hog's Ear Trace. At first it was little more than a whisper, and he mistook it for wind whistling through the trees. Soon he thought the whispers formed words and he listened more intently. The voice seethed through the car softly. Andrew's eyes darted back and forth between the road and the review mirror. He spun his head to the right and scanned the backseat.

Empty.

Still, the voice called out. A child's voice. A little boy's voice.

Andrew turned the radio on so loud his ears rang and his head throbbed. Still, he could hear the boy chattering away in the trunk, babbling endlessly, not making any sense but mumbling and muttering and ranting wildly. Speaking in tongues. His mother always said that. Speaking in tongues.

"Shut up!" Andrew screamed. "Shut up, shut up, shut up, dammit!"

He never meant it to come to this. Something had to be done. The boy was clearly possessed. His mother—the whore—had seen to it. Andrew did not blame her, though;

it was that cult. They had turned her against him. They had turned his whole family against him. And little Andy, oh what they had done to him.

Andrew had never been a violent man. Never had an angry bone about him. He had to find a way to release his son from his torment, to get the demons to relinquish their claim. He could not bring himself to shoot the boy, though; could not take the knife to him like he had done to Shelly. He waited, waited until the nightfall, waited until Shelly's father went inside to answer the phone (which was only ringing because he was calling from his cellular), waited until the boy was alone. Andy made it so easy for him, running out into the road like that.

Andy was free now.

But the demon inside him was still there, still in the trunk, chattering away.

Andrew slammed on the brakes and the car careened off the road and into the forest. He stopped just short of a dropoff, and he gazed down into the moonlit ravine.

The chatterer in the darkness giggled.

Andrew threw open his door and marched around to the back of the car, keys in his hand. He flung open the trunk and gripped the towel-wrapped corpse. It shuddered beneath his clutching hands. It hissed as he pitched it onto the cold ground.

"Die goddammit die," he shrieked as he wrenched the towel free and the thing writhed and squirmed on the forest floor.

The dog yelped once and died.

Victrola's Way to Pay

Athena Workman

"What? What?" she whispered . . .
"What would he want?"

Victrola sat on her rocker and wondered if it was possible for the rays of the sun to melt sweaty skin right off the bone; to cause it to slip and slide off the way a translucent chicken skin will fall off a drumstick after it's boiled. She didn't know the term, but she'd heard of folks spontaneously combusting, and as the sun mercilessly pummeled her even in the shade of her front porch, she imagined her skinny body bursting into scarlet flames, the lanky dishwater hair on her head standing up straight like the flame on a birthday candle.

Mama snorted inside the house, the piggy noise drifting through the open window, and Victrola quit her ruminations and smoothed down the skirt of her threadbare red dress, lifting her legs a moment later and studying them. Tan from always working in the garden, making sure the carrots weren't eaten by the wild varmints and the okra didn't get too long, turning its sweetness bitter and its innards tough to eat. Her pinky toe had a scab on it, and she wiggled all her toes, hoping that the movement would shake it loose. It didn't. Victrola laughed and raised her head in time to see the stranger on the dirt road just beyond the dooryard.

He was moseying past the dented mailbox, hands stuffed in pockets and face up toward the seamless sky as if Life hadn't given him a good goosing in a long time. He was a honker, as Mama was wont to call all handsome men, and Victrola straightened up fast as she took in his tufted blonde hair, tan skin, and such a good build that it was evident under his long-sleeved white shirt and dark blue trousers. His black shoes, city shoes, kicked up miniature clouds of dust as he turned into the dirt driveway and made his way to the porch.

Victrola smoothed down her hair and smiled, revealing teeth that were long past a relationship with a toothbrush, although all still stood in their picket fence places. The stranger, a man into his twenties and past the age of reckless stupidity, stopped just beside the rickety steps to the porch. He returned her smile, turned his face back to the heavens.

"Nice day, huh?" he asked, and his voice was pleasant, low. Victrola's belly gave a grumble.

"Oh, yeah." A trickle of sweat began to sneak down her left temple, and she flicked it away. "It's a beaut."

"Uh-huh." His smile slipped, and he bit his lower lip. His teeth were as white as Grandpa Johnny's dentures fresh from the Sears catalog, and Victrola found herself aching for them. She leaned forward, her hands clutching the arms of the rocker, not realizing she was doing either.

The stranger was studying the house, his gaze roaming between the attic, second floor, and the floor just beyond Victrola's chair. Finally, his smile bloomed again, and he gave a nod.

"Think I'll go help the neighbors," he said, and tipped an imaginary hat. "Have a good day."

A sound escaped Victrola's slack lips—a mix of a groan and a grunt that she was helpless to stop, but he didn't hear her and turned around, making his way back to the drive. She emitted the embarrassing noise again. He couldn't leave—he'd just gotten there! In a wave, all the feelings of loneliness that had teased her throughout the past five years rushed over her: when Daddy had passed and gone on to the Lord's land, when she'd had to quit school in ninth grade and all her old friends moved on, when she'd had to quit her job sewing for Mrs. Watson and tend to Mama after she fell down the stairs to the root cellar; they all swept by in flood, causing her to call out.

"They don't need no help!" she yelled, and the stranger stopped, turning and cocking his head. The belligerent sun caught his hair and made it shine ethereally. "They got a boy—a couple of 'em. I ain't got nobody here to help me." She shrank back a little then, abruptly shy. "You wanna stay?"

His grin returned, easily creasing his face, and he walked back to the porch, taking a meandering path, kicking pebbles out of his way. Miraculously, his shoes were clean, untainted by the red dust of the clay.

"You want me to stay?" he asked, when he'd once again reached the steps to the porch. "Why? Ain't you got any friends?"

"No," Victrola answered, sullenly. "They all got their babies and husbands now."

"Ain't like city women, huh, who got time for friends."

"And workin', and drinkin'!" Victrola said, indignantly, although she secretly wished she could be that way; free and wanton, lost in the concrete of the big city.

"Well, I don't know." His gaze settled on the bowed second floor. "It don't look like you can pay me for my services."

"I can pay! I got money!"

His liquid blue eyes fixed stonily on hers, but his smile was still jovial. "Now, come on—you ain't got no money! If you had money, you'd be wearin' shoes."

"Ain't no need for shoes out here," she said. "Nobody need stand on attention with fancy footwear."

He threw back his head and laughed then: a rich, throaty sound that made something south of Victrola's belly growl. She put one hand to her stomach and waited until his chuckles subsided.

"Oh, darlin'," he said, shaking his head. "You're a card. What you got to pay me with?"

"I got some carrots and red potatoes, and some canned relish . . ." Her voice drifted away as she saw him shaking his head again.

"None of that interests me," he said. "What else you got?"

Victrola opened her mouth and laughed. She'd hoped

that it would sound as his did, but it came out cracked, garbled. Quickly, she cut it off, and decided to joke, lifting her leg and pointing her toes his way. "You can have my scabby toe. I sure don't want it."

He came forward, taking the two steps up and leaning over, putting his hands on his knees and inspecting her foot, looking very much like a jeweler inspecting an exquisite diamond. Surprised by his scrutiny, Victrola dropped her foot. It landed on the porch boards with a soft splat, and he straightened up, becoming very tall and lean.

"I'll take it," he said, and whipped out a pocketknife with a yellowed ivory handle.

"Huh?" she asked, and he grinned.

"I ain't gonna beat around the bush. That's a fine-lookin' toe you got there. You give it to me, and I'll fix the shingles on the roof."

"I—I was jokin'!" she said, appalled, drawing her feet under the rocker, twisting them together for protection. "I cain't give you my toe!"

"It's just the little one," he said, quietly, his smile dissolving. "You don't need it as much as the big one. And you did say you wanted me to stay. Don't you still want that? Don't you want me to fix your roof?"

"Well, yeah, but . . ." Victrola stared at him. My, he had pretty eyes. As blue as a robin's egg. She wanted to sit and stare into them for hours. She wanted to talk to him, too, for Mama couldn't talk anymore, the postman didn't stay after trucking all the way out to their stead, and the milkman didn't come anymore at all, even though he had never spoken much when he did. He'd come and gone much the way the rest of the world had. Nobody remembered that poor old Victrola was stuck out here in the sticks, with her sickly, sleeping mama and silent vegetable patch. Victrola sighed.

"Why don't you like potatoes?" she asked, abruptly.

He shrugged. "Ain't very tasty. Too gritty and grainy. We got a deal, darlin'?"

It seemed they did, after one more look into his luminous eyes. Reluctantly, she nodded and lifted her foot to him. "Is it gonna hurt much?" she asked. Tucked well behind the jumble of her dullard mind she figured it would, but that cautionary voice remained a ghostly whisper.

He grinned and knelt down, unfolding the blade from the handle. The stainless steel gleamed, winking off the blade and shining in her eyes. She shut them, and when she reopened them, he had her foot propped on his knee, the knife mere inches from her toe.

"Not much, darlin'," he said, and began to slice.

She hobbled around for a few days, but after the first twenty-four hours, what he'd said was true: it didn't pain her too much. After sawing off her toe, he'd taken a match and burnt the bloody stub, stating that he'd learned the technique from Al-Zahravi, whoever that was. Breathlessly, tears oozing out of her eyes to mingle with the beads of sweat already congregated on her face, she'd said he sounded like someone from that story Arabian Nights. The stranger had laughed again, and her belly became a flip-flopping horny toad. She didn't tell him that it relieved the aches more than the cauterization, though she mightily wanted to. Oh, there were just so many things she wanted to share with him: how difficult it was, being out there all by herself taking care of Mama; how sometimes it seemed that the only living things left in the world were her and the chickens; that she wished Daddy had been buried close by so she could sit on his grave and talk with him. But once the stranger managed to rope a long piece of twine around her toe and fashion it into grisly necklace that hung around his neck and banged against his chest, he wasn't much in the way of conversation. Victrola had asked him to stay, had given her toe for that very reason, yet she stood out in the dooryard for two days, sunlit sweat trickling through her limp hair, the heat turning her dress into another layer of skin, and watched as he tacked tarpaper over the holes, nailed the old shingles flush again, intent and mute even as she asked him if he wanted a glass of lemonade or a mess of collard greens.

He did speak once, after she asked what his name was. Sitting on the apex of the house, he paused in his hammering, wiped sweat from his forehead, and grinned. "David," he told her.

"Peter," he said a moment later, after she'd opened her mouth to tell him that was a nice, simple name; nothing like Victrola, a moniker that made everyone laugh and tease. Victrola's mouth remained agape, confused.

"Michael," he continued, letting his arms dangle over his knees. Through his hands she could see her toe, idly swinging north of his belly button.

"Huh?" she managed, and he laughed, further numbing the throbbing pain in her stump.

"Whatever you want it to be, darlin'," he called. "Which one do you like?"

She thought about it as carefully as the wet heat would allow. "Michael," she finally said, and he gave her a curt nod.

"There you go, then," he said, and returned to his repairs, leaving her once again to issue her futile invitations of food and drink.

Where he went those two nights she didn't know, and she dragged the rocker in Mama's room over to the window, leaving skidding trails in the dust, and stared into the starry darkness until her eyes felt grainy and protuberant, wishing that she'd included an invitation to stay with them. The barn's loft was still nice, even if the hay was old and musty. Her own room was comfortable as well, if the water stains on the walls and the moth-eaten quilt was overlooked. When she thought about him in her room, Victrola flushed and made herself leave her watch at the window to get to work: changing Mama's bedpan, forcing chicken broth down the old woman's throat and wiping away the dribble that leaked out of her mouth, standing over the bed after her mother fell asleep, the knife unrealized and dull in Victrola's hand.

No thumping or pounding sounds echoed through the house on the third day, and Victrola retired to the porch after gathering pink and blue chicken eggs and spindly, stunted carrots, sulking and watching the muddy sky roil over the horizon. As he had before, Michael came sauntering up the lane, his face to the storm sky, the unnatural breeze playing with chunks of his hair.

He stopped by the mailbox and called, "Nice day, huh?"

"Oh, yeah," Victrola growled, her hands gripping the rocker's arms. "It's a beaut."

Dressed in the same natty suit that she'd first spied him in, Michael cocked his head and crossed the dooryard. "Victrola," he said, stopping by the steps. "What's got you all crabby?"

"You enjoyin' my toe?" she burst out, leaning forward, stilling the rocker's short, furious arcs. "I outta rip that off your neck!"

Comically mortified, he put a hand to the twine around his neck. Her toe hung above his tie, shriveled and brown. "Now, why would you wanna do that?"

"You didn't talk to me!" she whined. "I gave you that toe so you'd stay, but all you did was sit up on that roof and work! I shouldn't have given it to you at all!" Angrily, she thrust out her wounded foot. "Look! Now I ain't got all my toes, and it was for nothin'!"

"For *nothin'*?" he scoffed, dropping his hand, his smile vanishing. "Darlin', that wasn't part of our deal. Did I ever say I'd stay to *talk* to you?" She opened her mouth, but he held up his forefinger, shushing her. "You think carefully now. I said I'd stay and fix the roof. I never said nothin' about entertainin' you in any other way."

Victrola clenched her jaw and concentrated, and

slowly realized that he was right. The agreement had been the roof for her toe, and nothing else. A slow blush to match the thunderheads darkened her face.

"Yeah, now you see," Michael said, and came up the steps to lounge against the splintered porch post. "You wanted conversation, you should've asked for that, too."

"I want conversation," Victrola muttered, her embarrassed gaze on her mutilated foot.

"What's that?" he asked, leaning forward, cupping an ear.

"I want . . . conversation," she admitted, and Michael nodded and straightened up, turning to study the road.

"Well," he said at length. "I really think I ought to get over to the neighbors. I noticed their hen house was fallin' down. Guess their boys got too much else to do to get to it."

"No!" Victrola cried, standing up, pushing back the rocker, making it squeak loudly as if mice were trapped in the rising winds. "You got to stay! You got to do that for me!"

"Now why would I *have* to?" he asked, nonchalantly, as if the whistling storm could not be heard or the color of the mud glutting the sky wasn't turning to pitch.

"You got my toe!" She would have stamped her foot if it wouldn't cause a flash of agony.

"Yeah, I got your toe." Briefly, he fingered it. "What else you got?"

Victrola stared at him, strands of her hair tickling her face, whipping across her nose. And inspiration struck. "I got my hair!"

Michael left the porch post to come to her, lifting a hand to rub a chunk of it between his fingers. So close, his heat was intense, and Victrola shut her eyes as a wave of pleasurable warmth tightened her scalp and swept slowly through her body.

"Your hair," he mused. "You like your hair a lot?"

"I do," she said, before opening her eyes and immediately amending, "I did! I *did*! But you can have it! You can take all of it if you want it!"

"All right, then," he said, dropping her hair and stepping back, leaving her space cold and wanting. Dipping his hand into his jacket pocket, he emerged with a pair of scissors. The snicking sounded hungry.

"You go tie it up, Victrola," he whispered. "I want to do this right."

She limped into the house, letting the screen door slam after her, unmindful that she might wake Mama, send her into one of her pained spells that lasted well into the early morning hours, and ran to the kitchen, finding an old black ribbon in one of the kitchen drawers. The mirror in the front room was cracked, the induced bad luck well into its fourth year, but Victrola crouched down and watched through a large triangle as she tied a loose ponytail at the back of her skull.

"Perfect," she breathed, seeing not a dirty, skinny girl with dullard eyes and dishwater hair, but a lively, vibrant woman in the peak of her prime. On legs that seemed lighter than they were, she limped back to the porch. She had a flash of fear that he'd left, that it had all been a cruel joke, but he was still waiting for her, his form silhouetted against the raindrops that had just begun to fall.

"Get on your knees," he told her. Victrola looked up and saw his smile, but her answering one trembled.

"You'll stay?" she asked, clasping her hands between her flat breasts. "You'll stay and talk to me?"

"I'll stay and talk to you," he said, and pointed the scissors at the porch boards. "Now get down, darlin'."

Carefully, she lowered herself to her knees and shut her eyes as he lifted the ponytail, grasping it tightly and yanking.

"Ain't you lucky?" he mused, just before the scissors began to eat. "This ain't gonna hurt one bit."

After her beribboned ponytail disappeared into his pocket, he dragged the other dilapidated rocker next to hers and fulfilled his promise. And my, did he ever; chatting through the rumbles of thunder and rainwater that occasionally sprayed the porch and their faces, misting them like morning dew. He talked to her about the swampland he owned in Florida and his investment in the Brooklyn Bridge, and as he did, Victrola sat demurely beside him and primped, fluffing up her newly shorn hair with the tips of her fingers and batting her stumpy eyelashes. Occasionally she shuddered, for the winds stung and her head was chilled without its protective long cap of hair.

"I got short hair!" she exclaimed once, and he laughed, and then she forgot about her haircut, propping her chin on her hands and giving him a look that no man would mistake for mere friendship. Not that he noticed, and he continued to chatter on about pyramids he'd climbed in Egypt and a box he found in Asia that he claimed once belonged to God. She pshawed him; he put a hand over his heart and solemnly swore it the truth. He talked about things foreign and unbeknownst to her, things that her sheltered, stunted mind had never dreamed of, and when the storm drifted on to the north and the night skies were free of their cloudy prison, he said it was time for bed, and rose to leave.

"Wait!" she cried, reaching out to snatch at his jacket sleeve. Deftly, he moved out of reach, stuffing his hands into his pockets. "You're gonna be back, ain't you?" She scowled. "My hair's worth more'n just one day of company, ain't it?"

"Sure it is," he told her, before his gaze drifted to Mama's bedroom window. The woman had snorted and coughed throughout the day, but Victrola had been too absorbed in Michael's stories to attend to her. "But a girl's gotta get her beauty sleep, and your mama needs tendin', don't she?"

He left then, traipsing off the porch and disappearing

into the darkness before she could offer the loft or, better yet, her own bedroom for the night. Victrola slowly rose and limped into the house, the pain in her toe returning (and now how his voice was just as much a numbing agent as his laugh!), and made a vegetable broth for her mother. So distracted was she, reliving the melodious songs that were his stories, that more broth ended up on the bed sheets than the old wasted woman, and Victrola cursed as she mopped up the mess.

"Why don't you get better?" she hissed, her question slithering through the low light of the kerosene lamp to slink across Mama's face. But the wrinkled skin remained slack, the white, veined eyelids closed, and Victrola went to bed, lying down and playing with the blunt ends of her hair while the stump of her toe throbbed in a crimson nimbus.

Michael returned the next morning, strolling up the lane like he always did, but instead of musing that the neighbors must be in dire need of his services, he took the rocker next to her and launched right into a tale about a man he once knew in Europe: a man who had not believed in the Holy Trinity, and had been chased down and subsequently burned at the stake. Forgetting about her clipped hair, Victrola gasped.

"Burned at the stake?" she echoed, horrified. "They don't do that no more!"

"Did I say it happened *yesterday*, Victrola?" Michael had asked, mildly, leveling his glorious blue gaze at her. When she dumbly shook her head, he went on, informing her that burned human flesh smelled much like crispy pork.

His stories unwound as the morning waxed toward noon, and when the sun reached its zenith Victrola could no longer ignore the growling of her empty belly, and served them both chow-chow and crackers. Watching him dig into what she'd made with her own two hands did her proud, for there was nothing like a man enjoying a woman's hard work. So involved was she in making sure he had his fill that she didn't see how his jacket was soon covered with crumbs, chow-chow juice dribbling and running down his chin. It would not have mattered if she had noticed, for her only other concerns were drinking in his eyes, waiting for and wanting that rejuvenating, exciting laugh.

When he let out a ringing belch that signified the end of his meal, she laughed and clapped delightedly, running back into the house only to put up the plate and check on Mama. The old woman slept on, oblivious to the heat or the loud conversation just outside her window. Victrola returned to Michael's side, and he asked, "How is she?"

"Sleepin'," Victrola answered, waving a hand dismissively.

"Oughta feed her," he said, watching her carefully.

"Oh, I'll get to it," she answered, and twisted in her rocker until she faced him. Propping her hands on her chin, she said, "Go on—tell me another story!"

So he did, and told her of the speakeasies where he'd danced the night away, the fear of being discovered and jailed only part of the thrill; the time he'd met a man deep beneath Berlin, sitting in a bunker with a gun to his head; how he'd overheard two boys talking about committing the perfect murder. But as his stories grew darker and more ominous in nature, Victrola continued to stare at him, hanging on every word, not caring what he talked about as long as he talked. Once she wondered about her hair, and if it was still in his pocket, close to him in a way that she was not, and once her gaze fell on her toe, still hanging on a string around his neck. The bruised nail, the same shade as the skin, seemed to grin at her, and that was all that made her shudder that long, sunny day.

He rose at nightfall. This time, she did catch the rough fabric of his sleeve, hooking it in her fingers. "Stay, why don't'cha?" she begged. "The hay's soft in the loft . . . but my bed's softer."

"I bet it is," he said, winking. "But that wasn't part of the deal, was it now, Victrola?"

"It could be!" she said, voice rising near to a screech. "It sure as rain could be! What do you want?"

She saw his bright gaze flicker momentarily toward the bedroom window, but then he moved out of her grasp, leaving her hand hovering in empty air. "I want my sleep," he told her, and walked to the steps. "An' you need it, too. Don't worry, darlin'—I'll be back in the mornin'."

After Mama's dinner, most of which again ended up on the sheets and pillow that propped up her wasted, empty head, Victrola paced the house, her gaze wild like a trapped animal's. What did she have left? Nothing in the house was of any value; everything was old, wrecked, covered with greasy grime or a thick film of dust. There were pictures, but what would he want with portraits of her family? She had some clothes, but he was a man—surely he was not *funny* that way. Once she stopped in Mama's doorway and peered in at the comatose woman. Would he want Mama's hair, too? She could offer to braid it with the hank of hers that he now owned. But Mama's hair was brittle, gray, lifeless, and the knife that had been reaching for it faltered. Victrola flung it away to a corner and stomped out of the room as best she could on her injured foot.

"What? What?" she whispered, standing in the middle of the front room while outside, the crickets chirped in response but offered no soluble answer. "What would he want?"

His arrival came as the sun's fingers finished their creep over the horizon, and Victrola sat forward in her rocker, gripping the arms and greedily grinning. Oh, how his face had filled her dreams, plastering her with more kisses than a girl like her had ever known, filling her body with such an energetic heat that she thrashed on her bed and moaned thickly, repeatedly. She wanted that in real life, there under the sun, but instead of joining her on the porch, he stopped by the mailbox and leaned against it.

"Cain't come up there today, Victrola," he called, crossing his arms over his chest. "All out of stories. Plus, I saw those boys got to the henhouse but the well needs new stones. Damn thing's fallin' apart right under their noses! So, I best be gettin' on. You take care now, you hear?" Wearing a wicked grin, he raised one hand to tip an imaginary hat, and turned on his heel.

"*No*!" Victrola screeched, leaping out of the rocker and across the porch, unmindful of the searing pain coursing through her foot or the way her limp made her lurch most unattractively. She bounded down the steps and the drive, stones biting painfully into her tender soles, dust coating her feet. Michael waited, and did not speak when she stumbled to a halt before him.

"Don't leave," she panted. "I got somethin' for you."

"You got somethin'?" he mused, giving her a beatific but suspicious smile. "What you got?"

"Anythin'!" she yelled, flailing her ropey arms. "Anythin' you want—just name it and I'll give it to you!"

"Victrola," he whispered, and reached out a hand to finally give her what she'd always wanted, ever since he'd first sauntered past her dooryard: a touch. His forefinger trailed down her cheek, stopping at the tip of her chin, and Victrola's vision abruptly narrowed to only include his face, her body tingling as if set on fire. "Now what could you possibly have left? I took your nasty toe; I got your hair. I don't want your breasts or your cooch, 'cause then, what would I have left to suck on or dip my wick into? And that's what you want, ain't it?"

Breathlessly, she answered, "Yes."

"I don't want your nasty old chow-chow or relish—girl, you can't cook to save your life," he went on, his gaze hardening as he pinched the skin of her chin between his thumb and forefinger. She remained unmindful of the pain or his hurtful words, trapped in the fathomless blue of his eyes. "Don't want your chickens—don't want that kinda blood on my hands. An' you can't grow vegetables for shit." He cocked his head, considering her mouth. "Could take your tongue—that'd sure shut up your prattlin'—but then again, maybe I need some suckin' on, too." His grin was lascivious, his tongue darting out to lick his lower lip. "So, I ask you, Victrola—what you got left for me?"

Only one thing swam to the murky surface of her mind, and she let it out immediately. "Mama," she whispered, and he pinched her again, the action spreading his smile even wider.

"Mama," he said.

Afterward, when Mama's last breath remained unheard under the pillow and her withered body finished its thrashing, Michael took Victrola's hand. She was standing in the doorway, had watched it all through foggy eyes, but began to cry when she realized Mama was dead and truly gone, just like Daddy. But Michael would not allow her to shed a tear, and instead of shushing her, he stuck a finger in her mouth, silently commanding her to suckle. His skin was soft, salty, and his fingernail nicked her gum. When he pulled it out, the tip of his finger was scummy with slimy blood. He held it before her face. She licked it away and matched his grin, the corpse on the bed forgotten.

"Good girl," he murmured, then led her through the house to her bedroom, pulling her along as certainly as if he'd lived within its walls his entire life. Beside the bed, Victrola came as soon as his hand cupped her secret place, gasping aloud and rocking against him, and when he laughed and pulled her to him, she came again, crying out this time as her knees buckled. Michael threw her onto the bed and removed his jacket, grinning as she curled up into a ball, holding her throbbing belly. Soon his clothes were in a pile on the floor and he was parting her legs, his stiffness a divining rod heading for utopia.

"Gonna git what you asked for, Victrola," he said, sinking into her, and she grunted and clasped her hands around his neck, grasping his hips with her thighs, crying out as he plunged into her again and again.

They went on that way as the day melted like the one before it, the intolerable heat snaking into the darkened bedroom, turning their pores into puddles, the bed sheets into a soggy slide. Victrola's clipped hair was mashed to her head, but Michael held onto it occasionally, taking away more of it each time he lifted to orgasm. Sometimes he left her to take a piss, and she collapsed on the sheets, a demure smile curving her lips, exhausted from the inside out but unable to halt the craving of more of the undulating, intoxicating waves that he created deep within her. When he returned, her legs were loose, waiting for him, her arms extended, and each time, he accepted her unspoken invitation with the same smile, the same dancing light in his blue eyes. For Victrola, the day was heaven, the ensuing night on a plane even higher, if such a place existed in the universe, and when he finally let her go as the full moon hung at its apex in the sky, she immediately drifted into slumber, curling up on her side and dreaming of how he'd so gloriously rid her of her virginity.

The insistent crow of the cock awoke Victrola, and she opened her eyes, smiling until she found herself alone. Sitting up straight, her bare breasts jiggling, she cast a wild glance around, but the room was as empty as her bed.

"Michael?" she called, and winced as the sore spots between her thighs rubbed together. He'd worked a number on her, but even through the pain small fireworks erupted in her belly, and she couldn't wait to have him inside her again. Victrola eased herself off the bed, pulled on one of her dresses, and limped out of her room.

"Michael?" she repeated, looking around after she reached the first floor, but he was neither in the kitchen nor the front room. Mama lay in her bed, the pillow still over her face, her body stiff and beginning to smell in the heat, but Victrola spared her only a cursory glance before going to the front door and pulling it open. Bright, harsh sunlight poked her in the eyes, making her squint as she went to the edge of the porch and looked up the road. Her dull face broke out into a grin when she saw him. There he was, her beloved! Sauntering up the road in that happy way he had, his glorious face turned to the heavens! What was he thinking about? Victrola smoothed down the tufts of hair sticking out on her head and smiled his way, hoping his thoughts were on her, and how he would spend the day giving in to her every whim and demand. After all, she'd given him the most important thing in her life, hadn't she? She was entitled.

Michael finished his jaunt and stopped by the mailbox, nodding at her and stuffing his hands into his pockets. The cuffs of his pants and his shoes were untouched by dust, shiny and pristine. "You feelin' all right today, Victrola?" he asked, conversationally, in a tone better suited to discussing the weather.

"You know I am," she said, shyly but suggestively.

"Well, I just had to make sure," he said. "I gave you exactly what you wanted, didn't I?"

"You did, you did that!" she answered, laughing, rocking on her heels as if he'd just said the funniest thing she'd ever heard. Michael nodded, satisfied, a small smile playing at the corners of his lips, then looked up the road and sighed.

"Well, I best be goin'," he said. Victrola's laughter cut off as if she'd been slapped. "That well really needs tendin', and those boys're nothin' but lazeabouts anyway. You have a good day now."

"What?" she breathed, and sputtered, "You—you cain't go! We—we got business to attend to!" Jerkily, she took a step down, her feet meeting the warm wood of the porch step. "You—you're supposed to stay with me!"

"I didn't say that," he said, arching his eyebrows, feigning a surprised look. "I didn't say that at all, Victrola.

You wanted me to give you pleasure, and that's what I did. That's *all* I had to do. Not one time did I say that I was gonna stay here forever, and you didn't *ask* me that, either." He shook his head. "A man has his limits, you know."

"*No!*" she screamed, bunching her hands into fists and beating her thighs, the cords in her neck standing out lividly. Michael frowned.

"Now, don't go gettin' all upset," he scolded her. "You shoulda known. Now, I got to get goin'. There ain't nothin' left here for me to do, and you ain't got nothin' to make me stay." He nodded toward Mama's bedroom window. "You best get goin', too. You got an old lady that needs a proper burial."

He moved away, his gait jocular, his gaze upturned to the perfect cerulean shade of the sky, and when he began to whistle "Happy Days Are Here Again", Victrola began to scream: an insistent shrill that split the calm morning air. But he did not turn, did not look over his shoulder, and when he disappeared over the rise in the road, she was left alone again: a choppy-haired woman with a missing pinky toe and a smothered mother lying dead in her bed. And before the final vestiges of her mind ripped to shreds and she hunkered down on the steps like a cowering, beaten dog, Victrola realized that Michael had taken something else with him; something that he hadn't asked for but had stolen nevertheless.

All That's Left After the Big One Drops

Nick Mamatas

The car felt like it was driving over the very curve of the world.

They came for Harold as the war began, just before dawn, when the moon was gone and a defeated sliver of sun poked through black smoke clouds to paint the walls of the bedroom. They were gentle but brusque. "Get up!" A command from a voice that rarely spoke in any other way. "We're leaving, and you're coming with us. You won't be having to pack." The other's small hand touched his arm.

Harold lifted his head and blinked away ocular phenomena and the crust of sleep but still saw only shadows over shadows. The presence was there, though, the aura of authority and fear that had haunted him for all his days. ". . . father?" Harold asked.

"Let's go."

The first cockroach was coerced. It had been only a month ago. Three older boys held Harold down and mashed the bug against his lips, tried to strain the white pulp and flaky exoskeleton through his braces and teeth. That's how he told it, anyway, though really two of the kids were only standing there giggling and Big Keith just told Harold to open his fucking mouth, then grabbed his jaw and popped the roach in. "Chew it. Chew it good." And Harold, more out of surprise than anything else, did so. It took three hard chomps to get the roach to stop wriggling, and it tasted like a broken thermometer leaking mercury, but Harold swallowed it.

The ride to the bunker was silent. Usually in the car Abby

would sing and Harold would jab her with his elbow and she would screech and call him Chubsie Ubsie and Dad would thunder at them from the front seat. And Harold would glare into the rearview mirror, but Dad never made any sign of noticing. Abby was quiet, though, huddled in the far corner of the sedan, her eyes wide and unblinking. She looked over at Harold and sniveled, ready to cry. It seemed to Harold that Dad's thin-lipped smile kept anyone from making a sound. But she seemed so small in her big empty half of the backseat, ready to say something, to ask the big question, but too afraid to be willing.

The car rolled over the empty road like a well paved dream. On the shoulders of the road stood soldiers, M-16s ready, and little silver boxes. Radar detectors? Pass-boxes or something, Harold decided; then he curled up in a ball. At least he'd never see the assholes from school again, but he'd never see Beth again, either. Maybe she was just a sizzling puddle by now, with two sharp eyeteeth sticking out of the goop. Harold kept his eyes shut tight, letting them fill with tears. The car felt like it was driving over the very curve of the world.

Three weeks ago. The second cockroach was a dare. *Whatever doesn't kill me only makes me stronger.* Harold had read that in a comic book.

"Bullshit."

"Eeeeew!" The girls in class were at that stage where any stray molecule could spark an "Eeeeew!"

The roach was just hanging around the corner of the Formica lunch table, not doing a whole hell of a lot. The lunch line wasn't moving, and Harold actually felt a hot, sweaty burst of . . . something. A girl was looking at him. He snatched up the roach, tossed back his head, and clamped his hand over his mouth. It scampered down Harold's tongue, and the boy choked on it for a second. He could only think of how pissed Dad would be, having to pick up a corpse from the school, so he swallowed hard, coughed again and again, and then finally held up his arms.

"Eeeeew!"

"How was it? Was it good?" some kid asked. "Freak."

"Eeew, eew, eeeew, I can't believe he did that," the girl announced to nobody as she actually wandered off the line and through the cafeteria, shuffling like a mental patient.

Harold turned to the kid, shrugged, and said with a pretend world-weary sigh: "Women!"

The kid snorted and poked his friend. "The fat turd thinks he knows about girls. He said *women*!" Turning back to Harold, he asked, "Who are you, Al Bundy or something?"

"King Kong Bundy, more like it."

For a few days, Harold was either Bugman or Hey, Bundy! Either was fine with him, really.

Bombs went off like flashbulbs in the sooty distance, so far away from Harold and the little sedan. Harold hummed to himself, *"hmmmm, hmmmm hmm-hmm hmm-hmm . . . this corrosion"* to keep from being annoyed by Abby's occasional whimpers and the rustling of her jumper. He could have rested like that forever, smiling in a half-sleep on a smooth road, but the sedan hit grating eventually, tires rumbling, and overhead lamps illuminated the car as it drove beneath them.

Dad said, "We're here. Safe." They drove for miles, deep under ground. Harold opened one eye and watched the ceiling of the tunnel zip by. The place smelled of exhaust and Lysol.

The third roach was a challenge. One he initiated, not one merely accepted. Two weeks ago. Harold found it crawling along the side of the red-painted stall in the second-floor boys' room and scooped it up to let it run and play across his fingers and palm as he walked back to Physics. The teacher shut up, impatient for Harold to sit down, but instead of scuttling to his seat, Harold held up the back of his hand. A few of the kids muttered; someone squeaked. The roach stood between two knuckles, waving its antennae curiously. Then Harold slid it into his mouth with tongue and hungry lips and walked back to his desk chewing. He enjoyed all the muttering and the special intensity with which Mr. Teufel ignored him while explaining momentum until the bell rang.

A note was sent home. Dad fumed quietly and asked Harold to please try not to stand out so much with his nonsense, and he took away screen privileges for a week. They didn't speak of it again.

Families were separated and led to different parts of the massive honeycomb. There were no sharp corners, Harold noticed. The whole complex seemed to be made of huge arches and round rooms. Even the doorways were oval. A soothing female voice, the sort he'd heard counting down to self-destruct in every space movie he'd ever seen welcomed him and everyone else to "temporary quarters." Technicians in orange jumpsuits handed out Fruit Roll-Ups, then lined up all the boys. They were all white, most of them taller than Harold, all with short haircuts and the doughy potato faces of the Midwest. Harold looked around for a mirror, or some reflective surface, to see if the mascara he forgot to wipe off before crawling into bed had run. As if the faces of the other boys didn't tell him what he already knew. They were too stunned to say anything, though, or even to give him one of those looks.

They were marched down a hall, then made to turn a corner. Then waited. Then another corner. Like a line at Disneyland, where they fool you into thinking you're almost there. Separated again into groups of five, Harold and four stick-straight high-schoolers were led into an examination room for poking and prodding. Like the usual checkup, then body cavity searches, finger-prick blood tests, eye exams, running a treadmill. No questions, though—Harold guessed that the medics already had everyone's charts. Their hands were so cold and firm. One noticed his hickey and peered at it. Hmm.

"Nazis," Harold muttered, so quiet, but not quiet enough.

"No, son. We're the good guys. You're safe now. We just don't want everyone in the honeycomb catching your cold. This is a sealed environment. No germs, no vermin, no pets. Just people, ordinary people like you and me."

After, Harold and the four other boys were led into a small auditorium, handed booklets, and told to read.

Last week. The sink was a mess, Harold's hands looked like he had spent the morning juggling Shinola, and black tears streaked down his face and belly. He did manage to mostly dye his hair, though. And he had cut it himself, too, trying to get that spiky look, but mostly he just looked like he had just gotten up. A roach scuttled over porcelain. Harold smashed it with a finger, then licked off the glop absentmindedly. Keeping in practice. *Learn to like it!* he commanded himself, popping the remnants of the roach into his mouth and watching himself in the mirror as he chewed.

"Eh, good enough for freshman year," he said, and left the house through the window so Dad wouldn't catch up. He'd have all day at school and most of the afternoon to screw his courage to the sticking place and fight off the crew cut he knew was coming.

School wasn't too bad. No snickering at all, just a bunch of dumbass comments: "What happened?" "Did you do that *yourself*?" "*Dude,* you shouldn't have stuck your head in that shoe-shining machine." Harold smiled at that. *Dude* was better than *faggot*, after all. He went to the boys' room between every class, wet down his hair, and ran his fingers through it to keep it looking punk or whatever.

At lunch, Lance buttonholed him. Lance was a lacrosse-playing jock, but not too bad. He'd lent Harold a mixdisc once, and said hi in the hallways unless he was with his girlfriend. He was a tall guy, two heads taller than Harold, and could get a good look at the clumsy haircut. "You know what they say, Har. A man who cuts his own hair has a fool for a client. It's a good try, though. Standing out, kinda goth, kinda punk. I get it. Changing your image. Let me know if anyone fucks with you. I'll kick their ass or something." Harold giggled, and they shook hands.

Some dirtbag named Ivan, he of the face full of acne and an overwashed Hatebreed T-shirt did snort at Harold later, tried to spit on him—Harold flinched out of the way—but when Ivan called him Bugman Bundy, Harold just stuck out his tongue and said, "How about I lick the pus off your pimples? That'll taste much better than a cockroach. Or maybe not?"

Ivan was just nonplussed at that, so Harold got away without a beating.

The war was going exceptionally well, have no doubt about that. Command and control was still intact, the honeycombs were impenetrable, and soon all would be able to return to the surface. This is temporary. There are no *if*s, only *when*s. When the jet stream pushes the radiation out to sea. When we get the all-clear from Washington. Sooner than you think. Not tomorrow or next month, but soon. Victory is already ours; we're just arranging the final details of the parade.

Everything will be completely normal again, and until then, the honeycomb is your new home and new school. That's what they told Harold and the other boys, with the help of PowerPoint slides and the friendly sort of smile one sees only at press conferences. Everyone got free PDAs with maps and beeper numbers and homing devices in case anyone got lost. And there were games on them, even a mini-version of Sandstorm III. No time to play now, though, the flak said. Her name was Amy, and she was even shorter than Harold. "Use the mapping feature to find your family's quarters. They've all been briefed, too, and are waiting for you. Have some dinner and get some rest. Y'all have the rest of the week off, but we are going to have a full curriculum of your grade here in Auditorium 23. That way, when y'all get to go home, all y'all will be caught up."

Amy went on for a bit about this and that—she was very concerned about recycling. Harold wanted to turn to the kid next to him and whisper a joke, but he couldn't remember any. Really, he just wanted to grab someone by the collar and demand answers. *Why are you so special? What does your dad do that you get to live?* but he couldn't even meet the eyes of the boy next to him. Instead Harold looked down at the guy's nail-bitten hands. Was he a jock up on the outside, a nerd, or a dirtbag who got his head shaved by his one-star general daddy on the trip over so he'd blend in?

Eventually, Harold knew, the boys would sort themselves out. Some would study hard; others would steal their notes. Some would do the work; others would take the credit. A few would play the games; Harold would hand out the towels. Some kids were born to be kings and lived, remora-like, off the sweat and fear of others. And Harold couldn't even be the Kid Who Ate Cockroaches anymore.

Amy didn't offer to answer any questions after she was done, and she left by pushing on the whiteboard; it swung open like a secret entrance and revealed another rounded hallway. Harold and the other kids left through the doors like normal people.

Three nights ago. "You know who my hero is, Father?" Harold said at dinner. Abby had to do a book report on heroes and had picked Madyson Fontana, a fifteen-year-old superstar who wore a thong and pretended to sing. Her memoir, all fifty-two pages of it, accompanied her first single on the download, so it was really easy to get information on her.

"I don't know, Grandpa. Who is your hero? Dracula?" Dad said, bored. He shoveled some mac and cheese onto his plate. Grandpa was Harold's new nickname, because he looked like Grandpa Munster, whoever that was.

"Charles Manson!"

Dad smiled. "Oh? And why is that?"

"Because . . . he had followers. And charisma. He threw society's laws aside!"

Dad looked at Abby, who was more interested in molding her mac and cheese into some kind of gloppy yellow castle than in the conversation, then pointed out: "He ordered a pregnant woman killed for no reason. He was a dirty drug addict, retarded, and spent most of his life rightfully rotting away in prison." He was calm, like a telemarketer.

"Why did he want the lady killed?" Abby asked conversationally. "Was he the papa?" Most of her attention was still on her little engineering project.

"He's still my hero. They should have let him out and made him president for life!" Harold giggled and peered at Dad.

"You think he'd have been a good one, being a mass murderer and all?" Dad put down his fork and straightened up in his chair.

"Better than the asshole you work for!"

"Bad word! Five-dollar fine!" Abby shouted.

"I think Reynolds is doing fine."

"We're at war with like five different countries. Manson only killed like five people."

"We're defending ourselves."

Harold took a gulp of soda and said, "You're in the CIA, aren't you, Dad? Have you killed five people?"

Dad snorted. "You know I'm not in the CIA. I'm a civilian consultant. And no, I would never kill anyone, unless somebody came in here and tried to hurt you or Abby. I'm sorry if that disappoints you, Harold, but I'm a man of peace."

"Then why couldn't I come to work with you for Career Day? It's because you torture and kill prisoners of war! Spike reservoirs with LSD! I bet your department brainwashed Manson and made him a sleeper agent. That's why he died of a stroke in prison!"

"He was ninety-two years old. That's why he died of a stroke in prison," Dad said. "And I didn't want to bring you into work with me because I have to spend a lot of time with my colleagues, and occasionally have to talk to high-powered officials."

"So?"

"So, my son looks like a chubby homosexual vampire. How am I supposed to work with that?"

Harold tipped over his plate and howled, "God damn you!" Abby laughed, then cried and screeched when Harold pushed her glass into her lap. He kicked the chair, almost tripped over it, and barreled out of the room and down the steps to the playroom. Real loud, now, he screamed again, "Goddamn you! Goddamn you!" Harold thought about dropping the ol' F-bomb, but he had already taken a big risk using *asshole* in front of Dad and didn't want him to coming down to the basement.

He played video games for a while, and cried and thought about going upstairs once everyone was safe in bed and killing Dad and Abby both while they slept with the longest kitchen knife he could find. Dad first, of course—he snored, so it would be easy to sneak up on him. Then Abby, and he could live here alone till food ran out, staying up, drinking, shitting on the linoleum, staying in bed all day. Whatever he wanted. Will To Power. Yeah!

But Harold was afraid and cried some more. He threw down the controller and curled up in a little corner under the vent and sobbed loudly enough, he hoped, so Dad could hear him upstairs, through the shaft.

A waterbug crawled out from somewhere and presented itself majestically. Harold blinked away his tears and saw that it was much bigger and blacker than the others. At least as long as his thumb and twice as wide. He glanced up at the door at the top of the steps; it was open just a crack, and there was a sliver of light pouring in from the living room. Harold grabbed the insect quickly and shoved it into his mouth. He didn't gulp. He chewed. Nice and slow. Crunchy and gooey, like candy made from a cold puddle of meat. Gross. Disgusting. He kept it in his mouth, forcing himself to taste every tangled leg and thin wing. Then he gulped it down, and sucked on his tongue to enjoy the flavor.

When Harold found his quarters, Dad wasn't there, but Abby was, sitting on the couch like a stuffed girl in a historical museum.

"Hi," he said.

She turned to him and peered with big eyes.

"Did you go to school?"

". . . yeah," she said. "Where's Daddy?"

"I don't know."

Harold scoped the place out—three small bedrooms, two about the size of the walk-in closet back at the house, with twin beds, and a slightly bigger setup for Dad. The main room, with the screen, a couch, and a little round table. A kitchenette. The fridge and cupboard were stocked, but with nasty shit—who the hell eats whole wheat? Off-brand spaghetti sauce? Government-issue cola? Christ. The doctor was right, though; there were no bugs to be seen, and no droppings either.

"Where's Daaa-deee?" Abby screeched. She hadn't moved from the couch. Harold slammed the fridge shut, marched into the room, and said, "I. Don't. Know. Don't ask me questions you know I don't know the answers to!"

"Why are we here? What about the other people?"

Harold fumed, but tried to keep it in check, "Don't ask me questions you *do* know the answers to, either! This is a bomb shelter." He held his hands up over his head, pantomiming an umbrella. "We are thus sheltered from the bombs."

Abby sniffled. Then she asked, "What about the people not in the shelter? Are they okay?"

Harold didn't answer. He plopped down on the floor, pulled out his PDA, and started playing a game instead.

When he got to level three, Abby asked what he was doing.

"Killing sandniggers."

"Can I play, too?"

"No."

"Why not?"

"It's a boy's game. Turn on the screen."

"I'm hungry."

He turned off the game. "I can make you a sandwich, but they only have whole wheat bread." Abby made a face. "Or pasta."

"Let's wait for Daddy," she said. "I'm not hungry for real."

She turned on the screen and watched it for a bit. Some show with exploding puppets. When she fell asleep, Harold turned it off, messed around with the PDA for a bit, then forced himself to eat a bologna sandwich with whole wheat.

They were both asleep, curled up together, when Dad came in, and still that way when he left.

Just last night. Harold knew right away that black mesh and baby fat didn't really go together. "But you know what," he told the mirror, "Fuck it." He didn't look half bad when he sucked in his belly. He just had to remember to never ever exhale.

Harold had gotten the e-vite only twenty minutes before, so he had no time to really fret about his wardrobe. Dad was away, Abby asleep, so he was able to walk right out the front door and grab the city bus at the end of the block. The bus was empty except for a strangely agitated bus driver and the tinny rumble of AM radio. Looks like the U.S. launched first, but didn't strike hard enough to knock out all spoilsport ballistics hidden under the Persian Gulf. And China was well enough to shoot back, too. Harold was amazed at how calm the news-reader was, then remembered that it was probably just an AI.

Before he left, Harold decided to go into his father's room, which had always been off-limits. He had a work terminal in there, and even one of those neat garbage cans that disintegrated the paper right as it was tossed in. The air was still and smelled like brand-new shoes from the mall.

Harold sat down at the computer, ready to crack it, ready to find out what Father was up to. He slid his palms all around the tower, looking for the power switch, but couldn't find it. The little orange switch on the power strip was glowing, but that was the only real button anywhere near the setup.

"Turn on," he said. Maybe it was a verbal model. "Open sesame. Russell 42. Harold 15. Abigail 10. Abby 10. Grandpa Munster. God. Jesus. Password! Kill Whitey! Fuck Iran!" Nothing. The damn walls were so well-built that

Harold had never heard a sound coming from Father's room, even when he would press his ear to the door in the middle of the night. It was like Dad never even breathed. And *he* called Harold a vampire. Even if he knew the commands, his voice cracked too much to pass for Father's anyway.

Harold looked around the room some more, for a stray piece of paper, or a chipdisc, or something, and found it. A crumpled pink Post-it note with a phone number hid on the floor by the power strip. Harold stared at it, blood roaring up to his head. This could be the number for the Red Phone. The president's desk line. A contact number for some perfumed whore who did espionage work on the side. Maybe it was someone who could tell Harold what the hell was going on. Were the missiles really on their way? Maybe his father would even pick up the phone and say that he'd be home soon and that it was all right.

You did a good thing, son, finding that number. Now here is what you need to do . . .

Harold *had* to call it! But first, a little confidence-booster. He tiptoed past Abby's room and down the steps to the kitchen. It was dark, and Abby had left the crumbs from her English muffin behind, so it was easy to find a cockroach. Harold smacked it down against the counter with the fat palm of his hand, then shoveled it into his mouth. He didn't bother chewing, but just gulped it down, like a movie star doing a shot of booze. Then he dialed the number.

"Yes," said the voice on the other end.

"Gah . . . heh—heh!" He hung up quickly.

The phone rang. Harold's heart nearly shot out of his chest. Then the screen turned itself on, in vid-conference mode. Harold threw his hands over his face and ran out the door and into the wilds of suburbia.

Harold had some time alone in the new quarters after morning lessons. The rounded walls would have been pretty cool in other circumstances, he decided. Harold daydreamed a kiss from a brown-haired girl on a park bench. He had never liked the park, because crabgrass made him wheeze. He could watch screen, but guessed it would all be news or endless cheerful instructions from Amy or an Amy-skinned AI. Instead he looked at himself in the dark glass and tried willing his reflection to disappear till an escort dropped off Abby and told them that they could have hamburgers or fried chicken for dinner that night if they wanted.

After the escort left, Abby looked at Harold pointedly but didn't ask where Papa was. Harold didn't say he didn't know either. They waited together, alone.

Midnight. The lampposts and ranch houses were all dark under General Orders, but it was still too cloudy to see any stars or rocket-red streaks headed his way from overseas. Harold didn't know if that was supposed to be ironic or just sad, but if he stopped peering out the window, he'd have to see the dead looks on the faces of the other passengers. *Fuck that. Fuck them.*

Harold got off at the last stop and walked three blocks to the Stanton Bridge anchorage. Already he could see the bob and weave of kids waving glow sticks and hear the thump of deep bass. Kids, all ages were there, some dancing, or at least whipping themselves around like whooping cranes ready to mate. Most skulked in corners, or bobbed their heads in time with the DJ. Harold loved the anchorage; if he were in shape and not afraid of heights, he'd have scaled the pitted stone pillars and explored the catwalks and suspension cables all night. Instead, he just stared up at them and made his way to the bar.

"Coke," he ordered. "No. Rum and coke." The bartender poured it blankly, not smiling conspiratorially as Harold had hoped. "*Yeah, you're fourteen, but what the fuck, it's the end of the world, right? If we don't drink it now, we're just gonna leave it for the cockroaches. They're all that'll be here after they drop the big one!*" That's what Harold had imagined the bartender would say. He also imagined that she'd have a nice rack like the girl on the e-vite and not be an old man with a bull-ring though his nose. Ah well, at least he got served.

Glargh! Rum and Coke tasted awful. Like roaches and Coke, really. Harold dribbled some out onto his chin, and spilled a bit, too, so it would look like he had drunk more of it. It felt warm in his empty belly, though, and he sipped at it, and stirred the ice with a swizzle stick to make the cubes melt faster. Harold tried to sway to the music, testing the edge of the dance floor, but never diving in.

He wished he had Doc Martens or those fucking awesome bondage boots with the big-ass platform heels and thick buckles instead of black Chucks.

Nobody sneered or made faces. Nobody noticed. Strip-mall goth kids just stared right through him and bent sideways to slip past him, without even an "Excuse me," or a "Move it, you fat faggot!" to acknowledge his existence.

Harold managed to drink nearly all his rum and Coke, and ordered another plain Coke to wash the taste off his tongue. Then a gentle touch on his elbow. He turned and saw her smiling at him. It was . . . Beth! From computer camp, two years before, not fat camp from last year. She looked a bit silly—a mop of brown curls, owl-round glasses, and a corset that shoved her breasts and the fat deposits around them into a little pile under her chin.

"Would you care to be made immortal?" she asked in a deep TV-vampire accent. Harold blinked, so she reverted back to her normal squeak. "Harold! Hi, it's Beth, from camp."

"Yeah!" Should he hug her? He'd have to put down his drink. "I know. I'm just . . . you know, a little drunk.

What are you doing here? I didn't know you liked goth stuff."

"Oh, I'm very in touch with my dark side, Harold," she said. "Check it!" She opened her mouth and stuck her fingers under her eyeteeth. They were pointy fangs now, much whiter and more pronounced than the rest of her teeth. "Sweet sixteen! Made from real enamel, too, not plastic! And they're permanent."

"That is *so* cool," Harold said. "Is it real enamel from real people? Like cadavers and shit?"

"Eeeew!" Beth said. "No, they grow it in a petri dish."

"Heh," Harold said. "I know." *No I didn't,* he reminded himself. "I was just teasing you." He smiled wide.

"C'mon!" She grabbed his hand and pulled him deeper into the party. They barely knew one another, and she was a bit chunkier and lamer than he hoped his girl would be, but she was friendly and they could talk computers if the making-out thing didn't go too well, so Harold trotted along after her.

They held hands. Harold told Beth that his father worked for the CIA. "Mine's a truck driver," she said.

They are all so *dead,* Harold thought, while Beth went on about some flame war she was a part of about the Goddess and Islam and who was more punk rock: The But I Love Hims or Spanky 77.

Finally they kissed. She initiated it. Her tongue tasted sour, like a sip of cheap wine. Harold hugged her like he hugged his sister, and felt the folds of flesh under her corset. She wasn't complaining about his pudge, so fuck it. They kissed for a while, occasionally getting nudged or bumped by the bigger kids.

"So, what do you say?" Beth asked, her voice deep and funny again, her smile serious. "Care to live forever in the eternal night? To sleep in a crypt underground under the bastard sun, and to rise under the moon and master the earth?"

"Uh . . . sure," Harold said. His crotch tingled. She

stroked his hair and bit him with her factory-fresh enameled fangs, hard in the neck. Harold swallowed an "Ow!" and then stroked her hair in return as her tongue darted in and out between her wet teeth. The pain was good, cleansing. Hot! In the distance he heard a scream, one louder and longer than anything else. His eyes fluttered and he nearly passed out when he remembered that it was the air siren.

Beth pulled away. "You'll remember me, right? We're together now?" she asked, desperate and sad. "Don't forget any of this." It was quiet for a moment. "It's important," she told him.

Harold nodded and hugged her hard. They kissed quickly, just two seconds of fat, mashed lips, and then they parted, following the crowd as it evacuated the party and scattered like vermin under the glare of the dawning nuclear sky.

Harold got home with the bus, tiptoed up the steps, and managed to squirm out of his goth gear and into pajamas. Under the blankets he hid, and squeezed his eyes shut hard, trying to will himself to sleep. It seemed like only a few seconds passed before they came for him. It was nearly dawn.

Dad wasn't in quarters the next morning either. Harold fed Abby and showed her how to two-way him with the PDA. Then he went to go looking for their father. The halls of the honeycomb were cold; Harold's lips were numb and legs heavy from dread. People he passed in the hallway weren't much better off, but mostly they were together in families. A mother leading two children past him, her palms flat against their shoulder blades. A young couple, the man's head tucked under his girl's chin. They walked like they were in a three-legged race where coming in last was the goal. Only the staff, all in orange jumpers and quick smiles, walked with purpose. They knew his name.

"Hi, Harold!"

"Hi. Can you tell me where my dad is? His name is Russ."

All the staff had that same practiced shake of the head—once left, once right. Very efficient. "Can't help you. Why don't you go back to your quarters and rest. He'll be there soon, and you can catch up with him then!" Very chipper. Harold wondered if they were being given drugs to keep them happy.

Most of the hallways were empty, and even with the PDA's automated maps, Harold found himself walking weird curves or doubling back on himself. The school auditorium was cold and dark, but unlocked. The secret whiteboard door was secured, though.

He was walking back to the exit when he saw his father through the window. Harold ducked low, not wanting to be seen, then scuttled to the door and cracked it open.

"Too many," Dad said.

"Pffft, I say not enough." It was some other guy. Younger than Dad, with a better haircut and a silvery collar. *Hipster CIA,* Harold judged him.

"Two would have been sufficient," Dad said, an edge in his voice.

"Look, Russ, it's an academic argument at this point. We managed to take out three, we'll get another half through infrastructural collapse, and that's it. It's all already over. We won't know the final score, though, till the Chinks and the Arabs start crawling out of their own honeycombs."

"If they even have any," Dad said.

"Yeah! Not if we're lucky!" The hipster patted Dad on the shoulder, clucked his tongue, and made the little finger-gun sign. "See you at eighteen hundred hours. Go home, eat something. Hug your kids."

Dad just stood in the hallway, watching his colleague walk deeper into the honeycomb. He didn't even notice Harold opening the door and walking up behind him.

"Three what?" Harold asked.

Dad jerked and gasped, his hand to his chest. "Harold!"

"Three what? Million people dead?"

Dad shook his head. "Three billion," he said. Harold stared. "People I killed just last night."

"Oh."

"I'm sorry."

Harold clenched his jaw, ready to cry. Dad just took his shoulders, turned him around, and with a hand between his shoulder blades led Harold back to quarters. They hid under for a long time, waiting for when they could scamper up and out, into the daylight—a family.

A Ragnarok Without Gods

Michail Velichansky

"Please remain calm."

The sky burned. There was no night; fire cast the roads in red and made the asphalt look like marble. Thunder rumbled in the distance.

Ruth found the gas station where she worked abandoned. The night manager had left the place unlocked. Ruth checked the power and found the electric lights still worked. She clocked in, checked out her own cash drawer. She tried to drink some coffee, but found her hands shook too much to hold the cup. She worried she would not be able to work the register. Not that it mattered: people filled their cars without paying, leaving the nozzles on the ground.

On the small black-and-white Ruth watched the local news:

"Remain calm," the anchorman said. "The safest place is your own home. The phenomenon will pass. Please remain calm. Emergency responders are taking action. We can all get through this."

Ruth liked to watch the anchorman on the local news. Had he come in early too? Unable to sleep as firelight spilled through his curtains? Light that had made her room seem alien. She spent so little time at home, so much more at the counter watching him report on local happenings. Did he have nowhere else to go? She muted the sound and turned on the radio. They played no music. "Please remain calm."

At 5:30 Mr. Charlie came in to buy a cup of coffee and a plain donut, as always. He paid for ten dollars and thirty-seven cents worth of gas with a twenty-dollar bill and waited for his change. Out of his suit he took a sleek black handgun and checked and rechecked the clip, the safety, the sights. He was careful to point the gun away from Ruth. His hands were covered in liver spots, and wrinkled. The gun looked strange in them.

Working at the gas station, Ruth had been robbed several times—usually local kids, sometimes folks on the run. The gun did not scare Ruth; Mr. Charlie did.

"The world's coming to an end," Mr. Charlie said. "It doesn't matter if I kill him now. The motherfucker. He's going anyway, but I want it to be me that sends him off."

Ruth had never heard Mr. Charlie swear before, not even when that woman hit his car while he was pumping gas. He swore clearly and succinctly. He had always been well-spoken.

"Steven. He's a motherfucker. I'm going to kill him now. Finally."

He counted his change, then separated out the pennies and dropped them in the tin marked Take-A-Penny, Leave-A-Penny!

"Thank you, Ruth. Good morning."

"Good morning, Mr. Charlie," Ruth said. She watched him sit straight and rigid in his station wagon. He checked his gun again, then laid it in his lap. Mr. Charlie drove off onto the side of the road to pass the other cars.

"Please remain calm," the radio urged.

The earth shook. A gale stripped the leaves off trees and battered at the station's windows.

Ruth remained calm. As she went through the aisles, straightening the mess earthquakes made, she thought that she did not care how soon the world would end. Let the station burn. Let her trailer burn. Even before the sky burned she had had no place to go.

There was some duct tape underneath the counter. She stuck X's on the windows.

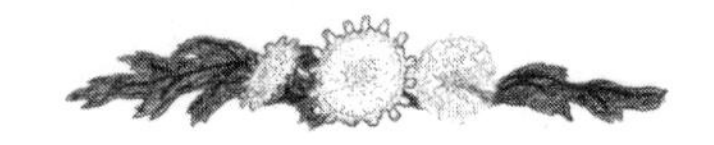

Cars sat abandoned by the pumps, the metal growing warm beneath the sky. There was no gas left. Ruth covered each of the nozzles with a yellow bag. Someone was breaking car windows, and a fight broke out down the road. Ruth called the police; the number rang and rang, and then the line went dead. The news station had been replaced by an emergency broadcast screen.

Ruth found a girl sitting cross-legged next to the fridges in the back. Chocolate wrappers lay strewn about her. She took a sip from a can of beer, choked on it, sobbed, and drank again.

"Hello," Ruth said.

The girl looked up. "I'm sorry. I was trying to get home, and I got stranded." She took another drink. She spat it out onto the glass and wiped at her face with her sleeve. "It's supposed to keep you mellow, right? Please let me stay. I can't make it home now, the roads are all blocked."

The girl looked too young to drink.

"You can stay," Ruth said. "It's no good running anyway."

The girl nodded and took another sip. This time she managed to hold it in her mouth. "Do you live around here?"

"I work here."

"Do you want some?" She offered Ruth a can. Ruth shook her head. "I'm Natasha."

"Ruth."

Natasha nodded, toying with the can. Her lips trembled. Ruth knelt down next to her and took the can away.

"How long do you think it'll be?" Natasha asked, trying not to look outside.

"Not long."

Natasha nodded. "I thought maybe I could make it home, see my folks . . . I wish I could at least call someone, but all the phones are dead. The ones that haven't been broken. They're looting already." She laughed—her voice broke and she rubbed at her eyes. "What for, huh? There's nothing they can do with any of it."

"Maybe they don't realize that," Ruth said.

"It's obvious, you know? It's obvious, and they still

want to steal and fight and all that." She struggled with a candy bar. "I was trying to watch my weight—you know, before. I was always watching my weight. It never worked. I should have eaten all I wanted. I wish there were a steak in front of me right now."

"You shouldn't have bothered. You look nice." It was a lie. Natasha's face was red, swollen from crying; she was dirty; her breath smelled of beer, her body of flowery deodorant and sweat. But Ruth thought she would have looked nice in better times. Ruth took the candy bar out of Natasha's hand and tore the wrapper for her.

"Why're you at work anyway?" Natasha asked. "Don't you have a family or something?"

"Nowhere else to go."

"That's pathetic," Natasha said. "That's goddamn sad and pathetic." Her face scrunched up as though she would cry again, but she didn't. "You know what? I'd do it too—loot. I bet it'd make it easier. If I could just break something, if—" she threw a can against the glass front of the refrigerator. The can bounced, landed on the floor. Beer spread out into a puddle.

The lights flickered and died. It made no difference. The firelight had overpowered the electric lights an hour ago. The radio hissed quietly behind the counter.

"We can wait it out together. All right, Natasha?" Ruth liked the name. She remembered when she had wanted to change her name to something exotic like that.

Natasha nodded. She took Ruth's hand. "We'll wait it out," she said. Then she kissed Ruth. Her lips had been chapped by the wind and her mouth tasted bitter. But she kissed as though no one else remained in all the world.

It had been a long time since someone had kissed Ruth like that.

"I'm sorry," Natasha whispered in Ruth's ear.

"Don't be," Ruth said. Natasha's breath felt hot against her cheek. "Will you kiss me again?"

"Sure."

Ruth held Natasha close, helped her stand. They went into the back room. Red light seeped between the doorframe and the door. It made the room seem small and bloody. There were rags, and cleaning supplies, and stacks of soda. For a little while they fucked. The motions were familiar to Ruth, yet she found that it still felt new. Natasha felt new. Natasha kissed and licked and bit with passion and without skill. Some of the time, Natasha cried. She came twice, each time her orgasm shaking her like the final earthquake in the final hour. Ruth held her, and they did not start again.

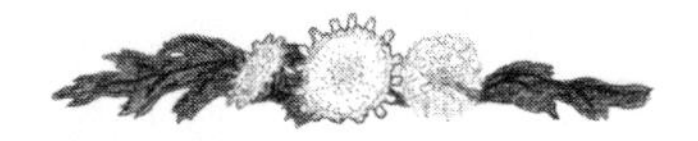

They listened to looters stealing food, cigarettes, liquor—anything they could take. It felt strange to know that the station would be gone. It stirred some halfhearted anger in Ruth, though not enough to make her want to stop it.

"How can it all be gone? How can it just go away like that?" Natasha said. "Like . . . like I've never been to Argentina. I've never even cared about goddamn Argentina, but now it'll be gone, and I'll never be able to see it. No London, no Paris, no . . . no little Shinto shrines in Japan . . . I won't be able to see any of it anymore."

"Do you think you would have gone to see them all?" Ruth asked.

"I don't know. Maybe not."

"I always thought I might have seen more of the world. But I don't think I could have, or I wouldn't be here. Neither one of us would be here."

Natasha said nothing. Her back was warm against Ruth's breasts and belly. She held Ruth's hand against her chest. "I'm scared. I don't want to not exist, and I don't believe in Heaven, and . . . Ruth? Do you think what we did was wrong? I don't believe in Hell either, but I don't want to go there."

Ruth said, "Probably not. Not now."

They dressed, even though the room was hot. Ruth

thought she smelled smoke, and she wondered if their hour had ended. She worried for Natasha.

"It's worse knowing it'll die with me," Natasha said. "I don't know, I've never died before. But it feels worse."

Ruth thought about what Natasha said. "I don't think it's so much worse. Maybe there's no such thing as a Shinto shrine. It's just something we made up so we'd have somewhere else to go. Maybe there's nothing but this place, and us, and we're the only ones who'll go. That's not so bad . . . that's not so bad at all."

Ruth could hear the fire outside the door. Natasha heard it too, and turned so they were face-to-face.

"I went to Japan once with my folks. A long time ago. They took me to a Shinto shrine, and I got to watch some kind of ceremony. I was bored. The whole time, I was bored and I didn't understand, and now it'll burn just like this goddamn station. This is it, huh? It's all burning. I wish the roof would fall and crush us. I just don't want it to hurt, you know? Tell me it won't hurt, Ruth."

"It won't hurt," Ruth whispered.

Then, over the fire's growing roar, she heard someone cry, "Look at it burn! Fuck yeah—went right up!"

So the world was not yet burning. Looters had set the station on fire. Something fell in the store and drowned out further cries. Ruth thought Natasha had not heard.

I won't say anything, Ruth thought. *This is a good time. It might as well be over.*

"Natasha?"

"What?"

"You could try to get out. There's still some time left. It's only looters. The station's burning, but not the rest of it—not yet."

"I'd rather wait with you," Natasha said. But the fire roared loader, and something large collapsed. Natasha cried out at the sound. She opened the door to an inferno. All of the shelves burned, and the ceiling. Black smoke billowed from the plastic. Natasha turned and said something, but

Ruth could not understand her. Maybe, I don't want to die. Or maybe, Thank you.

Natasha stepped out into the flames, ready to run towards the door—and she hesitated. Heat licked her skin, and Ruth could see her scream. It seemed wrong the girl should die even that much sooner than the world itself. It seemed wrong that she should die at all.

Ruth grabbed some rags and ran after Natasha. She beat at the flames around them. Natasha pressed her face against Ruth's shoulder, hiding from the flames. A ceiling beam collapsed in front of them. Ruth pressed on, almost carrying Natasha now. Her skin burned, and she breathed in smoke, and choked on smoke, and saw only smoke through watering eyes. She felt her way along the shelves though it burned her hand. She slammed sideways through the door and they tumbled out into the open air.

Ruth waited for her eyes to clear. They didn't. Fire fell from the sky. All around them, the world began to burn. The station collapsed as if bowing to the powers of destruction. People ran down the road, screaming, looking back, looking up.

"Let me go!" Natasha groaned, her voice ruined by the smoke. "Let me try to run!"

"There's nowhere to go."

"Don't you care? It'll all be gone soon, we'll all be gone soon—if it doesn't matter, can't we at least try? Can't we do that much? Please?"

"Sure," Ruth said. She let Natasha go. "Sure you can try."

Natasha took a step. "Come on. Maybe we can outrun it for a little while at least. At least something. At least anything."

Then she ran to join all the frightened others. Ruth forced herself off the ground. She ran after Natasha. And when she lost Natasha, she ran after herself, because she thought that maybe Ruth should not die before the whole world died—and maybe not even then.

Afterword

And so concludes our journey through the realms of everyday strangeness to uttter madness to the very end of days. What follows is a tour of the terrain we've mapped, some points of interest and insight.

"White Shrouds of Memory"

This was one of our earlier submissions, and from line one, we knew it had to be the first story in the book. The image of the woman simply falling out of the sky and into Thomas's life, into his tree, for us epitomized the sudden and devastating emergence of the odd. Skeptics and critics out there, please note that the Lockerbie incident, mentioned in the story, was real and did have the result of entire and sometimes living bodies falling to the earth.

"An Average Insanity, A Common Agony"

What is horror? That's a question that has been—and will continue to be—debated for many moons. Yes, horror is the thing that goes bump in the night. It's the gleaming eyes in the darkness, the gleaming blade opening flesh. It's the inhuman beast and the clawing, decayed fingers of the living dead. But it's also the loneliness, the fear, and the longing that radiate from a squandered life, and the need and desperation they produce. With a lyrical sadness, Tom Piccirilli realizes this ubiquitous and mundane desperation better than any writer working today.

II

"Wednesday"

The voice in this piece is wonderful. Amusing, even seductive, but Canfield expertly exposes the character's flaws through his imaginary foil. The *Twilight Zone* nature of this piece comes not only from the fact that the women disappear from this misogynist's world, but from the fact that it keeps turning without them. And, really, why *is* it just him?

"Running Rain"

Brian's creation is both poetic and devious, intensely focused, as challenging to the reader as a skilful whodunit but startling to the core. Hitchcock would be pleased; we know we are.

"Whatever Happened to Shangri-La?"

Radix omnium malorum cupitidas est, indeed. This was the first story which, after we had finished reading, caused us to look at one another, sure in the knowledge that it would be in the anthology and also that we might well be hanged for it. Larry's a groovy guy (Harlan Ellison called him one of America's great humor writers) who lives beyond his means in the heart of San Francisco. He acknowledges the absurdity of the premise, but agrees with us that the entertainment is in the telling, which we find to be superb. It serves as a lesson to writers that most traditional horror villains are preposterous anyway, from the reanimated dead to shapeshifting lunatics, and that a story about any of these subjects is made quality by the writing alone.

"Windows"

This story struck a very close chord with us as two people longing to be homeowners. For MacKay's character, desire grows into desperation and desperation into disease, but even for the observer the home remains alluring. We love the ambiguity of the evil: her madness? seductive specters? a hungry house?

"Hexerei"

Not every story needs to be set in New York or Ohio. "Hexerei" is intriguing, poetic, terrifying and somehow accessible despite its German setting. Every one of us has trespassed, every one has feared punishment, every one has felt the relief of that retribution slipping silently away. The witchcraft element is put to excellent use here, powerful but unaggressive, simply a pastoral fixture, without dark robes or red candles. We were delighted to read about these zombies in the original sense.

"Mysteries of the Colon"

Tem wrote this story specifically for *Corpse Blossoms*, and really hit the mark. The protagonist exemplifies the pathetic, nervous, and self-destructive manner in which we attempt to suppress our fears, even those that threaten us. It is worth mentioning that R.J., who had been secretly convinced for some time that he was developing colon polyps, made a same-day appointment for an exam after reading this piece. The story might have saved his life—that is, if the doctor had found anything other than compacted stool and hemorrhoids.

"The Man in the Corner"

Eric graced us with a handful of stories, and we think we chose the most elegant and satisfying one. It's almost painful to experience this through the protagonist he chose, to feel the whipcrack as the piece whirls to highlight your own morbid, perverted, and somehow worse guilt. Eric had no professional credits to speak of when he first contacted us, and in the many months that this project has consumed, he has ascended to a position on Shocklines' bestseller list. We look forward to his future successes.

"Disposal of the Body"

The casual, authentic voice of this story is entrancing, almost like a detached and bewildered confession. It's hard to look away. We'll admit we're still unsure of what's happening at the end, but a mystery is fine with us.

"The Smell of Fear"

This was the first story we received, and Bev was a great sport about revisions. "Make it crazier, Bev." "Okay, now not so crazy." And so on, until we reached a happy mean. We suspect that our haranguing contributed in a psychological way to the success of this story as a humorous peek into dementia.

"Feed Them"

We've had complaints that this story leaves readers right at the cusp of the action, but that's precisely what we like about it. The creatures are the eeriest we've read of in a long while, and possibly harmless, but it's the main character and her choices which give the story strength.

"The Weight of Silence"

Our baby was two months old when we read this subtle nod to "The Tell-Tale Heart," right at the peak of SIDS season. As a result, it terrified us beyond reason. Scott chronicles a mother's journey into *utterly*, employing grief as a show and guilt as an addiction. He marks where his seed is sown and carefully reaps each plant. The fruits of his labors are cold, bleak, and dizzying.

"Skeleton Woods"

Near sunset. Autumn. Overcast sky. Barren trees. The path lost. Is anything more quietly terrifying, more full of the promise of wickedness, than the woods at nightfall? No horror writer working today captures our innate fear and dread of the forest as Ramsey Campbell does. "Skeleton Woods" is eerie, atmospheric, unexplained. This short story is an excellent companion piece to his novel, *The Darkest Part of the Woods*, which was originally to be titled *Skeleton Woods*.

"Need"

Gary's story is the most elaborate and rewarding of the batch. We invite you to read it multiple times—slowly—to get the full effect. He wrote this "After-the-Fact" piece just for *Corpse Blossoms*, and it shows. The cops' angry regret over a lost chance mirrors our own and is palpable. The dawning of the final scene rushes on like labor pains, fated and unstoppable. Seems likely that this will garner him yet another Stoker nomination.

"The Last Few Curls of Gut Rope"

Steve let us really run this one through the mill, but the original attitude—sharply poetic, eerie but moralistically fairytale-like—remains. Aesop reincarnated and in bad need of psychotherapy.

"Finding Father"

We're haunted by Little's chronicle of familial anxiety and genetic destiny, disturbing in daylight, awfulness in the mundane. The message of hope to be found in the end, of the protagonist simply walking away from the futile, evil matter in which he has entangled himself, is very refreshing.

"Empathy"

Kealan queried us regarding this tale, worried that its 7,700 words were a bit much, our announced word limit being 5,000 words. Sure, we told him, we'd give it a look. Originally titled "Grand Guignol," it had been inspired, Kealan explained, by "the most horrific thing" he'd ever seen. I (R.J) read it first, taking it to bed, wondering what that horrific thing could have been. This train of thought led me to the most horrific thing that *I'd* seen: prone to morbid curiosity, I'd recently looked at online stills fromthe first videotaped beheading to make the news, post-Iraq invasion.

It haunted me. For days. I'd close my eyes, and there

it was, a progression of images charting one man's final, bloody journey from *alive* to *no longer alive*—the look of fear and pain as the blade began to open flesh; the head, still connected, wrenched back; the end result—heavy lids and empty eyes, nothing beneath the line of the jaw, and—

I shook these images away and began reading Kealan's tale. A page or so in, I stopped, chilled. And that's not hyperbole. This story chilled me to the core.

Afterward, Kealan and I swapped tales. We'd both made a horrible mistake, choosing to view something we weren't meant to see, and we paid for it.

The story itself grew and changed, becoming more intense with each pass. And so the 7,700-word "Grand Guignol" became the nearly 10,000-word "Empathy," and Kealan Patrick Burke continues to establish himself as one of the most promising emerging voices in our horrific little industry.

"The God of Discord"

Humor may be a strong element to "The God of Discord," but there are some dark and disturbing creatures swimming just beneath the surface. The bastard lovechild of H.P. Lovecraft and Jeff Strand.

"Because Afterwards, They Pull the Shades"

We can't say enough about this piece. Combining the real-world terror of Harlan Ellison's "The Whimper of Whipped Dogs" with the nightmare carnivals of Ray Bradbury, it both captures and evokes apathetic guilt . . . the rubbernecker's desperate rationalizing of inaction. It makes us wonder why the elderly aren't used as characters more often in the genre, or perhaps aren't used as well, given the heartbreaking scenes Brooks delivers. While we were at first hesitant, we decided that any horror anthology can benefit from one slime-covered psychic parasite. Brooks's doesn't lessen the impact of the story's gritty emotions.

"The Chatterer in the Darkness"

Zumpe accomplishes dizzying terror quickly and effectively in this dark psychological piece. The tenderness, the cruelty, the confus-ion, the truth: all whirl together in a pulse-racing nocturne.

"Victrola's Way to Pay"

Within the anthology, we think of this story as the last respite before a journey's end. The leisurely pace and dusty pastoral setting render it timeless. Victrola is so petty, so worthless and foolish, and yet we pity her in her demise. As emotionally involving as tales of Faustian bargains can get.

"All That's Left After the Big One Drops"

There's a lot going on in this piece, so if you didn't get it the first time, go back to it and pay attention. The chronology is brilliantly indirect. One of R.J.'s favorites, and one that slowly climbed to the top of Julia's preference list between first and last read. *Corpse Blossoms* has been described as downbeat, even heartbreaking—Nick's story is one of the few with a positive message, obscured as it may be behind black makeup and concrete walls. Nick is a fireball, very vocal in the genre and even aggressive, but one look at this story and you'll understand that he has a right to be: he's just that good.

"A Ragnarok Without Gods"

Quiet despair. Simple survival. Desperate intimacy. Velichansky captures all of these in his personal snapshot of the end of days. This speaks to all of us, living in this fast, dangerous 21st century world, where war, poverty, technology, disease, radicalism, hatred and ping-ponging nationalistic revenge all swarm together and frenzy like locusts to promise a swift delivery of Armageddon. Which will cause it? We don't know, and Velichansky doesn't tell us, but one thing is certain: nobody is surprised.

locusts to promise a swift delivery of Armageddon. Which will cause it? We don't know, and Velichansky doesn't tell us, but one thing is certain: nobody is surprised.

Contributors

Gary A. Braunbeck

Gary A. Braunbeck is the author of nearly 200 published stories, as well as the collections *Things Left Behind, A Little Orange Book of Odd Stories, Escaping Purgatory* (co-written with Alan M. Clark), *From Beneath These Fields of Blood, X3, Graveyard People: The Collected Cedar Hill Stories, Volume 1,* and *Home Before Dark: The Collected Cedar Hill Stories, Volume 2.* His novellas and novels include *In the Midnight Museum, In Silent Graves* (a.k.a. *The Indifference of Heaven*), *Keepers,* and the forthcoming *Prodigal Blues* and *A Cracked and Broken Path.* A six-time nominee for the Horror Writers' Association Bram Stoker Award, Gary received the Stoker in 2003 for his short story, "Duty". He has recently been elected president of the HWA. He lives in Columbus, Ohio, where no one has ever heard of him.

You can learn more at www.garybraunbeck.com.

Clifford Brooks

Clifford Brooks lives and works in a small apartment overlooking San Francisco's Golden Gate Park. Though often, looking out his window, he doesn't see the trees.

Kealan Patrick Burke

Described by *Publishers Weekly* as "a newcomer worth watching," Bram Stoker Award-winner Kealan Patrick Burke is the author of *The Turtle Boy, The Hides, Vessels* and *Ravenous Ghosts*. He is also the editor of *Taverns of the Dead* (which received a starred review in *Publishers Weekly*), *Quietly Now, Night Visions* 12 and the charity anthology *Tales from the Gorezone.*

He can be reached at elderlemon2003@aol.com, or visit him online at: www.kealanpatrickburke.com.

Ramsey Campbell

The *Oxford Companion to English Literature* describes Ramsey Campbell as "Britain's most respected living horror writer". He has been given more awards than any other writer in the field, including the Grand Master Award of the World Horror Convention and the Lifetime Achievement Award of the Horror Writers Association. Among his novels are *The Face That Must Die, Incarnate, Midnight Sun, The Count of Eleven, Silent Children, The Darkest Part of the Woods, The Overnight,* and *Secret Stories.* Forthcoming are *The Grin of the Dark* and *Spanked by Nuns.* His collections include *Waking Nightmares, Alone with the Horrors, Ghosts and Grisly Things* and *Told by the Dead,* and his non-fiction is collected as *Ramsey Campbell, Probably.* His novels *The Nameless* and *Pact of the Fathers* have been filmed in Spain. For more information, visit www.ramseycampbell.com.

Michael Canfield

Michael's first dozen stories have appeared at SonandFoe.com, StrangeHorizons.com, futurismic.com and LenoxAvenue.com, in Tim Pratt and Heather Shaw's fine e-zine *Flytrap,* in the magazine *Realms of Fantasy,* the PDF anthology *Daikaiju!2: Giant Monster e-Tales,* as well as the anthologies *From the Borderlands,* and *MOTA3: Courage* edited by Karen Joy Fowler. At the tail-end of the twentieth century he attended the Clarion SF and Fantasy Writing Workshop in East Lansing, Michigan under the tutelage of Professor Lister Matheson and many fine writers. He lives in Seattle and maintains the requisite writer's blog at michaelcanfield.net. He also reports on celebrity bloggers for CelebrityPundit.com. He maintain steady employment, usually, but as of this writing he's out of a day job and looking for a nice, steady, interesting gig.

Brian Freeman

Brian Freeman's fiction has appeared in *From the Borderlands* (Warner Books), *Borderlands 5* (Borderlands Press), *Shivers, Shivers II, Shivers III* (all from Cemetery Dance Publications), and many other magazines and anthologies. His first novel, *Black Fire*, was written under the pseudonym James Kidman. Published in 2004 by Leisure and Cemetery Dance Publications, the book was nominated for the Bram Stoker Award by the Horror Writers Association. Cemetery Dance Publications recently published *Blue November Storms*, a new novella, and *The Illustrated Stephen King Trivia Book*, which Brian wrote with Stephen King expert Bev Vincent. Glenn Chadbourne created over fifty unique illustrations for the book. Brian lives in Pennsylvania. More books are on the way.

Find out more at www.brianfreeman.com.

Bentley Little

Rejected by his family, hated by everyone who has ever met him, Bentley Little lives in self-imposed isolation on the grounds of a former cattle ranch, where he listens obsessively to the music of Daniel Lentz and awaits the death of T.M. Wright. He is the author of numerous novels and hundreds of short stories.

Erin MacKay

Born in Mobile, Alabama, and raised all over the Southeastern United States, Erin graduated from Wesleyan College in Macon and later earned a master's degree in linguistics from the University of Georgia. Erin currently lives in Atlanta with her husband and two dogs. She loves college football and gourmet beer, preferably at the same time.

Look for Erin's short fiction in Fantasist Enterprises' *Cloaked in Shadow: Dark Tales of Elves* and upcoming *Modern Magic*; L. Marie Wood's *Hell Hath No Fury*; Sam's Dot Publishing's *Potter's Field*; and in an upcoming issue of *Surreal Magazine.*

Nick Mamatas

Nick is the author of the Lovecraftian Beat road novel *Move Under Ground* (Night Shade Books, 2004) which was nominated for both the Bram Stoker and International Horror Guild awards in the First Novel category in 2005, and which was named to the Locus Recommended Reading List for first novels published in 2004. He lives in Brattleboro, Vermont.

Joseph Nassise

Nominated in the same year for both the International Horror Guild Award and the Bram Stoker Award, Joseph is the author of four novels, a fiction collection, and a number of short stories. He has also done work in both the comics and role-playing game industries. Joseph was elected President of the Horror Writers Association in 2001, the twelfth individual to hold this post. After two terms and the longest running service of any HWA president, Joseph has recently resigned. Past presidents have included Dean Koontz, Charles Grant, and Brian Lumley. Born and raised in Boston, Massachusetts, he currently lives with his wife and four children in Arizona.

Visit him at www.josephnassise.com.

Scott Nicholson

Scott is the author of *The Home, The Manor, The Harvest,* and *The Red Church,* as well as the story collection *Thank You For The Flowers*. His next novel, *The Farm,* will be released in summer of 2006. Nicholson has worked as a painter, musician, radio announcer, dishwasher, baseball card dealer, and journalist.

His website, www.hauntedcomputer.com, contains a journal, fiction samples, and articles.

Ward Cary Parker

Ward's short fiction has appeared in *Indy Men's Magazine, Twilight Showcase, Harpur Palate* and several other publications. His story in the HWA anthology *Bell, Book & Beyond* received an honorable mention in the *Year's Best Fantasy & Horror*. He has recently completed both a horror and a mystery novel. He lives in Florida with his wife and works for an advertising agency where he writes stuff even more disturbing than horror.

Tom Piccirilli

This three-time Stoker Award-winner is the author of more than a dozen novels including *Headstone City, November Mourns, The Night Class,* and *A Choir of Ill Children*.

You can learn more about him and his work at www.tompiccirilli.com.

Marion Pitman

Marion was born and brought up in North London, and lived in and around London until 2004 when she had to move out to Reading. Marion had a secondhand bookshop for many years until it burnt down in 2000, and now tries to sell books on the internet. She has also worked as an artist's model, and for some years was assistant editor of a magazine on advertiques and other collectables, *Collector's Mart*.

After the fire, Marion took advantage of having no fixed abode to travel, spending a good deal of time in New Zealand and Zimbabwe, much of it following cricket. Other hobbies include broadsword fighting and folkdancing. She has two stepdaughters and two step-grandchildren. She can't drive, has no television, and no cats.

Marion has been published the following works in anthologies: "Easy Way Out" in 1978's *Superheroes,* "Dead and Alive" in 11th *Fontana Book of Horror* in 1978 and "The Seal Songs" in *Animal Ghosts,* from Hutchinson in 1980. "The Seal Songs" also appeared in *19* magazine in 1979, "Amenities" in *The City* magazine in 2000, and "Sunlight in Spelling" in *3SF* magazine in 2002. She has two novels doing the rounds and is halfway through another.

Patricia Russo

Patricia has been writing for 25 years. It passes the time. She has been published in many small press zines, most numerously in *Tales of the Unanticipated* and *Not One of Us*. Recently she has had stories published in *Surreal* and *City Slab*. When not writing, she teaches ESL to adults, a practice close to torture (for the students), which she enjoys. Her only hobbies are playing the recorder, very badly, and 'cursing the music on the radio that the neighbors play…'

Julia and R.J. Sevin

The Sevins are relative newcomers to the industry. R.J. has been reading and writing horror and only horror ever since he can remember. He is working on completing two novels. Julia studied literature at the University of California at Santa Cruz, where she also co-edited a campus literary paper. She has no works professionally published yet, and probably never will if she doesn't get off her behind. As of this printing, the couple has been forced by Nature out of southwestern Louisiana and are officially homeless. They have a one-year-old son who responds facially to "Where's Wolverine?" and "Where's Jabba?" and will point to a picture of Sid Haig in response to "Where's Captain Spaulding?" He has recently mastered toddling but is philosophically opposed to the oppressions of sensible speech. He's still conceptualizing his first novel. R.J. and Julia write, edit, and create art full-time and so are very appreciative that you purchased this volume.

Eric Shapiro

Eric debuted in 2002 with *Short of a Picnic,* a fiction collection about mental illness that enjoyed critical and commercial success. *It's Only Temporary,* his second book and first novella, opened to terrific reviews, and was a Top 10 Bestseller at Shocklines.com upon release. In 2005 alone, new fiction by Eric is slated to appear in seven different multi-author anthologies.

Darren Speegle

Darren has recently moved back to the States from Germany, where he lived for six years. Many of his tales are set in, or were inspired by, his experiences in the Old World. He hopes to find in Alaska, his new home, a whole new breed of story. Darren's often-dark and always-unusual fiction has been characterized as "evocative" and "literary" and has sold to such publications as *The Third Alternative, Cemetery Dance, Crimewave, Brutarian, Flesh and Blood,* and *INHUMAN*. He is the author of two short story collections, *Gothic Wine* and *A Dirge for the Temporal,* both released in 2004. He has just wrapped up his novel *Relics,* which is set in a far future, post-cataclysmic Europe. Darren enjoys hiking, cycling, and the outdoors.

Find out more at www.darrenspeegle.com.

Steve Rasnic Tem

Steve has sold over 250 short stories to date to such magazines and anthologies as *Twilight Zone Magazine, The Magazine of Fantasy & Science Fiction, Weird Tales, Year's Best Fantasy & Horror, Best New Horror, Shadows, Borderlands, Gathering the Bones, Cutting Edge, Taverns of the Dead, Quietly Now* and scifi.com. Some have been collected in the volumes *City Fishing* and *The Far Side of the Lake*. Forthcoming work includes fiction in *Mondo Zombie, Dark Arts,* and in the British magazines *Crimewave* and *The Third Alternative.* A new chapbook from Wormhole Books, *The World Recalled,* which he also illustrated, will be ready in the fall.

Steve has been awarded the Bram Stoker Award, the British Fantasy Award, the International Horror Guild Award, and (with his wife Melanie Tem) the World Fantasy Award for his fiction. He has also been nominated for the Philip K. Dick Award. His novels include *Excavation* and 2003's *The Book of Days* (*Publishers Weekly* said "This contemplative odyssey is easily one of the more risk-taking and rewarding books of fantasy published this year.") He has created illustrations for Wormhole Books, the Imagination Box multimedia CD, and his short animated film "The Swimmer". A recent turn to painting has resulted in appearances in several Colorado gallery shows.

Steve has a master's degree in Creative Writing from Colorado State University, where he studied poetry under Bill Tremblay and fiction under Warren Fine. Last summer, Melanie and Steve team-taught the fifth week of the Odyssey Fantasy Writing Workshop in New Hampshire. The Tems live in Denver, a short distance from their four children and three granddaughters.

Learn more about the Tems at www.m-s-tem.com.

Larry Tritten

A veteran freelance writer (*Scriptor horribilis*), Larry migrated from the backwoods of North Idaho to San Francisco. He has several separate identities as a travel writer, humor writer, writer of erotica, and writer of scifi, fantasy, horror, and mystery. Larry has been published in *The New Yorker, Harper's, Vanity Fair, Playboy, Travel & Leisure, National Geographic Traveler*, etc., and in just about every major metropolitan newspaper. He has had some 150 genre stories in most of the best magazines and several anthologies including *Year's Best Fantasy*.

Michail Velichansky

Michail was born in the former Soviet Union, but left with his parents when he was five years old. After living in Austria and Italy, Michail's family received political asylum from the United States. This was less exciting to a five year old than things like Legos and gum and ripe bananas, which were all quite new and delicious (except, possibly, the Legos). Michail has been writing for five years. He recently received 1st place in the 1st quarter 2005 Writers of the Future award. *Corpse Blossoms: Volume I* is his first professional sale. He is a graduate of the University of Maryland in College Park. He also attended the Odyssey writing workshop in 2003.

Steve Vernon

Steve was born and raised in the wilds of Northern Ontario. He is currently living in Halifax, Nova Scotia. He makes a living as a palm and Tarot reader and is married to the best bellydancer in the province. He has been published in such markets and magazines as *The Horror Show, Cemetery Dance*, Karl Edward Wagner's *Year's Best Horror, Flesh & Blood,* and *Horror Garage*. Look for his novella of wild west terror and zombified buffalo—*Long Horn, Big Shaggy*. Steve has a long repressed fear of poultry and all manner of free verse.

Visit Steve at http://users.eastlink.ca/~stevevernon.

Bev Vincent

Bev is an expatriate Canadian living in Texas for the past sixteen years. In 2005, he and his wife went through empty nest syndrome when their only daughter fluttered off to university, choosing one of the three campuses on the North American continent farthest from home. They are trying not to take her decision personally.

Bev is a contributing editor with Cemetery Dance magazine and Accent Literary Review. NAL published his Bram Stoker Award-nominated, authorized companion to Stephen King's Dark Tower series, *The Road to the Dark Tower*, in September 2004. He is the author of over thirty short stories, including appearances in *From the Borderlands* (*Borderlands 5*), *Best of Borderlands 1-5, Cemetery Dance, Shivers II & IV, Red Scream, Who Died in Here?, Dark Discoveries*, and *Sex, Lies and Private Eyes*. He and Brian Freeman co-edited *The Illustrated Stephen King Trivia Book*, which features several dozen kick-ass illustrations by Glenn Chadbourne.

You can visit Bev at www.bevvincent.com.

Steven E. Wedel

Wedel is a lifelong Oklahoman who grew up in Enid and now resides in Moore with his wife and four children.

He holds a master's degree in liberal studies, creative writing emphasis, from the University of Oklahoma and a bachelor's degree in journalism from the University of Central Oklahoma.

Wedel is the author of *Call to the Hunt, Seven Days in Benevolence, Murdered by Human Wolves, Shara* and *Darkscapes*. He also has published numerous pieces of short fiction, several how-to articles for writers, literary criticism, and has taught a course in horror writing at Moore Norman Technology Center.

You can learn more at www.stevenewedel.com.

Athena Workman

Athena is a thirty-five-year-old married mother of two living in Tennessee, but she's split her life equally on both sides of the Mason-Dixon Line. In addition to her motherly and wifely duties, she enjoys careful gardening, experimental baking, playing with her crazy cats, and feeding her blue ribbon habit by entering multiple categories at the state fair. From 2003 to 2005 she was the editor-in-chief of the now-closed horror and dark fantasy e-zine *Lost in the Dark*, and now serves as co-editor of Apex Science Fiction and Horror Digest.

Since late 2003, her work has appeared in sixteen publications, including *The Harrow, Black Petals, Neverary, The SiNK, Dark Krypt, Chick Flicks, Apex Digest, Chaos Theory: Tales Askew, ScienceFictionFantasyHorror.com,* and *Nocturnal Ooze*. In 2005, her novella appeared in the print anthology *Darkness Rising 2005*. Upcoming works include a story in *Twilight Times* and book reviews for *Apex Digest*. This is her first professional sale. She is currently on hold while agents look over her recently-completed Southern novel and decide if she is worthy enough for representation.

Lee Clark Zumpe

Lee is prone to fits of creativity between 2 and 6 a.m. During these seizures, he locks himself in a room in a remote corner of the house and writes. His work has appeared in magazines including *Weird Tales, Book of Dark Wisdom* and *Horror Express* as well as the anthology *Horrors Beyond*. His second collection of poetry, *Feed Me Wicked Things,* will be published in 2005 by Naked Snake Press.

Lee works for award-winning publisher, Tampa Bay Newspapers, serving a dual role as proofreader and contributing writer. He also edits the Lovecraftian journal *Dark Legacy*. Living on the west coast of Hurricane-plagued Florida, Lee and wife Tracey enjoy scouring antique festivals for vintage toys, Victorian ephemera and linens.

Visit Lee at http://blindside.net/leeclarkzumpe or write him at clark1@gte.net.

Post Script

On September 1st, 2004, shortly after announcing our guidelines for *Corpse Blossoms: Volume I*, we received our first submission: Bev Vincent's "The Smell of Fear".

On August 31st, 2005, mere days after having been driven from our New Orleans-area home by Hurricane Katrina, Bev treated us to a nice Cajun lunch.

A lot can happen in a year.

As we write this, two months since Katrina devastated the Gulf Coast, from New Orleans to Biloxi, Mississippi, we're still homeless. The last nine weeks have found us living a nomadic life. Our first stop was a dirty hotel in Houston where for two weeks we would not let the baby crawl on the floor. Next was a single-wide trailer in Sulphur, Louisiana, provided by our generous friends, William Bolen and his family. It was here that our child immediately took his first steps. We excitedly made preparations to stay there for some time, until Hurricane Rita appeared on the horizon and forced us, the Bolens, and many others to flee north, east, west, anywhere. The trailer is now on its side. The Bolens are well.

We felt targeted.

We returned to New Orleans to find our town and our homes devastated. It's been difficult, to say the least, but we've been blessed—with friends and family. We lost quite a bit, from trivial items to our sense of security. But we had each other—we lost no one.

And we had our project, our other baby, the endeavor that dominated one year of our life—the book you now hold in your hands. It has served as something to take our minds off of mold-covered walls and ceilings collapsed under the weight of gallons of rainwater. It's been something on which to focus, a goal, a signpost, a destination.

We hope you've enjoyed it—that is, as much as one can enjoy a collection that's been called "downbeat" and "depressing"—and we want to know what you thought. What did you like? What didn't you like? Drop us a line at admin@creepinghemlock.com and let us know.

If you're reading this in early 2006, please consider giving a little something to a committed relief or rebuilding charity such as the Red Cross or Habitat for Humanity, even ifyou've already donated (which you have, in some way, by purchasing this volume). Katrina and Rita aren't in the national news anymore except as an explanation for the price of gas—CNN has moved on to topics of greater concern to the world at large. But we've been back home, we've seen it and we've lived it. Along the Gulf Coast, Katrina and Rita are going to be the only news for a long time.

If you've plucked this book off a dusty library ledge in 2012 or 2074 (may these tales and their tellers enjoy such a shelf life), please find somewhere to donate some of your money or time. Help someone in need in any way you can, as often as you can.

Human suffering didn't begin and end with a Superdome full of citizens in distress. It's always been with us. It always will be with us.

Just like compassion.

Julia & R.J. Sevin
Grapevine, TX
October 31, 2005